The Nation of Merchants

Sembia is a realm ruled by coin, where power rests in the deepest purses and feeds on the most carefully tended secrets.

The City of Thieves

In Selgaunt, some thieves haunt the dark alleys, some haunt the cavernous manor homes, but all are seduced by the glint of gold.

The Distant Desert

The sands of the Calim Desert and the crowded byways of the city of Calimport are a world away, unless you know the right threshold to cross.

The Uncertain Friends

In Selgaunt, trust is a rarer—but less prized—commodity than gold, and knowing who to trust can be the difference between a long life and an early grave.

The Daughter

Thazienne Uskevren, determined to make her own life in a family where few options are offered, sets out on a mission of revenge and exploration that takes her farther than she ever imagined.

D1570507

THE COMPLETE
SEMBIA
SERIES

THE HALLS OF STORMWEATHER

SHADOW'S WITNESS
Paul S. Kemp

THE SHATTERED MASK
Richard Lee Byers

BLACK WOLF
Dave Gross

HEIRS OF PROPHECY
Lisa Smedman

SANDS OF THE SOUL
Voronica Whitney-Robinson

LORD OF STORMWEATHER
Dave Gross
MARCH 2003

SANDS
—OF THE—
SOUL

Voronica
Whitney-Robinson

To Roderic,
Still my darkest knight.

SANDS OF THE SOUL
Sembia

©2002 Wizards of the Coast, Inc.

Distributed in the United States by Holtzbrinck Publishing. Distributed in Canada by Fenn Ltd.

Distributed to the hobby, toy, and comic trade in the United States and Canada by regional distributors.

Distributed worldwide by Wizards of the Coast, Inc. and regional distributors.

Made in the U.S.A.

Cover and interior art by Terese Nielsen
Map by Dennis Kauth
First Printing: November 2002
Library of Congress Catalog Card Number: 2001097179

9 8 7 6 5 4 3 2 1

US ISBN: 0-7869-2813-1
UK ISBN: 0-7869-2814-X
620-88622-001-EN

U.S., CANADA,
ASIA, PACIFIC, & LATIN AMERICA
Wizards of the Coast, Inc.
P.O. Box 707
Renton, WA 98057-0707
+1-800-324-6496

EUROPEAN HEADQUARTERS
Wizards of the Coast, Belgium
P.B. 2031
2600 Berchem
Belgium
+32-70-23-32-77

Visit our web site at **www.wizards.com**

THE
MOONSEA

THE DALELANDS

THE VAST

SELGAUNT

CORMYR

SEMBIA

SEA OF
FALLEN
STARS

THE DRAGON COAST

THE VILHON REACH

AMN

TETHYR

THE LAKE OF STEAM

CALIMSHAN

CALIMPORT

N

W   E

S

TASHALAR

0   450

MILES

PROLOGUE

The Month of Marpenoth
1372 DR

The fog rolled in. Ebeian Hart pulled his light-weight cloak closer around his slim shoulders. The red-haired elf did it more out of nervous habit, not really suffering any chill this unseasonably warm night. He didn't like it when things were out of the ordinary, even the weather, especially when he was in the middle of a theft. And tonight was something special.

Ebeian crouched lower behind a rather muscular statue and surveyed the rest of the inner courtyard. With his slim hands grasping granite biceps, he cautiously peered around the carved elbow of the bygone Soargyl and scanned for more guards. A pair of ill-equipped sentries had trudged past him a few moments earlier, and the Waterdhavian elf counted past one hundred to see if there would be more, but no others made any rounds.

Ebeian shook his head. Things had certainly changed at Sarntrumpet Towers, he mused sadly, and not for the better. There was a certain shoddiness to the manor and grounds. While the Towers had never been known as a great beauty, at least in the past it had been well kept. That was obviously not the case anymore. Ebeian was nearly ready to change his mind, toss the escapade aside as worthless because there was no challenge, but he hated changes in plans even more than he hated events out of the ordinary. He had gone this far and would go farther before the night was over.

Fairly sure that he would encounter no other guards, Ebeian lightly hopped off the granite pedestal, gave a quick bow to his carved, temporary partner in crime, and began to pick his way toward the five stone towers that rested in the center of the courtyard.

"Doesn't look like I'll need this tonight," he whispered to himself as he tucked his enchanted glass in a hidden pocket. "No need to waste my 'seeing eye' when there's clearly nothing to be seen."

He had discovered that only simple glow spells were being used to illuminate the sundry statues and fountains that littered the courtyard, and none were for protection or alarm. Ebeian had heard from "colleagues" of his that Lord Rorsin, head of the Soargyl family, was no longer paying top coin for his magic, and it appeared that they were right. The young Soargyl had let many things fall into disarray, including much of the family fortune. Ebeian shook his head sadly. He was sure Lord Rorsin's father would have been the first to agree that the lad was not ready for the early leadership that had been thrust upon his hulking shoulders. But death had taken no notice of qualities like readiness.

Ebeian shivered again and tugged the dark gray cloak tighter still. This time it was to ward away the unpleasant memories of more than a year past. Horrible events transpired then that had contributed to the second-rate condition of Sarntrumpet Towers and had actually led Ebeian there this night, in a roundabout fashion.

Obscene shadow monsters had invaded the home of the Uskevren during a gala, not to mention the Soargyl manse as well. It was as though he could still sense their lingering touch. The wraiths had left a huge swath of destruction in their wake. Many party goers lay dead after the attack at Stormweather Towers, the Uskevren family home, but a few were left worse than dead. Lord and Lady Soargyl, Rorsin's parents, were murdered in their own bed that same night. Ebeian, after viewing what those shadow monsters were capable of, fervently hoped that the Soargyls had been asleep when it happened, but somehow he doubted that.

A slick sweat was forming under his leathers. Ebeian took several deep breaths of the heavy night air, trying to clear his head. He could taste the tang of Selgaunt Bay, though it was not too near. Of course, he reasoned, changing the direction of his morbid thoughts, there was another rationale why the garden and, most likely, the manse was not overly protected and it had nothing to do with Rorsin's competence or lack thereof.

Families such as the Soargyls and the Uskevren controlled Selgaunt. It was practically a sacrosanct rule that the homes of such elite families were inviolate. Burglaries simply weren't done. That was why Ebeian Hart was there this sickly evening, when the delicate elf would have much rather been sitting comfortably in his rooms at the Lady's Thighs Inn, sipping some mulled wine and perhaps regaling some lady of the eve with one of his many tales.

He was there for a prize that only one particular woman would appreciate—one woman who would understand the irony and the value of stealing something from one of the Old Chauncel, a family from whom stealing just wasn't done. That woman was Thazienne Uskevren.

For just a chance to bring a smile to her lips or hear her laughter he was willing to do this and a fair bit more.

"Ah, Tazi," he whispered at the thought of her raven hair and sea-green eyes, a green much deeper than his own.

She was also one of those attacked on that fateful evening not so long ago. Not killed, she was left, in Ebeian's opinion, much, much worse. It had taken song priests most of that night to reunite her torn soul with her body. Even twenty-one months later she was still not herself, was still almost a shadow. Her shape and form was right, Ebeian thought, but her substance was wispy.

Of course, the only daughter of Thamalon Uskevren continued to go about her daily duties—and a few of her more risqué night callings—as she had before, but Ebeian could tell that some of Tazi's fire was gone. He sincerely hoped that passion was simply resting . . . dormant. Like a flower waiting for spring, perhaps Tazi only needed some warmth.

I would warm you again, he thought, if only you'd let me back in.

Ebeian shook his head to clear the reverie.

I can reminisce some other eve, he chided himself. Tonight, I have work to do.

Picking his way through the garden of stones, not a single plant in sight save for a few weeds that were spidering their way over the flagstones, Ebeian reached the center tower. How Rorsin was able to sleep in the same tower, let alone the same bed, where his parents were murdered caused Ebeian to wonder once more if the boy was addle-brained. What dreams plagued him was not something Ebeian wanted to contemplate for very long.

Ebeian decided not to use a levitation spell to raise himself the distance up to what he suspected was the bedroom window. After all, he reasoned, he didn't want whatever bauble he pilfered to simply be handed to him. Everything else had gone far too easily so far. If this was going to be worth it, he decided, he was going to sweat for the prize a bit.

Scanning the steep side of the tower, Ebeian could discern large chinks in many of the stones. A smirk played on his face. He had just the right tools with him this particular jaunt. Of course, he prided himself on always having the right tools for every occasion.

Reaching into a satchel belted to his waist, Ebeian pulled out a pair of enchanted metal claws and stuffed his cloak in their place. Each claw had four talons and a pair of leather thongs attached to the crossbar where they joined. It had been some time since he used them, but they glinted in the sparse light as though new. Carefully wrapping each one of them over his slender hands, Ebeian was soon ready.

The lower stones that made up the tower were beginning to crack badly. With relative ease, Ebeian hoisted up his light frame and, like a lizard, began to methodically work his way up. His fingers always unerringly discovered a handhold, no matter how insignificant. Years climbing around the great city of Waterdeep had honed his skills. This was almost second nature to him.

The higher he ascended, though, the more difficult it became to find a grip. Without as much weight resting on the upper stones, the less damaged they were. Cracks were fewer and far between. This was when the talons came in handy. The thin yet sturdy metal was able to slip into the slightest of scratches and afford Ebeian a handhold.

"Perhaps a bit of the old levitation *was* in order," he muttered, growing sweatier.

The damp air didn't help, and Ebeian was certain that the only way he was going to remove his thin leathers at the end of the night was to peel them off . . . or maybe get some willing barmaid to peel them off for him. That was something pleasant to contemplate.

Ebeian was so engrossed in trying to decide which

barmaid he wanted to assist him that he didn't notice that the notch he had wedged his hand into was close to crumbling. The moment he began to raise himself up with that hold, the stone fractured apart and Ebeian started to drop.

Clawing wildly at the tower side, Ebeian slid a good story or two before one of his talons caught in a chink of a marble slab. He winced as the momentum of the sudden stop wrenched his left shoulder, and hissed in pain as his arm tried to leave its socket.

"Dark," he moaned. "That's going to slow things down."

He dangled by his left hand for a moment.

"By Fenmarel, I must look like some beast from the jungles of Chult, swinging here."

Needing to catch his breath, Ebeian looked down as best he could. By some good fortune, the guards had still not made another pass, and the mild enchantment on the claws had kept them silent on the frightening slide down the tower. When Ebeian realized that the fog would block the sentries' view of him, if they did come by, he breathed a little easier.

It took Ebeian twice as long to recoup the distance he had lost. When he finally reached the ledge under what he believed to be Lord Rorsin's bedroom window, what little good humor he had possessed was long since gone. Once again the thought crossed his mind to toss the whole plan to the wind and try again another night. But, despite some of the things he said and did, Ebeian was determined. Tazi meant more to him than he let on, even to himself. He wanted to be the one to reach her, when it seemed that nothing and no one else could. He firmly believed that what he stole from this place would be the gift Tazi needed to restore herself.

His resolve strengthened, Ebeian swung his right leg up and hooked the ledge with his ankle. With only slightly less grace than normal, thanks to the throbbing ache in his injured shoulder, he pulled himself up. Taking advantage of his narrow perch, the elf rested his face against the cool rockwork. There wasn't much of a view at his elevation, he realized vaguely, what with the fog obscuring the city lights. In fact, Ebeian noticed with some unease how that same fog had covered the Soargyl grounds like a shroud. The various statues and figures were indeterminate ripples under the mist. Yet again he found himself shivering.

Each breath was an effort, and that concerned him. The pain from his shoulder was excruciating and Ebeian was afraid that it might slow him down.

"It's probably the heavy air tonight," he told himself. "I could cut it with my eating dagger, it's so thick."

Using that poor theory to mollify his concerns, Ebeian turned toward the window casement and untied the talons from his hands. He rubbed the tattoo on the side of his neck with his declawed right hand. It was his way of offering a silent prayer to Fenmarel before he began any caper.

A dim light flickered within the room. By its uncertain glow, Ebeian was able to make out a large bed. Mountains of pillows were heaped upon it as well as several large blankets. Ebeian thought unkindly that it looked like Lord Rorsin was unable to convince anything living to keep him warm at night and relied on the extra bedding for his company, but the bed was unoccupied.

"I wonder what the dull lad is up to? I was certain I was going to have to step lightly around his big form."

It was simply one more piece that didn't fit into Ebeian's plans for the night.

Gingerly, he removed a set of lockpicks from a strap on his left forearm, careful to jostle that shoulder as little as possible. The lock on the casement opened in short order. Since no one was there, the elf didn't have to concern himself with the breeze created by the open window. As Ebeian slipped noiselessly into the room, he marveled once more how easy everything was to get into.

At this rate, he thought, the boy might as well leave the doors open!

The situation didn't sit well with the thief. Why indeed leave everything so unprotected? Could Rorsin feel so certain those unwritten rules would protect him from common thievery? Even if he did, how could he ever feel safe after those heinous shadows killed his parents? Or did he have something *inside* the tower to keep him safe? There was food for thought.

Ebeian allowed his eyes to adjust to the dim lighting of the master bedroom. There was a large trunk at the foot of the bed, but he dismissed rifling through that.

"Some moth-eaten blanket wouldn't draw anything but a moue of distaste from Tazi," he reasoned correctly, "and I am not some chambermaid, bearing fresh linen!"

Padding softly through the room, his pointed ears straining to hear the slightest noise, Ebeian moved toward the dressing table. He was hopeful that there might be some shiny trinket worth his time. Sifting through the pile of coins on the tabletop, though, Ebeian began to feel somewhat disappointed. He wanted something that screamed the Soargyl name to present to Tazi and he was turning up nothing at the moment. The pain in his shoulder was making him impatient.

Unwilling to sift through too many of the drawers of the table and make unnecessary sounds, Ebeian noticed a set of double doors to one side. He was curious if they led to a study attached to the bedroom, which would be a logical assumption. The "colleagues" he had consulted the other night did not know many details of the layout of the interior of the Soargyl manse. Perhaps there might be some paperwork of the Soargyls' most recent dealings lying about. Rorsin struck him as the unorganized type. Ebeian knew Tazi appreciated information as much as, if not more than, some twinkling gem.

He walked carefully, avoiding a few of the worn floorboards, and leaned cautiously against one of the doors.

After a suitable amount of time passed without hearing anything, Ebeian cracked it open.

He could see that a fire was burning in a marble fireplace along the east wall and that was the only light in the room. There was a leather sofa and a few divans as well as a table, but no desk or the like to be seen. A carafe glinted ruby-red in the firelight and two empty glasses rested nearby. Just like the bedroom, there were pillows everywhere. Ebeian wondered at Lord Rorsin's decorating tastes. Either he didn't have any of his own or he had simply left everything the way his mother had chosen.

More and more, Ebeian was sure Rorsin wasn't ready for leadership. He seemed to be the kind of boy who simply followed. Ebeian was so caught up in his analysis of the young Soargyl that he almost didn't catch the tread of footsteps in an outer hallway. Luckily for the elf, Lord Rorsin was a lumbering clod and the elf was able to skitter back out of the room as soon as he heard the sound. Ebeian started to shut the door, but an icy voice froze him in mid motion.

Through the tiny sliver of space between the doors he afforded himself, Ebeian peered into the sitting room. He could see Rorsin nearly stumble in, so intent was the young lord on his visitor. The blond-haired Soargyl kept peering over his shoulder at the dark figure behind him. From his vantage point, what he saw caused Ebeian's heart to skip a beat. If the figure was whom he thought, Ebeian understood why Rorsin hadn't bothered with any magic inside the house. He wouldn't need it tonight.

That silky voice spoke again and was unmistakable to Ebeian, even from a distance. Though he had only seen the man, to use the term loosely, from afar on a few occasions, Ebeian didn't need to see the dark, close-shorn hair or the goatee to know it was Ciredor.

What is he doing back with the Soargyls? Ebeian wondered.

The elf didn't know much about the mage—Tazi had

Sands of the Soul • 9

preferred to tell Ebeian very little about her last encounter with Ciredor—but what he did know was enough.

At one point nearly two years past, Tazi's mother had tried to match her wayward daughter with this man. It was not her first attempt at matchmaking, but as far as Ebeian knew it was the first real error in judgment the Uskevren matriarch had ever committed. Shamur had been under the mistaken impression that Ciredor had the potential for a good match with Thazienne. Playing the dutiful daughter, Tazi agreed to meet with him, as she did with all her mother's selections, and, as was her way, Tazi proceeded to steal something from him.

On the night of a celebration to Lliira, Ebeian couldn't remember which one, Tazi had set out to steal a diamond stud from Ciredor that she had presented him with on a previous occasion. What happened beyond that Ebeian never found out for certain. All he did know was that Ciredor disappeared and Tazi was a changed woman. She immediately dismissed her closest companion and refused to speak to Steorf since. Ebeian had tried a few times to ply her with drinks and find out the whole story, but the icy looks she shot him stopped him dead in his paces. The only piece of information he ever got was from Steorf.

The mage-in-training let it slip out that Tazi nearly died at the hands of that necromancer and wouldn't say more. Ebeian didn't pursue the matter, secretly glad that Steorf was no longer a part of Tazi's life—he detested competition of any sort—but if Ciredor was back, that didn't bode well for Tazi.

"Can I offer you something to drink?" a nervous Lord Rorsin asked his guest.

"It's not what you can offer me that intrigues me this evening," Ciredor replied smoothly. "It is what I might be able to offer you."

A slow smile curved his lips. Ebeian watched as Ciredor motioned Rorsin to sit, as though it were the mage who was master of the house.

And perhaps he is, mused Ebeian.

"I have something for you, something special."

With that, Ciredor reached into a hidden fold of his dark red doublet, and pulled out a crystal flask. He placed it carefully onto the teak table beside the couch with the slightest hint of a flourish.

Lord Rorsin studied the amethyst-hued flask for a few moments. Ebeian thought he was probably not looking at it so much as trying to work up the nerve to speak to Ciredor again.

"What is it?" the Soargyl finally asked.

"I thought you'd never ask," came Ciredor's easy reply. Ebeian sensed that the mage was simply toying with the slow lord and enjoying it.

"It is something your father hired me to do, before his untimely demise. His last wish, so to speak."

Ebeian watched as Lord Rorsin's head dipped slightly at the mention of his father's death and saw how that reaction did not go unnoticed by the dark mage.

The bastard, Ebeian thought.

"Within this crystal is something very unique. One might call it a one-of-a-kind piece."

The elf could see Ciredor lift the flask off of the table and allow the firelight to play on its many facets.

He is a good showman, I'll give him that, Ebeian grudgingly admitted to himself. He knows how to work the angles. Lord Rorsin is very much out of his league here.

As Ebeian predicted, the blond man could not outwait Ciredor. He didn't grasp the rules to this undeclared game.

"You still haven't told me what it is," he said, with a touch of petulance.

"I would have thought you would have guessed by now," Ciredor answered, and as though he couldn't resist the twist of the knife, he added, "and I would have thought your mother would have taught you better manners when speaking to a guest."

The elf realized that Ciredor was not someone he wanted to be on the opposite side of. Ebeian could see that he had an unerring ability to find his opponent's weak spot and dig in. He wondered even more what this mage had done to Tazi and what it had taken her to drive him away. He listened even more closely, the pain in his shoulder all but forgotten.

"What I have here is both precious and useful. Mark my words, boy, that combination does not occur in this life very often." He carefully placed the flask back on the table. "That"—he pointed at the container with one long finger—"holds part of Thazienne Uskevren's soul."

It took all of Ebeian's self-control to remain silent at that revelation. How could that be, he wondered. When and how would the mage have been able to take *that* from her? His fingers practically bit into the doorknob as he, like Lord Rorsin, waited for an explanation. Even as it came, Ebeian realized when Ciredor could have accomplished it.

"I'm sure you recall the night your parents left this mortal coil," Ciredor began.

When this produced a nod from Rorsin and—Ebeian wasn't sure if it was a trick of the light or not—what appeared to be a tear from his pale, blue eyes, Ciredor continued his narrative.

"On that fateful evening, the Uskevrens," Ciredor began, and Ebeian noticed the subtle insult to Tazi's family name, "were hosting a party. As you know, many attendees were slaughtered just like your parents. The shadow creatures seemed to draw the very essence from their victims."

Ciredor paused for a moment, and Ebeian wondered if it was only for effect or if the necromancer actually appreciated the creatures.

"I am also quite certain you would remember that the Uskevrens nearly lost their only daughter during the attack. Or were you too overcome with grief to assimilate that fact at the time?" he questioned solicitously.

Ebeian could see that Rorsin was becoming flushed. The elf was silently rooting for the Soargyl to actually display a little backbone, but that didn't seem to be in the cards. He could also see that Ciredor recognized he wasn't going to get a bite from the lad this time. He hurried along with his story.

"With Thazienne gravely wounded and the household in disarray after the evening's slaughter, I saw my chance."

Ebeian watched in fascination as Ciredor continued as though he were alone.

"I had been waiting forever, it seemed, for just the right moment to claim that little bitch. I owed her so much. . . ."

Ciredor absently rubbed his chest for a moment before he realized where he was and regained his composure.

"Word spread quickly among the survivors of the debacle that Thazienne had been gravely wounded and her father had sent for High Songmaster Ammhaddan. It was simple enough for me, disguised as that very priest, to intercept Thamalon Uskevren's servant and be escorted inside. In they led me to poor little Tazi's bedroom, begging me to save her."

Ebeian's lips twisted in anger at the casual way Ciredor used Thazienne's special nickname.

"Her soul had been partially torn from her body, but still it lingered nearby. It was a difficult decision, whether to simply send that part of her to the Abyss and help the rest to follow or to take what was lost for myself."

He glanced at Rorsin to see if his audience was still hooked, and he wasn't disappointed.

"And all the while," the mage continued, pacing back and forth before the fire, "she lay there, so very . . . vulnerable."

Ebeian noticed how Ciredor savored that last word, as a cat might some delectable morsel.

"So I decided to take what was available for myself. I saw the value in it, and now I offer that to you," Ciredor finished, turning to stare at Rorsin.

Ebeian held his breath as he waited to hear what the Soargyl would say in response. All the while, his mind worked at how he could return Tazi's soul fragment back to her. This is what had been wrong with her all along, he reasoned, and now the elf could save her.

"I-I don't know what to say," Rorsin stammered, obviously frightened to anger the mage.

"Well, try, dear boy. I don't have all night."

With that, Ciredor seated himself in a cloud of maroon velvet back onto the couch.

"What I meant to say was that I wouldn't know what to do with something so 'precious,' as you phrased it. I have to wonder why you would be willing to part with it to someone like me."

Ebeian smiled from his hidden vantage point. Perhaps Rorsin might have a backbone after all.

"Here," the mage began, "try to follow along. If you have possession of part of Thazienne Uskevren's soul, you will have the ability to scry through her."

Both the elf and Ciredor realized Rorsin was confused.

"A window through her eyes," Ciredor explained. "You would have the inside view to all her family's dealings. I think even you," he added derisively, "can recognize what that could mean for you and your family."

"I guess I'm not making myself plainly understood," Rorsin interjected. "I don't understand why you would ever part with something that special?"

Good question, thought Ebeian. The elf had been wondering that himself. If Ciredor hated Tazi so much for that mysterious, past offense, why sell her so cheaply? Surely the dark mage could come up with a more interesting fate for her than this.

"I have to admit," Ciredor grudgingly revealed, "that you pose a good query, boy." He stood up and his maroon clothing turned black against the firelight. "I was never able to fulfill my bargain with your father and I find loose ends to be . . . annoying. As delightful a morsel as the splinter of little Tazi's soul is, I cannot be bothered with fragments right now. They have no worth to me."

Ebeian saw that Lord Rorsin was curious, and that curiosity emboldened him.

"No worth?" the lord asked.

Ciredor turned to gaze into the fire, and when he spoke again, Ebeian recognized that he did it more for himself than anyone else in the room.

"I have been collecting flasks such as these for some time now, and one like hers would be worthless. It would sully my offering. I wouldn't risk that when I only need three more to complete my objective."

"You've got more of these," Rorsin pointed to the flask on the table, "here with you?"

Warming his thin, long fingers by the fire, Ciredor did not even turn around when he responded, "Not here, but in hot Calimport. I need only collect one more and I will be quit of this frigid city. Fannah's is the last, and I need find only two other, minor souls."

Ebeian's green eyes grew wide at the mention of one of Tazi's only friends.

"Though tonight," Ciredor added as he turned to smile at Rorsin, "I find it quite comfortable here."

Rorsin made no reply, not knowing how to. His smile fading, Ciredor became brusque.

"Enough dawdling, boy. Do you want what I have to offer, or has this evening been a waste of my time?"

Ebeian could sense Rorsin's fear of Ciredor coming off of him like waves. His own mouth was drying out at the prospect of this bargain and what part he would have to play.

"I can't refuse such an offer, can I?" Rorsin astutely answered. "But what amount could I possibly pay you?"

Ciredor's easy smile returned at the sound of acquiescence.

"Don't trouble your blond curls at this moment, dear boy. One day, I will come for my payment, and have no doubt, you will be able to pay."

With that, he reached for the flask, covered it with both of his hands, and closed his eyes.

"A few words," he told Rorsin, "and this bit of Thazienne Uskevren is yours."

Ebeian could feel his bowels turn to water as he watched Ciredor close his eyes. The pain from his shoulder was already a memory. This was the moment, and there was no turning back, even if part of him might want to.

Ciredor had only spoken a word when the elf hurled himself from his hiding space. The double doors slammed open from the force of his explosive leap. Ebeian saw confusion register on both the faces of Rorsin and Ciredor, but surprise was his. Before Ciredor could react, Ebeian smashed the crystal flask from his grip. The momentum of that leap brought both necromancer and elf to the ground, upsetting the heavy teak table. The flask shattered on the floor.

Ebeian watched as gold wisps rose from the shards of the broken container, and he almost laughed aloud at the picture Ciredor presented, scrambling over to the pieces and his hands closing on empty air. The wisps stole their way to the fireplace and, in a deafening roar, they were gone through the chimney, extinguishing the flames in their wake.

"She's free," Ebeian whispered, forcing himself to his feet in the darkened room. He knew his moment was at hand, but he had given Tazi a gift no one else could.

Ciredor turned wildly in the elf's direction. He stretched out his arms, and two green balls of light exploded from his fingertips. Ebeian was helpless before the spell and was flattened to the ground under its weight.

In two angry steps, Ciredor was at the elf's side. Through a haze of pain, Ebeian saw Ciredor raise his hand in what was sure to be a killing blow, but he hesitated.

"What have we here?" asked Ciredor, almost gently,

the glow from his hands having revealed the thief's pointed ears.

Ebeian could feel Ciredor's icy hands on his face. Between the suffocating weight of Ciredor's magic and the pain from his shoulder he was nearly unconscious, but the elf could tell that Ciredor had raised his head from the floor and was lightly turning it this way and that.

"It is almost too impossible to be true," came Ciredor's shocked response. "An elf in this city . . . and one who bears the mark of Fenmarel Mestarine?"

Ebeian watched as at the wave of Ciredor's hand the heavy table righted itself. He could see that Rorsin had finally found his feet and was nearly to the door to the outer hallway, clearly out of his element. Ebeian could have laughed at the sight the boy presented. He looked for the entire world like a child waiting for the punishment of a schoolmaster, if he could have made any sound at all.

Ebeian was rapidly losing consciousness. His thoughts drifted back to Tazi. He could see her green eyes and smiling mouth, and he could hear her joyful giggles.

"You have no idea how special you are," Ciredor said, "and what is in store for you."

Ebeian was startled awake from his dazed vision to see black eyes boring into him. Turning his head slightly, he realized he was stretched out on the heavy table. Almost against his will, tears slipped from his eyes to run their course into his pointed ears.

In a low, melodic voice, Ciredor began a heinous chant. Pain exploded both inside and out of the elf's body. Rorsin crouched in the corner, unable to look. Gut-wrenching screams tore from Ebeian's lips. Outside, the sickly fog swallowed all light and sound.

CHAPTER 1

A TENDAY LATER

"Dark and empty," Tazi spat out.

Her hair was plastered to her face, and the rain showed no sign of slowing. It was difficult enough trying to keep her balance on the taut rope but the winds added another element she had to compensate for. She couldn't even afford to wipe her hair away from her eyes. She needed her arms positioned right where they were for balance.

"This seemed like such a good idea a few hours ago," she shouted over the wind, to no one in particular.

The only thing Thazienne Uskevren was not concerned with was discovery. In such foul weather, no one in their right mind would be out, let alone looking up between the tallhouses of this quarter of Selgaunt. There was nearly no chance she would be seen, let alone heard, balanced as she was on a thin rope stretched between two of the more reputable buildings in the area.

She inched her way across the slick rope, with her night's reward clutched tightly in her right hand. It was her first theft in almost a year. The glass figure Tazi had pilfered was meant to be a gift but was quickly turning into useful ballast. With that in one hand, and her sack of tools in the other hand, arm outstretched for counterbalance, she was nearly to the opposite tallhouse and relative safety. Her lips began to curl upward in a slightly demented smile as her "wilding" neared its successful end. If the wind hadn't been howling so, she probably would have heard the telltale creak that rope makes just before it gives way, but she couldn't hear anything over the roar of the wind.

With only a few more paces to go, the line snapped near where it was tied off on the first roof. Tazi plummeted toward the ground with no time even to scream. Without thinking, she immediately let go of both her sack and the glass bauble she had so recently liberated. Using a move the family butler, Erevis Cale, had taught her a few years back, Tazi twisted to one side and curled herself into a tight ball. She began to tumble through the air in a more managed fashion and gain some control. She broke out of her somersault when she caught a glimpse of a pole screaming into view. It was fastened to the side of the second tallhouse.

Normally, the tallhouse owner's colors would have hung there, but the banner had been taken in due to the weather. Tazi grabbed onto the wooden staff and spun around it madly for a few revolutions. The rain, of course, as well as some moss had made the wood slick, and her dismount was uncontrolled, leaving much to be desired. Fortunately for her, the ground was not too far below.

Landing hard on her rump, Tazi lost her breath in one whoosh. Momentarily dazed, she could only blink water from her eyes, a mostly useless exercise in the deluge. Even if she weren't dressed as a not-so-respectable young man, part of her normal, "evening" clothing when she was on jaunts such as this, anyone who knew her would have had a hard time recognizing her. The only daughter of one of Selgaunt's wealthiest families had come to rest ignominiously in a puddle of mud in the alleyway between the two tallhouses.

Regaining her composure, Tazi stood and disgustedly tried to wipe her leathers clean with her gloved hands, as she flexed this part of her and that to assess any injuries. Realizing there was little chance of cleaning off the bulk of the filth, Tazi allowed a foul expression to fix itself on her face. Acknowledging to herself that it was her pride that was wounded and nothing more, she began looking for her prize.

It only took a few moments of foraging for her to discover her sack, half hung up as it was on one of the lower window casements of the second tallhouse. The broken end of the rope swayed mockingly nearby and Tazi cursed herself for not examining her equipment more closely earlier in the evening. She decided to berate herself later and salvage at least something from this miserable night.

With a quick jump, she reclaimed her sack with slightly more grace than her previous endeavor. The glass figurine did not fair so well. It had smashed into a few large shards. Tazi held one piece up for a moment and examined it absently, then let the piece drop to the street and kicked at the remains viciously, lucky that her boots were tough leather.

"I quit," she cried aloud and began to make her way out to Rindall's Way.

As she had rightly suspected, Tazi passed no one on her slow march back to the Oxblood Quarter and the Shattered Kit Fox. With the unusually warm weather passed nearly a tenday ago, the blustery and wild conditions of Marpenoth had returned. Only the most destitute or desperate would have no choice but to brave the inclement weather that night. And, of course, the serious sellers that Selgaunt was famous for. The climate, as it turned out, was a perfect match for Tazi's mood: stormy. The cloak she kept in her sack provided little cover and practically no warmth. All she wanted was a warm mug of wine and some dry clothes—and to be left in peace.

Such a simple job, she chided herself, and I still failed. What's wrong with me? she wondered, but she had no answer.

Soon enough, she was on Larawkan Lane, with the Kit in sight. The tavern had been her home away from home for nearly the past five years. Stormweather Towers, the Uskevren mansion, was spacious enough most of the time, but Tazi had discovered that keeping rooms at the Kit afforded her a certain amount of freedom that she found almost nowhere else. It was a place where, even though she was disguised, Tazi could be herself.

"There is privacy in anonymity," the family butler had once remarked to her. Like so many of his lessons, Tazi had taken it to heart.

She reached the battered door of the Kit and pushed at it, her anger fueling her. The door slammed open, drawing bemused stares from the few patrons inside. The foul weather had made for a slow night at the normally bustling tavern. At the sound of the clatter, the barkeep shot the newcomer an angry look. Tazi returned his glare for a moment before turning to close the door behind her. As Tazi passed under one of the glow lights fixed near a support timber, Alall, both barkeep and co-owner, was able to get a better glimpse of the sopping wet intruder. Recognition lit across his face, and his gray-grizzled jowls softened as he began to smile.

Ignoring his welcoming look, Tazi made for a table in the northwest corner of the bar. She shook off her wet cloak and slung it on a nearby stool with her sack. Slumping into a chair against the wall, she began to peel off some of her outer garments, but not enough clothes to ruin the illusion that she was a young man. She was always careful about that. As Tazi began to scrub ineffectually at her soaked hair, a dishrag was suddenly thrust under her nose.

"Here you go, poppet," Alall offered. "I believe you've brought in enough water tonight to rival the River Arkhen," he chuckled good-naturedly.

Tazi quietly accepted the cloth and began to towel dry her short, dark locks.

Not too put off by her silence, the barkeep continued, "What can I offer you to warm yourself? Some hot cider or a mug of mulled wine?"

"Just some hot wine, Alall," Tazi replied abruptly, not looking him in the eye.

"Right away," he cheerfully answered, but the cheer was somewhat forced.

Alall had a keen, albeit somewhat aged eye, and he knew something was troubling the cleverly disguised woman in front of him. In fact, he suspected something had been bothering her for some months. He decided to try another tactic.

"I'll see if I can scare up my good-for-nothing wife and get her into the kitchen for you," Alall said, as he lit the gutted candle on her table.

Tazi looked up sharply until she realized that Alall was teasing with his "good-for-nothing" remark.

"Don't trouble Kalli on my account," she said.

"No trouble for you, poppet," he replied.

He walked away before Tazi could come up with another reason not to eat.

Tazi sighed and leaned back in her chair as she watched Alall bustle off. She shook her head disgustedly. There was just no stopping the innkeeper once he had a notion fixed in his gray head. Normally, she felt comfortable and safe there. Nevertheless, she was antsy and agitated.

"It must be these wet things," she mumbled and tried to dry herself with Alall's dishrag.

As she blotted her throat and shoulders, Tazi winced when she ran the cloth over a section of her chest. She dropped the rag and ran her hand along her breastbone. Once more she realized that the wound had long since healed over. There was hardly any trace of the scar left after all this time, just the memory of pain. Almost against her will, though, Tazi found her thoughts drifting back to that fateful evening nearly two years past.

It had all started out well enough. The typical family response to a semi-important festival day: over the top and all the most elite of Selgaunt in attendance. Tazi had again favored a Cormyrean-styled gown chosen to drive her mother, Shamur, to distraction. Some details were vague but Tazi smiled slightly as she was sure Shamur had been angry about her clothing selection that evening. Tazi was also certain her mother was angered by the fact that her daughter was once again ignoring the eligible men Shamur carefully positioned before her. Tazi had chosen to give most of her attention to the daughter of a family friend: Meena Foxmantle. Tazi had chosen this course for its aggravation value alone.

Meena was not the most exciting company, being rather a mousy sort of girl. Normally, Tazi would have only spent time with her if she had been forced to, but more than anything she enjoyed being contrary where her mother was concerned. Talking to a girl all evening was not what Shamur expected her daughter to do.

As the evening and Meena's ceaseless prattle dragged on, Tazi recalled letting her eyes wander. She remembered her elf friend Ebeian had been in attendance, but he was too busy working the room to do more than nod in her direction. Of course, Erevis Cale managed to catch her glance more than once that evening.

Erevis . . .

"What can I fix up for you?" a warm voice interrupted.

Tazi was startled out of her reverie by the question. She looked up into the hazel eyes of Alall's wife Kalli.

The tall woman loomed over Tazi, who sat hunched in the corner. Almost as old as Alall, Kalli stood a good head taller than her husband. Tazi could tell that Kalli, like Alall, was trying to mask the concern etched on her face with little success.

"Please don't bother, Kalli," Tazi said with a half-hearted smile. "I told Alall not to trouble you, but he just doesn't seem to listen to anyone but you once he gets an idea stuck in his head."

"He knows well enough to mind me," she replied jokingly, almost distracted by Tazi's comment. But too many years in the Sembian army had trained the woman well. She could recognize misdirection when it came her way. "It really is no trouble. You should have something substantial inside you, especially if you've been up to no good." At this, Kalli gave a slight nod to Tazi's cloak and sack. "Even a bit of stew would do you good."

Tazi would have bridled if her mother had talked to her like that, even though their infamous quarreling had softened over the past year to something more like gentle fencing. But with Kalli, she had never felt anything other than companionship. Tazi respected and even envied the quiet discipline the older woman possessed. It went beyond her years of military service and training. Tazi recognized that Kalli felt complete in herself and with who she was.

"Maybe just a little stew, if it isn't too much trouble," she relented, mostly to please Kalli but also to buy herself some time alone.

The tall woman brushed a strand of her slightly graying blond hair from her eyes, and her strong features relaxed some at Tazi's acquiescence.

"No trouble where you're concerned." With that, she headed off to the kitchen.

Tazi's gaze drifted to the flickering light of the candle, and she shivered slightly. She could hear the rain pounding outside. It would take some time before her leathers would dry out after the night's failed escapade. While it would only take a few moments to wander upstairs to her rented room and change, Tazi found that she was suddenly too tired to bother. Her failure weighed her down. Nothing seemed to go her way and hadn't since that night. Involuntarily, her fingers trailed lightly across the faint scar on her chest. Once again, Tazi was caught up with memories.

That night had carried on so uneventfully. Tazi's only recollection of her conversation with Meena was her saying something about Steorf. That had captured Tazi's full attention. It had been many months since Tazi had seen or heard much about the mage-in-training. She had broken off their relationship after she had discovered in a most foul manner that the young man had been hired by her father to keep her out of harm's way and clean up after her. Tazi wasn't able to get past the sense of betrayal she felt. She could number on one hand those people she counted as friends, and she had thought he was one of them. She couldn't take the fact that it appeared that he was a hired friend.

As much as that stung, still she found herself scanning the room for him at Meena's mention. While her sea-green eyes were not able to find his tall, blond figure that didn't mean he wasn't somehow there. He was a formidable enough mage in his own right that a cloaking spell would have been easy enough to manage. That night wasn't the first time that thought had crossed her mind. Sometimes she just sensed he was near, somehow, but before she could look much more, all hell was unleashed in the main hall.

Black shadow creatures descended on the unsuspecting guests as well as a veritable army of ghouls. While the ghouls fought in the expected fashion, those revelers the shadow demons managed to slash paid a horrible price. Tazi had watched as one victim after another fell under their claws. As the victims were ripped open, wispy vapors escaped their bodies. The fiendish wraiths seemed to feed on the vapors, and as the mist left the wounded person's body, the corpse itself shriveled away, leaving nothing but a dried husk behind.

Tazi couldn't remember how many of those creatures invaded her home. Defensive pockets of people formed as both ghouls and shadow monsters made their way through the crowds. Some of the guests fell while others tried to protect themselves. She recalled grabbing Meena by the hand, who had became immobilized at the sight of the creatures. Tazi had planned to drag her over to where her parents were circled by the family guard. She thought they would stand a better chance there. Only a few ghouls stood in her way. Since Tazi had defied her parents' orders, she was not unarmed as were so many others in the main hall.

She had hidden an enchanted dagger beneath the folds of her dress. It only took a moment to grab it and free herself of a few of those folds at the same time. Without the long skirt of her gown tripping her up, Tazi had been able to move more freely. It was a good maneuver on her part, for a ghoul was eyeing Meena and herself. Realizing her companion was helpless, Tazi knew it was up to her to save them both.

The ghoul was formidable, and it did an insidious job toying with Tazi. As soon as she saw her opening, Tazi had slashed the creature's throat and drove her dagger home as the ghoul writhed on the ground, gushing purple blood. Seizing Meena once more, Tazi again tried to reach her parents and the guard, but a shadow had other plans.

With her parents only a few paces away, a shadow demon descended in front of Tazi, cutting her off. She immediately shoved Meena behind her and brandished her enchanted dagger. Of everything that happened that night, Tazi most remembered the icy yellow eyes of the shadow and how they bored into her very being—and how hungry they were. She felt caught by their intensity. The only thing that snapped her to awareness had been the sound of Cale shouting her name.

Overcome by the horror, Meena fainted dead away. Tazi had no choice other than to position herself over the insensate girl. She couldn't abandon Meena. She slashed at the shadow, which swirled around her, to no avail. Once more, she heard Cale scream her name and she recalled fearing he was somehow in mortal danger. Perhaps those thoughts distracted her enough, she wasn't sure, but the shadow moved in with lightning speed to rake her with its talons. Though she was agile enough to sidestep the brunt of the attack, the creature still tore open her shoulder. The blow brought Tazi to her knees. She dropped her dagger and clutched at her shoulder. Once again the shadow swooped in and sliced across Tazi's chest.

Instead of the warm blood Tazi thought she was going to feel ooze down her chest, a chill stole over her. It was as though she was sinking in cold waters. She could vaguely make out the face of Erevis Cale, but it had an unreal quality to her. A gray mist obscured her vision then, and everything became darkness.

Tazi couldn't remember much after that. Her parents later told her what they were able to learn about the shadows. It seemed that they fed off the souls of their victims. Many had perished that night, but Tazi was spared, thanks to Cale's brave intervention. She was told he managed to stop the shadow demon before it was actually able to feed on her soul. Furthermore, after he successfully wounded and drove the creature from the Uskevren mansion, most of Tazi's essence flowed back into her. It took song priests many hours to reunite the rest of her soul and life-force with her body. Tazi recalled the long and painful months of recuperation that followed.

She trained tirelessly, trying to regain her former strength and agility, but every day was a struggle. She was amazed to discover how weak she had become, and she was too frightened to admit it to anyone. Those closest to her saw how tired and pale she was, but she persevered through her own self-imposed training and had reached a point, or so she thought, when she was ready to try her hand at some of her more larcenous activities. When the winds of Marpenoth turned cool again, Tazi woke up feeling oddly refreshed. She took it as a sign that she was ready again, but she had failed tonight.

"Sorry to interrupt your daydreams," Kalli said, "but your stew's ready."

Kalli looked at her, clearly disturbed by the vacant look in Tazi's eyes.

"It looks good," Tazi replied after a moment's hesitation. "It should be fine," she added, sensing Kalli wanted her to say something else.

Kalli placed both her hands on the wooden table and leaned closer to Tazi.

"Child, what is wrong?" she whispered.

Tazi looked up into Kalli's face. She could see how worried Kalli was. Glancing past the older woman's shoulder, Tazi could see that Alall was watching the scene from behind the bar. As soon as Tazi caught his eye, he turned his attention back to the mug he had ostensibly been polishing for the past five minutes. If everything had been normal, Tazi would have laughed at the two mother hens clucking over her, but all she felt was suffocation.

"Just leave it be," she whispered to Kalli and saw the hurt register on the woman's face.

Kalli straightened her back and turned to leave. Tazi shot out her hand and caught the woman's wrist lightly. Kalli turned at her touch.

"One day," Tazi promised, "I'll try to explain."

If I'm ever able to explain it to myself, she thought.

"When you're ready, child, I am always ready to listen. You know I . . ." but the older woman was unable to say more. Tazi's words had been enough to soften Kalli.

"I know," Tazi said sincerely and squeezed Kalli's hand once before letting go.

Kalli smiled at her and walked away, leaving Tazi to her solitude.

She picked absently at the bowl of steaming stew, one of Kalli's finer concoctions, with little interest. She knew if she didn't at least play with the bowl for a little bit, either Kalli or Alall would find some excuse to come back over and worry over her. Tazi really didn't want to say something to either of them that she would regret later. They had been too good to her over the years to deserve that kind of treatment. The only other person outside her family that she had known longer than the Ulols was Steorf.

Why does his name keep floating up tonight? she wondered.

Pushing the bowl away from herself, Tazi reached for the mug of wine. She sipped at it slowly, feeling its warmth start to spread through her. She warned herself not to drink too much without food, but Tazi had already decided she would spend the night in her rooms here. Her condition, inebriated or otherwise, really wouldn't make any difference. She hoped the wine would help her forget the evening's failure.

Tazi set the mug down and pushed her fingers through her drying locks. She leaned her chair back against the wall, balancing herself on its back legs, and closed her eyes. Her mind would not stop replaying her fall from between the buildings. Like a dog worrying a bone, she kept playing the scene over and over. Abruptly, Tazi slammed down the chair with a thud. She balled her hands into fists and stared at them as they rested on the wooden table, as though they were separate entities.

"Why can't it be like before?" she whispered plaintively, suddenly shivering again.

She reached for her mug, hoping to drive the chill away, but a strong hand grabbed hers. Without looking to see who it was, Tazi used her free hand to reach for the dagger she kept secreted in her boot. Gripping its worn handle, she drew the small but deadly weapon out in a flash. Her unwanted guest didn't flinch at the blade brandished before him.

"I've faced worse," he said simply.

Tazi froze at the sound of his voice. She glanced past him and saw that no one seemed to notice him standing before her. Tazi stared up at the hooded man in shock and amazement. She didn't need him to pull back his black hood for her to recognize him, but as though he read her last thoughts, the stranger used his free hand to pull the hood away from his face. Tazi found herself staring into the gray eyes of a man she hadn't seen in two years: Steorf.

His blond hair was a little longer, she noticed, and slightly unkempt. It gave him a wilder look, Tazi thought. Even though his black cloak still obscured most of his body, Tazi could see he was just as muscular as she remembered. She found herself momentarily curious as to how much more powerful his magic had become since they were last together. It didn't take long, however, for her surprise to be quickly replaced with anger. Though she might wonder about him and his abilities, she had neither forgotten nor forgiven his betrayal.

Not lowering her dagger, Tazi replied, "While you *think* you might have faced worse, do you really want to find out?"

Steorf didn't even blink at her bravado. He yanked Tazi to her feet. While she stared at him in a stunned fashion, he reached over with his free hand and passed it across her sack and cloak.

"You'll need those," he said.

Too startled by his actions to speak, Tazi removed her gear from the stool. She noticed that both items were bone dry, and a quick pass of her hand over her vest revealed that all her clothes were dry as well.

"Just what do you want?" she asked the mage.

She wondered what could have possessed him to act

in this manner. He took her arm and led her from the taproom into the stormy night.

"There is something you have to see," he answered enigmatically.

CHAPTER 2

THE LADY'S THIGH INN

"How?" was the only word Tazi managed to choke out as she stood in the doorway of Ebeian's room.

For the entire march from the Oxblood Quarter to the Lady's Thigh Inn, Steorf had not spoken one word to her. The only thing he had done to acknowledge her presence was to extend the ward that kept him dry to cover her as well. Tazi found herself wondering if he was simply playing at being the silent type for some sort of effect, marching a step ahead of her the whole way. Standing in Ebeian's door, she understood that there would have been no words for him to describe to her what lay in this room. She would not have believed him.

Tazi recalled that she had always teased Ebeian about his almost insane penchant for neatness. He had explained to her once after an evening escapade of theirs that there was a method to his madness.

"It's like this," he had told her. "If I keep the room impeccable, it's much harder for someone to nose around through my things without my noticing." He shot her a pointed look at that before snuggling closer to her and adding, "By maintaining everything scrupulously precise and to a minimum, there's less of a chance of leaving telltale clues as to my business."

In fact, it was when Tazi was snooping through his things that he'd caught her in the act. He had, in turn, discovered a few of her secrets that day. Since then, they became slightly more than friends.

Her father, of all people, had once tried to pair her up with the elf "silver trader" when Ebeian first appeared in Selgaunt. Tazi decided to do a little investigating of her prospective beau. Before Ebeian stopped her, she'd discovered that the elf was a fraud, simply accepting payments from clients in Waterdeep to fund his travels. He was no more than a glorified servant, running errands for the wealthy with no real fortune of his own. But she discovered he was ambitious and was always looking for a deal. Ebeian was made for Selgaunt, or, rather, he *had* been made for Selgaunt. All that remained of her sometimes lover was scattered about his rented room.

As Tazi stepped across the threshold into the dimly lit chamber, she was almost overcome by the smell of rotting flesh. It took all of her control not to gag on her own rising gorge. Against the far wall was Ebeian's bed and Tazi saw what looked like his head and part of his torso. The rest of him was scattered in between. There were flies buzzing everywhere.

As though moving through a dream, she carefully picked her way around and over what turned out to be chunks of her friend, littering the floor. Tazi had to duck under one of the cross beams because it was festooned with ribbons. She paused to stare at the innocuous sight, so out of place in the chamber of death, and Steorf, who had never left her side since she entered the room, murmured something. His right hand immediately started to glow and he held it up closer to the ribbons. Tazi blanched at what his light revealed.

The ribbons hanging the length of the timber were entrails. She squeezed her eyes shut and swayed slightly, stepping on something decidedly spongy. Steorf grabbed her upper arm, fearing she might stumble. As soon as he did this, Tazi whirled to face him. His touch had galvanized her into action.

"Who did this to him?" she demanded fiercely, her sea-green eyes blazing. Steorf involuntarily took a step back at her vehemence.

"I haven't been able to discover that yet," he replied, "but I wanted you to know what had transpired without delay. Considering the nature of your friendship—" he paused, almost tripping on that last word—"what happened to Ebeian could come back to you."

He looked down at her with his solemn gray eyes.

It took a moment for his words to sink in. When they did, Tazi was indignant.

"Are you saying you or someone else could think I did this to him?"

"Once again, Thazienne Uskevren, you misunderstand me," he answered gravely. "When I discovered Ebeian like this, I was concerned there was the possibility that you might be in jeopardy as well."

Tazi peered up at Steorf closely for a moment, weighing his words a little more carefully. What she said next was somewhat difficult for her to tender.

"Thank you for that. We need to find out who did this to him, though, and why."

Tazi could see various emotions briefly flicker across the young mage's face. He looked both pleased and sheepish at her words.

The mage said, "I believe the best way for us to do

that is to bring in a cleric of Mystra. He would be able to speak with the dead.

"It is one of the necromancy spells," he added quietly, "that I have not yet mastered."

Ignoring his look of discomfort, Tazi ordered, "Then do it now, before any more time passes. Judging by the smell and the flies"—she motioned to the clouds of insects—"we've already lost enough of that. I'll pay whatever they ask."

Steorf looked hard at her.

"Coin," he said evenly, "has never been an issue for me. Will you be all right here with him?"

Tazi turned to face Ebeian's bed and nodded briefly. With that, Steorf turned like some great bird of prey and was gone, leaving Tazi alone.

She stood staring at the bed a few paces away, collecting herself. With Steorf gone, the room took on a menacing air. Every creak the floorboards made as Tazi neared the bed she had often shared with the elf was like a scream. Her nerves were stretched to their limits. Death was something she didn't see much of, but when Tazi did, it was always horrific, and this time it had claimed someone close to her.

Tazi reached the bed and could feel the sting of tears behind her eyes. She rubbed at them and forced herself to look closely at what was left of her friend. Carefully, she sat down near his remains and rummaged through her sack. She was surprised to find she had stuffed Alall's rag in there without realizing it.

Almost gingerly, even though she knew Ebeian couldn't feel anymore, Tazi began to wipe his face free of the caked blood. She wanted to do something for him, to see his face as it had been, but she also needed to keep busy for her own sake. The coppery smell of blood was overwhelming and nauseating, and the entrails strewn about recalled a gruesome night for her. She found herself dragged into memories she had desperately tried to forget.

Nearly two years before, on a night a little drier than this one, Tazi had gone out to play a trick on another suitor of hers. She had meant to pilfer a small gift she had presented him with, but she walked into a living nightmare instead.

Her suitor, a mage named Ciredor, practiced a dark magic with a high price. Tazi had discovered his hidden sanctum and found that Ciredor had committed a heinous act. He had split open a young boy from Selgaunt Bay and pulled out various organs and entrails from his body but had left the child alive. He was using the boy's life-force as an energy source for his magic.

Various clues had proven to Tazi that a then recent acquaintance of hers, a young woman from Calimport named Fannah, would likely be his next victim, and Tazi wouldn't let that happen. She realized that she needed to kill the boy to stop Ciredor, but he discovered her before she could take her first life.

Tazi found herself in a fight to the death with the mage, but she wasn't alone. Steorf had followed her and he managed to temporarily distract the dark wizard.

Steorf's concern for her safety proved to be a crucial error. Ciredor easily bound her friend against a wall and turned his attention to Tazi once more.

She could still remember the excruciating pain when one of Ciredor's minor spells caused her hair to grow immediately to its former waist length. He had toyed with her mercilessly, and Ciredor delivered the final blow when he revealed that for the preceding seven years, her friend Steorf had been on Thamalon Uskevren's payroll, no more than a hired hand. Her father was buying her friends for her.

Despite how devastated Tazi was by that discovery, she didn't let it stop her. She was able to use her emerald ring of protection to thwart the killing bolt of magic Ciredor had thrown at her. He was stunned that she had been able to stop him, and that was his downfall. Tazi, though blinded by terrible pain, managed to throw the small dagger she kept secreted in her boot into his chest. While he was incapacitated, she killed the young boy who had been his energy source. Weakened by the wound and the drain of the battle on his magic, Ciredor vowed revenge and fled, never to be seen again. Tazi was left alone with the ashes of the child she had killed and Steorf's betrayal.

She shook her head violently. The smell of decay brought Tazi back to the present and was suddenly so overpowering that she ran to the window of Ebeian's room and flung it open. Leaning heavily on the casement, she breathed in the damp air and let the rain cool her face, but she could still taste ashes in her mouth when she thought of Steorf's betrayal. Nothing could wash that away. Tazi turned from the window and leaned against the wall, raking her hands through her short hair.

What's happening? she wondered. How is it that Steorf is in my life again?

Glancing at Ebeian's body once more, Tazi tried to determine what had transpired. Someone had killed him—that much was beyond obvious—but she started to look more carefully around the room. She rummaged through the wardrobe and his desk. Nothing was out of place and nothing gave her any answers. She felt sure Ebeian wasn't killed in his room. Someone would have heard all the noise if it had happened there. Ebeian would not have gone down quietly, Tazi was certain of that. Of course, a mage might have been able to cast a spell of silence while Ebeian was killed. Steorf had been the first to discover him and it looked like Ebeian had been dead a tenday at least. Steorf . . .

"I haven't spoken to him in two years and now he shows up for this," Tazi wondered aloud. "What would he have been doing with Ebeian?

"Dark and empty!" she yelled as she threw her hands in the air. "Why this now, when I'm next to useless?"

Tazi paced back and forth, unwelcome thoughts

pouring in. She couldn't fathom what kind of dealings Steorf might have had with Ebeian, but Tazi was certain that this was not a chance encounter between the two of them.

Why wouldn't Ebeian have told me if he and Steorf were working on something together? she thought.

It was true that she had cooled many of her relationships after her injuries at the hands of the shadow demons, and it had been many months since she and Ebeian had shared any real time together. She'd shut everyone out as she struggled with her loss of ability and confidence. When she thought more seriously about it all, Tazi realized that she had let all of her associations drift away and she really didn't have any idea what any of them were doing with their lives. The more that fact sank in, the more she realized she didn't know what some of them might be capable of.

"Look at Steorf," she pondered aloud. "In just the short time we were together tonight, he demonstrated more skill than I've ever seen in him before. Everything he did came so easily. Granted," she argued with herself, still pacing, "they were all minor spells but just how strong has he become? Just what is he capable of doing?" She moved back over to sit on the bed and looked down at Ebeian's delicate face.

"I know you would be absolutely mortified if you could see what a mess this place is," Tazi chuckled, trying to keep a grip on her emotions.

In a twisted way, it did seem as though someone had scattered his remains as though, in death, he wanted to mock the way Ebeian had chosen to live.

And how many knew that quirk about him? she pondered.

"I will find out who did this to you and make him pay," Tazi vowed quietly.

"This doesn't seem to be working," Tazi whispered.

"Give it some more time," Steorf replied.

"It's nearly moondark now, and you arrived with this cleric—" she nodded her head toward the disciple of Mystra—"around midnight. How much more time do you need?"

"This is not an easy spell," he answered. It was hard to tell, but Tazi thought Steorf sounded irritated. "I already explained that to you. Have some patience, for once."

Before Tazi was able to shoot back a retort, the cleric of Mystra interrupted them.

"It would be very helpful if one of you could tell me who Ebeian's patron deity was."

"Thazienne should know that," Stcorf said, turning to face the fuming Uskevren. "I believe you were closest to him."

His almost sarcastic tone was not lost on Tazi. The night was weighing on both of them, and it showed.

"It may have been Lathander, but that was something we never talked about," she said, directing her answer to the cleric. "I'll see if there's anything among his possessions that might give us a clue, but don't count on it."

As Tazi started to rummage through Ebeian's meager personal belongings again, she looked at Steorf with new eyes. In the hours that had passed since he had gone in search of the cleric, Tazi had played out several scenarios in her mind. She finally concluded that Steorf would not have gone to all the trouble of finding a cleric if he himself had had a hand in Ebeian's murder. It would have been near to impossible to find a liar amongst those who served Mystra to aid him in some type of subterfuge, but she was troubled that it took the presence of a priest to prove Steorf's innocence to herself. While she might grant him the benefit of the doubt regarding Ebeian's death, she was still too proud and angry to ask what his business with the elf had been. Perhaps that was best left a mystery, for what would it matter now?

She also knew she was becoming unjustly impatient with the cleric. These things did take time. While Tazi didn't bother much with religious matters, she was not ignorant of them. Still, it had been many hours, and the first thing Steorf and the cleric did when they arrived was to shut the windows and fill the room with burning incense. From the stench of decay to that perfumed odor was not an improvement. It was enough to make most sick to their stomach and Tazi probably would have been ill had she eaten much at the Kit. She almost wished the two would ask for a brief break . . . anything to step out of that place for a moment or two.

But if the men wouldn't leave, neither would Tazi.

"I'm afraid there's nothing here," she said to the cleric.

The older man turned to face her. Neither Steorf nor he had bothered with any introductions, so Tazi didn't know his name. His purple robes with the seven stars and red mist clearly marked him for what he was, and that was enough. Tazi wished everyone could be so clearly labeled and known, inside and out. She was half-sick of secrets.

"I am sorry it distresses you to be here," he told her, and Tazi was startled that her discomfort was so obvious to him, "but this is difficult."

Steorf smiled when the cleric seemed to confirm his earlier statement, but his satisfaction was short lived.

As though reading Steorf's mind, the cleric continued, "The spell itself is not too difficult to cast for someone who is accomplished. What makes this challenging is the length of time your friend has been dead and the condition of his body."

The cleric's use of the word "friend" instead of corpse was not lost on Tazi. She was touched that the older man didn't refer to Ebeian as a carcass or some kind of object. He was able to see the elf as a person—or at least recognize that Tazi still did.

"Please keep trying and ignore my impatience," she

apologized with a forced smile, and the cleric returned to the task at hand.

With renewed attention, the old man turned to his makeshift altar. Tazi and Steorf had pushed the small dining table in front of Ebeian's bed for his use. The cleric had proceeded to cover that table with several thick, pillar-style candles and a small incense burner. Tazi watched as he pulled a small leather pouch out from under the yoke of his tunic. With a quick snap, he broke the cord that fastened it to his neck and emptied the pouch's contents onto the center of the table. Tazi tried to move forward to get a better look as the cleric fingered through the various baubles, but Steorf motioned for her to hold still. She gave him a dirty look but kept her ground.

The priest studied a small blue crystal he held near the candlelight and seemed satisfied with his selection. Intoning a few words, he tossed the stone straight up into the air. As it fell, he brought his hands together thunderously over it and ground the stone to powder in his clasped grip. Murmuring a prayer to Mystra, he emptied the contents of his hands over one of the candles. The room began to fill with a blue glow. Where Ebeian's head and torso lay, a vague shimmering began.

Tazi let out her breath, unaware until that moment that she had been holding it. With wonder-filled eyes, she turned to the cleric but was startled to see the strain he was already under. His face was covered with a slight sheen of sweat. He kept his hands together in supplication and his eyes squeezed tightly closed. She couldn't quite make out the phrase he kept repeating again and again. Steorf gently touched her upper arm, and she turned her attention back to the glowing shape. A gasp escaped her as she saw Ebeian open his eyes.

"We don't have much time," the cleric whispered, teeth clenched. His pain was obvious. "Something is blocking my attempts to reach your friend more clearly. Hurry and ask what you can!"

With that, the cleric began chanting quietly again.

Tazi looked at Steorf. He shook his head and said, "I think it would be better if you talked to it."

"All right," Tazi hissed, "I'll talk with 'it'!"

She turned to the shimmering face of her lover.

"Ebeian?"

There was a moment of silence, and Tazi felt a touch foolish speaking to the elf's torn face. She cleared her throat and was about to speak his name again when a whisper almost like a breeze carried across the room.

"Who's there?" it asked.

"It's me, Eb. Tazi."

At the mention of her name, Ebeian's eyes became more focused beneath the enchanted shimmer that coalesced over his face and remains.

"Where are you?" he asked, unable to turn his head. "I can't see you."

Tazi moved closer to his bed and after a moment's hesitation sat down where she had been keeping vigil a few hours earlier. She reached out and touched his face.

"I'm here," she told him, looking straight into his green eyes.

Steorf stepped closer to her and whispered in her ear, "Hurry, Thazienne, we don't know how much time you have with it."

Tazi was still angered that Steorf kept referring to Ebeian as "it," but she also realized he was right.

"Who did this to you, Eb?"

Ebeian seemed surprised by her question.

"You're the one who's done this to me."

Tazi was at first shocked and puzzled by his response. Steorf recognized her confusion.

"When you ask a question, the corpse takes it literally. The answer was correct. You are the reason the corpse is reanimated. You must be very exact," he explained.

She gave him a quick nod and said, "Ebeian, who killed you?"

"It was Ciredor," he stated simply.

The silence in the room was deafening.

Tazi's blood turned sluggish in her veins at the mention of that name. Her senses threatened to reel out of control and yet a part of her had known since she first saw Ebeian's body that there was no one else who could have done this. She felt Steorf place both his hands on her shoulders and, for the moment, was grateful for the contact. It was the only way she knew she was really there.

"Ciredor is here?" she asked, still finding it hard to believe that the dark mage was back in her life.

"I don't see him," Ebeian answered, trying to turn his head with his partially severed neck.

"Remember, ask carefully as he takes your questions literally," Steorf reminded her gently. "I know it's hard," he added, and still he held on to her.

"How did you come to clash with Ciredor?"

Ebeian looked her in the eyes and answered, "Because of you, Thazienne."

Tazi could feel the sharp stab of tears but bit back on them.

"What did I have to do with it?" she asked, almost afraid of the answer.

"I went to the Soargyls' mansion to steal you a pretty to make you smile. Ciredor was there with Lord Rorsin, and he was trying to sell a fragment of your soul to the young Soargyl. I freed that part of you, and he killed me because I was useful to him."

The elf's voice was almost emotionless.

"How could Ciredor have a part of my soul?" Tazi whispered, more to herself than Ebeian's body, but the elf answered, nonetheless.

"I heard him tell Rorsin that he disguised himself as a priest when you were hurt last year. Instead of healing you, the disguised Ciredor took that part of your soul that was lingering around you."

"When did this encounter between you two happen?" she asked cautiously.

"At the beginning of Marpenoth," the corpse replied.

Tazi was flabbergasted. The beginning of Marpenoth was when she had awakened feeling refreshed, more like her old self than she had since her injury. That was a tenday past.

"I knew I felt something," she mumbled.

"What?" Steorf demanded.

Tazi reached up and placed her left hand on his, which still rested on her shoulder. Without looking back at him, she told Steorf, "I'll explain it to you later."

The glow surrounding Ebeian's corpse began to flicker.

"You've got to be quick," the cleric urged. "I'm losing him. Something is fighting me, and I don't think it's him."

Tazi was fairly certain who was responsible for the interference. Her mind raced to ask the right questions while she struggled with the fear that was just below the surface.

"Why did Ciredor need you?"

"He told me, right before he killed me that he was collecting complete souls for a ritual he has planned in Calimport. Mine fit into his plans because of who I worship."

"Has he gone back to Calimport?" Tazi questioned.

She realized that a tenday had passed since Ebeian was attacked and she had not heard or seen anything having to do with Ciredor. He must have returned to Calimport or crawled into some other hole to hide. It was the only course that made sense.

"I don't know where he is," answered the elf.

"Thazienne," Steorf reminded her kindly, "Ebeian's body can only tell you what he knew when he was alive."

She turned back to look at him.

"This isn't Ebeian anymore," Steorf explained. He could see Tazi wanted to protest. "All this is now is a shell. Eb's soul has already passed on. The cleric simply reanimated Ebeian's body."

"Then what have I been talking to?" she asked.

"You've been able to access the memories that were imprinted in his body. Hurry now," he warned at the sight of Ebeian's flickering torso.

Tazi looked back at the elf's remains. In the glow of the spell, she had almost fooled herself into believing Ebeian had come back to life. The more she had questioned him, the more he'd responded like his old self. Even understanding what she was talking to, Tazi found it hard to believe it wasn't her friend any longer. The glow was fading.

"What does Ciredor plan to do with your soul?"

"The pain was very severe while he was killing me," Ebeian explained, "so I couldn't hear everything that he was telling me."

"What could you hear?" she implored, seeing the magical glow that surrounded him start to waver.

"He said my soul and the others were to be used for the 'Skulking God,' whoever that is."

The last few words were very hard to hear.

Trying to eke out every last bit of magic, Tazi leaned in and spoke one last question into Ebeian's pointed ear.

"Does he have all the souls he needs?"

She had to strain to hear his response.

"No," he whispered. "He still needs Fannah's."

Horror-struck, Tazi sat up as though a lightning bolt had passed through her body. She looked first at Steorf then to the cleric. The older man let out a grunt and collapsed onto the floor. She and Steorf rushed to his side. Tazi could tell that he was breathing, and Steorf began ministering to him immediately. In a few moments, the cleric started to come around, and Steorf guided him to a chair.

"I'm fine now," he assured Steorf and Tazi. "That was much more draining than I'd anticipated. I don't think I'll have the energy for my obligations on the fifteenth, but somehow I think Mystra will forgive me."

"It looked like you were struggling the whole time," Steorf observed.

"Something very strong was trying to prevent me from completing the spell. You,"—he turned to look at Tazi—"have a very powerful enemy."

Tazi, who had returned to sit by Ebeian, answered, "Yes, I do." She began to play with the emerald ring on her left hand. "I've faced him before and won, though. I can do it again if I have to."

But her voice lacked conviction even to her own ears.

Steorf, assured that the cleric had recovered, moved to stand near Tazi again.

"I didn't see any of this," he offered. "Not Ciredor's hand, not Fannah's part in it . . ." he trailed away. When she didn't say anything, he tried once more. "What do you want to do now?"

Tazi stroked Ebeian's face.

"I wish I could've asked him one more thing," she whispered, "but I wasted that."

The glow was gone from his body, and Tazi could see that all that was left of him was a shell. Ebeian was gone forever, his soul stolen away. She got up and faced Steorf.

"What would've been that last thing?" he asked her.

Tazi just shook her head.

"I've lost him, but I'll be damned if I let that bastard take Fannah, too."

Steorf nodded slowly and asked, "What do you plan to do?"

That simple question stopped Tazi in her tracks. Her momentum was cut short, and she floundered.

"There's someone I have to speak to," she finally said and turned to leave, everything else forgotten.

Steorf started to follow.

"No," she said, stopping him with a light touch of her hand on his thick chest. "I need you to get Fannah and bring her back to my rooms at the Kit. Don't leave her side for a moment. Where I have to go now, I have to go alone."

With that, she slipped into the night.

CHAPTER 3

STORMWEATHER TOWERS

Tazi held her fist poised in the air. She chewed her lip for a moment, trying to decide if this was the right course of action.

I can't see any other way, she said to herself.

Having made up her mind, she brought her fist down on the thick door. One rap, silence, then two raps.

"Come," a deep voice invited.

Tazi swung open the heavy door to Erevis Cale's bedroom. She had been there just a few times before. The only other semi-private room in which she ever spent time with Cale alone was in his pantry, occasionally sharing some brandy with him. Of the two rooms, Tazi preferred the pantry. His bedroom was decidedly uninviting.

The only light in the room came from a

tarnished oil lamp on Cale's oak night table. Tazi found her eyes had a hard time adjusting to the dim lighting. She understood that Cale didn't need much light as he kept his furnishings to a minimum, more austere than even her elf friend. Aside from his long, wrought-iron bed and night table, there was just an overstuffed leather chair and a pine trunk near the foot of his bed. Tazi's eyes lingered for a moment on the trunk and found, despite the way the night had passed, that she couldn't resist a quick smile at an old memory.

When she was about twelve years old, Tazi began to cut her thieving teeth. The most obvious place to start practicing, she discovered, was at home. With so many rooms and so many people coming and going from the household, there were many opportunities for her to acquire the odd, sundry bauble. One of her mother's jewels here, a silver candlestick there . . . and so it went.

She worked her way through most everyone's quarters, and when the items went missing, the staff took the brunt of the blame. No one suspected her.

Feeling fairly confident, Tazi one day decided to filch something from Erevis Cale's room. While most of the staff and even a few of her family were somewhat intimidated by the new butler, Tazi was fascinated by the gaunt man. She didn't hesitate to sneak into his quarters.

Even then, Cale kept his personal effects to the bare essentials. The young Tazi was somewhat disappointed that there were such slim pickings in his bedroom. Her eyes lit up, however, when she caught sight of his pine trunk. Finding it locked, Tazi took out a crude pick and began to work on the catch, certain that there would be something of value hidden inside.

This was the sight Cale discovered when he walked into his room.

"Having some trouble?" he asked the young Thazienne.

"As a matter of fact, this lock of yours is giving me a

difficult time," she replied, not showing a hint of surprise or fear at being caught.

Cale walked over to where Tazi was kneeling, crossed his arms over his chest and fixed her with his most menacing expression. The effect it generated was not what Cale expected. Tazi looked up at him for a moment, solemnly, then clamped her hand over her mouth to stifle the giggles that threatened to escape. She could see Cale was momentarily caught off guard by her reaction, but he quickly recovered.

"So it appears I have found the rat that has been pilfering the mansion coffers for the last few tendays," he said.

"It seems you have," Tazi replied, matching him measure for measure.

She could see that a part of him was not angry with her at all. In fact, she thought he was even a little pleased with her response. She stood up, but even though she was tall for her age, Tazi came well short of Cale's six-foot-two frame. She had to crane her neck to look up at him better.

Cale stared at the black-haired Thazienne for a moment with an unreadable look on his face, as though he were weighing several options. He reached down and took the lock pick from Tazi's unresisting fingers. Tazi watched as he turned it this way and that in his hand, scrutinizing it closely. A small part of her dreaded the fact that she was going to have to explain herself to her mother and father after Cale turned her in. Her mind was already racing for a good excuse when Cale interrupted her scheming.

"Do you think your parents will be pleased with the 'hobby' you've taken up?" he asked.

Now was the time for Tazi to start laying some kind of groundwork for the story she would later spin for her parents in her bid to escape punishment. But she found she didn't want to play the tearful, contrite child for Cale.

"I didn't do any of this for them or what they might think of me. I did it for me and me alone. It seemed the—" she paused, searching for the right word—"natural thing for me to do."

Cale slowly handed the pick back to Tazi.

"This is really very poor quality," he observed, noting that he had startled the young girl by his actions. "If this is going to be the kind of life you chose for yourself, then you should do your best."

Tazi's jaw dropped open when he offered his support and Cale couldn't help but smile.

The smile softened his chiseled features and he looked very young to Tazi just then as she realized he was only twenty or so. Without thinking, she playfully jabbed him in the side as she often did her younger brother, Talbot, when he pulled a good prank on her.

"All right," he said, seeming to ignore her touch, "let's gather up your things. Your first lesson will be the value of proper tools," he told Tazi as he escorted her from his chambers.

Tazi turned and glanced back at his trunk.

"What about that lock?" she asked with a quick jerk of her head.

Cale led her from the room.

"We'll save that one for another day. It is far trickier than it appears."

Tazi walked over to that same trunk so many years later, still smiling from her reverie. A low voice reminded her she was no longer that young girl.

"Can I do something for you, mistress?" Cale asked.

Tazi turned to see that Cale had been sitting in the leather chair the whole time. She simply hadn't seen him until he spoke to her. She was momentarily embarrassed that he had caught her daydreaming. There was a time when it wouldn't have bothered Tazi if he had found her lost in an unguarded moment, but those days had passed for her. She didn't want anyone to find her exposed.

She sat down on the trunk, resting her elbows on her knees with her hands laced loosely together.

"I'm sorry to bother you so late," she began lamely, realizing she hadn't awakened him as he was still dressed in his ill-fitting servant's garb, "but some events have transpired and I need some advice. Ebeian . . ."

"Ebeian is dead," Cale finished for her.

He didn't bother to rise or offer Tazi anything to drink. He sat rigidly in his chair with his fingers steepled under his chin.

"I suppose I should be surprised that you know that," Tazi replied after a moment, "but you have always been 'well connected,' haven't you?"

Cale merely tipped his head in acknowledgement. Since he first started training her, Tazi recognized that Cale had a network of associates with ties to the less-than-respectable element of Selgaunt. Because he never seemed to use those connections for anything other than for the Uskevren's benefit, Tazi never mentioned it to her parents. If her family had been in jeopardy, it wouldn't have mattered to Tazi what dark secrets of hers he possessed. She would've handed him over in an instant. However, he was always true as far as she knew, and she was fully prepared to use him and his connections.

"Then you are probably already aware of the manner of his death," she continued, not waiting for a reply. "I was doubly surprised myself. First to have Steorf, of all people, drag me away from the Kit, and of course, to then find Ebeian dead."

A small part of her hoped that she might have wounded Cale at the mention of Steorf's name.

In the aftermath of her initial encounter with Ciredor, Tazi knew Cale was somewhat pleased that she had broken off her friendship with the mage-in-training. For as long as she had known either one, Tazi was aware of an unpleasant undercurrent between Steorf and Cale and was certain there was no love lost. Cale's pleasure, however, soon dissipated as Tazi shut him out over time as well. Between that and the long months of recovery since her injuries, a wedge had come between them.

"Steorf and I discovered that it was Ciredor who was responsible for Eb's death," Tazi told him. "That bastard plans to take Fannah next for something I don't completely understand, but I won't allow it. I've got Steorf keeping guard over her in my rooms at the Kit while I get ready to take this battle to him . . . in Calimport."

"You remember your lessons well," Cale finally answered her.

" 'Always face your enemy at a time and place of your own choosing,' was what you taught me. Well," she said, "the place is not quite one of my choosing, but maybe with Fannah's knowledge of Calimport, I can turn it into one."

Tazi felt the need to move. She stood up and began to prowl around Cale's room again. She had often teased him that he chose to live like a cloistered monk. Since the incident with the shadow demons, Tazi thought his room, like his manner around her, had grown even colder. Glancing at the deep shadows in every corner, Tazi noticed the room was more secretive than she ever remembered.

It might just be a façade, she thought, just as my room is. Perhaps this darkness no more represents Cale than the lace doilies and pastel paints reflect who I really am.

"Cale?" she finally asked with her hand outstretched.

His words stopped whatever question she was going to pose, and even Tazi wasn't sure what that would've been.

"I cannot possibly go with you," he said with closed eyes. "There are certain matters here that demand my attention."

Tazi turned away, shoulders slumping. Whatever she thought he might have said, a refusal was not something she had expected. Tazi wrapped her arms around herself as though suddenly chilled. She wished she was anywhere but there, unexpectedly feeling abandoned.

Stupid girl, she chided herself, what did you expect him to say?

That didn't change how she felt. With her back turned, Tazi didn't see what Cale did next.

He slowly rose from the chair, a suddenly tender look fixed on his severe features. He reached a long, muscular arm toward Tazi but stopped within an inch of brushing her short locks with his fingertips. Instead, he balled his hand into a fist and lowered his arm to his side. In a militaristic fashion, Cale squared off his shoulders to deliver his next lesson.

"The name Uskevren means 'too bold to hide,' as you well know. You should remember the most important example I ever taught you: Finish whatever you begin," Cale reminded her. "You must finish this with Ciredor."

Tazi kept her back to Cale but stood up a little straighter at the mention of the necromancer's name. "I know that," she replied quietly.

"Though I can't go with you," Cale continued and Tazi wasn't sure but thought he sounded a little sad, "I can help you somewhat. Among the papers on your writing desk, you will find an address. It is a dwelling in one of the more dubious quarters of Selgaunt that houses more than it seems." He paused, but Tazi didn't turn. Cale continued, "In this residence, you will discover a gate to Calimport. It will save you many days—even months— of travel, but the gate is not without cost."

"I know about costs," she whispered.

Cale nodded at her response but the acknowledgement was lost on Tazi. She kept herself rigid like a wall and refused to face Cale while so many emotions coursed through her. It was the only way she could keep herself in check. She wasn't going to allow Cale to see her turmoil. Undeterred, he continued his counsel.

"I also think it would be fortuitous to bring the scrolls

you took from Ciredor with you. After your grueling encounter with him, I still marvel that you had the presence of mind to take them with you," he admitted proudly. "I have a feeling that their meaning will become clear on this journey."

" 'Better to be prepared than caught empty-handed,' " she quoted with a touch of sarcasm.

"Always," he answered. "The last thing I would advise is that you have both Fannah and Steorf accompany you."

Tazi tilted her head and almost looked over her shoulder at him when Cale mentioned Steorf by name. She stopped herself, feeling that it would somehow be a defeat to turn. If he was going to send her off without him, then so be it. She would be on her own.

"Fannah will be much safer under your constant care," he told her, and Tazi swelled a little at the compliment. "And you might find that in this journey you will need a mage you can trust."

Cale sighed wearily. Now it was his shoulders that sagged as if under a great weight.

"Steorf," he nearly whispered, "is a mage you can trust, Thazienne."

With that admission, Cale turned and walked over to his chair. He stood beside it and lightly rested his hand on its arm, the same hand he had wanted to touch Tazi with earlier.

Once again, Cale had shocked her. Tazi never thought he would've recommended Steorf for anything, let alone as a comrade on so deadly an undertaking as this. She swallowed hard and turned to face him only to discover that Cale had moved away and presented his straight back to her.

"If you think that is the course of action to take," she finally replied, "then I'll follow it."

"You have to do what you think is the wisest, Thazienne," he reminded her. "For in the end, you live only with yourself."

"Thank you for everything," she told him quietly.

Cale didn't turn, only nodded his head slowly in response. Tazi felt torn, wanting to go to him but also fearing to trust him, or herself, completely. When the awkward moment stretched out too long, she finally moved to go. She swung open the heavy door but paused in the doorway, not wanting to leave things between them like this.

Tazi glanced back, half hoping to find him looking at her, but Cale still presented that rigid back to her. She found the sight oddly heartbreaking, the emotions he triggered in her a surprise even to Tazi. As she turned to leave, her eyes caught sight of his pine trunk. Closing the door behind her, Tazi realized that in all these years she never had found out what he kept in there—or in his heart.

At the sound of Tazi's departure, Cale turned toward the door.

"Safe journey, dear heart," he whispered.

Shamur Uskevren watched for a moment longer and silently slid the viewing panel shut. Once she was certain it was sealed tight, she re-lit her lamp. She was especially cautious because she knew how observant Cale could be. If neither her daughter, Tazi, nor Cale had been aware that she had been witness to their whole conversation, she was probably safe from discovery.

Though she was barefoot and dressed only in her silk nightclothes, Shamur ignored the chill. Her mind preoccupied with the events she had just observed, she made her way through the passage automatically. As far as Shamur knew only she and her husband, Thamalon, had any knowledge of the intricate, hidden routes that honeycombed Stormweather Towers. The spy portals had come in handy on many occasions when Shamur needed to test the loyalties of the various servants and guards the Uskevren hired from time to time. Tonight, they had revealed much more than loyalty.

Shamur's feet were so numb with cold by the time she returned that she hardly noticed as she crossed from the stone floor to the luxurious carpeting of her private bed-room. But she was not so distracted that she didn't observe that her fire was dying. She moved over to the ornately carved fireplace and added a log to the smol-dering embers. A few moments of fanning and the wood was crackling cheerfully again.

Certain the fire was stoked, Shamur padded around her canopied bed to her wooden armoire. She let her hand slide down the left side of the chest, her delicate fingers searching the various carved figures. Using a combination known only to her, Shamur pressed several of the indentations in the designs at once. With a tiny click, a panel swung open.

She reached into the shallow compartment and with-drew the only item that was inside. Shamur held the note carefully in her hand, as if it was some precious artifact. The faintest trace of her daughter's perfume still lingered on the parchment.

She settled herself onto the settee near the fireplace and looked over the note with her keen gray eyes. There were only a few lines scrawled on it, and Shamur had read them so many times, she knew them by heart. Still, she read them aloud once more.

" 'Whatever good is in me exists because of you,' " she quoted. " '*Ai armiel telere maenen hir*. Cale.' "

As she had for so many months, Shamur once again sent up a silent prayer that she had discovered the note before her daughter had.

That night of Thazienne's grievous wounds, Shamur couldn't sleep. She had needed to see her daughter's chest rise and fall one more time to reassure herself that Tazi still lived, regardless of what the priests told her. Only then would she be able to rest. Since she didn't want to have to explain herself to anyone, let alone the servants, Shamur had quietly slipped into Thazienne's bedroom after she saw Cale depart that night.

Walking over to her daughter's bedside, Shamur was amazed to discover the sudden, romantic confession Cale had left behind, written on her daughter's personal stationary.

Shamur was slightly in shock from the culmination of events that evening, and the note was too much for her. She slid it into a fold of her robe and, when she returned to her chambers later on, she hid the missive in the hollow panel in her wardrobe. She felt she needed some time to decide what was best for her daughter.

Now, a year later, she saw that some sort of divide existed between her daughter and Erevis Cale. Obviously, he had never spoken of his feelings for her except in that note.

Perhaps he has grown tired of waiting for a sign from Thazienne, the woman who "holds his heart forever," she thought, before coming to a decision.

Shamur looked a final time at the Elvish words of love written to her daughter from a family servant and threw the note into the fire. As the flames licked up the paper, Shamur felt certain she had done the right thing.

She loved her daughter fiercely and would do anything to ensure Thazienne's happiness. She wouldn't have her daughter trapped in a painful union if it could be avoided. Being linked to a common servant just wasn't right for her daughter, though it had taken this sad encounter between Tazi and Cale to cement her decision. Shamur had struggled for months with what was best and took this night as a sign. With the letter destroyed, she felt certain Thazienne's long-term contentment was ensured.

A soft knock on the door startled Shamur from her concerns.

"Come in," she said.

Thamalon Uskevren, wearing a maroon and gold robe, walked in.

"I'm not disturbing you, am I?" he asked.

For the first time that evening, Shamur smiled. With her ash-blonde hair loose about her face, she looked more her daughter's age. That fact was not lost to her husband's appreciative gaze.

"Come sit with me," she invited, patting the cushion next to her.

A year before, Shamur would never have extended an offer that intimate to her husband, but many things had changed over the past months, mostly for the better. She didn't have to hide behind a mask with him any longer. When all was said and done, there was no one else with whom she would rather share a moment like this.

Thamalon sat down beside her and wrapped his arm around her shoulders. Shamur settled against him and let a small sigh escape her lips.

"What keeps you awake, wife?" Thamalon asked kindly.

"I'm just thinking of our children," she finally replied. "There are so many things that could go awry for them."

The Old Owl, as he was known to many, kissed his wife on her head and replied, "With you guarding them, nothing horrible could ever happen."

"I hope you're right," she answered and hugged him close.

❂ ❂ ❂ ❂ ❂

"How utterly perfect," Ciredor chuckled aloud as he watched Tazi step out of Cale's bedroom.

There were very few unanswered questions in his life, but the room Ciredor was in happened to contain many of them. Sometime during the Age of Skyfire, the chamber had been hewn out of the desert mountains while the djinn, Calim and Memnon, raged against each other. The walls were carved with an ancient script that defied all his efforts at translation, but beyond that, Ciredor had very few clues as to who else might have occupied it before him.

He had let his anger get the best of him many years before when he discovered the sanctum and killed its former guardians too quickly. Realizing that he had lost an opportunity for knowledge, the necromancer wrote off the mistake as one of many lessons of life and vowed never to make that mistake again.

At various points in the natural recesses of the room, glow lights winked in the darkness, but their illumination was outshone by the radiance of a multifaceted, amethyst no bigger than a man's fist. It rested on a natural rock pedestal, the focal point of the room. The eerie, purple light it emitted flickered oddly off of the jagged walls and the hollow caverns of Ciredor's cheeks. Behind him, the chamber connected to a passageway that was lined with ten figures of various sizes, all at least as large as an elf. The amethyst's brilliance played affectionately on those figures, caressing them.

But it was Ciredor who was enraptured. With an almost loving look, he reached out to the stone again and grazed it with his thin fingers. It blazed more intensely at his touch. He gazed deeply into the stone and began to laugh once again at what he saw within.

"My dear, dear Thazienne," he said to the gem, "how can it be that so much time has passed and you are still the same?"

But there was no one else to answer him. Not that he needed an answer, either. He knew well enough that Tazi had simply survived this long in her life due to luck and her family's fortune. He wondered just how many times her parents had had to pay to have her resurrected, she seemed to be so careless.

Obviously, her parents weren't all that cautious, either. They had, after all, made the mistake of letting him come into their home to "heal" their stricken whelp once. He felt he was soon to find out just how many other mistakes they had made with their daughter.

"How completely foolish and trusting you are, little girl," he persisted, staring into the gem. "Didn't you learn anything from our last encounter? So you think you are going to bring the battle to a . . . how did you so quaintly put it?" He paused for a moment before continuing, "a time and place of *your* choosing?"

He threw back his head and laughed again.

"Since when has any of this ever been your choosing? Do you think the boy-mage found your elf lover by his skills alone?" he asked the stone. "Oh, Tazi—" he shook his head—"how I wish you could see me as I see you right now. It would be rather exquisite to enjoy in person the pain that all of this would cause you . . . but that will come soon enough."

For a moment, Ciredor could again taste the bitter hurt Tazi had felt those years past when he revealed to her that her close confidant had been simply a hired hand. There was an undeniable sweetness to the pain she had emanated that night. Tazi had possessed a certain innocence then, despite the lifestyle she had chosen, and he had been the man to claim that innocence. More than once since then, Ciredor had found himself savoring that memory despite the hatred he harbored at losing to such a child. Finding he couldn't contain himself any longer, he began to pace around the chamber.

"Through clues and signs, I led your would-be-mage to that tableau I carefully staged just for you, dear Thazienne. I even hoped you might recognize my signature on this without any magical assistance, but you proved yourself unworthy again. I suppose I shouldn't be too disappointed in you. After all, in the end, I will get everything I need."

Absently, he stroked his goatee.

"It was rather entertaining to watch that old man you hired strain and groan and sweat as he struggled to animate poor, dead Ebeian," Ciredor said. "And, finally, that corpse told you just enough to whet your appetite and send you to me, bearing gifts, no less."

One side of his mouth turned up into a smirk.

"And still, you don't see."

Ciredor moved swiftly across the chamber to the gem, caught up in his own discourse.

"I was the one who allowed Ebeian to speak, as it were. It was only the words of my choosing that passed through his battered mouth. Will you miss those tender lips, little Tazi?" he wondered.

He kneeled before the dais where the amethyst lay. Stretching one arm across the platform, he allowed his head to rest against it and stared at the jewel as if he was watching a lover sleep.

"Once more, I pull your strings, sweet puppet," he continued softly, "and you dance for me most obediently. I'm waiting here with open arms to welcome you to my home. When you arrive, we will settle the debts between us, Uskevren. When I'm done with you and those you hold dear," his voice dropped to a deadly whisper, "you will wish I'd killed you that first night."

He sat up and tugged at his black tunic, as though he were readying himself for an evening out, brushing at various imagined stains and dust.

"I really can't be bothered by worrisome details right now, though. So," he said, directing his speech back to the gem, "pack your bags quickly and bring yourself and that Calishite beauty here."

He rose in a dignified manner and clasped his hands behind his back.

"I appreciate the aid your butler has given you, so that I am not kept waiting too long," he acknowledged as he began to walk around the stone like a schoolmaster delivering a lesson. "And I appreciate that the gate is all Cale has given you. I would not want him to give you more. In fact," Ciredor grudgingly admitted, "I would not want to have to deal with him to get to you. There is something about him . . ." he trailed away thoughtfully, "something I can't read."

Snapping himself from his trance, Ciredor studied the room and the figures beyond. Like a drill instructor inspecting his troops, he marched past each one. As if they were pieces of a puzzle, he made sure once again that each fit his needs. When he was satisfied with what he saw, the mage returned to the gem.

"Bring the crown for my queen here, little Tazi," he ordered. "Bring the last piece to my gift. Once it is here, I need only wait until the new moon. A tenday from now and everything changes. And, of course, you are mine."

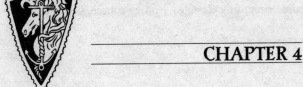

CHAPTER 4

PASSAGES

"Will this rain never cease?" Tazi hissed.

She, Steorf, and Fannah stood before a brick tallhouse on Morrow Street in the Edis quarter. It was well past night's heart, and most of the residences that lined the street were dark. A fine drizzle misted the air.

"It doesn't really matter whether it stops or not," Steorf snapped. "It's not as though you're suffering for it."

Tazi gave him a sharp look before turning to pace a little along the street as she ostensibly looked for guards. Steorf was correct, though. As well as having chosen the black leathers that she had spent the previous day oiling, Tazi also sported a travel cloak, as did Steorf and Fannah. From her head to her ankles, she was protected from the rain by the spell that was woven into

the fabric. The precipitation rolled off her. She wasn't
going to end up drenched like the other night, but Tazi
felt the need to say something, and complaining about
the weather was the most obvious and mundane topic of
choice.

"I'm going to climb the wall and see if there are any
guards we need to know about," she offered.

"I thought your *manservant*," Steorf stressed that
particular title, "guaranteed that this building would be
virtually empty for the night."

"There are no guarantees that you can trust," Tazi
reminded him. "You should know that by now."

"There are a few, Thazienne," he answered quietly.

Not having a quick retort, she moved past him and
crossed the street toward the low wall that surrounded
the tallhouse. In one fluid motion, Tazi swung herself
onto the top of the wall and crouched low. It felt good
to be in motion, even this little bit. She felt ready to
jump out of her skin and had a bad taste in her mouth.
Tazi knew she couldn't afford to make any mistakes
for Fannah's sake, if no one else's.

Glancing back at her two companions, Tazi studied
their differences. Steorf, tall and muscular, dressed head
to toe in black, looked most formidable, and, Tazi sensed,
he was wound tight as a spring. Fannah, on the other
hand, stood there as though she were waiting for some
visitor to come calling. While she was also dressed in
dark tones, with her thick hair tied back in a single,
waist-length braid, Tazi noticed there was nothing
furtive about her mannerisms. Fannah just seemed to be
waiting.

Nothing disturbs her, thought Tazi.

In fact, the only time Tazi ever recalled seeing Fannah
shaken was on the night of their first meeting. Tazi,
dressed in her leathers, was on her way to the Kit to plan
what turned out to be the terrifying rendezvous with
Ciredor when she heard shrill screams. She ducked into
the alley from which the sounds originated to see that

two sailors from Selgaunt Bay were accosting a beautiful foreigner. On a whim, Tazi decided to break things up when she saw how badly the foreigner was defending herself.

In the midst of the altercation, the woman had ample time to take advantage of the "young man's" rescue attempt and slip away, but Fannah had stayed behind. Tazi's first thought had been that the woman was in shock or fearful that her rescuer might be more formidable to deal with than the two drunk fish from the bay and was afraid to move. After some brief swordplay, Tazi left the men bloodied but alive and turned her attention to the object of their drunken desires to see why she still lingered behind.

The raven-haired woman's clothes had been torn, but other than that, she herself was free from injury. On closer scrutiny, Tazi saw that the Calishite woman had ice-white eyes, and she correctly deduced that the stranger was completely blind. Tazi had assumed at the time that Fannah had stayed in the alley while she drove off the attackers because she was sightless. She suspected that Fannah wouldn't have known where to flee. Over time, however, Tazi had been forced to reconsider that theory.

While it was true that Fannah was blind, she was more than capable of accurate vision. It had only taken a moment for her to "see" through Tazi's disguise that night. While so many of the sighted people around her thought Tazi was a young man, a disguise she was very proud of, Fannah knew differently through smell and touch. She had been able to leave the alley at any time during the fight. However, Fannah had chosen to remain. She had given her trust and safety to Tazi's abilities.

She's given it to me all over again, Tazi marveled. If she's this sure of me, then maybe I can be, too.

No one was in sight. Realizing that, once again, Cale was right and there was no exterior guard to the manse,

Tazi silently slid down the wall and rejoined her cohorts.

"It looks as though everything is quiet outside," she told them. "I think it would be best to have you, Steorf, check for the most silent way inside." Tazi spoke his name aloud in deference to Fannah's blindness. "You're the best one to figure out the right path to ease our way in."

It was Steorf's turn to look sharply at her.

"You want me to 'ease' our way in?" he asked a little incredulously. "We haven't done that in a long time."

"I'm sure you're still good at it, or have you lost your touch?" she asked with innocent eyes.

She wasn't sure but Tazi thought she saw Steorf's strong jaw twitch in the hint of a smile.

"Oh," he answered, "I think you'll find I'm still good at it . . . and a few things more."

With that, he moved off to survey the grounds with a different eye, leaving the women alone for a moment.

"So you and Steorf are back to 'easing' your way around?" Fannah questioned.

Tazi looked at her in surprise.

"I'm blind," Fannah explained in her melodic voice, "not deaf."

Tazi couldn't resist a giggle at Fannah's jab.

"You don't miss a thing," she replied. "You'd think I would remember that by now." Taking a deep breath, she continued, "It has been a long time since he and I have done something like this together. I'd be lying to you if I said I wasn't worried."

"You'd be a fool to ever say something like that," Fannah corrected her. Laying her delicate hand on Tazi's sinewy arm, she continued, "And you are no fool, Thazienne. You never have been."

Fannah wasn't able to see the slightly grateful look that Tazi gave her, but Tazi was sure she knew just the same. Since the beginning of their unusual friendship, Tazi had always felt that Fannah could look right through her, blind or not. That hadn't changed over time. She reached over and quickly patted Fannah's hand, almost embarrassing herself with the familiar gesture.

"Are you ladies ready?" Steorf asked with mock formality.

He had slipped up behind them noiselessly. Tazi knew he asked the question in jest, but it was appropriate nonetheless. If they weren't ready, this whole crossing would end disastrously. She weighed her options one last time and gazed hard at her companions. There was no other choice.

"Let's bring this to Ciredor," Tazi finally answered, "and bring it to an end."

"Then let's be on our way," Steorf said, tilting his head. "If you don't mind," he added after a moment, "I'll make a quick pass to muffle the clanging your rapiers are making, Thazienne, before you alert everyone that we're coming."

Tazi whirled to face him, an angry retort on the tip of her tongue. She knew well enough her Sembian guardblades were as silent as she was and was about to remind Steorf of that fact in no uncertain terms. But the expression Steorf wore revealed he had been teasing her.

That's twice now, she thought.

Her lips curved up in spite of herself.

"You are touchy, aren't you?" was all he said.

Steorf swung up onto the wall and reached a hand down. Tazi laced her fingers together and gave Fannah a leg up to him. Soon enough all three were crouched along the wall. Steorf motioned to what appeared to be a servants' entrance and through a series of quick gestures let Tazi know that was probably their best chance. Fannah remained silent throughout the whole exchange. Tazi passed along their plans to the Calishite by pressing her finger into Fannah's hand and drawing a few key symbols. Tazi knew Fannah would not speak aloud again until they did.

There was only a small garden of stones between the wall and the servants' door. Aesthetically pleasing with a very intricate pattern, the garden also made a very simple and effective alarm. It was much harder to cross silently than a garden of dirt and grass, and any rocks knocked out of place would reveal an intruder had been through it. Tazi touched Steorf's arm, but he was already one step ahead. With a practiced gesture, he made the magical pass he had earlier joked about. Thanks to that spell, the three were able to walk a few inches above the ground and not disturb a single pebble.

When they reached the door, Tazi motioned for Steorf to step aside. Certain there weren't any wards on the door, Tazi reached under her shirt sleeve, took out her picks, and began to work on the lock. Three quick twists and it sprang open.

The right tool for the right job, Tazi thought with some small satisfaction, sliding the picks back into their guard on her arm.

Steorf stepped into the inky blackness first and spread out his hands. After a moment of silence, he whispered, "I don't believe anyone is here."

"Just to be on the safe side," Tazi said quietly to Steorf, "let's limit the amount of magic you use."

She wanted to make no mistakes and part of her concern came from the fact that she wasn't certain how well Steorf could control his magic.

Taking her cue from her two companions, Fannah asked aloud, "Why should we do that?"

"Well," Tazi replied, "none of my informants have had any dealings with the sorcerer who controls this gate. We can't be certain that he doesn't have some kind of affiliation with Ciredor. If Steorf doesn't know anything about him, we have to assume the worst. The fewer traces we leave behind, magical or otherwise, the better."

Tazi couldn't see, but Steorf had stood a little straighter when she mentioned his name.

"Do you know where the gate is?" Fannah asked.

"Cale wasn't certain, but he thought it was located in the cellar," Tazi answered, swallowing hard.

Silently, she dreaded going down there. She had always harbored a fear of cellars, which were often traps. After the sight she had seen in the bowels of the one Ciredor had occupied, Tazi hadn't stepped down into a cellar since.

"We'll have to make our way carefully," Steorf warned, after bumping into a doorframe. "I believe the owner has some kind of shadow spell on the tallhouse. The darkness is absolute."

Before either Steorf or Tazi could say any more, Fannah took the lead. Out of all of them, she was the best equipped to maneuver through the house. She was the only one not affected by the darkness, having been blind since birth. Fannah lightly clasped Tazi's hand, and Steorf followed directly behind. Tazi was always caught off-guard by the depth perception Fannah possessed. Her ability to discern the dimensions and spatial relationship between objects bordered on amazing. This time was no exception. Fannah moved through the house as though she had lived there all her life.

Passing carefully through what was most likely the servants' quarters, the trio made their way to the kitchen. It reeked of rancid fat and mold. Tazi's stomach, already in turmoil, roiled at the smells. She wondered how long it had been since the kitchen had been cleaned, or how long it had been since any servants had passed through the building at all. She was hard pressed not to sneeze at the dust they stirred up.

A few more steps and Fannah led them into a pantry. Tazi dismally noticed it didn't smell much better there, either. Fannah felt along the shelves with deft fingers, passing over spoiled supplies and ruined goods until she discovered the door handle to the cellar. She opened it just a crack, to test the integrity of the hinges. They, at least, had been given some attention recently, and the door opened soundlessly. After one step down the equally noiseless stairs, Fannah stopped and Tazi nearly walked into her.

"What's wrong?" Tazi asked into Fannah's ear.

"Something smells down here," she replied.

"It's probably just more moldy food," Tazi reassured her.

Fannah still hesitated. "I can smell that, but there's something else," she said.

"What?" asked Steorf, who had moved to share the step with Tazi.

"I can smell old food and something else. Something like animal waste."

"We can't stop now," Tazi urged.

Steorf moved past Fannah and continued the rest of the way down the stairs, both Tazi and Fannah trailing in his wake. The moment he reached the base of the stairs, a light sprang up. Everyone froze.

Bathed in the weak glow, Tazi could see that the cellar was not very big. Only thirty feet long and twenty feet wide, the room didn't concern Tazi. She had been in bigger traps before. The walls were made up of dark, rough-hewn river rock and constantly seeped moisture. The stones were slick with mold and slime. The smell of decay permeated the entire room. Glancing around quickly, Tazi could see there was no other furniture or staples housed in there, save for the prize for which they had been searching.

A stone archway taller than Steorf and nearly as wide as it was tall nestled in the far corner of the room. Aside from its size, the archway was unremarkable to look at. Tazi was able to see through the opening of the portal and make out the far wall directly behind it.

"That's it," she said, moving to stand beside Steorf. "Let's go."

Steorf put his arm out in front of her.

"No," he said, "Fannah was right. There is something else down here. See?"

He pointed to a bowl near the gate that was overflowing with what looked like food scraps. Tazi could barely make out the dish.

"There's no creature here now," she reasoned. Turning around in a complete circle, she proclaimed, "We're alone. There's nowhere for anyone to hide."

Suddenly, a low growl filled the cellar. The threesome faced the gate in unison in time to see a large, gray creature slink around from behind it. Tazi was amazed and somewhat startled. Since she had been attacked by one long ago, she harbored a deep seated fear of dogs, but this was something more than a simple canine.

Slightly larger than the average mastiff, the dark-furred creature's eyes glowed a deep red. As its lips pulled back in a warning snarl, Tazi could see that its mouth was filled with what looked like an impossible number of teeth. As it swung its massive head from Tazi to Steorf to Tazi again, it clicked its teeth with deliberate slowness.

"But you could see straight through that gate," Tazi said, "and that thing wasn't there a moment ago."

"Gates can twist perception as well as time and distance," Steorf explained. "I'll deal with this."

No sooner did Steorf move forward than the dog-beast sprang from beside the gate. In two quick bounds, the hound, as large as a man, had covered the distance between them.

Steorf raised his arms and spoke a word that Tazi didn't recognize. A crackle of light exploded from his hands toward the animal. Whatever spell he thought was going to happen didn't, though. Undaunted, the beast knocked him flat, tearing a good chunk out of the leather gauntlet Steorf wore. Fortunately for him, he had thrown his hands in front of his face in a reflexive defense. The dog shook the glove mercilessly and circled around for another pass.

"Do something," Tazi screamed, but the burly mage

half sat and stared at his own hands as though dumb-struck. "Your sword!" Tazi yelled.

The beast, no longer content to shred Steorf's clothing, leaped once again onto the mage.

Steorf, knocked back onto the ground, grabbed the hound's collar with both hands. He was barely able to keep the snapping jaws from his eyes and was losing ground fast.

Tazi, realizing that Steorf couldn't draw his weapon to defend himself, jumped into action. Shoving Fannah back, she ripped off her travel cloak, wrapped part of it around her left arm, and threw herself at the tangle of fur and friend.

Landing nearly astride the animal, Tazi managed to lock her left arm around the dog's throat and throw part of her cloak over its muzzle with her right hand. Between that and the momentum from her leap, she was able to wrench the beast off of Steorf.

Tazi stole a quick glance at the young mage to see if he was all right. Steorf looked uninjured but still dazed. She wondered just when was the last time he had to rely on his physical abilities but didn't dwell on the thought. She didn't have time for more.

Barely able to contain the snarling monster that was at least twice her weight, Tazi found herself thrown against the wall. The wind was momentarily knocked out of her, and the dog was able to use the opportunity to free its face from the confines of her cloak.

Tazi thrust out her left hand and said the spell word that triggered her emerald ring, but there was no gray shield to protect her and no excruciating pain, as the ring had always demanded.

Tazi found herself staring into the beast's red eyes, eyes that glinted almost as much as its bejeweled collar. She could feel the dog's breath hit her face in short, hot blasts. Her right wrist still bore the scars of a dog attack from many years before, and faced with one of her bogeymen, Tazi began to sink into the mindless terror of childhood. She instinctively crouched against the wall and began crawling backward like a crab. The dog only watched her retreat and stood its ground.

It took only a moment for Tazi to realize that the gray beast wasn't following her. She whipped her head around to search for Steorf. Tazi saw that he had moved backward from the spot where he had been attacked and was crawling around, probably looking for something to use against the dog as a shield. Turning toward the stairs, Tazi could see that Fannah had stayed exactly where she had pushed her. Glancing back at the hound, she confirmed that the animal had not followed her. In fact, the beast was sitting right beside what was left of Tazi's cloak, unperturbed. She backed up a little more.

"Steorf," she cautiously whispered back over her shoulder, "I think the beast only attacks if someone approaches the gate."

The young mage was unsteadily rising to his feet.

"It doesn't matter," he finally responded. "The animal must be impervious to magic. I think that collar protects the canine. There's no way we can defeat it. We'll have to leave and think of another way."

Tazi detected a quake to Steorf's voice, and she was momentarily surprised by his quick defeat. She wondered if he actually meant that there was no way for *him* to defeat it magically, but part of her wanted to run as well. The most powerful tool she possessed was useless against the hound. A hasty retreat was appealing and seemed logical. She looked over to Fannah, though, and saw the raven-haired woman standing on the bottom step. She appeared serene to Tazi, but very vulnerable. Tazi's mouth tightened, and she stood up.

"No," she answered Steorf, "there is no other way than this. I'm not running away or taking the easy route anymore."

Tazi took a step forward.

As she suspected, as soon as the hound saw her move closer to the gate, the beast was in motion. Tazi could see its powerful muscles bunch in effort as the dog made its attack. With a vicious snarl, the guardian launched itself into the air, much as it had done with Steorf.

Tazi crossed her arms at her waist and drew her Sembian guardblades. Though she knew their enchantments would be useless against the guardian, the rapiers were still good steel. Not many things were impervious to that.

Tazi used the animal's might against itself. She held her right arm sturdy, and even though the dog saw the threat she posed, it was unable to stop its motion. The beast impaled itself onto Tazi's right rapier. She simultaneously swung across with her left blade and partially decapitated the thing. The momentum and size of the animal toppled both of them to the ground.

Straining against the animal's dead weight, Tazi managed to push the creature off of her. She rose just as Steorf, somewhat shamefaced, reached her side. Tazi didn't notice him as she checked to verify that the dog was truly dead, not completely trusting the copious amounts of its blood that covered her. She half-expected it to open its eyes and gnash its jaws. One look at its nearly severed head, however, removed all doubt.

Tazi grasped the blade that was still embedded in the guardian with both hands and began to tug. She finally had to place her foot against the animal's side to give her the leverage she needed to free her weapon from the meat of its chest. Steorf handed her the other rapier.

"It's safe now, Fannah," she called out as she retrieved what remained of her cloak.

She used the tatters to clean her blades before replacing the weapons in their sheaths. Soon enough, Fannah stood next to her winded companions.

"Something tells me you two must be a sight, indeed," Fannah said.

Tazi smirked at the comment, but Steorf didn't respond.

"Well," Tazi admitted, looking at the large carcass and the widening pool of blood on the floor, "we did a pretty horrible job of not leaving any kind of a trace behind."

She flashed a smirk at Steorf.

He stepped over to the dog and knelt by its side. Steorf slid his hands over the dull collar and deftly removed it with a small click. He placed his hands on the dead beast's side and closed his eyes.

Tazi watched in mute fascination as a blue glow enveloped the dog. The animal's wounds began to knit themselves shut, and the pool of blood evaporated. With only a few words, Steorf healed the hound. Soon enough, the animal opened its eyes and briefly thumped its tail as Steorf replaced the jeweled collar.

Tazi took a step back, but the dog merely rolled upright and padded over to lie by the far side of the gate as though it were a comfortable hearth. Fannah walked over to the dog and hesitantly touched it. The guardian thumped its tail once more. Tazi turned to Steorf with an amazed expression on her face.

"You said we shouldn't leave any traces, and once it was dead I was able to remove the enchanted collar," he offered in quiet explanation. "As soon as we leave, the creature will revert back to its former, unpleasant demeanor toward unwanted guests."

She cast a sidelong glance at him and said, "I thought you told me the other day that you weren't very adept at necromancy spells."

"I've been practicing for this journey," was all he would answer.

Tazi jabbed his shoulder good-naturedly.

"A good thing for us that you have been."

She smiled up into his face, trying to recapture some of their old camaraderie, for Fannah's sake if nothing else, but he didn't return it.

"I'm sorry," he said quietly and cast his eyes down toward his limp hands. "I just . . ." he struggled with the words, "seemed to have forgot myself during the battle."

Tazi moved a fraction closer and laid a hand on his forearm.

"Just because you forgot yourself for a moment doesn't mean that you lost yourself. Remember that," she told him earnestly.

He stared hard at her before laying his other hand briefly over hers.

"Thank you, Tazi."

Fannah walked back over to them and asked, "Is it time?"

Tazi looked at both her friends.

"I think so," she replied. "Steorf, do you have any idea what we might expect from this gate travel?"

"I've heard many stories," he replied, "but they have all contradicted themselves. Either none of them were true, or what they signify is that each gate is very different."

"Which do you think it is?" Tazi asked, valuing his thoughts on the matter.

This was not lost on Steorf.

"I believe every gate is very different," he answered seriously.

"Then I suppose the only way we'll find out is by going through," Tazi concluded.

She peeked over at the dog one last time. The beast simply lay to one side, snoring softly. She shook her head but kept one hand on the hilt of her rapier anyway. Old fears didn't just fade at the pass of a hand.

The three approached the archway slowly. The gate looked as if it was made from pink sandstone, the kind one might find in the desert. Tazi was still able to clearly see the other side of the cellar wall. Her heart started to beat a little faster, and her mouth dried out. It had been a long time since she felt like this. In the last year, none of her wildings had left her feeling so alive. Even though she and her friends were going off to risk death or worse, she couldn't help but grin.

"This is it," she told them.

In unison, Tazi, Steorf, and Fannah stepped through. Tazi's senses were immediately overwhelmed. She felt as though she had walked into a storm like the ones that battered the ships in Selgaunt Bay at year's end. All around her, various shades of blue and yellow swirled and howled. There was no dirt or sky where she found herself. Tazi was terribly disorientated with nothing to ground her senses. She didn't know if she was moving forward or backward. Fannah and Steorf were nowhere to be seen. She was beginning to panic just a little and bit back on that feeling.

Trying to move forward as best she could, Tazi could make out a shadow to her left. Desperately trying to focus her eyes, Tazi called out to the figure. As she squinted harder, Tazi was startled, and she let out a gasp. The figure was her elf friend.

"Ebeian!" she cried.

Tazi could see that he was whole again but suspended in the maelstrom of the gate. She watched as he writhed and moaned as if white-hot pokers were stabbing him. She could see he was in excruciating pain. Tazi stretched out her hand and tried to reach him.

"Eb!" she called out, and everything around her went dark.

Tazi crashed to her knees. She was breathing hard and had broken out in a cold sweat. She opened and closed her eyes several times until she realized the colors were gone, there was a solid surface beneath her knees and hands, and it was deafeningly quiet.

"Is anyone here?" she asked finally, breaking the silence.

She heard both Steorf and Fannah make weak replies. Tazi breathed a little easier after she heard their voices. The three simply sat where they were for a few moments and allowed their equilibrium to balance once again.

"Did you see anything in there?" Tazi asked as she rose on shaky legs.

"Nothing that made any sense," Steorf replied. "You?"

"I saw Ebeian," she blurted out. "He looked . . . tormented."

Steorf moved carefully through the dark to stand beside her.

"That wasn't him," he reassured her. "His soul has gone to its final journey. I think the gate picked up what was most on our minds and showed it to us."

"Do you think that was it?" Tazi asked hopefully, hating the idea that Ebeian could somehow still be suffering.

"I do," he answered confidently. "Don't you think so, Fannah?"

"I'm not sure," Fannah carefully replied. "I have been sightless since birth, but I saw something."

"What was it?" Tazi asked.

"What I saw was for me alone, I believe. However, I did not see Ebeian anywhere in that whirlwind," she confirmed for Tazi.

"Well," Tazi finally continued after a thoughtful pause, "let's see where we've ended up. At least this place doesn't stink."

The room was dark, but dry and clean. Fannah took the lead just as she had in the other cellar. In short order, she found a set of stairs and began to lead her sighted friends out.

At the top of the steps, Fannah felt a door latch. She opened the door slowly, and the room was bathed in harsh light. Both Tazi and Steorf winced in discomfort.

Fannah stepped out into a busy street and spread her arms. She closed her ice-white eyes, put her head back, and sighed before turning to face Tazi and Steorf. Tazi stood in the doorway and breathed in the smell of dust and sand. Still not having adjusted to the bright sunshine, she held up one hand to shield her eyes and squinted at Fannah. All she could make out was a black silhouette framed against gold.

She heard her friend's melodic voice say, "Welcome to Calimport, Tazi."

CHAPTER 5

CALIMPORT

Tazi was surrounded.

All around her, life swarmed and teemed. She, Fannah, and Steorf found themselves in a bustling section of Calimport. The warm sun beat down on them, and Tazi took in everything. Many men and a few women pushed past her. The men were clad in loose trousers, shirts, embroidered vests, and robes. Most of them wore some type of head covering, but that varied in style.

Perhaps it denotes station, Tazi thought.

The women were completely covered, even wearing veils over their faces. Tazi caught glimpses of trousers when their robes peeked open, but no more than that. Those more poorly dressed were leading beasts of burden pulling heavily laden wooden carts. Tazi had to move quickly to avoid getting a toe crushed by one of them. There wasn't a single creature that wasn't bustling.

Looking up toward the horizon, Tazi saw slim towers stab at the bright sky. Some of the towers supported incredible domes that glinted in the sunlight. The occasional flying carpet drifted from parapet to parapet. Lower down, the buildings were less than extravagant but wondrous nonetheless, a few sporting intricate mosaic designs. Tazi realized that she was standing in the middle of a throng of people, her mouth agape.

"I must look like a fish just hauled out of Selgaunt Bay, mouth opening and closing," she chuckled to herself.

"What was that?" asked Steorf.

Tazi was lost to her gazing again.

Men and women were shouting things down to the merchants at Tazi's level from atop the walls.

None of the stalls or archways had any names or signs that she could read, and she likewise noticed no identifying marks on the door they had stepped out of, which was set into a mud brick wall. When she heard a telltale click, she tried the handle and found that the door was locked behind them. Tazi suspected it would not open again. There would be no going back that way.

As someone shoved past her, Tazi realized that they needed to move.

Speaking loudly to be heard over the buyers above, Tazi yelled, "we shouldn't stand here too much longer."

Both Steorf and Fannah faced her expectantly.

"I would dearly love to tell you where we should go, but I can't even say where we are right now. I think Fannah is best suited to do that."

Steorf nodded at her logic, and Fannah moved a little closer to Tazi.

"Tell me what you see," the Calishite asked her.

"The mud walls all appear the same to me," Tazi admitted, "and I can't see any signs. In fact, the only thing I do see is a symbol cut high into the wall, but it's the same design as one over an archway nearby as well so I doubt it means much."

"What is it?" Fannah asked.

"It looks like the silhouette of a ship with one mast."

"Are the sails unfurled?" Fannah questioned.

"Yes," Tazi answered, realizing that the symbol might mean something after all, "the sails are full."

Tazi watched as Fannah smiled slightly.

"Tell me," she prodded further, "is there one building that stands out among the others near here?"

Tazi turned around and spotted a five-story building with a six-story minaret on top within a stone's throw from where they stood. She described the edifice to Fannah, a little perturbed that the Calishite never gave her a quick answer.

But she always gives me the right one, Tazi told herself.

"We are in the Piqaz Drudach within the Osiir Sabban. The entire area is known as Hook Ward. This is my home," Fannah said.

"Too much of a coincidence," Steorf muttered.

"You might be right," Tazi agreed, thinking she would mull that over later. "So what's the building in front of us?" she asked Fannah.

"That building is known as the Lighthouse of the Moon," Fannah explained. "Not only does it serve as the only lighthouse within the harbor walls, it is also a temple to Selûne."

"That's a temple?" Steorf asked.

"Yes. The priests of Selûne man the lighthouse," Fannah answered, "but for the last eight hundred years, they haven't had to do a thing to make it function. There's a mirror in the minaret that coalesces the moonlight every night and shines it out toward the harbor. No one has ever been able to extinguish that light. In fact, there is only one time every month when it doesn't shine: the night of the new moon."

Tazi stared up at the mirror. "How fortunate to have such a dependable beacon!"

Fannah smiled once more. "It's funny how many creatures mistakenly fear the night, as though blackness was somehow inherently evil. They don't realize they should look to themselves, that it is the darkness within that they should fear."

Fannah pulled the hood of her travel cloak over her head, and Steorf followed suit. All that was left of Tazi's cloak, however, was a pile of rags after her encounter with the dog. She realized she was a bit exposed.

"It would help if we could get some clothing less conspicuous," Tazi noted. She had already seen several men stare at her a little longer than she was used to, even dressed as she was.

"Like in all of Calimport, the merchants of Hook Ward sell most everything. It shouldn't be difficult to find some suitable supplies for us," Fannah informed her.

Tazi and Steorf flanked Fannah as they began to maneuver through the throng. As Fannah deftly wove amongst the sea of people, Tazi had a little time to notice more of her surroundings.

Much like Selgaunt, people were buying and selling every kind of merchandise possible, but what puzzled her was that several different priests were hawking their gods as though the deities were simply wares as well. In front of the lighthouse, proselytes of Selûne, dressed in their white and blue finery, were preaching to a group of slaves. Tazi suspected the slaves were listening merely to give themselves a break for a few moments, but then two other acolytes descended on the small congregation. One wore the black and purple robes of Shar and the other a pair of white bound hands, showing she was a follower of Ilmater. It only took a short time before the sermons turned to shouts between the three. Tazi had never seen any temple in Selgaunt tolerate that type of behavior.

"What's going on?" she asked Fannah.

Fannah turned slightly. "What do you mean?"

"Those proselytes over there are about to start fighting," she exclaimed.

"Oh, that," Fannah chuckled. "It's a well-known saying around here that 'Hook Ward has a holy war at least twice a day'!"

"I can't believe it's fitting for them to behave like that," Steorf added, breaking his silence. "Doesn't it shame their gods?"

"Steorf, you misunderstand," Fannah explained gently. "I think nearly every deity of Faerûn is represented here in Calimport. Many of the clerics have to compete for followers or their temples will suffer. It is their duty. In fact," she added, "it is perfectly acceptable for clerics to hold secular positions in the city, with their salaries going back to their respective temples."

"I guess I just don't understand," Steorf replied, shaking his head.

He glanced around uncomfortably, and Fannah smiled indulgently.

"It is a little hard for foreigners," she said. "Come along. Selamek's Warehouse is not too far away. We'll be able to pick up a few things there."

Traveling in a southeasterly direction, the three continued to push their way through the crowds. Tazi looked back over her shoulder one last time at the sermon to see if the priests had come to blows, but the crowd swallowed up the view.

Fannah expertly led the two through the mazelike streets and Tazi found herself shoved right up against her, the crowd was so thick at times. The Calishite woman didn't even appear to notice the close quarters, but as Tazi glanced over Fannah's shoulder, she could see that Steorf looked distressed as well.

Though Selgaunt was a busy merchant city in its own right, Tazi found she was almost suffocated by Calimport. The streets, such as they were, were very narrow, with mud brick walls dividing and subdividing every possible space. Though the streets opened to the sky, across many of the walls that separated the dru-dachs merchants had laid poles. From these poles, the ingenious peddlers managed to string up even more goods. Tapestries and rugs hung from some, while jewel-hued, freshly dyed yarns hung from others like cheerful spiderwebs. Hardly a breeze stirred the hot air. Tazi felt trapped and claustrophobic.

"Fannah," she whispered in her friend's ear, not wanting Steorf to know she was uncomfortable. She felt that, for the sake of the group, and since she saw his reticence with the dog, she couldn't afford to show fear or allow failure.

"Wouldn't it be easier if we went along the walls above instead of fighting our way against the tide down here?"

Tazi had been noticing how much room there was on the higher walkways, and how much airier they looked, too.

"If we did that," Fannah explained, "we would draw much more attention to ourselves. The upper walkways are for more 'noble' people. There is anonymity and safety for us down here.

"Don't worry," she added, "I can tell from the smell that we're nearly there."

Soon enough, Tazi understood what she meant. A sour odor filled the unmoving air, and Tazi found herself gagging. Without saying a word, Fannah motioned down one of the side streets and Tazi could see twenty large indentations in a clay platform as big as a house foundation. Each hole in the platform was the size of a small drinking well and was filled to the brim with a colored liquid. Every pot had a different color. A couple of robed men were leaning over the various holes like they were scrubbing laundry.

"Leather dyeing," Steorf offered.

"It is a rather unmistakable smell, isn't it?" Tazi replied, absently running a hand down her own leather vest.

The three rounded a turn and came upon one of Calimport's official bazaars: The Scarlet Cross Trading Coster Warehouse. Tents and stalls were pushed up against more permanent structures, and people were shouting to and fro. Merchants thrust objects mercilessly in their faces as Tazi and her companions ran the gauntlet of shops.

"A leather sack for all your treasures?" one seller called out.

"Something sharp and shiny for milady?" another cried.

Tazi was startled as the vendor simply levitated several swords and a mail shirt near her, twirling them around for her inspection. She saw Steorf flinch when the shopkeeper did it to him too.

Tazi also noticed that the types of items for sale changed the deeper they went into the market. The outermost shops had hard goods and weapons, while further in, the stalls were all full of coarse fabrics and different kinds of clothing.

A few feet into the melee, Fannah found what she was looking for. She struck up a conversation with one of the hawkers, and Tazi realized that the two were speaking in Alzhedo, the native tongue of Calimshan. It was the first time she had ever heard it spoken, and Tazi believed it was one of the most lyrical languages she had ever heard.

Only Elvish is more beautiful, she thought, remembering a few of the words Ebeian had said to her once.

The vendor and Fannah, after some obvious haggling, struck a bargain. The old man turned to the back wall of his shop and pointed a finger at several robes that were hanging up. One by one, the robes flew across the shop and were floating in front of Tazi.

"Pick a *jellaba* that suits you," Fannah told Tazi, switching back to the common tongue.

She chose a white and blue-stripped robe and paid the mutually agreed upon price. Tazi quickly covered herself and felt less vulnerable.

"I don't seem to be happy unless I'm in disguise," she whispered to Steorf, trying to draw him from the moodiness that had overshadowed him since his failure with the dog.

The mage didn't respond. Just as Tazi had stared at the people and architecture when they first entered the city, it was his turn to be mesmerized. Tazi thought he seemed fixated by all the magic surrounding them.

"I have to admit," she leaned closer to him as she flipped up her hood, "that they do seem to be more open about their abilities here in Calimport."

"Abilities?" Steorf scoffed. "They're more like simple parlor tricks. It's shameful behavior," he continued. "Just like in front of the temple of Selûne. And they call *us* barbarians."

Tazi looked at him with a little concern.

He's quick to judge, she thought, but then he's never been outside of Sembia, either.

"Fannah," she said, turning to her companion, "I'm counting on you to help us from making a mistake. From all I've read and seen, the customs of this place are very different from Sembia, and I'd like not to offend too many people."

"If I 'see' you starting to fall, I'll do what I can. But he"—she pointed unerringly at Steorf—"is the sorcerer, not me. There's only so much I can do."

The two women giggled, and Steorf relented a touch. Tazi, pleased that Fannah's words had the desired effect on him, got all of them moving again.

"There must be food somewhere in here," she said to Fannah.

"Farther in, closer to the warehouse proper," Fannah answered, "are the more precious and perishable items."

"Let's keep moving," Tazi urged. "Even with the robes, I still feel a little exposed. Also, it should be harder for someone to overhear us in this throng if we're on the go."

"Well, that's true," Steorf interjected, "as I can barely hear you myself."

Tazi smiled at his quip but was concerned that he still was somewhat preoccupied with the open displays of sorcery.

I'll deal with that later, she thought.

"When I mentioned what Eb told us after his death, you told me you were familiar with the Skulking God," she reminded Fannah. "Is his temple here in Hook Ward, too?"

"No, it isn't," she answered. Fannah ducked as a large basket of fruit passed rather quickly by her head. "On occasion, you might find some of his proselytes out in the wards, but there is no proper temple anywhere above in Calimport for the Lurker in Darkness."

She reached out and plucked several pieces of fruit for Tazi, Steorf, and herself from that same basket and flipped a coin in the direction of the farmer. Tazi was impressed.

"I could hear the basket whistling through the air," Fannah explained when her companions remained silent, "and I could smell the fruit within it."

"But how did you know where the merchant was?" Steorf demanded.

"Lucky guess," Fannah laughed. "I knew that someone within the bazaar would grab the tossed coin and if it wasn't the correct merchant, the rightful one would wrestle it back for himself."

Tazi laughed at her friend's clever solution.

Continuing out of the bazaar, the threesome passed through an archway into a most decadent area: the south end of Eraré Sabban. On their left was an obvious festhall with a stone façade, a little rundown but still opulent. What made the roomy building stand out were the seven pillars in front of the structure. Each carved column depicted a woman in various stages of undress. Tazi watched as Steorf became uncomfortable and turned away only to be equally embarrassed by what was to his right. Even Tazi had to blush at that.

"The building to your left is the Seven Dancing

Jhasinas," Fannah explained. "The name obviously came from the carvings in front of the building. The structure on this side is the Festhall of Eternal Delight."

"And the guests are obviously delighted to be there," Tazi managed to say.

Steorf was speechless, and Fannah hurried the two past the sybaritic scene literally spilling out of the doorways in front of them. The patrons, much like the Seven Jhasinas, were nearly nude. Fannah stopped them once they were a few buildings distant.

"That was rather a sight," Tazi exclaimed. "But you didn't have to run past so fast. I'm not that inexperienced."

"That was the temple to Sharess," Fannah explained.

"That was a temple, too?" Steorf blustered.

"It is the greatest one to my goddess. I was afraid someone might recognize me if we lingered too long."

"So that is the goddess you and your mother served," Tazi clarified.

"Yes, it is. I'm sure you were shocked by what you both saw, even briefly. The most pious there are the staff, and they are all dedicated to hedonism in the name of Sharess. Even the jhasinas who modeled for the pillars became priestesses of Sharess after she came to them."

"But it seemed so . . . disorganized," Steorf interrupted, trying hard to be diplomatic.

"Unfortunately, many visitors to the temple do have less than holy thoughts when they arrive. They take our doctrine and use it as an excuse for all types of behavior."

"We saw some of that," Tazi exclaimed.

"What they don't understand, or choose not to," Fannah continued, "is that to worship Sharess is to explore and indulge in one's senses."

Tazi saw that Fannah was becoming more animated than she had ever seen the blind woman before.

"To serve Sharess is to recognize the beauty in the world. To be fully alive and immersed in who you are through sight, smell, and taste. It was here," she continued, "that I was taught how to use my other senses to compensate for my lack of sight."

"Your mother was a priestess in this temple," Tazi remembered.

"Yes," Fannah answered, "but that was when Sharess was still under the influence of Shar. After the Time of Troubles, Sharess regained herself and became the bright goddess once more. This building was erected to celebrate her."

Tazi could see that Fannah was troubled by thoughts of her mother. She remembered Fannah telling her once that the only reason her mother didn't kill her at birth was because her religion forbade it. Fannah had survived her childhood simply because of her mother's religious fervor, not because of her love. Tazi changed the subject, troubled by her friend's distress.

"You mentioned a little while ago that there was no temple to the Skulking God," she asked. "How do we find him—or those who follow him?"

Fannah perked up at the question. "I said he had no temples *above* in Calimport. We will have to travel to Calimport Muzad, below the city surface, to find an obscure sect of humans I know of who still worship him."

"There aren't many followers left?" Steorf questioned. "I suppose that would explain why I knew nothing of him."

"No, that's not entirely true," Fannah replied. "Ibrandul has many followers both here and in Waterdeep. In Calimport Below, most of his followers are skulks, but I have dealt with his human Children before. I believe they will help us."

"Why are they below?" Tazi asked.

"The Lord of the Dry Depths is an old god," Fannah made clear, using one of the many titles of Ibrandul. "His worship extend back to the prehistory of Calimshan, dating before the founding of the Shoon Empire."

"And he's always been below the city?" Tazi inquired.

"At one time," Fannah replied, "a tribe of humans was

stolen from the Calim Desert by drow and forced to serve them for centuries. Finally, a monstrous lizard came to free them. Some of the humans stayed below in the Underdark, while others returned to the surface to spread the word of the Lurker in Darkness."

"So Ibrandul protects those trapped below," Steorf deduced.

"As far as I know, he does. He is supposed to keep safe any human who must travel through the dark regions, as well as keep safe and guide those who worship him. To some he appears as a red lizard, and to others he is seen as a chisel featured, bare-chested man with glowing eyes. And sometimes he is simply a wind in the tunnels below."

"And that's all?" Tazi interrupted.

"That is all I know," Fannah answered.

Tazi clucked her tongue and frowned.

"What is it?" Steorf asked her.

"I just don't understand what Ciredor would have to do with Ibrandul. It doesn't make much sense," she responded.

"Perhaps the followers of Ibrandul will be able to answer that," Steorf offered.

"I hope so," Tazi agreed earnestly. "I certainly hope so. How much farther?" she asked Fannah.

"We only need to pass through one more ward before we reach Crypt Ward. There, in the Forgotten Sabban, there is a passageway that will take us to the Muzhajaarnadah," Fannah told them.

"And the darkness below," Tazi added quietly.

"Which way?" Tazi asked Fannah.

"Toward the east," Fannah replied.

The three picked their way through Crypt Ward, carefully following Fannah's lead. Tazi had never seen such a large cemetery before, and some of the mausoleums were elegant in their ostentation. Scanning the ward, she was momentarily thoughtful.

"What is it?" Steorf asked her quietly.

"Look at that field to the east," she pointed.

Steorf followed her gaze out past the mausoleums to an area that was walled off only by metal spear fences. There were no buildings within the area, a sharp contrast with the other sections of Calimport that Tazi and her companions had passed through. Within the sabban, there were only a few obelisks and fountains visible and the occasional plinths to mar the view. After the hustle and crowds of the other wards, it was a peaceful change.

"What are you two looking at?" Fannah asked.

"I was just showing Steorf that park nearby," Tazi explained.

"That is the Forgotten Sabban," Fannah informed them. "While it has always been used as one of the most popular parks of Calimport, it is, in actuality, the home for many, many mass burials."

"It is also a cemetery?" Steorf remarked.

"Since the Sixth Age of Calimshan," Fannah replied. "And within that sabban is one of the hidden passageways to the Muzad."

"There are no real walls," Tazi observed, "and I don't see any of the typical sabban marks we've seen in the other drudachs."

"This ward is unique in that it doesn't have any true walls and no marks. That's one of the reasons," Fannah added, "how the ward came by its name."

Steorf moved behind Fannah, but Tazi stood a moment longer. Whether it was because she was overwhelmed by the realization that the land contained perhaps thousands of dead or because the vast expanse of green was like an oasis in the midst of the turmoil of humanity, Tazi was awed. She inhaled deeply, watched the setting sun turn the very air pink, and breathed in the smell of dust and grass. Shadows reached across the deep green with greedy fingers, and strange insects hummed softly. She felt as though she was momentarily caught up in someone else's dream.

"Coming?" Steorf called.

Tazi roused herself and trotted along to catch up with her companions. Fannah had reached one of the few markhouts in view, already obscured by the evening's growing darkness. She gently trailed her fingers along the sides of the mausoleum with her sensitive touch. When her hands recognized one of the carved phrases, she tilted her head like a curious bird.

"Someone you know?" Tazi asked, concerned that a friend or relative of Fannah's might be buried there.

Fannah smiled as she corrected her Sembian companion. "Not someone but some*thing* I know."

With a few deft moves of her fingers, Fannah tripped the door and it slowly swung open.

"In here," Fannah directed them.

Tazi looked around briefly but despite Fannah's insistence that the Forgotten Ward was a favorite commons, she saw no one nearby. She did have to admit to herself that the long shadows of the evening probably hid more than she could imagine, so she couldn't be sure just who or what might be watching. She hoped they remained undetected in this strange city.

She nodded to Steorf, and they entered the tomb after Fannah.

Inside, Tazi was surprised to find it empty. She had been prepared for a pocket of stale air laced with decay but found the markhout cool and almost refreshing. As she and Steorf glanced around, they both realized that the small edifice held no other occupants but Fannah.

"Not all of the mausoleums within Crypt Ward are quite what they seem, which is one of the reasons why the ward has become so popular," Fannah explained. "This is not the only one that leads to the Muzad," she continued, "but it is the only one I know of that will take us to the Temple of Ibrandul."

Fannah turned and keyed open another door. This one

was clearly a passageway down into the tunnels beneath Calimport, with its uninviting, dark depths.

Tazi took the lead with Steorf subtly illuminating a few feet around them. She debated about having him quench the light but decided to let it go. She was still unsure how to deal with Steorf at times, and that awkwardness made her hesitant. Part of her wanted and needed to trust him again. However, there was still that voice of doubt in the back of her mind.

Watch and learn, she told herself.

The inner doorway of the mausoleum opened up to a gently sloping tunnel that was cool, dry, and apparently empty. Once they passed the threshold, Tazi and Steorf discovered that not only was it wide enough for the three to walk abreast but also that his glow spell was unnecessary.

Every ten feet or so Tazi could see naturally occurring recesses in the rock wall, like sconces, that held small, shimmering spheres that did an adequate job illuminating the passage.

"Does this only lead to the temple?" Tazi asked Fannah quietly.

"If memory serves me right," Fannah replied, "I don't think there are any major forks until we get to the temple proper. That shouldn't be more than a short walk."

"Good," Tazi answered and firmly planted herself in the lead.

Steorf moved up just beside and slightly behind her, and Fannah trailed just behind the two of them.

Tazi was on guard and looked from side to side. She realized that the farther they traveled down the tunnel, the deeper underground they were descending. Just as the crowded streets of Calimport had gotten to her, the passageway was beginning to play on her nerves. She found herself turning at every noise, real or imagined. She saw from the corner of her eye that Steorf looked at her a few times, and she wasn't sure of the meaning behind the glances.

Does he know how wound up I am, she wondered, or is he just looking to me for leadership?

The tunnel snaked around to the left, and Tazi no longer had a clear view of what lay ahead. She dropped her hands so that they rested on the hilts of her blades, convinced that the direction of the tunnel was intentionally meant to obscure something. She could see that Steorf also grew sterner and more alert.

"Wait," Fannah warned them softly.

I knew it, thought Tazi.

Aloud, she whispered, "What is it?"

"I smell something, though it is only a faint trace. I smell something burnt and charred."

"A torch maybe," Steorf offered, "or some sort of residual magic, perhaps?"

Fannah disagreed. "I don't think that it's any of those things. While this temple has never had one in the past, I have heard that many of Ibrandul's temples have guardians."

"What kind of guardians?" Tazi asked.

"There is a kind of lizard, called an ibrandlin, which makes its lairs out of the temples. These lizards have the ability to breathe fire," Fannah explained.

"Steorf, keep an eye on Fannah, and I'll duck ahead to see what I can," Tazi told Steorf.

"Careful," he warned her.

She winked at him and replied, "Always."

Tazi moved away from her friends and slid flat against the side of the tunnel. She took a parting look at Steorf and Fannah before rounding the bend and losing sight of her friends. She cautiously stepped around some of the smaller piles of rocks and was careful not to knock a single stone loose. With her breath held, she reached around the second turn in the tunnel and felt a more noticeable breeze on her arm.

It must open up here, she thought.

She peered around the corner just enough to take a quick glance, but that was more than enough.

Fannah was right, she acknowledged to herself. There is definitely a guard.

Curled in front of a carved double doorway was a lizard, just as Fannah had suspected. From where she was hidden, Tazi estimated that the creature was nearly thirty feet long. Silvery-gray in color, the beast looked as if it was asleep. Folded over itself as it was, Tazi found it hard to be sure, but thought it had four legs as well as a serpentine tail. She could see a glimmer from one of its deadly claws.

And it breathes fire as well, she thought morosely.

Tazi stole one more glance at the beast and confirmed that there was no obvious way around the creature. If she and her friends wanted to enter the temple, they were going to have to deal with the ibrandlin, one way or the other. She eased her way away from the opening in the tunnel and just as carefully picked her way back to Fannah and Steorf.

When she returned, Steorf asked, "Was it there, like Fannah suspected?"

"That's the largest lizard I've ever seen," she informed them and detailed the creature's size further for Steorf.

After hearing the particulars, Steorf said to Tazi, "Between you and me, I think we should be able to kill it."

"That was my first thought, too, but I took it a little further," she replied.

"What do you mean?" Steorf asked.

"We need to enlist the followers of Ibrandul's aid. Just how are we going to look to them if we, as strangers, slaughter their watch lizard to get in to see them?"

Steorf was silent for a moment.

"I see what you mean," he agreed slowly, "but considering the beast's size, I'm not sure my spells could keep it at bay long enough for you two to get in without someone getting injured."

Tazi pursed her lips, frustrated by their dilemma.

"Fannah," she asked, "do you know how smart these lizards are? Could we trick one of them?"

"I'm sorry, but I don't know much about the ibrandlin," she apologized. "From what I've heard, they are not supposed to possess much intelligence."

"That'll help," Tazi said.

"They are smart enough to recognize worshipers of Ibrandul and obey their commands," Fannah added.

"What kinds of colors do the followers of Ibrandul wear?" Steorf asked.

"Typical wear is normally purple and black, though the clothing style is not specific. Higher-ranking members sport purple cloaks with a kind of circular design," she explained.

"Purple it is," Steorf stated and reached out to touch both Tazi and Fannah.

Tazi looked down at Steorf's hand on her shoulder. A purple stain began to spread from under his fingers to seep across the blue-and-white-striped shift she wore over her leathers. Soon the whole outer garment was stained a deep amethyst color. She let out a small gasp as she glanced up and saw that both Steorf and Fannah's clothing had changed as well to shades of purple and black. On Steorf's violet cloak, small circles covered the length of the garment.

"It's not permanent," he answered Tazi's unasked question, "but it should last long enough to fool the lizard ahead."

"This just might do it," she complimented him. "There's only one way to be sure, though."

Tazi led her friends around the sharp turns and stopped just before the tunnel opened up.

"If what you said is right," Tazi addressed Fannah, "then we should be able to just walk past this thing."

"That's what I have heard," Fannah affirmed.

The three stepped around the corner and started to cross the twenty feet that separated them from what must have been the main entrance to the temple. They hadn't even gone five feet when the gray lizard's eyes flew open. It flicked its head from left to right and unfurled its limbs to slowly rise on its tail, nearly twenty feet straight up.

Tazi resisted the urge to draw her blades, but it was a struggle. It was one thing to have a plan to remain passive, and it was entirely another thing to follow that plan when faced with such a fearsome creature.

"Do nothing," she whispered to Steorf and wondered if the next burnt smell in the chamber would be them.

The ibrandlin swooped down with lightning speed and stuck its large, flat head in Tazi's face. She held rigidly still as it moved its head from one side of her shoulders, over her own head, and down to her other shoulder. All the while, she could feel little hot spikes of air escape the two holes that was its nose. Tazi even thought she detected a hint of smoke in those puffs.

The ibrandlin followed the same procedure with Steorf and Fannah before crawling aside to clear a path for them through the threshold. Tazi hesitantly stepped forward and marched through the doorway, Fannah immediately behind her, and Steorf bringing up the rear. When they had all passed safely through, Tazi peered back at the ibrandlin. The lizard, however, appeared to have already forgotten them and was curling up once more like some great cat.

She shook her head and let out a sigh. When she turned back to her friends, Tazi saw that the purple colors Steorf had created were dripping off of them to evaporate into the stone floor without a trace. Before she had a chance to compliment him further, several young men appeared from a nearly invisible side chamber and intercepted them. Tazi saw that they all were Calishite humans and they wore the true colors of Ibrandul.

"Who are you?" one of them demanded.

It was not lost on Tazi that the worshipers had surrounded them.

"We have come seeking the aid of Ibrandul," Fannah told them.

"That may be," the spokesperson for the acolytes said, "but how did you get in here?"

Steorf took a deep breath, but before he could say anything Tazi squeezed his arm.

"We are here," Fannah replied easily, "and welcome as all should be who seek protection from those things that dwell in the dark."

She left it at that.

Good girl, Tazi thought. No need to tip our hand when we don't have to.

"The Lurker should know of this," one of the other worshipers muttered.

"If you seek the Skulking God's assistance, then follow me," the first worshiper told them and abruptly turned away.

Since the other followers held their ground, Tazi had a feeling that there was no choice in the matter.

"Please bring us before him," Fannah requested, playing along with the illusion of free choice as well.

The group made a silent march from the small, entry chamber into a much larger room. The entire chamber was hewn from rock, and all the decorations were natural indentations in the stone. The senior priest entered, dressed in robes of deep purple tied off with a black sash. His outer robe was covered in a silver pattern of circles that looked like scales to Tazi. His beard was shot with white, and his skin was leathered. Tazi wondered how he could look so dry and withered in the damp dark.

"What do you seek?" asked the old man.

"We are newly arrived in Calimport, Mysterious Lurker," Fannah correctly addressed him in the common tongue. "My companions are Thazienne and Steorf—" she motioned to each respectively—"and we have come on a most serious matter. Thazienne is best able to explain," she finished, startling Tazi by placing her in the forefront once more.

"I can see your companions are new to Calimport,"

the Lurker said, "but you are not." He spoke a few words in Alzhedo.

Fannah simply nodded.

When the ensuing silence stretched out, Tazi finally stepped forward from her companions and the few Children of Ibrandul who had led them there.

"I would like to thank you, Mysterious Lurker, for allowing us entrance," she began.

"Ibrandul opens his house to any human needing protection from the dark and offers sanctuary," he intoned benevolently.

"I'm not sure if we need the protection or if you do," she continued.

One of the Children of Ibrandul, just starting his first beard, stepped toward her, and Steorf moved to block him, but the Lurker waved the novice back. Tazi realized her mistake.

"I mean no threat," she explained. "I am afraid I'm bringing a warning to you and hope I am in time."

"Go on," he urged.

"My friends and I are pursuing an evil necromancer. He has already killed someone close to me, and I know he wants to kill this woman as well." She motioned to Fannah. "His trail has led here, to Calimport and to your god."

The novices murmured among themselves at that declaration, but the Lurker silenced them with a look.

"What do you mean, girl?" he demanded.

"All I can reason," she continued, "is that he is working toward some greater goal of his and he plans to use your god for his own, evil deeds. That has to be why he needed to collect so many souls. To be honest," she said with a touch of embarrassment at her lack of information, "I was hoping you might know what he could want with the Lord of the Dry Depths."

The senior priest was quiet for some time, and Tazi suspected he was weighing her words.

Finally, he announced, "Ibrandul protects all human

travelers who come to him in the dark. Here you have come to seek answers from him. Over the many years, there have been more than a few persons who have tried to subvert the Skulking God's powers. This necromancer of yours is not the first, nor, I suspect, will he be the last."

The Mysterious Lurker glanced behind himself before continuing, "Perhaps it is our book that this necromancer seeks. Over many years we have been collecting the sacred writings of Ibrandul. Even I have not read all of the words of the Lord of the Dry Depths, but I know there is great power in them. Power over the darkness."

With that, the priest turned and motioned to a stone dais behind him. Tazi could see a large tome resting on an altar. She approached it slowly.

"I wonder," she said aloud, "if this could have something to do with the scrolls I took from Ciredor."

The followers of Ibrandul looked quickly at one another.

Tazi drew near the dais and saw that a scaled cover carefully protected the portfolio of parchment papers. With a tentative hand, she reached out to touch the book. The novice of Ibrandul, who had taken offence at her first words, broke away from his companions and ran to the dais.

Before Tazi was able to lay a hand on the book, the Child of Ibrandul grabbed her fingers. He bent them back forcefully and twisted her hand hard. Tazi yelped in surprise and pain.

"No *gharab*, no foreigner," he explained roughly, "has the right to touch the Book of Ibrandul."

Steorf's anger exploded. He abandoned Fannah's side and launched himself toward the Child of Ibrandul. Tazi turned and saw Steorf raise his hands and shout a few words with no results. The Lurker ordered the other Children of Ibrandul to hold their places. The novice, ignoring his priest, laughed at the mage's obvious distress.

"No luck, *gharab*. Whatever magic you think you have will not work here in this temple."

When the youth saw concern cross Steorf's face, he laughed again.

"Have you forgotten how to fight?"

Steorf grunted and sprang at the slighter Calishite. The young man easily sidestepped Steorf, and Tazi took the brunt of his bull's rush. She was pushed back against the dais and knocked the tome over with a flailing hand. The parchments fluttered to the floor haphazardly amidst the cries of the horrified worshipers. Steorf glanced briefly at her before turning to face the Child of Ibrandul.

"What's the matter?" the young Calishite taunted him. "Not only can't you fight, all you manage to do is make more of a mess."

He was practically dancing around Steorf. The mage took a roundhouse swing at him, and the Child of Ibrandul just managed to duck and prance back a few steps. With his hands on his hips, the novice teased Steorf some more.

"You know, *gharab*, I'm starting to think even the blind woman could do a better job at this than you. And what do you think your woman"—he nodded toward Tazi—"thinks of you now that you've let her down . . . shown her just what kind of a man you are?"

Tazi could see that Steorf had reached a boiling point at the mention of her. The Child of Ibrandul moved a step closer to Steorf as his cockiness had made him careless.

Steorf shot his right hand out and grabbed a fistful of the novice's purple robe.

"I'll show you what kind of a man I am," he spat into the novice's face.

With his open left hand, Steorf delivered a wicked stab to the Child of Ibrandul's throat. He released him, and the acolyte doubled over, suddenly unable to breathe. As the novice was trying to take in a deep, wheezy gasp of air, Steorf brought his knee up into his face and Tazi saw her friend smile in grim satisfaction as they all heard the sickening crunch of bone. She realized Steorf was barely reigning himself in.

The novice pinwheeled backward, blood gushing from his broken nose. Steorf kicked out and struck the Child of Ibrandul in the kneecap, sending the novice crashing to the ground.

Steorf didn't stop there. He dropped down and straddled the young man's chest and continued to pummel his already bloodied face. The Child of Ibrandul was unable to offer any resistance. Steorf was lost in a blood-red haze.

Tazi was unable to stand any more. She rushed over to the two combatants and caught Steorf's raised fist, pulling at his arm.

"Stop it!" she screamed into his angry face.

He pulled his hand free and landed another blow onto the Child of Ibrandul's face. Tazi pushed Steorf off of the youth.

"He's finished!" she yelled, furious herself.

Steorf sat on the floor, breathing hard. He gave Tazi an unreadable look. Several of the Children of Ibrandul surrounded their comrade, blocking him from Tazi's view. Realizing there was nothing she could do for the fallen Child of Ibrandul, she walked slowly over to the stony-faced senior priest.

"I offer my sincere apologies for what just transpired," Tazi began slowly. "The only thing I might tender in our defense is that my friend acted to protect me *after* the novice made a threatening move. It is still no excuse, just an explanation."

A few moments passed before the priest answered. When he did, the old man did so carefully.

"Let me say this was a shameful transgression on both sides, but I am quite certain I understand why the two men did what they did. No apologies are necessary."

Tazi let out her breath gratefully.

"I was afraid that this might have destroyed any chance we had of retaining your help against Ciredor. That you might not believe in us and in what we're trying to do."

"Misunderstandings are just that," the Lurker replied. "I believe I know exactly what you are about. We will do what we can for you."

From the corner of her eye, Tazi could see Fannah kneel beside the fallen parchment papers. She gathered them up and carefully replaced the tome on the dais. Tazi sighed.

At least one of us, she thought, managed to keep her head and do something right.

"Where do we begin?" Tazi asked.

"You give up Fannah to us," he replied.

CHAPTER 6

CALIMPORT MUZAD

"What do you mean by that?" Steorf yelled as he regained his feet.

He started to move toward the Lurker, but Tazi blocked him and placed a restraining hand on his shoulder, giving him a warning look. She turned her head and questioned the priest herself.

"Just what do you mean by that?" she asked in a calmer tone.

"I will explain," the Lurker replied, holding up one hand, "but let me first attend to the Child of Ibrandul."

With that, he walked over to join the circle of Children of Ibrandul that had surrounded the injured novice.

Tazi quickly checked on Fannah. The blind woman stood near the dais, unperturbed by the unfolding events. Since she appeared fine, Tazi used the time to ensure that Steorf was all right. He held his ground, but Tazi could see that he was seething. She walked over to him and took his hands in hers. Normally, they were smooth and clean. She turned them back and forth and winced at the split knuckles and blood that was starting to dry in the cracks.

"Do they hurt much?" she asked him, in spite of her anger at his actions.

"Not nearly as much as I'm sure he's hurting," came Steorf's curt reply.

Tazi frowned at him.

"You know," she replied coldly, "you might have over-reacted just a bit."

"Was I supposed to stand around while he attacked you?" he snapped.

"I was hardly attacked," she retorted. "I think you just moved a little too quickly."

"I'm not going to let you get hurt again," he said through gritted teeth, "because I was too slow to act or was distracted for a moment. You have no idea what I went through when you were wounded that last time. I won't let that happen to you ever again if there's anything I can do to stop it."

Tazi stared up at him.

"I appreciate that," she finally replied. "I just think you might need to temper your actions with a little thought."

Realizing what he was trying to tell her, though, she added, "But don't think too long. I don't want to be hurt, either."

She looked down and lightly rubbed her thumbs against his bruised knuckles. When she looked back into his face, he was as close to smiling as he ever let himself get.

Tazi, struggling with her own mixed feelings, released his hands and turned in time to see several of the Children of Ibrandul carry their injured comrade through a side door out of the main chamber. The Lurker, with some blood on his robes, headed back to where Tazi and Steorf were standing.

"Let's see what he has to say," she whispered to Steorf. "If we don't like what we hear, grab Fannah and get out of here."

"Let me think about that one," he whispered back.

Tazi had to suppress a smile in spite of the situation.

"Will he be all right?" Tazi asked as soon as the Lurker was standing in front of them.

"In time, Asraf will be as good as new. However, I think I will have him carry a few scars as a reminder of the cost of acting hastily. One should always think before one acts."

Upon hearing those words, Tazi cast a sidelong look at Steorf.

"But enough on that matter," the Lurker continued. "What is done is done. We need to discuss what has brought you to us."

"You are correct," Tazi agreed, "but I would like to know what you meant about keeping Fannah."

"If this necromancer is as dangerous as you say—"

"Of course he's dangerous," Steorf interrupted.

"If he is that dangerous," the Lurker continued, though Tazi thought his patience was wearing thin, "then your friend is in the gravest of danger."

"That's why . . ." Steorf began in an exasperated tone but stopped short when Tazi surreptitiously squeezed his forearm.

"Yes, she is in jeopardy," Tazi finished more calmly. "That's why we're here."

The Lurker nodded in agreement.

"You've made it this far," he said, "but my reasons for keeping Fannah here are twofold."

"Please go on," Tazi asked, all the while keeping a light grip on Steorf's arm.

"The most obvious is to keep her as safe as possible. If something should happen to you both, Ciredor will not be able to find her exact location. There are some wards in place within this temple to thwart other magic, and they are fairly effective, as your young associate discovered just a short time ago."

Tazi dropped her eyes at that. However, she noticed that Steorf still looked unrepentant.

"There is something else that you may not have considered. This necromancer has had possession of the woman in the past. If he is as formidable as you say, he might have the ability to scry through Fannah's blind eyes, or have the means to use her against you somehow. Any plans that we form may be vulnerable to his abilities if the three of you remain together," he finished. "She will be safest without you."

Tazi was hesitant. Something about his logic didn't sit well with her, but she was loath to argue with a necessary host they had already insulted, to say the least.

Steorf was obviously not bound by the same compunctions.

"Are you trying to tell us that we can't take care of our own?" he barked. "We got this far, you know."

Tazi winced at Steorf's words. She felt he was overreacting again, just as he had taken too quick offense with the novice of Ibrandul. They couldn't afford to anger these people any more than they already had. Though she wished that she, Steorf, and Fannah could have had a moment alone to discuss the situation, she realized that wasn't going to happen. Tazi saw that Fannah didn't appear unduly distressed by their predicament. She was quietly chatting with one of the novices who had remained with her in the main chamber a few paces away from the dais.

She *did* say she knew them from before, Tazi thought, and Steorf *did* read the situation incorrectly just a few moments ago . . .

"I think you may be right," she finally said aloud.

The priest smiled at her choice, but Steorf was deadly silent.

"Let me just say a few words to her," Tazi said.

"Of course," the priest replied. "And don't worry, we will keep her safe from anyone who would do her harm."

Tazi looked him in the eye and nodded curtly. She could hear the sincerity in his voice during that last statement.

She walked over to where Fannah stood waiting. At a discreet motion from the priest, the novice moved away politely.

"The Lurker thinks you will be safer with them for a time," Tazi began.

"Do you believe that to be the best course of action?" Fannah asked her.

"His reasons are sound, and they have merit," Tazi replied.

Fannah took Tazi's hand in her own.

"Follow your feelings," she told Tazi softly.

"Steorf followed his, and look where that almost got us," she replied. "The walls nearly came crashing down."

Tazi could still see some of the debris from Steorf's skirmish littering the floor.

"That may be," Fannah agreed, "but he was true to himself. I can hear the anger in his voice right now, but he is in far less turmoil than you are."

"It's your life we're talking about!" she exclaimed. "I've got a reason to be confused."

"I haven't forgotten what is at stake," Fannah said softly.

"I'm sorry," Tazi apologized quickly, hating to see Fannah upset. "Of course you, out of all of us, know how important this is."

"If the Lurker's plan is sound, then follow it. I will be all right here and I might even slow you down. If he is wrong, however—" she paused—"then come back. We will find another way."

"I will find you no matter where you are," Tazi promised.

"I'm counting on it," Fannah replied, staring at Tazi with her ice-white eyes.

Tazi squeezed the blind woman's hand briefly and smiled. She released her grip, and a Child of Ibrandul escorted Fannah off in the same direction that the wounded novice was taken.

"We'll be back soon," Tazi called after Fannah. Then she added in a whisper, "You can count on it."

Steorf and the Lurker walked over to where she stood watching Fannah's retreating form.

"Shall we?" the Lurker said, making a slow gesture in a different direction.

Steorf was clearly still angry at the turn of events, but Tazi could see he was holding his tongue—at least for the moment.

"Please," Tazi replied, nodding in agreement.

The Lurker moved in front of them and led the two down a side passage.

"I didn't even see this hall before," Tazi quietly told Steorf.

He leaned toward her slightly and replied, "They've rather ingeniously used the rockwork to their advantage. Unless you knew where the opening was or you were standing at just the right angle, the entrance would look like just more shadowed rock."

The senior priest took them around a turn and down a short tunnel that led to a smaller antechamber. In the center of the room was a well-built oak table that would comfortably seat twenty, worn to a deep patina in many areas. The room was lit by thick candles and a few, subtle glow spells. All along the walls were shelves and shelves of books and scrolls. Tazi saw various maps hanging along some of the few free spaces and wondered if they were for the subterranean tunnels that Fannah had told them littered Calimport Muzad. Before she could get a closer look, seven of the Children of Ibrandul came in, and one set about rolling up all the open scrolls and putting them away.

"Friendly folk," Steorf whispered to Tazi.

"It's not as though we've given them much to trust," she replied.

Her eye was caught by a small tapestry that the Children of Ibrandul had left in place.

Within the intricate pattern, Tazi was able to see that some kind of a maze was depicted. She shook her head to herself as she tried to trace the way out of the maze.

I feel just as twisted and lost, she thought. Not sure who to trust in this room and not sure who to doubt.

"Everyone be seated," the Lurker said.

He took the chair at the head of the table. Tazi and Steorf sat to his right, and the other Children of Ibrandul sat in various positions around them.

"It is obvious," the priest began without preamble, "that this necromancer must be stopped. You two have mentioned that he is responsible for several deaths."

"Yes," Tazi added. "He killed one friend of mine and at least a few other innocents, and he means to kill Fannah as well."

She directed the last comment to everyone at the table, hoping they would understand the severity of the situation.

"For what purpose, however, you are not sure. Is that true?" one of the Children of Ibrandul asked.

"This man is evil. It's that simple," Steorf replied. "Whatever his purpose is, you can assume it will be monstrous, because it will be a reflection of him."

"A person's actions do reflect his spirit," one of the novices agreed, giving Steorf a long glance.

"It would still be advantageous to know the scope of his plans," the Lurker added.

He swept a stern look at the Children of Ibrandul, obviously not intending to tolerate their input.

"Knowing his intention would give us a clue as to where he is now or, perhaps, where he will be at some later point," Tazi added.

"I have a feeling that time is running out for you," the Lurker intoned.

"I think you're right," Tazi agreed. "Do you have any idea where he might be and how this connects to Ibrandul? Any idea at all?"

"I cannot even fathom a guess. Perhaps he has hidden himself in the tunnels here. After all, the Skulking God protects those in the lower depths, so he might be depending on that protection. It is impossible for me to say anything with much certainty."

"Then we're right back where we started," Tazi complained.

"We should get Fannah," Steorf interjected, "and try another avenue."

"You are quick to act," the Mysterious Lurker remarked. "Just because we don't know where Ciredor is now doesn't mean there isn't a way to discover his location."

"Is your power strong enough to find him here?" Tazi asked.

"No, child," he apologized, "but I know where you should go to seek out your answers."

"Where would that be?" Steorf asked.

"You will need strong, magical means to divine his plans and his lair. The only chance I believe you will have to find this man in time is if you go to the Dark Bazaar."

Tazi saw Steorf stiffen when the Lurker mentioned "strong, magical means." She knew he was not going to tolerate many more comments like those or the subtle jibes and looks that the other Children of Ibrandul were casting at him. She didn't think the Lurker was intentionally insulting him, but Tazi was certain that was how Steorf perceived the conversation, and she knew his pride was severely wounded.

"What is the Dark Bazaar?" she asked the priest.

"Didn't your Calishite companion tell you about it?" the Lurker inquired solicitously.

"There's been too much to see," Tazi explained, "and too little time since we arrived, I'm afraid, to learn all the secrets of Calimport."

The Lurker directed a severe look around the room and settled back in his seat.

He must not abide interruptions very well, Tazi thought, though he has tolerated our errors in judgment and etiquette.

"No one knows how the Dark Bazaars originated," the Lurker began with a slight smile, "but they have existed for many years."

"Is this some kind of night market?" Tazi asked. "In Selgaunt, there is always commerce going on to some degree, no matter the hour. Considering the size of Calimport, I would expect the same."

She had already forgotten her observation regarding the priest's tolerance of interruptions, but he seemed unperturbed by her question.

"While there are more and more night markets these days that take up business in the same locations as the permanent day bazaars, this is something different."

Steorf crossed his arms over his chest and leaned back against his chair. Tazi knew the position well. This was always the way he sat when he felt someone was spinning a story for him. He had struck the pose with her on more than one occasion over the years when her accounts of personal daring-do reached mythical proportions. She wished he wasn't so opposed to their dealing with the cultists. While under their roof, she felt the need to overcompensate for his rudeness.

"Go on," she urged, recognizing that the Lurker was passing along vital information, not some tavern tale.

"The Dark Bazaar is not populated by the common people. There are beings in attendance from not only all of Faerûn, but from other planes as well. I've been told that even some elementals can be found there."

"You've been told? Then you yourself have never been there," Steorf observed.

"No, I have not. The way to the Dark Bazaar is a difficult one and I have never had the need to attempt it."

"How do you know I will be able to find what I need there?" Tazi asked.

"I don't know for certain, but I do believe it is your best chance. The few words ever recorded about the bazaar speak of fantastic items—like dream vapor bottles or elven kiira—up for barter, but the most common item traded there is knowledge."

"Barter?" asked Tazi.

"Yes," the Lurker answered. "Barter is the only way to exchange items or secrets. As far as I know, there is really only one rule to the bazaar: One can only trade equal value for equal value. You can only ask or trade for one thing. The advantage, so they say, is that information gained there is always reliable."

"What happens after the transaction is concluded?" Steorf questioned.

"As I am led to believe," the priest replied carefully, "you are then escorted from the bazaar."

"By who?" Tazi asked.

"Again," the Lurker adjusted his robes almost nervously, "I do not know for certain. Most believe, however, that the bazaar is managed by the Temple of Old Night."

"The Temple of Old Night?" Tazi inquired.

"It belongs to Shar," Steorf answered.

"That is correct," the Lurker said with a small note of surprise in his voice. "You know of the Temple of Old Night?"

"I know some," Steorf answered mysteriously.

Tazi watched the two men closely. She had also been surprised that Steorf was familiar with the Temple of Old Night, but her admiration of his knowledge was quickly turning to exasperation. She could see that he wanted to play games of bravado with the Lurker and this was not the time. It looked like the Lurker was up for the challenge.

"Does it matter who runs the bazaar?" Tazi asked, interrupting their staring match.

"It's always wise to know what you're walking into," Steorf answered, keeping his eyes fixed on the Lurker.

"As much as you can, at any rate," the priest added.

The Children of Ibrandul remained silent, and Tazi saw that several kept their eyes lowered.

"If this is the best chance we have," Tazi decided, "then it is the one we have to take."

"I can not think of a better one," the Lurker agreed. "I have a vested interest in this as well. I and the other Children of Ibrandul do not want our faith sullied by any dark rite."

"How do we get there?" Tazi inquired, ready to get on the move.

"The way is rather perilous, and only the most skill-ful find the entrance," the Lurker explained. "Because we are as concerned about stopping Ciredor as you are, I am going to have three of the Children of Ibrandul accompany you through the tunnels. They can take you to where the last Dark Bazaar was held and follow the signs to where the new one will most likely be."

Upon hearing those words, the novices looked around at each other.

"You could give us directions," Steorf told him. "If the way is truly so treacherous, we wouldn't want any of your 'Children' to come to harm."

Tazi kicked him under the table, not at all pleased with what sounded at best like an insult and at worst, a thinly veiled threat.

"It will save much more time to show you the path rather than try to explain it to you," the Lurker replied.

Secretly, Tazi was grateful he had not outwardly taken any offense at Steorf's words.

"That would be best," Tazi agreed, before Steorf could add anything else. "I think the sands are running out for us."

The Lurker rose from his chair and smoothed his robes. He motioned to one of the Children of Ibrandul to approach him. When the novice reached his side, the senior priest spoke softly in the Child's ear. The novice nodded vigorously several times before the priest finished.

Steorf looked at Tazi during the exchange, concern plain in his expression.

"I don't think we have a choice," she whispered in reply to his unasked question.

"There are always choices," he whispered back. "Sometimes only wrong ones, though."

Tazi chewed her lip thoughtfully.

"One of the Children of Ibrandul will take you to a small chamber where you can prepare for the excursion," the Lurker explained. "You will find food and water, and an assortment of weapons and supplies."

"Weapons?" Steorf asked, with one eyebrow raised.

"Ibrandul helps those who are in need, but it never hurts to be ready for anything," the priest added.

With that, the Mysterious Lurker retired to a chamber beyond their counsel room. The glow spells glinted off the silver circles covering his outer robe, and Tazi was once again reminded of how much they looked like scales.

Without further conversation, one of the Children of Ibrandul motioned for them to follow him. He led them back through the main tunnel to another side room. Once inside, Tazi and Steorf saw that it was just as the Lurker had said. The room held several chairs, a workbench, a smaller table laid with a minor feast, and a wall covered with an assortment of weapons. Tazi walked over to the wall and removed a small scimitar with an ornate handle. She admired the weight and balance of the sword.

"I will leave you for a brief while," the Child of Ibrandul informed them, "before returning with two others for the undertaking."

Tazi thanked him, and he left, shutting the door behind him.

"What are you thinking?" Steorf hissed at her the moment the door shut.

Tazi placed a finger to her closed lips and made a circling gesture with her other hand to indicate the entire room. Steorf moved over to stand next to her. When he spoke again, he pitched his voice more softly though Tazi could see he was still angry.

"This room seems to be safe," he told her.

"I thought," she whispered back, "that Asraf said differing types of magic didn't work in the temple."

"I think he meant that they didn't work against each other," Steorf explained. "Since the Lurker took us to that inner chamber, I've been testing the waters, so to speak."

"What did you learn?" she inquired.

"As long as I'm not too intrusive, I do have limited use of spells. I've been able to detect magical artifacts, for instance, and devices for eavesdropping. That council room had several of both."

"Well?" Tazi asked and looked at him expectantly.

"We should be free to talk," he reassured her. Without hesitation, he added testily, "What are you thinking?"

Tazi shook her head at him and walked away a few paces. She briefly checked for less magical means of spying and, satisfied that there weren't any of those either, she returned to Steorf's side.

"If you could manage to keep your temper," she replied with equal frustration, "I might have time to actually do some thinking calmly, instead of having to soothe ruffled feathers."

"What do you mean?" he asked, genuinely puzzled.

"Between you and that priest baiting each other," she explained with a touch of ire, "I've felt like some kind of juggler, simultaneously trying to keep you calm, him happy, and listen to everything that was being said. But more importantly, I've been trying to hear what wasn't said."

"So you don't trust them," he replied, pointedly ignoring her assessment of his behavior.

"I don't know what or who to trust," she replied honestly.

She sat down on one of the stools near the workbench, rested her elbow on the table, and rubbed at her lip thoughtfully.

Steorf moved beside her and said, "I'm sorry I haven't been much help."

"I know you mean well enough," she answered, "and I know at times I'm hardly one to talk about bridling anger, but we're walking a slippery slope here."

"You didn't answer my question. Do you trust them?"

"As I said, I have some doubts about a lot of this. The Lurker," she elaborated, "definitely appears uncomfortable, but whether it's because he's apprehensive of us or anxious what role his god and, perhaps, his people might play in all of this, I just don't know."

She rose from the workbench and went over to stare at the wall of armaments.

"Fannah seems at ease with them," she continued. "I'll tell you—" she paused to face him, knowing her next words would wound—"I'm basing my decisions on her instincts."

Steorf pursed his lips together and was suddenly preoccupied with the inventory on the wall. The uncomfortable silence stretched out between them.

"I suppose," he finally commented without making eye contact with her, "that is the wisest course of action you can take. Out of all of us, she is the only one who really knows Calimport, and she has had dealings with these cultists before." He laughed ruefully. "Not only do I have nothing unique to offer you in this city of sorcery, I've already let you down."

Tazi suddenly understood why he was so quick to jump at every opportunity. It was to impress her.

"You," she said into his face, "have not let me down this time. You are right that sorcery is on every street corner, and thank Selûne that I know yours is the kind I *can* trust. You don't have to prove anything to me."

Steorf finally looked her in the eye.

"Keep in mind," he prompted her, "that Fannah has been away for some time. Things may have changed, and they may no longer be what she remembered."

"There are many things that have changed," she replied quietly.

More loudly, she said, "Once again, you make a good point. Don't think for an instant that I don't value your judgment here as well."

Suddenly uncomfortable, Tazi turned her attention back to the wall of weapons. She scanned the collection until her eyes came to rest on an unusual pike. She touched it briefly and turned to face Steorf.

"Remember the night we went out on one of our first wildings?" she asked. "We ran afoul of that fishmonger and he tried to run us through with his pike. And I thought he was going to be such an easy mark. If you hadn't stepped beside me, I would've been skewered for sure."

She laughed a little, but in retrospect thought that his actions then might have been a little more than just those of a bodyguard. Perhaps many of his actions had been more than just services rendered.

"I still carry the scar," he told her.

"You do?"

"I carry many things, Tazi."

The moment lingered between them, and he moved very close to her. Steorf took her hands in his, and Tazi didn't resist. He rubbed her delicate fingers in almost the same manner as she had done to his wounded ones earlier. Tazi stared at him solemnly, not certain what was going to happen next. Then a realization dawned on her.

"Your hands," she exclaimed softly, not quite breaking the mood.

Steorf smiled ever so slightly as she examined them, though he didn't release his light grip on hers.

"They're smooth again," Tazi noticed with delight. "Not a scratch on them! You have been testing the waters, haven't you?"

Steorf merely shrugged, but Tazi knew he was pleased that she had noticed. His subtle smile faded, and he squeezed her hands again. Tazi tilted her head to one side and parted her lips. She regarded him questioningly, and her heart beat a little faster. Steorf leaned forward, and the door behind them suddenly swung open. They broke apart, startled by the intrusion.

Tazi took a step back and watched as three of the Children of Ibrandul entered the room. The first was the novice who had brought them to the room, the second was one Tazi hadn't seen before, and the third was Asraf.

"Are we interrupting?" Asraf asked. Tazi thought he sounded somewhat mocking.

"We were just discussing our next move," Tazi answered him, afraid of what Steorf might say and also glad to have a moment to consider what had almost happened between them.

She glanced at Steorf and was relieved to see that he looked calm. In fact, he startled her by going over to Asraf and inspecting the young man's face.

Tazi thought that except for his nose, Asraf appeared fine. His nose, though it was no longer bloodied and discolored, definitely had the telltale lump indicating it had been broken.

That must be the reminder the Lurker said he was going to leave, she thought.

"Not bad work," Steorf commented easily, turning the novice's face from side to side.

"You had doubts?" the youth retorted, though he winced at Steorf's touch .

"Of someone else's work," Steorf answered, nodding his head slightly, "I always have doubts."

Tazi sighed but the youth took no umbrage with Steorf's insult. He tried to straighten and look Steorf in the eye. Tazi could see that though there had been some cosmetic work and he was cleaned up, the youth was not yet recovered entirely from Steorf's attack.

Asraf gave him a lopsided grin and Tazi realized he was younger than she had originally thought. While his body was not completely healed, his attitude had improved. Either the Lurker had admonished him or he had just decided not to be bothered by what the *gharabs* said any longer. He caught Steorf's hand in his and returned the favor.

"I could compliment you on your work, as well," he said, not missing the fact that Steorf's hands were no longer injured, either.

Steorf extracted his fingers from the acolyte's inspection.

"Yes," he answered, "you could."

Tazi shook her head and realized not much had changed after her discussion with Steorf. He was still proud and stubborn.

Would I really want him to change all that much? she wondered.

"What's next?" she asked Asraf.

"If you two have had enough time to refresh yourselves—" he paused and looked at them both shrewdly— "we should go."

Before Steorf could say something Tazi was certain would be in anger, Tazi asked, "You're coming with us?"

She could see from the corner of her eye that Steorf's jaw had tightened.

"Of course," Asraf replied easily.

"Oh," Tazi muttered. "This is going to be an interesting trip."

CHAPTER 7

TUNNELS OF THE MUZAD

"Which way now?" Tazi asked.

She, Steorf, Asraf, and the other two Children of Ibrandul had been maneuvering through the lower tunnels for just a short time. Already Tazi felt some disorientation. Every tunnel looked the same, with very few distinguishing features. The rocks were just rocks to her, no different from each other than blades of grass in a meadow.

"I don't understand how you're able to tell one tunnel from the next," she marveled.

"You wouldn't," replied the only clean-shaven novice in the group.

Tazi wasn't certain if he was being condescending to her or not. She did notice that none of the Children of Ibrandul had bothered to give their names to her or Steorf. In fact, they only knew Asraf's name because the Lurker had referred to him by name in front of them.

Are they not supposed to tell us their names, or is it a subtle way to snub us? Tazi wondered.

"That's why we're fortunate to have you to lead us," she said diplomatically.

When she received no response, she turned to Steorf and raised her eyebrows as if to say, "I tried." But he maintained his silence as well and she gave up her attempts to make conversation.

I wonder how my father manages to manipulate a room full of different merchants and get anything done? she wondered as she started to envy his ability to maneuver others so expertly. A compliment didn't work, so maybe a somewhat pertinent question might.

"Just how long ago was the last Dark Bazaar?" Tazi asked.

None of the Children of Ibrandul were quick to respond. After a look passed between the three, the beardless novice finally answered her.

"More than likely, it occurred last night."

"But you don't know for certain," Steorf remarked.

Tazi knew he was pleased to show her that their guides were far from omniscient.

"We've never been to one," Asraf chimed in.

"Why not?" Tazi asked, glad that at least Asraf was willing to offer some information without too much solicitation.

"They are very grave occasions," the beardless novice interrupted him. Tazi watched as he cowed Asraf with one serious glare. "As our Mysterious Lurker tried to explain to you, we have never needed to resort to these measures for information."

Tazi was definitely sure that the beardless acolyte was belittling them.

"Desperate times call for equal measures," Tazi replied, tired of the verbal fencing and insulting innuendo. "We aren't afraid to take any chance to save Fannah, no matter what the cost."

Steorf nodded in agreement.

She and Steorf marched on in silence for a while after that, behind the three Children of Ibrandul.

Tazi shivered occasionally as they descended into the cooler depths, and she thought longingly of her *jellaba* back at the temple. While her leathers would not slow her down like a robe might, her arms were left bare, and she shivered.

She also tried to look carefully at the different rock formations to see if there were discernable landmarks. In a few of the tunnels they went through, the group had to pass single file as the walls were extremely narrow. Others opened up into comfortable passageways that allowed them all to walk abreast of each other. Most of them had a little light, and Tazi recognized some of the first tunnels they walked through as main thoroughfares of sorts. They were lit with semi-permanent glow spells.

As they progressed deeper into the system, the lights grew more sporadic. Tazi relied completely on the Children of Ibrandul's unerring ability to navigate in the darkness.

"Do you really know these tunnels that well?" she finally broke down and asked Asraf.

The young Calishite fiddled with his black and purple robes and sneaked a peak at the other Children of Ibrandul. Tazi realized he did want to talk to her but was hesitant to speak, so she slowed her pace imperceptibly. As a result of that, she and Asraf fell a bit behind Steorf and the other two.

"I think I would probably get lost down here if I were alone," Tazi said. "Did it take you long to learn the layout of all of these tunnels?"

"Oh," Asraf answered after he saw that his two companions were just beyond hearing, "I haven't learned about all of the tunnels. I don't think I could know them if I dedicated the rest of my life to studying them."

"There are that many under Calimport?" Tazi asked, wanting to keep him talking.

"There are as many tunnels as there are grains of sand in the Calim Desert," he answered with a little reverence in his voice.

"And yet you know your way well enough in these," she replied.

"I know many," he answered proudly. "And I certainly know where most of the dangerous ones are in our area, but even some of the ones we're passing through right now are new to me."

"But you move through the darkness as though it were day," she said.

Asraf gave her a smirk in the gloom and answered, "That's because I walk the Dark Path of Ibrandul. It's a very basic spell that all the novices know."

"It let's you see in the dark," Tazi deduced.

Asraf laughed.

"You're quick," he complimented her, "but that's not quite it. The spell doesn't let me see in the dark so much as it lets me know where things are. You recognize the difference?"

Tazi tipped her head.

"Of course I do. I'm quick," she said, smiling warmly.

Asraf laughed again, and Tazi thought his voice had some of the same musical qualities that Fannah's possessed.

Steorf heard their merriment and dropped back to join them. Tazi could see that the beardless novice and his silent companion didn't notice their exchange. The two had switched to speaking Alzhedo and it looked to Tazi as though they were arguing over some marks on the wall. The silent novice was motioning back, but his beardless friend shook his head fiercely and pointed forward.

Wouldn't it be funny if they were lost for a change? Tazi laughed to herself.

"What trouble are you brewing back here?" Steorf asked Tazi, but included Asraf with a glance.

Tazi could see that he was trying to make amends for his first encounter with Asraf.

I don't know if Asraf will understand what he's doing, she thought.

"Nothing that any quick person couldn't work their way out of," she said aloud, with a wink to Asraf.

"Are you both going to wink your way to the Dark Bazaar?" he asked them.

"If that's what it takes, that's what we'll do. Right, Asraf?" Tazi asked as she clapped him on his shoulder.

The smiling Child of Ibrandul grew silent. Tazi was afraid she might have offended him either by making a joke of the Dark Bazaar or by using his name or both. She was about to ask him which was true when the other two Children of Ibrandul backtracked to them.

"What are you standing here for?" the beardless novice demanded abruptly.

"It's my fault," Tazi volunteered. "I tripped in the darkness, and my companion and this Child of Ibrandul stopped to help me."

She pointedly avoided using Asraf's proper name.

The normally silent novice chuckled condescendingly and the beardless one replied, "Watch your step. We can't carry you all the way, you know."

Tazi squeezed Steorf's hand and before he could say a word answered, "I'll try to be less clumsy."

"See that you do," the beardless Child of Ibrandul replied and turned with his comrade to continue the march.

Steorf and Tazi fell in behind them, and Asraf brought up the rear.

"Why did you say that?" Steorf asked softly.

"I can tell those two," she nodded ahead, "already think we're foolish and incompetent, so it was a story they'd believe easily enough. Truth is, I didn't want Asraf to get into trouble for talking so much with us."

Steorf raised a corner of his mouth and looked down at her with a gentle gaze.

"You're all right," he said, "sometimes."

She intentionally bumped gently into his side with

her body and replied, "So are you . . . sometimes."

She giggled quietly.

Asraf heard and watched everything that Tazi and Steorf did, and a troubled look crossed his face.

After a long and silent hike, the group turned a corner and the tunnel opened up into a huge chamber nearly as large as the main room of the Skulking God's Temple. Massive stalactites and stalagmites littered the space, and the darkness would have been absolute if the whole chamber hadn't been covered with phosphorescent lichen. It looked like a clear night sky just missing a moon.

"It's beautiful," Tazi said in a hushed tone.

"It is," Steorf agreed. "Do you hear something, though?"

Tazi listened closely.

"I hear water dripping. How can that be?" she asked Asraf.

"I'm not sure I hear it," he answered, and Tazi thought he sounded troubled.

"I'm not making it up," she defended herself. "I do hear water dripping in the distance."

"There is no water down this deep," Asraf explained. "But—" he paused for some time before continuing— "that sound is one of the ways Ibrandul can manifest himself here in the more arid regions, or so I've been told."

The other two novices moved off to examine something that Tazi, as closely as she scrutinized, couldn't see in the dark cavern. She took the opportunity to ask Asraf another question.

"Is there anything you could tell us about the Skulking God that might be of importance to us? I realize," she added to make certain he was not offended, "that everything about him is very important to you."

Asraf made sure the other Children of Ibrandul weren't close enough to hear then said, "Ibrandul rose in the form of a great lizard to free humans who had been enslaved for centuries by evil drow. He prefers to walk alone through the tunnels, sometimes appearing to others as a great lizard, and sometimes as a man who looks like he's made from obsidian with burning eyes."

"Does he do much besides roam the tunnels?" Steorf questioned.

"The Lord of the Dry Depths always aids humans who travel in the hostile underground, and protects those who worship him from ever being harmed by the drow again," Asraf replied.

An albino moth, the size of a bird, fluttered by, and Tazi gasped slightly at the sight of the nocturnal insect. She chuckled at her foolish reaction, and Asraf laughed.

"It is different down here. Don't you have creatures like that in the Land Above?" he asked.

"Don't you ever venture up there?" Steorf inquired, before Tazi had a chance to answer.

"I have never seen the sun," he answered seriously.

"Never?" Tazi exclaimed.

"When we are initiated into the Enveloping Darkness, as our worship is more properly known," Asraf replied, "we learn that there is absolute freedom in absolute darkness. We are not bound by some arbitrary rising and falling of a glowing orb to dictate our days. Things are not good or evil in the dark, they just are."

"But to never see the Land Above . . ." Tazi started to say.

"You never knew of the Underdark before you came here, did you?" he asked simply.

"No, that's true."

"Did you think your life was shallower or that you were somehow cheated because you were never in this perfect darkness?" Asraf challenged her without reproach.

"I don't think I was cheated," she answered carefully, "but I'm certainly glad I came here and saw this."

"Just because I can't see all the colors of this stone,"

the young novice explained, "doesn't mean I don't realize its beauty." He slowly rubbed his hand against the smooth rock. "The coolness of the stone, the texture under my fingers, those are all part of its uniqueness that is not lost on me. My parents made the right choice when they left me as an infant in these tunnels."

"They abandoned you here?" Steorf exclaimed.

"They placed me under Ibrandul's care," Asraf corrected him. "Here is where I live, and here is where I will someday die."

The quiet pride and contentment in his voice was not lost on Tazi.

"And it will be a full life," she added.

"You are quick," he teased.

Tazi laughed at their shared joke and moved a little farther away, her hand trailing along some of the stalagmites, suddenly appreciating the feel of the rock. She watched as more of the winged insects fluttered between stalactites like shooting stars.

Asraf studied Steorf and finally said, "You still don't understand how this can be enough for me."

"No," he admitted honestly, "I guess I can't."

"All of us have forces that guide us, and drive us as well. It's just that sometimes other people can't see them and so they have a hard time understanding."

"I suppose," Steorf agreed.

"For instance, I don't really know why you're here," he solemnly asked, "on this complicated mission."

"I'm here because my friend asked me to come. There's nothing complicated about it," Steorf answered.

The young Calishite leaned closer to the mage and whispered, "She's a little more than a friend, isn't she?"

Tazi could feel Steorf's eyes burning into her back. She pretended to be fascinated by a stalactite formation and unaware of the very personal conversation carrying on behind her. She didn't want to embarrass Steorf by teasing him, but there was also a tiny part of Tazi that wanted to hear his honest answer.

"What are you talking about?" Steorf asked Asraf, discreetly lowering his voice.

The young man smiled guilelessly and said, "You announce your feelings with every act you commit near her."

"What?"

"You jumped to protect her when you thought I might have done her harm, and—" Asraf began.

"I would have done that for any of my friends," Steorf interrupted. "And you wouldn't have been able to harm her," he added rather seriously, raising a finger in warning.

"You think not?" Asraf questioned, but Steorf could see that he was speaking in jest, and he relaxed a little. "Even that statement shows how you feel."

"I am a loyal man," Steorf stated simply.

Unseen by either of them, Tazi winced a little. Ever since Steorf had told her of Ebeian's death, she had started to feel some of the old closeness growing again. After all, seven years of friendship and wildings had forged a unique bond between them that she didn't share with another living soul. It was hard to forget. The two-year pause in their relationship hadn't changed much between them after all, Tazi was slowly realizing. She found herself slipping into a comfortable rhythm with Steorf again and there had definitely been a moment between them just before the Children of Ibrandul had come for them.

But when Tazi heard Steorf use the word "loyal," it was as if someone had torn open a newly healed wound in her. All the accusations Ciredor had made two years before regarding Steorf's paid companionship came crashing in on her again, and she wondered if she could ever really move past it all and trust Steorf completely again.

Unaware of her turmoil, Asraf continued with Steorf.

"I see you are a loyal man. That's my point. You're here with her on a deadly mission, you protect her whenever you can, and most importantly, I see the way you look at her."

"And how is that?" Steorf asked lightly.

"At certain moments like she is some precious jewel that has bewitched you," Asraf explained, "and at other times, you gaze at her like a man in the desert looks at an icy pool of water."

Tazi laughed to herself.

Asraf certainly has a flowery sort of way with words, she thought. Some of those books in the council room must be filled with romantic fables. He really does need to get above ground now and then.

Not caring to hear Steorf's sarcastic reply to that one, Tazi moved a little faster to catch up with the older Children of Ibrandul and passed out of earshot.

Steorf silently regarded Asraf.

After a few moments, he replied, "You do see well. There is something about Thazienne that cools the turmoil within me."

Asraf was surprised.

"I didn't think you'd admit to it so easily," he said.

"In all likelihood, we won't survive this encounter with Ciredor, so my secret will die with you."

"I'm pretty hard to kill," Asraf said glibly, "so your lady friend might just find out your deep, dark secret."

Not knowing how to respond to that, Steorf abruptly said, "We best catch up with your comrades, before they get too exasperated at having to wait for us foolish Land Abovers."

He and Asraf walked quickly over to the two other Children of Ibrandul. Steorf bumped into Tazi.

"I didn't see you," he said.

"I'm getting better at this maneuvering in the darkness," she answered seriously. "Maybe Ibrandul is on our side after all."

Tazi couldn't see Asraf's frown at her words.

When they came up beside the Children of Ibrandul,

the beardless novice startled both Tazi and Steorf by his next statement.

"I'm sorry it took us so long," he began apologetically, "but we wanted to make certain that we—" he indicated his silent companion and himself—"had read the signs properly. We realize how important it is to find the Night Market."

"Just there," he continued, motioning beyond the cavern, "the path goes on for about twenty feet or so and it splits in two directions."

"You must take care to walk along the right side," the normally silent novice finally said to them.

As they exited the cavern, the darkness grew rapidly. Both Tazi and Steorf had to rely on tactile sensations to navigate, and Tazi was rather pleased with herself that she actually was becoming more adept the longer they traveled in the tunnels. She wasn't aware that the older Children of Ibrandul were lagging after them.

Tazi could barely see Steorf in her peripheral vision, so deep were they now. Close behind she heard Asraf muttering. Tazi squelched a smile at that.

He certainly is a chatterbox, she thought and was suddenly very glad of his company.

He was as different from his companions, she realized, as day to night.

If the only guides we'd had were the two nameless ones, I wouldn't be as certain in finding the Dark Bazaar as I am with Asraf along.

Tazi was so caught up in feeling her way into the next passage along the right that she didn't notice that she and Steorf were on their own.

Asraf stood at the crossroads. His young face twisted up in confusion and he chewed furiously on his lower lip. A glance to the left revealed the retreating shapes of his fellow Children of Ibrandul, men he had studied and worshiped with for years. To the right, he could just barely separate Tazi's slim form from the clutching darkness of the shadows. He knew she and her companion were not the danger he had been led to believe they were.

After a heartbeat more, his face resolved into a determined set. He moved rapidly down the tunnel after Tazi, but the screams started soon after.

In a chamber deep beyond the counsel room that he had let the *gharabs* enter, the Mysterious Lurker sat behind an ornately carved stone desk. He had removed his outer robe and left it draped over a divan pushed against the side of one wall. Other than those two pieces of furniture, the room was bare of decoration. The only other item was a lone bookcase. Unlike the meeting room that was stuffed with books and scrolls, this set of shelves only contained a few pieces of parchment, but these were carefully tied up, not left as haphazardly open as the ones the strangers saw.

While he sipped from an obsidian chalice, he wondered briefly how far along in their journey the Children of Ibrandul and the strangers were. The priest shook his head and knew Ibrandul's Children would not disappoint him. He leaned back, sure that his novices were leading the two exactly where they needed to go and their part in all of this would be done.

The Lurker removed a small stack of papers from a niche in the desk and began to study them closely. He rubbed at his eyes and moved a candle closer so that the papers were in the ruddy pool of light.

"These eyes of mine are weary," he murmured finally and set the papers down.

The Lurker rested his head in his hands and did not hear the slight rustle behind him. A figure in black stepped out of the shadows along the far wall.

"Tired?" the black figure asked silkily.

The Lurker whipped around in his chair and squinted defensively at the voice.

"Who's there?" he asked.

The dark shape moved into the circle of candlelight. While still dressed in black, Ciredor had exchanged his tight fitting leathers for the loose silks of Calimport's elite. His vest had gold threads embroidered in strange patterns, their meaning known only to him. His outer robe billowed behind him like a storm cloud as he descended on the senior priest of Ibrandul.

"What are you doing here?" the Lurker inquired, sounding somewhat fearful.

"I am just here to keep my part of the bargain," Ciredor answered easily.

Without any further preamble, he withdrew a sheaf of papers. The Lurker wiped his hand across his lips and shakily accepted the bundle of parchments. He reached for them as a drowning man would an offered hand. It was hard for the priest to hide the gleam in his eye and the Lurker was certain his eagerness was not lost on Ciredor.

After carefully paging through the stack twice, the Lurker looked up at him with barely concealed awe. There was a bit of a quaver in his voice when he spoke next to the necromancer.

"I-I don't know how you managed to find these pages," the Lurker began.

He watched as Ciredor nodded benevolently in response, but he did not offer to explain where the velum sheets had come from.

"For the last few months," the Lurker continued when he realized that Ciredor was going to remain taciturn, "you have so diligently searched out these lost words of Ibrandul. If you hadn't come to us, who knows whose hands these pages might have fallen into. Even I was unaware of their existence."

"I have long been a supplicant of the Lurker in

Darkness," Ciredor finally replied. "It has been not only my duty, but that of my father and my father's father to spend our lives in search of these artifacts."

"I am only the first in my family," the priest said with a lowered head, "to embrace the Lord of the Dry Depths."

He was humbled in front of someone so dedicated to Ibrandul. The priest felt an icy finger under his chin tilt his face upward.

"I am glad," Ciredor said with some emphasis, "to have discovered a sect of Children of Ibrandul so devout to my god. Only in Waterdeep have I come close to finding followers a fraction as pious as yours."

The Lurker sat a little straighter, bolstered by this sincere compliment. He did believe that his novices were most accomplished and that bit of pride gave him the ability to respond.

"It only serves to follow that we would be the most loyal," the priest explained. "After all, Calimshan is the home of Ibrandul. He rose from our desert."

Not wanting to insult any other group of followers—and he realized that Ciredor must come from one of those—he hastily added, "The other sects are also fervent in their devotion, but we live in the heart of the mystery."

The Lurker watched Ciredor expectantly, looking for any sign that he might have insulted his benefactor. However, all the necromancer did was slowly smile.

"You are right," Ciredor agreed, "that our heart is within the Calim Desert."

The Lurker was relieved that Ciredor was not offended, though he was puzzled at the mage's reference to the heart. The Lurker thought Ciredor might have said more correctly that their origin was in the desert, but he was not going to chance saying the wrong thing again or nit pick over the turn of a phrase. To further smooth things over, he recounted his meeting with Tazi and Steorf, knowing the outcome would please Ciredor.

"Those foreigners arrived just as you said they would," he told Ciredor eagerly, and he saw the first spark of excitement appear in the mage's black eyes.

"Really?" Ciredor drawled.

"The two from Selgaunt and their Calishite companion arrived just a few hours ago," the priest clarified, spurred on by Ciredor's interest.

"Were they like I described?" Ciredor asked carefully.

"As soon as the woman with the short black hair heard of the sacred writings, she dashed right over to the book."

"Just as I told you she would," Ciredor agreed kindly. "What happened?"

"One of my young but very dedicated novices kept her from touching the lost writings," the priest answered. "That's when they truly revealed their colors."

"How so?" Ciredor questioned.

"The woman's burly young companion attempted to attack the Child of Ibrandul with magical means. Of course," the priest added, excited that his words were having a pleasing effect on his patron, "that was to no avail."

"Not in this sanctum," Ciredor agreed. "What was the outcome?"

"The beast had to resort to physical combat on an opponent much weaker than himself." The Lurker shook his head in distaste. "In fact, the man turned quite savage in the end, and his woman had to pull him away."

"They haven't changed," Ciredor chuckled, and the Lurker wasn't sure if the laugh was for his benefit or not.

"And the woman also let slip that she was carrying on her person several scrolls that she had stolen from you."

Ciredor only nodded slowly at this revelation.

"That is the only thing that concerns me," the priest added. "I am not sure that we will be able to recover those."

"Why not?" Ciredor asked, but the Lurker saw that he was not unduly distressed.

"Those two *muzha-dahyarifs* are on their way to a most fitting end. Several of the Children of Ibrandul, including the novice who was beaten by the young mage, are as we speak leading them into a trap deep within the tunnels of the Muzad," the Lurker explained. "There I am sure they will discover what it means to have betrayed the Skulking God."

"I know they will," Ciredor quietly agreed, "and don't be too concerned about the scrolls they have. I might have made copies of some of the writings elsewhere. What of their Calishite companion?" he added and the Lurker thought Ciredor was almost anxious.

"She is quite safe, Lord," the priest reassured him. "We were able to separate her almost immediately from her foreign companions. She is in a chamber located just beyond our main hall."

"Wonderful," he replied.

"She has been very acquiescent since she was separated from her companions," the Lurker noted, "and she knows several of the Children of Ibrandul from her own youth."

He himself had been amazed by that discovery.

"Why should that surprise you?" Ciredor keenly noticed.

"I'm astonished that a Calishite could be so easily deceived, I suppose," the priest admitted. "For all purposes, this young woman is every bit at home amongst us and yet she was traveling in their company."

"Try to understand," Ciredor explained easily, "that those two from Selgaunt are very persuasive. Fannah had been traveling with me some time ago in Sembia as I searched for the lost words when we became separated. She fell into some minor danger and the Sembian woman, Thazienne, took advantage of the situation."

"What happened?" the Lurker asked.

This was the most verbose his benefactor had ever been, and the priest was enthralled.

"Thazienne picked Fannah out of a crowd, an obvious

foreigner and unfamiliar with the commercial ways of the people of Selgaunt, and made arrangements for several of her less than reputable friends to 'attack' Fannah so that Thazienne could then conveniently rescue her. While Fannah is a very astute young woman, she is far too trusting at times."

"I am sure that will improve with age," the Lurker added. "When she approaches my age and has more experiences with life, as you and I have had, I am sure she will be much wiser for it."

Ciredor broke into a wide smile at the priest's theories and the Lurker was pleased that he was finally connecting with the man he knew would change the worship of Ibrandul forever.

"But I have interrupted you," the Lurker noticed.

"There is not much more to my story," Ciredor continued. "Fannah, being the pure soul that she is, felt a great deal of gratitude to Thazienne. My understanding is Thazienne used her hired mage to befuddle Fannah, and she inadvertently ended up giving those two the location of some of the scrolls we had saved from the greedy merchants of Selgaunt."

The Lurker hissed at that.

"Horrible to contemplate," Ciredor agreed, "and Thazienne would have dearly loved to have gotten her hands on all our words. I'm sure visions of jewels and immeasurable fortune were dancing in her head when she saw the collection on your dais."

"That will never happen" the Lurker promised solemnly, and Ciredor smiled again.

"You have done an excellent job protecting the sacred words. The only thing that we need to do is await the Foreshadowing that is less than a tenday away," the mage proclaimed.

"The time of the new moon," the Lurker said in a reverent voice.

"Yes," replied Ciredor. "That time when the Land Above is pitch black . . ."

"And we celebrate Ibrandul's promise to envelope the Lands Above and Below in utter darkness," the priest finished for Ciredor.

He could feel his heart beat more quickly at the thought of the upcoming ritual.

"Fannah may have fallen away from her roots," Ciredor added, "but she will play a pivotal role in the Foreshadowing. I would prefer that she be kept cloistered away until that time," he instructed.

"Don't you wish to see her?" the Lurker questioned.

"I would prefer if she had some time alone," Ciredor explained. "That way, she may be able to purge the effects the Sembians have had on her. Surrounded as she is by the familiar smells and touch of her home, I believe she will come to her senses without any magical intervention."

"Everything will be done as you request," the priest told him. Ciredor smiled at his fealty.

"I knew when I first met you," Ciredor added, "that I had found the true home for Ibrandul's lost words. This Foreshadowing will be like none other."

"Is that when you will read to us from the scrolls?" the Lurker nearly begged the mage.

"I will do that and so much more," Ciredor promised.

CHAPTER 8

THE DEEPEST TUNNEL

"Stay close," Tazi whispered.

The near total darkness of the tunnel made her cautious. She felt her way along the wall.

"I'm beside you," Steorf replied. "Are the Children of Ibrandul behind us?"

Before Tazi had a chance to answer him, a large shadow slithered ahead of them. Tazi felt something hairy lightly brush against her extended hand. She froze in her tracks and threw her other arm protectively across Steorf's chest.

"There's something in here with us," she warned him.

"Then let's see how well my sorcery works down here," Steorf nearly growled.

He shook off Tazi's shielding grip and raised both his hands, and Tazi could tell by the sound of his voice that he was thrilled to exercise his powers. A few words escaped his lips and dazzling light enveloped his hands. The light seeped from his fingers, and the tunnel was illuminated by radiance as bright as the morning sun.

The glare from Steorf's hands showed that the tunnel went on for about fifty feet beyond where they were standing. The rock was unremarkable. There was nothing to set the tunnel apart from the many others they had traversed, except that this one had other occupants; other, rather large occupants.

Just a few steps away from Tazi and Steorf crawled a dozen spiders. Each one was nearly as wide as Steorf was tall. Some stood on the floor as Tazi and Steorf did, but a few scuttled up the cavern walls.

That wasn't the end of it. Tazi watched in amazement as several of the largest spiders transformed into drow before her eyes. One was something in between an arachnid and a dark elf. Without any further warning, the pack of creatures fell on them.

Tazi turned with a scream and ran from the closest spider. From the corner of her eye she could see Steorf wearing an expression of shocked disbelief at her flight. She didn't have time to worry about that. One of the largest spiders ran after her, just as she had expected and hoped it would. After covering only a few feet, Tazi started to tumble to the ground. The spider descended on her.

As Tazi struck the ground, she tucked herself into a ball and rolled forward. As she did so, she freed the dagger in her right boot. When the spider landed on her, Tazi was just finishing her roll. That brought her face up directly under the center of the beast with her blade drawn. The momentum of the roll helped her to thrust the blade directly into the spider's belly and slash it fiercely.

Black blood flowed from the wound Tazi inflicted, and she instinctively knew those fluids were just as deadly, if not more so, than the spider itself.

Tazi moved away from the twitching monster as fast as she could and tossed her soiled dagger away. She withdrew both of her guardblades with a fierce shout.

"One dead," she called to Steorf.

There was no time for congratulatory remarks as both of them were immediately caught up in heated struggles. Tazi found herself surrounded by three spiders, and Steorf had to contend with several drow.

Tazi brandished her right guardblade at two of the spiders and flipped the left one up so that she held the sword like a javelin. With one powerful toss, she threw the weapon and impaled the other spider against the wall. It screamed and wiggled to no benefit. The point of Tazi's blade was wedged tight into a crevice. The animal's squeals started to increase as its weight slowly pulled its body down while the blade was held fast.

The noises stopped abruptly as the spider's head was sliced up the center by the sword. Tazi dispatched the other two fairly easily.

They must be the front lines, she correctly guessed.

She could see that Steorf had his hands full with the drow. She observed him as he grabbed the one closest to him and hit her in the face with the palm of his hand. Tazi was surprised that he was leading with his fists and not his magic.

Perhaps he doesn't want to make the same mistake that he did with the dog, she concluded. Or he's enjoying this.

As in the Temple of Ibrandul, Tazi heard the snap of bone but was startled when the drow Steorf had struck fell over dead. Then she realized Steorf must have shoved the elf's nose bone directly into her brain. He turned to another drow and slammed him into a wall, crushing his skull. The third drow proved a little more elusive, skipping just out of the human's reach.

"Fine," Steorf snarled, and released a bolt of magic.

The discharge passed through the drow and blasted away a portion of the wall behind the elf. Steorf watched as the figure winked out of existence—then he felt himself smashed in the back of the head by a wave of force. He turned to see the same drow now standing behind him.

"So," he called out, "you know some magic, do you?"

"I know more than enough to kill the likes of you," the drow taunted.

"We'll see," Steorf replied as he wiped a small trail of blood from his mouth.

Tazi started to join him when several more spiders dropped in front of her.

"Think you can stop me, stupid creatures?" Tazi mocked them.

She slashed at one of them, and it died straight away, but when Tazi turned to the others she realized the first spider had only been buying time for its comrades. The other two transformed into drow in front of her. Both of the dark elves drew their own blades.

Tazi knew she was in for a real battle. She vaguely thought that the Children of Ibrandul would even up the numbers and wondered where they were. She couldn't believe they were turning out to be so incompetent.

Neither Tazi nor Steorf could see Asraf running down the tunnel toward them. Before he could reach either of them, he was set upon by the hybrid creature. It stood only a little taller than Asraf and had two pairs of eyes, one set where a human would normally have them and a second pair higher on its temple. As well as having a pair of human arms, the creature had three pair of spider limbs along its side, beneath its humanlike arms. Each finger on its eight hands had an additional joint as well as fully functional spinnerets. A vicious set of fangs protruded from its human mouth.

It tried to block Asraf from coming any farther down the tunnel, not attacking him outright. Clicks and moans escaped from the dark elf head as it spread its spider arms, barring the Child of Ibrandul's way. Asraf feinted to the left and tried to slip past the half drow-half spider, but one of his arms was caught by several of the hybrid's hairy claws.

Terrified, Asraf pulled his scimitar from its scabbard and chopped off three of the clawlike hands that held his left arm. The hybrid screamed in rage and pain and lunged at Asraf.

But the Child of Ibrandul, over his momentary fright, confidently decapitated the beast with one stroke. He pulled off the two claws that were still clinging to his robe and ran to help Tazi and Steorf.

Tazi had underestimated just how cunning the two drow were. They managed to slowly turn her away from Steorf's direction. As one dark elf stabbed at Tazi, the other slipped behind her, changed back into a spider, and began to spin webbing furiously across part of the tunnel. When the drow saw that his companion had gotten enough strands across the passageway, he dropped his knife.

Tazi wasn't sure why he had done it, but she wasn't about to let the opportunity pass. She neatly ran him through and turned to help Steorf. She darted directly into the cleverly placed webbing and found herself trapped.

Every part of her that touched the web, whether it was skin or clothing, was held fast.

"Damn," she screamed.

Her struggling made her entrapment worse. She still had her guardblade drawn in her right hand, but it did no good. Through the spaces between the webbing, Tazi could see that Steorf was locked in a deadly battle with one of the more magically adept drow—and he was losing.

She tugged harder at the ropes and only further tired herself. Tazi was close to weeping tears of frustration. All she could do was helplessly watch Steorf die.

A chattering sound above Tazi made her look up as best she could. The other drow-turned-spider was sliding its way down to her on a cord no wider than her thumb. Tazi could vaguely see herself reflected in the two black orbs that were the creature's eyes as it hung suspended above her. She uselessly fought one last time against the silken restraints. She could hear its fangs clicking and feel a bristly arm push her head sideways against the web.

"Just get it over with!" she screamed to the creature, and squeezed her eyes shut.

She felt a sharp sting as its pointed tooth punctured her neck, and heat began to radiate outward from the wound.

"Tazi!" Asraf cried from out of nowhere and slashed at the webbing imprisoning her.

Tazi felt her sword arm fall free, and even though the rest of her body was still stuck, she wasted no time. She swung her arm straight up in front of her and the webbing to skewer the spider.

It fell, shrieking in its death throes.

Tazi smiled grimly, and Asraf cut her completely free.

"Glad to see you," she said, flashing him a quick grin as she bent over to pull her blade free of the spider. She felt a little dizzy straightening up.

Asraf smiled in return but he noticed she was covered in a slight sheen of sweat.

"Did the aranea bite you?" he asked worriedly, inspecting Tazi closely.

Tazi didn't get the chance to answer him. Another spider slid toward them.

Asraf shoved Tazi away from the remaining strands of arachnid silk and shouted, "I'll take care of this last one. Steorf needs you."

Tazi hesitated for a moment. There was a strange sensation in her throat, both numb and burning at the same time. She absently rubbed at the spider scratch below her chin, trying to collect her thoughts.

No, she corrected herself, not a spider, an "aranea." I wonder if Steorf knows about them?

The mage's name began to reverberate in her head, and she marveled at how she could have forgotten his quandary, even for a moment. She turned to face the other section of the chamber and saw that the drow had Steorf pinned to the ground and was drawing his sword for a killing blow.

"No!" Tazi yelled with a voice that sounded torn from her soul.

She ran as fast as she could over to the drow and was terrified to feel how unsteady she already was on her feet.

I can't believe that little scratch is taking its toll on me, she thought.

Steorf had strained his skills beyond belief. The drow had matched him spell for spell and had inexorably forced him to the ground.

Caught up in the struggle, the young mage was surprised to find himself distracted by the smallest minutiae, as if his mind refused to accept his impending doom even as his body surrendered. He noticed that emblazoned on the drow's tunic was a black disc bordered by purple.

"What is that symbol?" he whispered even as the drow's shield spell crushed him to the ground, realizing that he had seen the mark on every dark elf and every spider there.

"Take a good look. It's the last thing you will ever see," the drow spat back snidely and, with a wicked grin, raised his sword high.

"I seriously doubt that," Tazi retorted.

Even in his compromised position, Steorf was able to recognize the weakness in her voice.

The startled drow could only stare down in stunned disbelief as he watched the point of Tazi's guardblade burst free from his chest. She had deftly impaled his heart in one stroke.

He had only enough time to partially turn his head at the sound of her angry voice and glimpse her ominous sea-green eyes before toppling over like a felled tree. The dark elf struck the ground, hitting so hard he nearly forced Tazi's blade back out.

Steorf, free of the dark creature's enchanted restraints, looked up at her gratefully.

"It's about time you showed up," he teased her.

He held out his hand—joking—as if he needed help to rise, but Tazi didn't say a word, and Steorf could see that she was sweating profusely. He wasted no time scrambling to his feet.

Tazi's vision doubled and doubled again before finally clouding over completely. She could feel herself swaying and knew there was nothing she could do about it. She dragged a hand uselessly across her eyes.

"Steorf," she slurred and started to reach out toward him with her other hand.

Before she could grasp him, she collapsed like a marionette with her strings cut. Steorf caught Tazi just before she hit the ground. He held her under her arms and lowered her delicately to the cavern floor.

"Tazi!" he cried as he knelt beside her.

She didn't respond to Steorf's voice or his gentle shaking. She was completely drenched in sweat and convulsing. Steorf licked his lips nervously and rapidly ran his hands over her body. He could find no major wounds on her. Her lips whitened and she slipped into total unconsciousness, her breathing almost undetectable.

Steorf, not knowing what else to do, lifted her in his arms and rocked her slowly. The change in position caused her head to loll against his chest, and Steorf was then able to spot the cause of her condition.

Just below her chin was an inflamed cut and he realized that she must have been bitten by one of the spiders. Cradling her shoulders with one arm, he placed his other hand, palm down, on Tazi's wound.

"I won't let go of you," he whispered.

Steorf gazed at her ashen face and closed his eyes.

During the few days between discovering Ebeian's body and his journey through the gate, Steorf had studied madly. He had gone through his mother's extensive collections of spells and tried to learn as much as he could before leaving Selgaunt. The only problem was that though he had expanded his realm of knowledge, he hadn't had enough time to practice some of the new spell abilities fully. His skills were lacking. What he was about to attempt was untried, but he knew he had no choice. Steorf's hand began to glow slightly white and darkened to brown as he drained the poison from Tazi's system. The torn flesh on her neck started to knit under his touch until no trace of the small wound remained.

Steorf slowly opened his eyes and looked expectantly at Tazi. Her eyes were still closed but Steorf could see that her chest rose and fell evenly. A rosy stain began to spread over her chalky lips. Steorf tenderly brushed a strand of her ebony hair from her eyes and held his breath expectantly. Soon enough, Tazi's eyes flew open and she wildly clawed out, disorientated. Steorf effortlessly caught her hands with his free one and made soothing sounds, trying to calm her.

"It's all right now, dear heart," he whispered.

"What happened?" Tazi asked with some confusion.

Steorf didn't release his hold on her.

"I think the fight just caught up with you," he told her easily, but his words belied his expression.

Tazi could see the worry lines still etched on his face. "I think it was a little more than that," she replied, her voice growing stronger by the moment. "I think I was dead."

"I wouldn't ever let that happen," Steorf responded.

Their eyes locked briefly.

Seeing that she was rapidly gaining strength, Steorf released her hands and stood up, helping her to rise as well. When he was certain that she was steady, he let her stand unaided.

"You don't have to watch me like a hawk," Tazi told him after she caught him studying her while she stretched her limbs experimentally.

"Don't I?" he asked.

She had shaken off most of the effects of the poison, thanks to Steorf, and she scrutinized him. He looked tired, and she knew whatever he had done to expel the venom from her body had taxed him immensely. It was one more strength that she hadn't known he possessed. The tunnel was not nearly as bright as it was earlier and Tazi realized that was because Steorf was much weaker. She pushed some of his unruly, blond locks from his eyes, unknowingly mimicking his earlier gesture.

"Maybe I should keep an eye on you," she said gently.

Asraf, having dispatched his last opponent, was breathing hard. He watched as Steorf clasped Tazi's hand, the Sembian woman seeming to have recovered completely under the mage's ministrations. He was so caught up in their plight that he lost track of his own surroundings. An aranea in spider form, forgotten by all three of them, scuttled after Asraf and clambered up the rock wall behind him. When the spider was on the cave ceiling directly over the Child of Ibrandul, it dropped a silken strand of webbing down ten feet until the thick thread was level with Asraf's neck. Then the creature waited for the inevitable and it didn't have to wait long.

Asraf took a step back a moment later and sealed his fate.

The instant he brushed against the strand of webbing, his neck was caught. Instinctively, Asraf spun around to see what he was trapped by and that only exacerbated the situation. He had wrapped the silken cord mostly around his neck and he was held fast.

That was all the aranea needed. It hauled Asraf up as though he weighed nothing. Tazi and Steorf, both still recovering from their clash, didn't see his perilous predicament.

Face to face with the fanged horror, Asraf called out, "Ibrandul, deliver me from this beast," but the prayer failed to reach the notice of any deity.

Tazi heard his plea, though, and turned at Asraf's shout. She watched, horror-struck, as the spider enveloped Asraf in its multi-limbed embrace and bit down on his shoulder. Asraf hissed in pain, and Tazi rushed to free her guardblade, which was still embedded in the back of the dead drow.

Steorf, too, had recovered enough to realize Asraf's predicament.

"No!" he shouted, and a bolt of flame leaped from his outstretched hand.

As soon as the flame touched the aranea, it dropped Asraf. He fell to the cave floor with a dull thud. The aranea squealed as its carapace burst into flames, and it followed Asraf's descent to the ground. Landing on its back, the spider screeched pitifully for a brief time as its limbs worked futilely in the air. Eventually, its arms stopped their twitching. The cavern filled with the acrid smoke of burnt arachnid flesh.

Tazi sidestepped around the fiery remains of the spider and rushed to Asraf's unmoving form. Steorf followed close behind. Tazi dropped to her knees and rolled Asraf over with trembling fingers. His eyes were shut tightly against the pain of the poisonous bite. Tazi gently lifted his head and placed it in her lap. She hardly noticed that Steorf had dropped down beside her. He reached across Asraf's shoulders and tore aside the robes that covered the place where the spider had inflicted its venomous bite.

Tazi grimaced as Steorf's actions revealed a shoulder already horribly swollen, with purple lines of toxin running toward Asraf's neck, head, and heart. She looked helplessly at Steorf as Asraf writhed in pain. He returned her glance and looked determinedly at the wounded Child of Ibrandul. She didn't want Asraf to die, but she was afraid the strain of saving him might prove too draining for Steorf.

"Steorf," she started to say, but he shook his head.

Decisively, Steorf tore more of Asraf's robes away to further reveal the injured site and laid his hands on the wounded man. Asraf's eyes flew open at Steorf's touch. He weakly reached up with a palsied hand and grasped Steorf's wrist.

"Don't," he pleaded to the young mage, a desperate look in his fevered eyes.

"Why not?" Steorf asked.

"Because this is the way it should be," he reasoned weakly.

"What?" Tazi asked.

Asraf tried to smile at her but couldn't. Instead, he whispered, "This is my punishment, and I accept it willingly."

"Why should you be punished?" Steorf argued.

His anguished helplessness made his voice harsh. However, he had come to respect Asraf and Tazi realized Steorf wouldn't intervene if Asraf refused his assistance.

"Because I betrayed Ibrandul," Asraf answered with a fading voice. Tazi stroked his young face, and his eyelids flickered at her touch. He did manage a final smile.

"I just didn't believe that you two were evil," he said, then his breath rattled for the last time.

Tazi and Steorf kneeled in stunned silence for a few

heartbeats. Finally Tazi gently removed Asraf's head from her lap and got up. Steorf remained where he was with his legs crossed and his head in his hands. Tazi looked down at Asraf's body and whirled to pace the cavern, gently lit by the still smoldering body of the last spider to fall. That was the only light left as Steorf's spell of illumination had all but faded away. It was enough light to see that the cave floor was covered with unmoving aranea bodies. She strode over to a pile of three corpses and began to kick at them viciously.

"That won't do any good," Steorf finally told her.

"It won't do any harm, either," she growled back viciously and kicked at a still twitching spider limb.

"Dark and empty," she yelled accusingly to the cavern ceiling. "I thought he protected his Children from monsters in the dark."

Eventually, exhausted from both the battle and her anger, Tazi stormed over to a wall, placed her back against it, and slowly slid to the ground. She sat with her legs bent and her arms propped on her knees, hands dangling limply.

She heard her own ragged breathing, felt her heart trying to burst from her leather vest, and she knew no tirade would do anyone any good. She wouldn't risk undoing all of Steorf's healing efforts. Tazi thumped her head against the wall and silently cursed all the gods.

Not budging from his spot, Steorf said, "If his own god couldn't save him, perhaps he wasn't meant to be saved."

Tazi bit off the angry retort hanging on her tongue. She realized that Steorf was just as exhausted as she was, if not more so, and had the added burden of knowing that he might actually have been able to save Asraf.

Tazi stood up as if in a dream and began to walk around the chamber again. She glanced from Asraf to the many bodies of the aranea. Slowly a thought began to grow.

"This isn't right," she said.

" 'There is no right or wrong in the darkness,' " Steorf quoted the dead Child of Ibrandul bitterly.

"That's what I mean," she replied. "This is exactly the kind of enemy his god was supposed to save him from. Asraf was one of the most dedicated people I've ever come across. You could hear it in the way he talked about his faith."

She stood in front of Steorf and pointed to Asraf's unmoving form.

"He should have been protected," she said, "and he wasn't."

Seizing on that thread, Tazi rapidly searched the tunnel. She turned over every corpse and discovered they were all aranea—monstrous spiders that could transform themselves into the likeness of drow or other humanoid creatures to confuse and intimidate their prey. These were intelligent creatures that couldn't have just been creeping around in the dark at random, for no reason at all. The whole mission had been puzzling her, and the pieces were falling into place.

"The other two Children of Ibrandul aren't here," she said slowly.

Steorf stood up and surveyed the room.

"I don't think they even followed us in here," he said.

Tazi balled up her hand and thumped the wall with the bottom of her fist.

"That's what they were arguing about in the last cavern," she realized.

"Those scheming bastards were trying to decide which trap to send us down," Steorf added bitterly.

Tazi's faced blanched.

"And they've got Fannah. They separated us right from the start," Tazi realized sickly, "and led us down the wrong path. And we went."

"We'll get her back," he vowed, "even if it has to be over every one of their rotting bodies."

He started to storm back the way they had come, but Tazi caught him by the arm and pulled him to a stop.

"I don't think they're entirely to blame," she told him.

"What?" Steorf said, shocked that she could even consider that. "Are you sure you're fully recovered?"

"Remember Asraf's last words? He said he didn't believe we were evil."

"So?" he answered, too angry to follow her train of thought.

"That must mean that the others *do* believe we're evil. Someone got to those Children of Ibrandul and spun a vicious lie for them so he could use them for his own devices," she explained. "I know of only one man capable of that: Ciredor."

"You think he manipulated them?" Steorf asked, cooling somewhat.

"I know it," she answered with absolute certainty.

Before Steorf could say anything else, a hooded figure dressed entirely in gray robes moved out of the deepest shadows of the cavern. The figure was as tall as Steorf but neither he nor Tazi could distinguish if the figure was even human, let alone male or female. They held their ground as it approached, but Tazi's left hand slid down to the hilt of one of her guardblades.

"Who are you?" she called out to the figure when it was about ten feet away.

"Lady," the figure began in a deep and resonating voice, "I have come to call for you."

The Gray Caller slowly raised one arm draped in smoky hues and pointed at Tazi.

She could tell Steorf was tensing up, at the ready.

"What do you want from me?" she asked, as the Caller had made no overtly threatening moves against them.

"Lady," the Caller answered, "in seeing through those things that were deceiving you, you earned my attention as a worthy soul. I have come to offer an invitation and my services."

"An invitation to what?" she inquired as she took a step away from Steorf.

"I am here to escort you to the Dark Bazaar, if you care to go," the Gray Caller replied.

"I do very much wish to go," Tazi answered, after considering the figure's words and trusting her intuition.

As she and Steorf both approached the Caller, the figure made no move to lead them anywhere, and held its ground.

"The invitation is only for you, Lady," the Caller explained.

Tazi turned to Steorf and clasped his hands.

"Stay here, and I'll be back as quickly as I can," she told him. "You should be safe enough. The other Children of Ibrandul have probably left us for dead."

"How can you trust this thing after what just happened?" he asked her.

"It feels right," she explained, releasing his hands. "Trust me."

Turning to face the Gray Caller she said, "I'm ready."

"This way, Lady," the figure said, and motioned to the far end of the cavern.

As they slowly walked together, Tazi turned to the Caller and remarked, "There isn't some set road one could follow as the Children of Ibrandul led me to believe. This is the only true way into the Night Market, isn't it?"

The Caller nodded, and she tried to catch a glimpse under the hood but she was unable to see anything other than more shadows.

"Only those who are invited may enter the Dark Bazaar to trade secret for secret. Only those who can see through deception or prove themselves worthy in some other manner are ever invited. Your insight serves you well when you let it."

Steorf debated with himself for a few moments before he decided to follow them. He broke into a trot and nearly caught up to Tazi and her guide.

"Tazi," he called out.

When she didn't turn around he reached out to grab her shoulder, but his hand passed through thin air.

Both Tazi and the Gray Caller had disappeared.

CHAPTER 9

THE DARK BAZAAR

Tazi couldn't believe her eyes. The Gray Caller had simply rounded a brief corner in the tunnel, and it opened up into an eerie, twilight market. She stopped in her tracks.

Tazi thought that the cavern was larger than any she had ever seen. Somewhere in the distance she could hear the steady drip of water. Even in her wonder, she realized that her perceptions were somewhat skewed.

The whole area was distorted by a light mist that covered everything. When she looked down at herself, her semi-nude arms had a faint purple tinge to them. The Gray Caller appeared almost black, with a red cast to its cloak. From where they stood, she could hear the low murmur of many voices, but they were indistinct. There were shadowy forms, but she couldn't make out any people. Tazi knew there was only a fine line between reality and illusion in this place.

"Is this it?" she asked quietly.

The Gray Caller nodded.

Tazi started to pick her way down through the winding stalagmites to the main chamber. She felt strangely apprehensive descending the natural stone staircase, like a young woman making her debut into society when all eyes are upon her. But there was no fanfare and no gawking admirers or even the crueler sort waiting for a slipup.

Slightly disorientated by the muted quality of the place, she could hear her own footsteps, but they seemed very distant. Small rocks gave way under her feet, and she knew the stones fell, but she didn't quite hear the clatter they made. Tiny pinpricks of light twinkled sporadically around her.

Moving through here is like walking alone in a field of snow, she thought.

When Tazi reached what she assumed was the floor, she could just begin to separate different shapes in the fog. Stalagmites and stalactites formed natural partitions, and the pockets they shaped littered the huge grotto. Tazi could see small groups of figures, made hazy by the halo of candlelight in each that she passed.

There was more.

As she approached the "stalls," Tazi heard the voices more clearly, but the languages were all different. Having grown up in a city of commerce, she recognized the tone of the various conversations and knew that bargains were being struck, but as she neared a stall close enough to peek in and snatch a glimpse of the occupants, suddenly the language switched to Common and made perfect sense to her. Her eyes grew wide.

"How can that be?" she asked her escort.

The figure walked just a pace behind her down through the cavern as though it was her shadow—and she wasn't the only one with a shade in her wake.

Many folk wandered around with their own Gray Callers trailing after. Tazi watched as one Caller faded into the background after its guest was seated with another trader and played no further role in the bargaining. Tazi suspected that was one of the rules of the marketplace.

"Here there are no barriers, not even language, to stop the trading," the Caller explained. "We leave your choice of partners entirely up to you."

As they walked past a stall, Tazi gasped in awe. A very elderly man with long, white hair, with a moustache and a beard to match, was deep in a serious conversation. It was his companion that had startled her.

The man was talking to a very large, very angry black dragon. Tazi was able to catch bits and pieces of their discussion.

"I don't know how Storm Silverhand convinced me to try and deal with thee," the older man sputtered, "but I do have a hard time denying her any request, even one like this."

The dragon flexed its wings furiously.

Before Tazi could hear the obviously irate dragon's reply, the Gray Caller subtly moved her along. As soon as she was unable to see the two, their words became undecipherable again.

"I would have liked to have heard what a dragon had to say about anything," she told the Caller a trifle wistfully.

The wraithlike figure was silent. Judging by that response to her curiosity, she figured that unless she was an active participant in the discussion, she wasn't allowed to linger. Nevertheless, it was still hard to resist.

As she progressed deeper into the Dark Bazaar, she found that there were many sights to distract her. Some of the dealers were humans and creatures that she was able to recognize, but not all of them were. Tazi saw several humans arguing over what looked like an infant no more than a few tendays old, and she couldn't resist slowing her pace to see more, regardless of what the Caller might think.

The baby was on the center of the table and at first Tazi thought the child had very strange tattoos all over her body. As she approached the debating consortium, Tazi realized that the baby was not lying on the table so much as she was reclining on it, and it was the tiny creature who was directing the flow of conversation.

A closer inspection revealed that the marks on her body weren't tattoos at all. Every place on her body that should have had a fold of skin had a rosy crack instead. Her entire torso was crisscrossed with the bloody lines. The creature's eyes and lips, as well as her eyelids, were a bright red. Tazi shivered at the odd spectacle.

"Who is able to make all of this possible?" Tazi asked in awe.

"That is not for me to say," the Gray Caller advised her. "I and the others simply lead those worthy enough here and maintain the sanctity of the Dark Bazaar."

"But you must answer to some power," she continued.

The Gray Caller stopped and raised its hand.

"We are a part of something Faerûn does not even have a name for yet. Save your questions for your own bargain, Thazienne Uskevren," it warned her, "and don't waste them on me. I do not deal."

Chastised, Tazi moved from the Caller's side and walked farther along. Each step she took revealed more and more stalls and intimate nooks. Tazi noticed that the Gray Caller continued to follow her discreetly. She gave up questioning her companion for the time being and realized that she was on her own.

Passing another heated discussion between a distinguished looking man with a receding hairline and a beard with a single gray streak and a woman whose crimson cloak announced her as a Red Wizard of Thay where the only word Tazi heard was "Waterdeep," Tazi saw an old woman sitting alone behind a rickety table in another stall.

Tazi thought she looked a little like the fortunetellers that performed at the fairs that occasionally played in Selgaunt. The woman's abrupt movements reminded Tazi of a bird, and she was struck by the familiarity of the gesture.

Where have I seen that before? she thought.

She filed that away for future pondering.

She looks like she's from Calimport, Tazi reasoned, so perhaps I should start here.

"Well," she said to the Gray Caller, "she's the only person I could say I even vaguely recognize and connect with."

"The choice," the figure replied, "is always and only yours, lady."

She nodded curtly to the figure and strode over to join the woman. Tazi realized that she had grossly underestimated the woman's age. The misty effects of the Dark Market had softened the stranger's features. As Tazi approached the woman, she was shocked to see that the stranger was covered with lines, but these were common wrinkles, albeit plentiful, nothing like the crimson lines on the infant she had passed earlier. The woman's hair was mostly white, with only the occasional strand of black, and it hung loosely below her waist. Her skin had a leathery appearance, and Tazi thought it might split open at any moment. Her clothing was decidedly Calishite but was extremely faded and even torn in a few places. The only word that came to Tazi's mind as she sized up the woman was "weathered."

At the hushed sound of Tazi's footsteps, the wizened Calishite looked up. Her eyes were a dull brown, but Tazi detected a hint of shrewdness in them.

"May I join you?" Tazi asked.

"For now," the aged woman answered.

Tazi drew up a chair and looked hopefully at the woman across from her. A few moments passed, and Tazi realized her companion was not going to speak first.

"I'm not sure what I'm supposed to do," Tazi finally admitted.

"Then perhaps you should leave," the Calishite suggested in a cracked voice.

Just listening to her speak made Tazi thirsty.

"I've traveled a long way," Tazi informed her. "Too long a way to turn around and leave now."

"Little girl, I don't think you know the meaning of a long way," the crone cackled.

"Maybe I don't," she conceded, "and again, you could be wrong about that."

The aged Calishite nodded.

"I could be," she told Tazi ruefully, "and it wouldn't be the first mistake I've ever made."

"So you're saying that you're open to possibilities?" Tazi said.

The older woman leaned her head back carefully and began to laugh. Buried beneath the arid chuckle, Tazi could hear a lilt to the other woman's voice that was almost beautiful.

I wonder what she looked like when she was younger? Tazi speculated.

"You're staring," the woman noticed.

"I'm sorry. I'm just curious," Tazi answered.

"Curiosity can be a curse," the Calishite said in a parched tone, "and one often pays enormously for the luxury."

"Sooner or later," Tazi replied ominously, "we all pay, don't we?"

The elder woman regarded Tazi carefully.

"You have learned a few lessons, haven't you?"

"A few in my lifetime, and they've been costly ones," Tazi told her in a voice absent of bravado.

"It took me an eternity to learn mine," the Calishite said mostly to herself, "and I only had to give up the thing I loved best."

She seemed lost for a moment, and Tazi wasn't sure how to proceed, but the woman soon shook herself from her daydreams.

Or are they nightmares? Tazi pondered.

"So, little girl, have you come for a story, perhaps, or have you come to learn the secrets of the Calim desert?" she crackled.

"I have come for something very important," Tazi began, "but I don't know what form it will take."

"The rules are simple here, *gharab*," the Calishite explained. "You get to buy one treasure. What form that treasure takes depends on you. It can be a map, a gem, a dagger—" she paused and leaned across the spindly table to whisper—"or a secret."

Tazi thought the elder woman had sand lodged in her throat, the last part was so raspy.

"I'm not sure what it is I need," Tazi offered lamely.

The woman sat back abruptly and snapped, "Move along then, little girl. This market is not for tourists but those who come to deal. I don't have time to take you by the hand and lead you to water."

"Look," Tazi snapped, "this is life and death I'm dealing with, and all I want to do is not make a mistake. I want to do the right thing."

"All of this," the woman gestured to the room and beyond, "is about life and death. Sometimes you can make all the right choices and still lose. You'd do well to remember that.

"Now," she continued rapidly, "tell me quick: What is it you want?"

"There is a necromancer I believe is from Calimport. You might know of him and you might not. His name is Ciredor."

Tazi paused to see if the woman showed any sign of recognition. The wrinkled woman's face gave nothing away.

She grew frustrated and blurted out, "I need to know what he's up to!"

She waited breathlessly, but the woman didn't answer her question.

"You will have to pay for that," she informed Tazi.

Tazi was once again reminded how dry the woman sounded and looked. It was as though she had weathered a lifetime in the desert. The old woman looked at her expectantly.

Tazi rummaged through the small, outer pocket attached to her leather pants near her thigh. She withdrew a handful of "suns" and stacked them on the table. The metal made a muffled thud when it struck the wood. Tazi once again marveled how everything about the market sounded hushed. The older woman spilled the column and sifted through Tazi's coins with a withered finger before leaning back in her chair.

"These coins," she motioned to the pile of gold, "are not the things you value."

"It's all I have with me," Tazi apologized, suddenly fearful that she had traveled this perilous route for naught. "I don't have anything else to offer."

"That's where you are wrong," the old Calishite answered with a glint in her brown eyes. "The rule is equal treasure for equal treasure. What you ask is invaluable to you, isn't it?"

"I think it's my only hope," Tazi replied honestly.

"Then you do have one item to barter with," the older woman told her.

She tapped Tazi's left hand.

"My ring?" Tazi whispered.

"That is all I will accept," the other woman said. "It is the only material item of value you possess that I truly desire."

Tazi looked down at the emerald ring on her hand. Durlan, a moon elf, had given her the ring of protection when she was a small child growing up on the streets of Selgaunt. She had used it once successfully against Cire-dor. The pain the ring caused her had been nearly unbearable, but she was certain the band was the only thing that had stopped the dark mage two years past.

How will I stop him now? she thought plaintively.

"Tick tock, tick tock, goes the clock. Time is running

out," the white-haired woman reminded her. "This night is only so long."

Tazi clenched and unclenched her left hand a few times. Finally, with a quick movement, she pulled the ring off her finger and laid it on the table, but she kept her fingers on it.

"Well, little girl, are you going to strike a bargain here or not?"

Tazi chewed her lip and said finally, "I have never parted with this ring but if it's all you'll take, then take it."

Tazi removed her fingers from the gem.

With a speed that contradicted her advanced years, the elderly woman snatched out with her clawlike hand and pocketed the ring. Tazi already regretted her actions, but it was too late. The older woman looked Tazi directly in the eye and tilted her head like a bird. Tazi was once again bothered by the familiarity of the action but dismissed the thought for later.

"Do we have a deal?" Tazi asked her.

"We most certainly do," she answered.

❧ ❧ ❧ ❧ ❧

Ciredor idly thumbed through one of the Lurker's tomes. The man had generously donated his inner sanctum to the necromancer for his private meditation, and Ciredor secretly suspected that the senior priest was a tiny bit terrified of him and had given him the space because he wanted to escape the mage's company. Whatever the reason, the solitude suited Ciredor perfectly. He used the time to savor his situation.

"It is almost time," he whispered and idly rubbed a medallion he normally wore under his clothing but had now exposed. The black disc gleamed amethyst at its rim.

There was suddenly a hesitant tap on the door and Ciredor slid the pendant against his skin, enjoying the feel of the cool metal next to his body.

"Enter," he commanded.

The Mysterious Lurker opened the door slightly and looked at Ciredor.

"Yes?" the mage asked after he realized the priest was going to continue to stare at him indefinitely.

"I have some news for you, Lord," the Lurker began tentatively.

Ciredor smirked at the title, but was secretly pleased by the priest's submissive behavior.

"And it would be?" he led the conversation helpfully, waving his hand in a circular fashion.

"Two of the Children of Ibrandul are back," he said with some hesitation, "and I think they should speak with you."

"Send them to me now," Ciredor ordered, starting to frown.

The fact that the Lurker did not want to deliver the information indicated immediately to Ciredor that it wasn't good news.

The Lurker pushed open the study door fully, and Ciredor was able to see that two followers of Ibrandul were standing to the rear of him. They wore stricken looks similar to their senior priest and were trying to hide behind his flowing purple robes.

"Get in here," Ciredor growled.

I'm too close now to waste time on these games, he thought.

The Mysterious Lurker generously stepped aside and offered some mumbled, parting words before disappearing into the shadows of the antechamber. The two followers trudged in and hung their heads.

"What has happened?" he demanded. Then he added icily, "My ire only grows the longer I'm kept waiting."

The two novices exchanged a look between each other before one stepped forward.

"My Lord," he started in a rich, baritone voice that didn't match his thin frame, "we are sorry to bring you unhappy word regarding the foreigners."

He fell silent, closely studying his sandals for imagined imperfections, and Ciredor idly regarded his nails before continuing sweetly, "It seems that I didn't make myself clear."

He flung his hand toward the novice like he would swat an insect. A bolt of green light tore from his hand and struck the young man in the throat. The Child of Ibrandul was thrown up against the rock wall and held by the green energy. Like a manacle on his neck, the spell held him a few feet above the ground. His legs kicked uselessly in the air, and he scrambled with his hands to hold himself up and relieve the pressure on his throat. Ciredor strode over to where he was pinned.

"What happened?" he demanded.

The Child of Ibrandul sputtered and coughed but couldn't choke out any audible answers.

"Fine," Ciredor replied and turned his attention to the beardless novice, leaving his partner to dangle.

The other Child of Ibrandul had tried his best to melt into the bookcase but there was no hiding from the furious mage. Another green bolt blew the bookcase across the chamber, turning it into kindling and exposing the young novice. Ciredor crossed the room in two angry strides.

"Your turn. What happened?" Ciredor hissed into the face of the frightened Child of Ibrandul.

He shot a look at his companion before he answered in a small voice, "We weren't able to kill them."

"What do you mean?" the mage asked, not unkindly.

His courage bolstered by Ciredor's sudden calmness, the novice continued, "We led them down the tunnel to the aranea, and they walked right into the trap, but the other Child of Ibrandul with us turned traitor and ran to help them."

"What occurred?" Ciredor prompted.

The novice's eyes wandered over to his fellow novice, whose face was going from shades of red to purple. His sputtering was becoming more sporadic. Ciredor made a disapproving sound at his lack of attention, and the Child of Ibrandul turned to face him again.

"Asraf joined the two in battle and even helped free the black-haired woman from sure death in an aranea web . . . but he was killed soon after. Obviously," the student priest surmised, "Ibrandul was able to make him pay for his act of betrayal."

"And the foreigners?" Ciredor tried calmly to keep him on track.

The novice licked his lips nervously and said, "They survived."

"Surprisingly enough, I deduced as much. Anything else?"

The Child of Ibrandul grew white.

"Yes, Lord," he whispered, and stole a glance at his hanging comrade.

The manacled Child of Ibrandul was finally silent, but some of his limbs occasionally twitched. Ciredor placed an icy hand on the beardless novice's face and twisted him so that Ciredor could stare into his hazel eyes.

"I won't ask you again," Ciredor warned him in a deadly tone. "What happened to the woman?"

"A Gray Caller came for her to escort her to the Dark Bazaar."

Ciredor screamed in rage and in one motion used his powers to fling the Child of Ibrandul into the Lurker's ornately carved desk, face first. The novice's skull shattered with the force of the impact, and gray brain matter speckled the writing tablet set on the desk. Ciredor stormed out of the chamber into the tunnel.

Just outside the study, the Mysterious Lurker waited, griping his robes tightly.

"My Lord, where are you going?" he asked timidly.

Ciredor whirled around and nearly struck him dead, but he decided the priest's death wouldn't serve his purposes, so he swallowed back his burning rage.

"I am leaving," he told the Lurker.

Ciredor could see that the priest was in despair, fearful of his rage and also fearful of losing the lost words of Ibrandul.

"Will you be back?" the Lurker asked.

"As soon as I conduct a little business," Ciredor replied, having nearly regained his icy composure.

"Are you going to the Dark Bazaar?" the Lurker inquired shyly.

"Since your Children failed so completely, I don't really have any choice, now do I?"

"But," the Lurker told him, "everyone believes that market is controlled by the Temple of Old Night. They worship Shar, you realize. Are you sure it is worth the risk, considering your allegiance to the Lord of the Dry Depths?"

For the first time since hearing of the Children of Ibrandul's failure, Ciredor's sly smile returned.

"There is no risk when your faith is strong," he informed the priest.

The Lurker gazed at him in frightened adoration.

"You truly would risk everything for your god," he said in quiet awe.

"Most certainly," the necromancer replied easily. "Oh, before I go," he added almost as an afterthought, "you might want to get someone to tidy up your study."

Before the priest could comment, Ciredor faded from view and reappeared only a few feet from Tazi.

❧ ❧ ❧ ❧ ❧

"If this will save Fannah, then it's worth it," Tazi murmured.

"Who did you say?" the elderly woman asked.

Tazi didn't realize the other woman had heard her.

"Nothing of importance," Tazi dismissed the subject, suddenly distracted herself. She felt an odd chill pass over her. "What I do, I do for a friend."

The older Calishite appeared suddenly distressed and wouldn't let the matter pass.

"Did you say 'Fannah'?" she asked in a scratchy whisper.

"Yes," Tazi answered and was suddenly suspicious that her friend's name should mean something to the withered woman in front of her. "What does it matter?"

Tazi didn't believe it was possible, but even more creases formed on the woman's brow.

"It's just that—" the woman began, but stopped when a Gray Caller slowly moved past them.

The hooded figure swung its head in the Calishite's direction, and she snapped her mouth shut.

"What's wrong?" Tazi asked.

"Nothing," the old woman replied. "We've struck our price. Now, what was it again that you wanted to know?"

Tazi took a deep breath and asked, "What is Ciredor planning?"

"Then I shall tell you, treasure given for treasure received.

"Ciredor," the Calishite answered gravely, "has been collecting souls as an offering. They are a dark gift for Shar, his goddess."

"Where is he keeping them?" she asked quickly.

Tazi wasn't sure but she thought the old woman looked sad.

"The deal is done," the woman replied. "One item bought with another. Those are the rules. Now you must leave."

Even as the words escaped the Calishite's lips, Tazi noticed the ethereal condition of the market beginning to spread and grow. Everything became murkier, and all the sound damped as the fog encompassed the cavern. A cold breeze passed over Tazi, and she shuddered. Her hand rose up to her throat instinctively, and she was suddenly filled with dread. Even the old woman looked momentarily startled. Still, Tazi tried to talk to her.

"Please," she pleaded, "tell me what you can. I'll give anything to save Fannah."

The Calishite was barely distinguishable from the miasma that occluded the whole market. She raised a hand toward Tazi and called out to her.

The sound was all but swallowed up by the mist, but two words made it through: "Fannah," and, ". . . daughter."

Tazi finally placed where she had seen such birdlike gestures before. Fannah made them as well.

"Ibina il'Qun!" Tazi shouted against the vapors, but Fannah's mother, along with the Dark Bazaar itself, had vanished.

Tazi found herself staring at a rock wall.

Ciredor had expertly transported himself to the tunnel his scrying had revealed as the precise location of the Dark Bazaar and Thazienne Uskevren.

"How easy this all is, little Tazi. You can't hide from me in my mistress's domain," he said confidently.

Ciredor was deep in the Muzad, in the same chamber as the Dark Bazaar. The mist was thick and whispered to the dark mage. He moved through it and thought he heard Tazi just a little ahead of him, but with every step he took the fog swirled more and more forcefully. He could see vague outlines and hear the low murmur of conversation, but nothing was clear to him.

As he approached what from a few feet away looked like a congregation of people, Ciredor found that he had merely passed through a collection of shadows. He knew they were near, but everything was just out of his reach. The necromancer started to grow impatient.

"Why won't you illuminate the way?" he beseeched the ether.

Almost on cue, a light glowed dimly off to his left. His confidence returned, and he licked his lips in expectation. He knew with unerring certainty that that was the direction he was supposed to go.

"Thank you, Shar," he whispered reverently.

Ciredor nearly flew toward the light, but as soon as he reached it the glow winked out only to reappear to his right, just a few steps away.

It must be my excitement, he told himself. It has me dizzy.

He adjusted his course and went to the glow's new location, but just as before the fickle light disappeared only to be found behind him. He whirled around, his fury growing.

"What trickery is this?" he demanded.

He attempted to scry the light, but every effort he made failed.

Finally, the radiance glowed softly within a tiny pocket of the chamber and he followed it grudgingly. The closer he got to it, the more the contents of the grotto were illuminated. From a short distance away, he thought he saw Tazi talking to another woman but the scene was blurry, as though Ciredor were watching something transpire underwater.

He could barely discern the two shadowy figures, though he knew something had changed hands between them. He wasted no time. Ciredor stormed into the middle of the tableau and made a lunge for Tazi, but his hands passed clean through the woman, and that image flashed out of existence just like the will 'o the wisp that had led him on the fruitless chase.

Ciredor pounded his fist into the wall behind the trading stall and shouted in fury. The whispering grew louder, and as he stepped from the grotto into the center of the foggy maelstrom, the sounds were all around him, tantalizingly close, but he could see no one.

Ciredor spun around the chamber and howled in rage. The scream echoed on and on.

CHAPTER 10

RETURN TO THE TUNNELS

"There you are," Steorf called to Tazi in a relieved tone.

"What?" she asked, completely disorientated.

Tazi turned from the rock wall and saw Steorf standing beside her. There was no trace of the entrance to the Night Market anywhere. Steorf laid his hand on her arm with some concern.

"Are you sure you're ready for this?" he inquired.

Tazi stared at him with no comprehension on her face.

"What are you talking about?" she asked.

Steorf looked at her closely and explained, "I want to come with you. I don't want you to do this with only that thing as your guide."

He motioned to the space behind Tazi and

the realization dawned on Steorf that the Gray Caller was gone.

"Where did he go?" Steorf demanded, adding, "I knew there was something wrong."

"How long have I been gone?" she inquired.

"Gone?" Steorf repeated in a perplexed tone. "You turned away from me just a moment ago."

"I've been there already," she told him, finally understanding his confusion. "I must have wandered for hours in the Dark Bazaar."

"Are you sure you were really there?" Steorf wondered with a touch of skepticism.

"Yes, and I know what Ciredor is planning," she told him single-mindedly. "I still don't know exactly where he is, but I have a fairly good idea. We need to go . . . now."

Tazi could see that he was still a little confused.

Remember, she told herself, he's still recovering from that battle and hasn't caught up with me. I've had time to rest.

"We need to return to the Temple of Ibrandul immediately and free Fannah," she told him.

"You know what Ciredor wants?" he challenged.

"Like Eb told us, he's taking souls. Now we know why: He's taking them to give as a gift to Shar."

"The spiders . . . the aranea . . ." Steorf murmured.

"What about them?" Tazi inquired, curious but clearly anxious to be on the move.

"I noticed they all bore the same symbol. I knew I should have recognized it then. The black disc rimmed in purple is Shar's holy symbol," he explained, then grew quiet.

"I know you're tired, but we need to get back as soon as we can," she prompted him.

"What should we do about Asraf?" Steorf asked, pointing to the dead novice's body.

Tazi was ashamed to acknowledge to herself that she had forgotten Asraf's noble sacrifice. She glanced down at his young face and was momentarily saddened. When she looked at Steorf, she knew exactly what he was thinking and what he was willing to try, regardless of the cost to himself. She touched his face fleetingly.

"No," she told him, shaking her head, "we can't do anything for him other than respect his wishes. He felt this was what his god wanted and demanded of him and we have to honor it."

With that, she knelt and carefully wrapped Asraf's *jellaba* over his body.

As soon as she stood up, Steorf made a pass with his hand and ignited the Child of Ibrandul's body. Unlike the spider he'd burned earlier, this fire left no odor. Both Tazi and Steorf maintained a solemn silence as the flames lit the chamber. Finally, Steorf broke the stillness.

"That's another one Ciredor owes us," he vowed.

"Let's stop him before there can be any others," Tazi replied.

Tazi and Steorf made a thorough check of the cavern and retrieved all their weapons. When they were sure they had everything, they started back the way they had come. Nevertheless, they both noticed rapidly that without the Children of Ibrandul to aid them the journey back was more tricky.

"I hate to admit it," Tazi said, "but it was a little easier with those Children and their Dark Path spells."

In response to that, Steorf cast a minor spell of his own that illuminated his right hand. The radiance it cast was enough for them to see for about six feet around.

"I can cast a brighter one," Steorf informed Tazi.

"I know you can," she reassured him, "but I don't want to overtax you just for this. Besides those two novices lurking about, who knows what else might cross our path?"

Steorf agreed. They left the mortuarylike tunnel and very cautiously re-entered the large cavern that was glowing with phosphorescent lichen. Tazi half-expected the remaining two Children of Ibrandul to ambush them there, but the chamber appeared empty.

"It figures those cowards would scurry back to their den," Steorf commented.

"Either they thought those aranea would finish us off, or," Tazi continued thoughtfully, "they might have run back to inform the Lurker or even Ciredor that we survived."

"Who knows what we might be walking back into?" Steorf pointed out.

"One thing's certain,' Tazi commented, "it won't be a pleasant reunion."

"Did you have any doubt?" Steorf asked with a touch of sarcasm.

"You were right," she grudgingly admitted. "We shouldn't have trusted them. Happy now?"

"Ecstatic," Steorf deadpanned.

The two exited the chamber and began the daunting task of remembering the route they had taken, only in reverse. Tazi was certain that Steorf wasn't any surer of the route than she was. They tried to pool their recollections.

"Which way?" Steorf asked at one of the first junctions they came to.

Tazi studied both routes and closed her eyes momentarily. When she opened them, she regarded Steorf with a modicum of embarrassment.

"I'm not sure," she told him. "Dark!" she shouted at nothing in particular and kicked a small pile of rocks.

The sound echoed down the tunnels mournfully.

"Not only am I not sure which path to chose, I also made a horrible mistake at the Dark Bazaar," she chided herself.

Steorf laid a comforting hand on her shoulder.

"You found out Ciredor's plan," he reminded her. "Now we have a much better idea what we're up against."

She looked at him briefly and averted her eyes.

"Yes, I did discover that, but I should have thought out my question more carefully. If I had been clever, I would have found a way to ask his plan *and* his location.

I paid dearly, and we're not really any better off than before."

She absently rubbed her bare finger.

"You might have asked more carefully," he agreed, "and by the time you and I reunited, Ciredor might have changed positions. I think you did the best you could, given the situation. You can do everything right, and sometimes it isn't enough. However, sometimes it is."

"Thanks," she replied, not sounding convinced. "The only thing I will admit is that the journey to the Night Market was useful. Perhaps more so than the bargain I struck while I was there. If we hadn't made the attempt, we would never have found out the truth about the Children of Ibrandul. Who knows what might have happened then? I do have something rather amazing to tell Fannah when we get back to her."

"What is it?" Steorf asked, intrigued.

Tazi started to explain her meeting with Fannah's mother, but before she could finish, a scuttling resonated in the tunnel a short distance away. Tazi and Steorf froze in their tracks. Each looked at the other, and they drew their weapons in silent unison, immediately on guard. They continued in the direction they thought was the correct way back but also searched for the source of the sounds.

The rats found them soon enough.

Larger than the rodents Tazi had seen many times scurrying around the docks of Selgaunt Bay grabbing at scraps of fish, these subterranean creatures were a sickly white and, Tazi guessed, partially blind. Of the fifteen or so in the pack, a few hurried away at the scent of her and Steorf, but most held their ground, and some even swarmed at them.

"Back, curs," Steorf shouted.

He managed to fend off a few as he thrust his glowing hand in their faces. Tazi could hear them squeal in pain and rage. She herself dispatched two right off, easily spearing one on each of her two guardblades. A third, however, slipped past her weapons and viciously tore at her ankle with its razor-sharp incisors.

"Bastard," Tazi hissed, more out of rage than pain.

She kicked at it, and the animal, almost as large as a dog, was flipped into the air and struck the tunnel partition. The rat's skull split open, and the dying creature spasmed on the ground.

No sooner had the rat's blood begun to spill then three other albino monstrosities turned on their packmate and began to tear it apart. The squeals of both the dying and the feeding rats nearly reached a deafening pitch. One ran off with a large chunk of rodent flesh clamped firmly in its jaws. In its place, two others fought for position in the feeding frenzy.

"Back away!" Steorf yelled to Tazi, who had been watching the spectacle with morbid fascination.

The moment she was clear, Steorf ignited the horde of rodents. Those that hadn't yet reached the cannibalistic banquet ran in every direction from the intense heat and light emitted by the bonfire.

"I'm growing a little tired of all the roasting today," Tazi joked as she massaged her ankle while leaning against the wall.

"How badly did it bite you?" Steorf asked as he reached her side.

Tazi flashed a rueful grin.

"I'm sure the beastie left me a nice bruise, but the tough hide of my boot kept it from puncturing my skin."

She plucked out a lone tooth that had been embedded in her boot and flicked it away with distaste.

"I wonder what else lives down here?" Steorf pondered.

"I hope we don't find out. This way, I think," Tazi said, pointing to her left.

She stood up, and they continued along the winding path.

Over time, Tazi and Steorf started to notice that they were subtly ascending with every turn they made. There weren't any other rats or spiders in the various tunnels through which they passed. Tazi took it as a good sign, though they kept their weapons drawn the whole time.

"How much longer do you think?" Steorf asked her.

"I'm not sure, but I think we're fairly close," she replied. "Do you think there might be any wards set up to alarm the Children of Ibrandul if we get too close? They've got to be expecting us."

"Good question. I would assume there's always the chance. I'll keep an eye out for them," he assured her.

"Then again, they might think that any one of the myriad creatures that live down here might be enough to do us in," she remarked.

"Not a chance," Steorf told her easily. "It will take a lot more than a few vermin to—"

Tazi turned to see what had caused Steorf to stop speaking so suddenly, but he was nowhere to be seen in the dim light.

"Steorf?" she called worriedly and almost didn't see the pit that had suddenly opened up in front of her.

At the last minute, she caught herself right before she would have plunged over the side, arms pinwheeling frantically.

Carefully kneeling by the edge of the precipice, Tazi looked down. About fifteen feet below, she could see Steorf dangling by one hand. He had managed to snag a small crack in the wall. Another fifteen feet farther down Tazi was able to make out several large stalagmites that had been sharpened to razor points easily capable of impaling a human.

"Hang on!" she shouted to Steorf.

"Do I have a choice?" was his reply.

She pulled a length of cord from one of the pouches on her leather pants. Tying one end to a stalagmite near her, she called out to Steorf, "Eyes sharp. Here it comes."

Steorf squinted up and saw the thin cord dangling a foot away from him. With his one free hand, he wound it several times around his arm and shouted, "Ready?"

Tazi held the cord with her left arm, passed the

excess behind her waist, and held onto the remainder of rope with her right.

She dug in her heals and replied, "Got you."

Steorf muttered an oath and started to climb back up. Tazi strained at the other end and helped pull him as best she could. She provided an anchor and was fully prepared to lock down on the rope if Steorf showed a hint of slipping.

A few moments later, his blond head cleared the drop, and he hoisted himself the rest of the way out of the pit.

"Are you all right?" Tazi asked as she untied the cord from the stalagmite and began to coil it up.

"I'll live," Steorf proclaimed, rubbing his shoulder.

"All jokes aside," Tazi said seriously, "are you sure you're all right?"

"Thanks to you," he told her.

She smiled up at him and dusted his black shirt playfully.

"Don't you forget it," she admonished with a wink.

They continued along, more aware of the potential pitfalls along the route. At the next crossroads they had a differing opinion as to which was the correct direction.

"It's definitely getting brighter in here," she told him, "and I know I've seen this design before." She pointed to a distinct pattern in the wall of the tunnel that branched to the right.

"Tazi," Steorf replied in an exasperated tone, "that's not a deliberate design. I've seen markings like that in every tunnel we've passed through."

"Trust me on this. You might as well save your strength, anyway," she added with a nod toward his illuminated hand. "I'm sure we're going to need it."

"All right," Steorf replied, agreeing to both of Tazi's directions.

Trying to add some levity, he said, "If you're wrong about the tunnel, you owe me a round of drinks at the Kit."

"You think we're going to make it back alive?" came her retort.

Steorf looked at her. Tazi tried to hide her worry in jokes, but she could see that Steorf saw right through her.

"I know we will," he answered her seriously. "So no hedging on the bet."

"You know me," she countered, a real smile slowly growing.

"I most certainly do. How many drinks do you actually owe me at this point?"

Tazi laughed, and they remained on the course she had chosen. For a short distance, the path started to slope downward, and Steorf pointed out that they should consider backtracking, but Tazi held firm to her certainty that they were on the correct course.

Soon enough, the tunnel turned upward again, and even Steorf spotted a few familiar signs. They both grew quiet as they knew the temple was not too distant. Tazi's heart started to pound harder, and her mouth dried out. One look at Steorf told her that he was affected as well.

Tazi and Steorf finally saw the carved entrance into the Temple of Ibrandul. They gave each other a curt nod and burst into the large receiving chamber.

They were not disappointed in the welcome they received. Two novices were in the main hall waiting for them. The Mysterious Lurker, however, was nowhere to be seen. Tazi and Steorf had no time to worry about that. The Children of Ibrandul split their forces, one attacking Steorf and the other charging Tazi. They both brandished scimitars like the one Asraf had possessed, but nothing else.

The Child of Ibrandul who cornered Tazi was one of the novices she had seen in the council room the day before. She regarded her enemy with new eyes. It was still difficult not to hate him. Asraf's lifeless face floated before her and Tazi was afraid that Fannah might have already met the same fate.

But he's been used, she tried to convince herself, like so many of Ciredor's victims.

He charged her with his blade held above his head with both arms. As soon as he was in striking distance, he swung his weapon down. Tazi crossed her Sembian guardblades over her head, stopped his killing blow, and used them to wrench the scimitar from his grip.

She grabbed him by his ears and brought his face smashing down into her knee. He fell to the ground hard, knocking the air out of him. Tazi dropped to one knee and slammed one of her blades, hilt side down, on his skull. She left him alive but unconscious.

While she was dealing with her novice, Steorf had his hands full with the other. The Child of Ibrandul and he exchanged several thrusts and parries until the novice got lucky. Steorf's blade had been slightly damaged during his battles with the drow, and the Child of Ibrandul managed to strike the flawed spot with his scimitar and shatter Steorf's sword.

Steorf screamed in rage and threw the remains of his weapon to the ground. He backhanded the novice and brought his other arm down on the Child's sword arm, causing the novice to loose his scimitar. The two were barehanded and evenly matched again. They grabbed at each other.

Steorf and the last Child of Ibrandul tumbled against the dais and knocked the sacred book to the ground. Distracted by the pages fluttering everywhere, the novice tried to protect the holy writings. Steorf used the opportunity to grab his opponent's shoulders and slam the novice's head into the dais. He slumped to the ground.

"Both you and your divine scribbling can roast in hell," Steorf swore, and spread his hands wide to deliver a killing bolt.

"Don't," Tazi screamed, grabbing Steorf's wrist.

She could see that he was nearly lost to his own bloodlust, and she had to force her way bodily between him and his intended victim. Only when he would have had to blast through her to get to the Child of Ibrandul did a small amount of sanity return to Steorf's cold blue eyes.

"Get out of my way," he growled, chest heaving.

"No," Tazi told him, partially shielding the unconscious Child of Ibrandul. "I won't let you do this."

"What do you mean?" he asked.

His temper showed no sign of cooling, and Tazi knew she was in an uncertain situation.

He's dangerous right now, she recognized, and I don't know what he might do even to me if I get in his way.

Aloud, she explained calmly, "This isn't you. You don't kill indiscriminately like Ciredor does."

Steorf looked at her for a time.

"This is war," he finally said.

"You're right," she agreed, "and war is full of innocent victims, but you don't have to kill this one. He can't hurt us now."

Steorf started to calm. He backed up a step and regarded the scene. Tazi seized the moment.

"They are as much victims of Ciredor as we are. He's lied to them and manipulated them . . . and who knows what other evils he's brought down on them."

"He has much to answer for," Steorf agreed, lowering his hands.

"Yes, he does," Tazi agreed. "So let's put an end to the evil for everyone's sake."

Steorf looked once more at the inert novice before saying, "You're right. Let's get Fannah."

"We'll start just beyond that council room they took us to," Tazi ordered.

Though they were ready for others to show up, Tazi and Steorf didn't have any more run-ins with the Children of Ibrandul. The council room was empty and looked much as it had when they were last in it. Steorf spotted a door in the rear of the room and silently signaled Tazi over. Neither one of them saw any wards on it, so Tazi opened the door carefully to reveal the Lurker's study. Tazi swallowed back bile and Steorf grimaced in disgust.

The bodies of both of the Children of Ibrandul who had led them into the trap were roughly where Ciredor had left them. The only change was that the quiet one had finally been released from Ciredor's sorcerous manacle, and his body was crumpled in a heap. The room was rank from the beardless novice's brain tissue. Tazi had to swallow hard.

"Gods, I hope Fannah is all right," she said shakily. "We've got to keep searching."

Seeing that the Lurker's study was a dead end, Tazi and Steorf exited back through the counsel room and entered the hallway. The next few doors exposed only innocuous rooms with no one occupying them. Tazi tried not to get discouraged.

"Ciredor might have moved her," Steorf said quietly, voicing both their unspoken fears.

"She's here," Tazi asserted. "She's got to be."

Almost at the end of the tunnel, there was one door left. Tazi breathed deeply and swung it open. The room was ordinary enough, almost a parlor. Besides a large divan and a desk, there were many bookcases and a few tapestries adorning the walls. Candles were everywhere and they lent the chamber a cheery glow. Toward the back of the room, Tazi could see a large loom with Fannah seated behind it, busy with a shuttle in her hand. Tazi nearly laughed aloud.

"Fannah," she cried with delight.

At the sound of Tazi's voice, Fannah raised her sightless face and tilted it.

"Tazi," she replied, "you're back."

While Steorf guarded the doorway, Tazi made her way to Fannah's side. The two women clasped hands briefly, and Tazi couldn't wipe the smile from her face.

"Did you find out what you wanted?" Fannah asked her.

"I think I discovered what we needed to know," Tazi answered, glancing down at Fannah's loom.

She was momentarily startled to see an elaborate tower with a blue glow radiating from it on Fannah's tapestry.

"What's this?" she asked her sightless friend.

"I hate to interrupt," Steorf called from the doorway, "but I really think we should be going."

"He's right. Let's get out of here," Tazi ordered. "We need to get somewhere safe."

Both she and Steorf flanked Fannah and they started to make their way out of the tunnels. In the main chamber, which was still deserted save for the unconscious bodies of the fallen Children of Ibrandul, they passed by the overturned dais. Fannah's sandaled foot struck a few of the papers. She stopped and knelt down.

"What are you doing?" Tazi asked, at first thinking that Fannah had lost her footing.

However, she could see that her blind friend was carefully gathering the fallen pieces of parchment from the ground.

"Just because we have not seen eye to eye, so to speak, with the Children of Ibrandul doesn't mean these people are evil," Fannah explained. "I would not wish these writings to be defiled unnecessarily."

"Make it quick," Tazi told her. "Steorf, keep a watch on the inner door there."

She motioned to the entrance they had just come from.

It took Fannah a few moments to collect all the dropped pages. Tazi stood guard over her with one blade drawn.

"Hurry, Fannah," she admonished, but saw that a frown had crossed her friend's face. "What is it?"

Fannah rose carefully to her feet with the bundle of writings stacked in her hands.

She handed them to Tazi and asked, "Are these all part of the book they spoke of?"

Tazi frowned as well but accepted the sheaf of vellum. After sheathing her sword, she flipped through them all carefully before she answered Fannah.

"As far as I can tell, they are all written in the same hand. Why do you ask?"

"Because," Fannah said slowly, "this bundle is significantly heavier now than it was yesterday."

"Are you sure?" she asked seriously.

Fannah looked at her squarely with her white eyes and said, "I am very certain."

Before either woman had a chance to comment on the implications of that fact, Steorf rushed to their side.

"Ladies, I suggest we exit as quickly as possible. There was definitely something slithering in one of the rear chambers," he told them.

Together, the three of them fled the Muzad.

CHAPTER 11

RITUALS

It's gone," the Mysterious Lurker nearly cried.
"It's gone."

The old priest wandered around the main
chamber, paying little attention to the two
injured novices who stood there looking nervous.
He had eyes only for the once again upright, but
very empty, dais.

"How could this have happened?" he moaned.

"How could what have happened?" a deadly
voice repeated from the darkness.

The Lurker whirled and nearly tripped on his
own robes that were tangled around his legs. He
watched with growing fear as Ciredor separated
himself from the deep shadows behind the dais.
The priest could see that the necromancer was
already seething with anger. Thoughts of running crossed his mind, but he knew there was

no choice but to face the dark mage.

"Lord," he cried, "those *gharabs* have fled with the sacred writings of Ibrandul. I cannot begin to . . . to apologize."

He clutched at his robes defensively.

"What happened?" Ciredor demanded.

"A-a few hours ago," the priest stammered out, "the two Sembians found their way back to this chamber from the Muzad and stole the book."

"I thought you were going to take care of them," Ciredor taunted him. "They escaped your trap with the aranea, but you swore they would never return here alive."

The Lurker dropped his robes and wrung his hands together.

"They wouldn't have," he nearly screeched, "if that pariah, Asraf, had obeyed his orders." He continued on a higher tone, having found someone else to share the blame with. "If these two—" he paused and pointed to the two Children of Ibrandul—"had been stronger in their faith, they would have stopped those Sembians here . . . permanently."

"Leave this room," Ciredor told the Children of Ibrandul, suddenly very aware of their presence.

When they hesitated, he hissed, "*Now!*"

They fled without a backward glance at the Lurker, who felt very alone.

Ciredor slowly paced around the priest. The Lurker bowed his head under Ciredor's deliberate scrutiny and came to accept the fact that it was his responsibility alone regarding the safekeeping of Ibrandul's tome. He couldn't blame the others.

"What shall we do?" Ciredor whispered silkily. "Now that the book is gone and, I assume, Fannah as well, what do you suggest?"

All the while, he circled the priest.

It was all too much for the disciple of Ibrandul to bear. He dropped to his knees and buried his face in his hands.

"It's my fault entirely," he sobbed. "You discovered those amazing words, dedicated your whole life to retrieving them, and now, in one moment, I've lost them." The Lurker prostrated himself on the ground and cried, "I have betrayed my god. I don't deserve to live!"

Ciredor stood over him and tapped his foot. Seizing on an idea, the mage slowly sank to his knees and gathered the Lurker's shoulders in his steely grip.

He flipped the priest around to face him and said, "So you wish to die? Very well."

The Lurker broke free of Ciredor's icy hands and scuttled, crablike, a few steps back. His heart was pounding. He watched as Ciredor rose gracefully to his feet and reached with his right hand into a fold of his black silks. The priest cringed as the dark mage withdrew a glowing, amethyst gem and held it in his outstretched hand. The sight of the unholy artifact froze the Lurker's blood in his veins.

Somewhere he found the voice to ask tremulously, "W-what is that?"

Ciredor smiled a smile that didn't quite reach his black eyes.

"Don't be frightened," the necromancer consoled. "You said you don't deserve to live.

"Well," he continued easily, moving closer to the Lurker, "I'm going to send you to join your cherished Skulking God."

When Ciredor mentioned Ibrandul's title, something pierced the fear that had settled over the priest's mind like a fog.

He even found the courage to demand, "What are you talking about? You wouldn't . . ."

Ciredor advanced on the priest and extended his left arm. A green bolt escaped his fingers and shot over to the priest. Hovering over his body, the emerald orb divided into four smaller spheres, and each one pinned either an arm or a leg to the stone floor. The Mysterious Lurker was held fast.

"What?" he screamed at Ciredor.

The dark mage walked over to the bound priest and unceremoniously dropped the amethyst onto his chest. The gem winked and twinkled in the light, and the priest found himself mesmerized by the stone in spite of the predicament he was in. He fruitlessly strained against the sorcerous bonds. He was at Ciredor's mercy.

If there is such a thing, he thought morosely.

Ciredor walked over to the Lurker's head and stood so that the priest was forced to strain his neck back only to view the mage upside down. He scraped his scalp in the process, but the Lurker had a sneaking suspicion that that injury was the least of his worries. Ciredor gracefully dropped to his knees and leaned in close to the priest's ear.

"Your Lord of the Dry Depths," Ciredor explained smoothly, "has been dead for several years now."

"Lies!" the Lurker shrieked. "What kind of lies are you spinning?"

He was no longer aware of his vulnerability, having heard his god was so maligned.

"Surely you recall the Time of Troubles years back, and the Godswar," Ciredor continued, undaunted. "I'll take your silence as an affirmation." The dark mage chuckled. "My, this floor is rough."

He rose to his feet, brushing the dust from his pants. The Lurker watched as best he could while Ciredor prowled around his prostrate form.

"While skulking about . . . if you'll pardon the pun," the dark mage said in a mock apology, "deep in the Underdark beneath Waterdeep, Ibrandul had an encounter with my goddess. Shar slew him on sight."

"No . . ." the Lurker denied, but without much passion.

There was something in what Ciredor said that rang true to the priest. He had noticed over the past few years that there were fewer and fewer encounters with the Lord of the Dry Depths. He had been vaguely uneasy for months since Ciredor had been feeding him Ibrandul's "lost words." It was as though he sensed at a subconscious level that something was wrong.

"How can that be?" he asked, still reeling from the realization that his god was indeed dead.

"It was a time of great change," Ciredor explained, savoring the pain the Lurker suffered as though it were a fine wine. "Ibrandul's avatar was no match for my queen. She seized his powers, his dominion, and his followers after his death."

"But we have seen some signs of the Lurker in Darkness," the priest argued weakly. "Not many signs, but there have been some."

He was desperate to cling to any hope that his god still lived.

Ciredor smiled playfully and shook his head.

"Always, it was Shar," he explained. "She maintained the illusion that your Skulker was alive because it suited her whim, and helped her in her ongoing battle with Selûne. She is so very wise," he added reverently.

"There is no point for me to continue to live," the priest told him.

Being so close to death, he realized that he was truly dedicated to Ibrandul and tried to garner some peace from that knowledge.

"I won't argue that," Ciredor agreed, "but don't be too sad. Your death will have some meaning yet. In fact," he added slyly, "I think it will have more meaning than your life ever did."

The Lurker could tell that Ciredor hoped he would ask the mage to elaborate, but in finding the strength of his faith the priest also found the strength to resist Ciredor's final temptation. He maintained his silence.

A slight frown creased the necromancer's face when the Lurker grew quiet.

"Afraid?" he asked sweetly. "You should be, for your soul is nearly the last that I need."

When the Lurker didn't even bat an eye, Ciredor continued, "I have been collecting these facets for my goddess over the last few years. Within this gem—" he pointed to the stone still resting on the Lurker's chest—"are ten souls. But these are not ordinary souls, by any means. These are the souls of beings who have all worshiped Shar in one aspect or another."

He walked around the Lurker, and the priest could see that the mage was caught up in his own narration.

"Some of the souls knew they worshiped Shar, but not all. There is an elf in here who literally fell into my hands and did not even realize his deity was a part of my dark goddess."

So absorbed was the dark mage that the priest was sure Ciredor had forgotten that there was someone in the chamber with him.

"Fannah shall be my crowning glory," he continued, "for she and her family are priestesses of Sharess, and that goddess was completely under the influence of Shar for many, many years until she broke free. I shall unite these souls and make the ultimate gift to Shar: a gift of unity. I will give her . . . herself."

The Mysterious Lurker saw that Ciredor was nearly in a state of rapture over his plan. Though he knew he was near death, he found he was actually curious.

"What do you get from this 'gift'?" the Lurker asked.

Ciredor looked down at the bound priest and said, "Shar will see that I, over all other mortals, understand her and know the secrets of her heart. Because of that, she will take me as her consort."

"This is what you have been planning for the Fore-shadowing all along," the Lurker deduced.

"Clever in the end," Ciredor complimented the priest. "The 'Foreshadowing' that will occur on the new moon is actually a night that has been declared a Kiss of the Lady by Shar's true Temple of Old Night. Within my desert stronghold I will honor her with my gift: my heart, if you will, and Shar will honor me."

"You will not succeed," the Lurker said. "I have made many mistakes in my life, and I shall pay for them all, but so shall you pay for yours. The Sembians will stop you."

Peals of laughter poured from Ciredor.

"How delightfully entertaining you are," the necromancer said. "I know my goddess will find you equally amusing as she has already enjoyed duping you these fourteen years. I think she will find you delicious."

Ciredor stepped back a few paces.

The Lurker watched with detached fascination as Ciredor closed his eyes and began a low chant. He still found the dark mage's voice sweet, even though his life was forfeit at the sound of it.

It will be good, he thought serenely, to finally join Ibrandul.

His serenity only lasted a heartbeat. As Ciredor's litany reached its crescendo, the Lurker's world exploded. Pain blossomed over every inch of his body, and he writhed in excruciating torment. His eyes rolled back in their sockets, and he wept tears of blood. He clawed at the stone floor until he reached the bones of his fingers and he ground those down too. He was beyond screaming, beyond any verbal expression. The gem pulsed on his chest.

The last living sight he saw was Ciredor's calm visage. The Mysterious Lurker felt his very essence ooze from each of his pores and vaguely saw a gray smoke rise from his body. That smoke was hungrily sucked into the waiting gem, and when the last wisp of his soul was seized, the Lurker's body went limp.

Ciredor's laughter echoed throughout the abandoned temple.

❦ ❦ ❦ ❦ ❦

"What do you mean I can't go with you?" Steorf demanded.

He, Tazi, and Fannah had escaped from the false Temple of Ibrandul and navigated their way back into Hook Ward. Though Fannah was distressed to learn that the Children of Ibrandul had been misled, she was not entirely surprised.

"You and I know how sweetly deceiving Ciredor can be," she had reminded Tazi.

Though she had been loath to admit it, Tazi recalled how infatuated she had been when her mother had first introduced her to the dark mage.

"There is something compelling about him," she grudgingly acknowledged. When she saw Steorf's stern glance, she hastily added, "Even though he is a monster."

Fannah had brought them to the Festhall of Eternal Delight, despite their blushing protests.

"This is the only place to rest in seclusion," Fannah had informed them, "for a number of reasons."

Tazi noticed that her Calishite friend hadn't used the word "hide."

"Since he is a minion of Shar, this temple of Sharess is our only choice," she had told them. "Shar's influence can not reach us here and we can fully prepare for the coming storm."

Fannah had spoken to an old acquaintance and secured rooms for them all. Steorf mumbled something about Fannah's old friends and traps, but Tazi sharply reminded him that Fannah had only said she knew *of* the Children of Ibrandul; she had never claimed any allegiance with them as she did the priestesses of Sharess. Tazi was content to trust her sightless friend once more.

With most of their gear, including the sacred book, safely stowed in their rooms, Fannah led Tazi through many halls of debauchery to a special room down in a lower level. Steorf adamantly refused to leave Tazi's side any longer and followed along, though the sights in the halls brought a rosy flush to his face. When they reached the door, however, Fannah placed her hand on his broad chest and told him he could go no farther.

"I am sorry," she explained at his shocked question, "but this is a place only for women. You can not enter."

She crossed her arms firmly. It was the first time Tazi had ever seen Fannah take a stand on an issue. She could see that her friend was resolute in her statement.

"Steorf," Tazi said as she pulled him aside slightly, "I will be safe here with Fannah. If you're not allowed, then you can not break their customs."

Steorf shifted his weight from one foot to the other but was as steadfast as Fannah. Tazi tried something else.

She pulled out of her satchel the scrolls she had stolen from Ciredor all those many months before—what felt to Tazi like a lifetime ago—and with a certain amount of gravity, placed the scrolls in Steorf's hands.

"I'm not exactly sure what Fannah has in mind for us two," she explained, "but we can't afford to waste any time. While I am involved in this—" and she motioned to the closed door—"I need you to decipher Ciredor's writings. I'm certain that what we need to stop him is in those scrolls and that false book of his."

Steorf tucked the scrolls into a fold of his cloak and stared at Tazi. She could see that he reluctantly agreed with her logic. She took a step closer and leaned up to whisper in his ear.

"There is absolutely no one else I would trust more with this task than you."

She stepped back to look him firmly in the eye.

"I won't disappoint you," he replied.

With a quick look at Fannah and the forbidden chamber, he turned back to their rooms.

"I'm ready," Tazi told Fannah after Steorf was gone from sight.

"No, you aren't," Fannah informed her gently, "but you will be."

With that enigmatic statement, Fannah opened the door to the chamber and stepped inside. Tazi followed suit.

The chamber was spacious and steamy. The entire floor and walls were covered with tiny tiles that formed incredible mosaics. Tazi had heard that parts of Calimport were decorated with this form of art, and she had caught glimpses of some of the famed Calishite talent during their first, rapid pass through the city, but nothing compared to this.

The tiles were fine, and Tazi marveled at their number. It must have taken years, a lifetime for this room to be so adorned, she thought.

Almost reverently, she traced her hand along the surprisingly cool tiles and admired the exquisite designs. There were writings—Tazi could only guess at the language—and fantastical creatures done in incredible detail. No windows broke the patterns along the walls, but Tazi did notice several discreet vents placed strategically in the room. Running alongside the walls were benches tiled in the same style and gleaming brass fixtures next to them. The majority of the room was taken up by a large pool of steaming water.

"Please," Fannah said, motioning to one of the benches.

Fannah sat down herself, and Tazi took her cue from the blind Calishite. When Fannah began to disrobe, carefully folding her clothes in a neat pile beside the decorated bench, Tazi did the same with her leathers. She noticed that beside every bench was a small pail filled with soapy water. She saw Fannah reach for a similar bucket and a piece of cloth. Using the rag, Fannah started to scrub the filth of the past few days from her body.

Tazi did the same and noticed that the water had a

tangy smell of spice and the ocean. She inhaled deeply of the aroma. Everywhere she scrubbed, Tazi felt her skin tingle, and she was glad to be free of the dust and blood of the Muzad.

After a suitable period of cleansing, Tazi watched as Fannah took a second pail of water and poured the contents over her head, rinsing away the last vestiges of dirt.

While Tazi sluiced off the grime, Fannah moved to stand near a special niche in the wall. She removed a small basket filled with dried herbs and walked deftly over to the edge of the pool.

"Tazi," she said softly, "it is time for you to enter the sacred waters of Sharess."

Tazi padded slowly over to the pool and saw that there was a series of steps into the water. She slowly entered, gasping at the intense heat of the water. She could feel her face flush because of the overwhelming warmth, and it was nearly too much for her, but she realized that this was significant to Fannah and forced herself to stand on the bottom of the pool. The water covered her to her shoulders, and the room was shrouded in the tangy steam.

Tazi wasn't sure if Fannah was speaking or chanting because her melodic voice was so low. She didn't recognize the language though she believed it to be Alzhedo.

Tazi watched as Fannah started to throw handfuls of the herbs into the water between breaks in her chant. Tazi merely stood in the water and slowly swirled her arms back and forth, finally starting to relax her limbs in the intense heat, waiting for whatever came next. When her basket was empty, Fannah set it back in the niche and entered the water as well.

When she was only a few feet from Tazi, Fannah stared hard at her with her ice-white eyes.

Finally, she said, "You are about to face your greatest evil. If you are to succeed, you must be purified for the coming battle. You must come to understand the various faces you have worn in your life. You must unite all of your selves and become whole if you are to defeat him and emerge triumphant."

With that, Fannah fell silent.

Tazi wasn't quiet sure what Fannah expected her to do. She noticed that the steam was growing and Tazi wasn't even able to see Fannah anymore through the heavy vapors. Tazi knew her friend was within arm's reach but the entire chamber was clouded by great billows of steam. Sweat started to pour into her eyes, and she blinked at its salty sting. The more she blinked, however, the more Tazi thought that the warm haze was lifting somewhat. She was even able to make out Fannah's outline again in the mist. As Fannah's shape grew sharper, Tazi jerked back in surprise.

The face in the mist was not that of her friend, but her own staring back at her.

It was not entirely a mirror image, it was the face she had worn at the age of six. There was a glint in her younger self's eye that the older Tazi recognized. It meant she had just pilfered something and was immensely pleased with herself, with her jet black hair in soft curls, tongue peaking out, and her young face screwed up with determination. The older Tazi felt like giggling at the sight before her, but she wasn't sure if the giggles she felt welling within her were because of the vision her younger self presented, or because that was how she had felt at that precise moment in her young life.

"I'm going to make you pay for that, you little rat," a voice threatened the girl-child.

The older Tazi suddenly found herself standing in the same hallway as the girl and she turned just like her younger self at the sound of the voice. The older Tazi recognized the owner of that voice. It belonged to her older brother, Tamlin, and she could see him storming down the hallway. Obviously, her younger self had done something to aggravate him.

And he surely deserved it, Tazi thought, but he'll make me pay for it. He always did.

Aloud, she shouted, "Run!" to her six-year-old version.

As though the girl-child could hear her, she tore down the hallway. The older Tazi found her heart pounding and a wicked grin spreading across her face.

"That's not right, Thazienne," Cale chided her.

Tazi turned to see herself when she was thirteen or fourteen. Teenage Thazienne was bent over a chest with a finer set of lockpicks in her delicate hand than the set she had first owned. Cale was standing beside her in his pantry, scrutinizing her actions carefully.

The older Tazi watched in fascination as Cale reached over and covered her young hand with his long fingers. Tazi could feel her heart skip a beat as though he was touching her hand now.

"There is a certain finesse to what you are doing," he told her in his deep voice. "You must trust your feelings."

Tazi watched as the teenager gazed up at Cale with admiration and the beginnings of something more. Tazi swallowed hard at the scene that was played out in front of her.

"I'll show her," Tazi heard herself say.

She turned and found herself in her bedroom in Storm-weather Towers. The version in front of her now was from only a few years back. She watched as the young woman stomped around before sitting in front of her dressing table. Tazi pursed her lips together angrily and knew what her other self was about to do.

"You show her," she egged the younger Tazi on.

The young woman grabbed a pair of shears from her collection of bottles and sundries on the dressing table and stared at herself in the mirror.

"Try to explain your daughter's latest shenanigans to that circle of hens you call 'friends,' Mother," she spat.

She gathered up a handful of her waist-length hair

in one hand and held the shears in the other. In one snip, the tresses fell to the floor. After only a few moments of hacking, the young Thazienne sported the hairstyle Tazi wore ever since, highly unfashionable in the ever fashion-conscious Selgaunt.

"Good work," she complimented the young Thazienne, and the two women wore the same expression in the mirror.

When Tazi turned away from herself and the dressing table, she watched as a still older version was by the window, dressed entirely in black leathers. Tazi could see down through the window a younger Steorf anxiously waiting for Tazi to join him. He was also suitably dressed for a late night wilding, and Tazi could feel her heartbeat quicken in anticipation of the night's events. She could see that her younger self felt the same way.

A scream tore through the room. When Tazi turned again, she found herself in the cellar of Ciredor's tall-house. Her blood turned to ice. She saw her other self hammered to her knees by Ciredor's magic. As she watched herself struggle with Ciredor, Tazi ran her hands through her hair, momentarily surprised that it wasn't waist-length again. When she fought Ciredor then, he had toyed mercilessly with her. One of the things he had done was to restore her hair to its former length. The process had been excruciatingly painful, as Ciredor had meant it to be, and Tazi rubbed her scalp as she watched those horrible moments from two years in the past once again unfold.

Her past self gazed from the view of the young boy Ciredor had disemboweled to feed his dark magic to Steorf manacled to the cellar wall. Tazi's heart was pounding, and her mouth was devoid of moisture as her other self whispered the word inscribed on the emerald ring that Durlan had given her.

She gasped as Ciredor's bolt was deflected by the gray

shield that had formed around her other self. Tazi, near to tears observing the old battle, realized that she didn't feel the resolve that she had felt in that moment. As she watched herself pull a small dagger hidden in her boot and expertly strike Ciredor just below his heart with it, she was not able to remember what her other self so obviously possessed: courage.

"No!" Tazi yelled, absolutely terrified.

She hoisted herself out of the sacred pool and stood shivering at its edge. Someone placed a calming hand on her shoulder, and Tazi wheeled around, breathing hard.

Not knowing what to expect, Tazi had to calm her beating heart. It was only Fannah who stood behind her, holding out a large, white towel. Tazi accepted it and wrapped the towel around herself with shaking fingers. Fannah motioned for her to sit on one of the benches and joined her there.

Tazi blotted at her face and tried to control the wild beating of her heart, not saying a word.

Fannah smiled at her and said, "It is always shocking to truly see yourself."

She patted Tazi's hand.

"As long as you encountered these ghosts of yourself bravely," she continued, "then you will be ready for what lies ahead. Just as a desert is not comprised of only a single grain of sand, you are not merely one facet, but thousands."

The steam had almost evaporated, and Tazi thought carefully before she answered, "I believe you're right, Fannah."

"Rest for a few minutes," she told Tazi, "and we will go up to Steorf and see what he has uncovered."

Tazi leaned her head back against the cool tiles and closed her eyes.

I didn't remember what it was like to know I possessed the ability to defeat Ciredor, she thought to herself. If I can't remember what it was like, how can I possibly beat him now?

She absently rubbed her bare finger.

I'm not the woman I was, she thought.

There was no one in the room who could argue otherwise.

CHAPTER 12

THE CALIM DESERT

"I think I've got a little more figured out," Steorf informed Tazi and Fannah.

Tazi nudged her mount with her knees and moved closer to Steorf's horse.

"Is that why you've been so silent these last few hours?" she asked.

"I've been trying to conserve energy," he told her. "And, yes, I've been mulling over those writings. I wish we'd had a little more time to go over them in Calimport. It was more conducive to study, and it was more comfortable there."

He shifted in his saddle, and Tazi smiled at his last remark. The three of them had been in the desert for two days, and comfort was no longer an option. When they had left Malikhan Gate in the Trade Ward and first glimpsed the massive expanse of the Calim desert, Tazi had been dumbstruck. Calimport had been fantastical enough for her, but in the end, it was still a city.

In the few days she spent there, Tazi began to catch the rhythm of the wards. Commerce was as much a part of life in Calimport as it was in Selgaunt.

The city was easy enough to understand, but she had no words to describe the barren wasteland that stretched before her eyes as she and her friends left the city behind. The Calim desert extended nearly two hundred miles to the north, east, and west of the city.

"How can this desert even exist?" she asked Fannah. "It's surrounded by the ocean."

"Many millennia ago, two powerful djinn, Calim and Memnon, battled for control of this area," Fannah replied. "They were finally bound by elven spells, and their captors felt the damage they did to their personal battleground was nothing compared to what they could have done if left free."

Fannah spread her arm to point at the desert.

"This," she told Tazi, "is the price of their confinement."

Tazi stared at the lifeless dunes of sand and the miles of salt flats. The golden-white vastness was something she had never seen. Her youth had consisted of towers and streets packed with nobles and the grimiest of urchins. Parks and forests, all things green and lush, were as much of nature as Tazi had ever seen until then, until she was faced with a sea of white. It was almost incomprehensible.

And she and her friends were going to have to cross it. Somewhere in the middle of the deadly wasteland, Ciredor was hiding.

They decided that using any type of magical means of travel in the desert would shine like a beacon and tip Ciredor to their location. None of them were too eager to trust other sorcerous types in Calimport after their tragic encounter with the followers of Ibrandul, anyway.

So they purchased horses and plenty of supplies to

take with them into the desert. Fannah had warned them that they would probably find little water and even less food so they had to be very careful with their provisions. They needed to pack every conceivable item they might need, and special clothing must be purchased as well, to protect them all from the harsh glare of the desert sun. They all sported light cotton *abas* and cotton head cloths.

Two days later, as Tazi also shifted in her saddle and winced at the ache in her muscles, she thought back longingly to the fleet of flying carpets tethered in a stall they'd passed. She placed one hand on the small of her back and attempted to ease the knot that had formed after two nights of sleeping in the saddle. Even she had to reluctantly agree that this was wearing on her.

"So tell us what you've figured out," she told Steorf. "Anything to get my mind off my aching bones."

Steorf knew her statement was only half jest. He took a sip of water from his flask and wiped his mouth with the back of his dry hand.

"As far as I can tell," he began, "we're still heading in the right direction."

"I would certainly hope so," Fannah chimed in, and both she and Tazi giggled.

Her horse was loosely tied to Tazi's mount. She had admitted that it had been quite some time since she had ridden and wanted to be close to one of her sighted companions. For the first time in their friendship, Tazi actually thought of Fannah as blind.

"I know now that Ciredor plans to complete his ritual tomorrow night," he told them.

"The first night of the new moon," Fannah remarked.

"Yes," Steorf answered, "when everything is shrouded in darkness. Ciredor's most recent addition in his sacred book reveals that this particular night has been declared a 'Kiss of the Lady' by the Temple of Old Night."

" 'Kiss of the Lady?' " Tazi asked.

"As best I can tell, that appears to be the most important holy day for those who worship Shar," Steorf explained. "It is supposed to be a night of horrific deeds done in Shar's name and ends with a feast at dawn."

"Have you deciphered where, exactly, this event is going to occur?" Fannah wondered.

"I am fairly sure he is going to conduct this dark ceremony in a specific set of minarets that are near the heart of the desert."

Steorf paused and scanned the horizon.

"I don't know which exact ones yet," he finished.

Tazi knew he was frustrated at what he perceived to be slow progress translating Ciredor's writings.

"You're working as fast as you can," she said, trying to console him. "I can only imagine the frustration, though. Every page you translate causes the next page's code to change, and you have to start anew."

Steorf merely grumbled. Tazi realized he didn't want anyone else making excuses for his ability or lack thereof. She tactfully redirected the conversation.

"Just how many towers could there be here in the Calim?" she asked Fannah. "How could anything survive?"

"Back during the Shoon Imperium, the Trade Way was constructed. Magic was combined with the stones used so that they would be almost impervious to some of the more natural problems associated with the desert," she told Tazi. "Every two miles, a pair of minarets was constructed. The towers are forty feet tall, and each one has what appears to be an open parapet at the top. There are elaborate arches that hold up the gilded roofs. Some say there is glass or other wards at the top that keep anyone or anything from reaching the braziers in the center."

"So nothing can extinguish the lights within," Tazi guessed.

"I have heard stories that when the braziers from each pair of minarets are lit with the blue crystals inside the minaret, something amazing occurs."

"What?" Tazi asked as she rearranged her head covering to keep more of the desert glare from her eyes.

"A blue glow encompasses both towers in a protective sphere that neither beast nor foul weather can penetrate."

"But if that's the case," Steorf asked, "why is it so difficult to cross the Calim Desert? I mean, I understand why we can't march down the paved road to Ciredor and announce ourselves," he observed, "but wouldn't other travelers and traders find the route convenient and faster even than the sea?"

"Many years ago, much of the road fell into disrepair as naturally occurring sinkholes broke many of the Way's enchantments," Fannah answered. "Some of the towers were partially or completely buried some time ago and the gems from many of the towers stolen away. Our *syl-pasha* would like to repair the road and has even made a tiny bit of progress, but the work is slow."

Tazi glanced at both Fannah and Steorf. While Fannah was spared the terrible brilliance of the desert sun bouncing off the reflective sand into her eyes, the blind woman was not any more immune to the intense heat than she or Steorf. The three had been riding for hours without a break, and Tazi decided to call one.

"I think we could use an hour to rest," she suggested.

"Good idea," Steorf agreed. "This will give me another chance at those scrolls."

They stopped the horses near an outcropping of rocks. The terrain varied slightly as they progressed deeper into the desert, but only slightly. They passed over miles and miles of rolling dunes only to have the terrain completely flatten out to salt flats with the occasional rock pile. The ground around the knoll was more salt flat than sand, and there was even a section between the rocks that was slightly marshy. The horses went immediately over to lick up what little moisture there was. Tazi gratefully slid out of her saddle and stretched her sore legs. It took a moment for her to move around any way other than bowlegged.

When she'd loosened up some, she helped Steorf stake down a silk cloth and attach it to some of the rocks to fashion a makeshift lean-to. They spread another on the ground, and the three collapsed in the temporary shade.

Tazi sipped greedily at her water skin. Though she had opted for a cotton *aba* to protect herself from the sun, she still wore her leathers underneath. She knew she was perspiring and had to keep up her water intake to prevent dehydration. There was no effective way to cover her hands that were exposed on the reins. They were turning a fiery red. She rubbed at them gingerly.

"Perhaps you should have considered taking some of the lighter clothes we saw in the market," Fannah remarked after she heard Tazi take a deep drink.

"It was a hard decision," Tazi agreed, "but I would rather sweat a little and have more protective gear than the reverse."

Tazi refused to part with her leathers in the market, secretly fearing to lose anything else she had come to rely on, like the ring she no longer possessed.

"We brought more than enough water, so you should be all right," Fannah said thoughtfully.

Tazi turned to Steorf, wondering why he was so quiet. While she had been talking to Fannah, he had pulled out all the parchments they had of Ciredor's and spread a few across the salt flat. He was now lost in his studies. Tazi shook her head.

He doesn't give up, she thought.

She ran her hand through her short locks and was startled by how stiff they were. She studied her hand and saw that it was lightly sprinkled with sand.

"This stuff is insidious," she said to no one in particular, and rubbed her hand against her leathers.

She pulled off her boots and shook them out. To her dismay, a small amount of granules emptied out onto their ground cloth.

"It's everywhere."

While Fannah checked on their provisions and prepared a light snack for them, Steorf said, "I've got a better sense where those minarets are."

Tazi crawled over on her hands and knees to where he had propped himself up against the rocks. She looked at the parchment he was studying, and recognized it as one of the few she had stolen from Ciredor two years before.

"From what I can tell," Steorf told her, "those minarets are somewhere near a place called Teshyll."

Tazi studied the words he was translating. The elaborate scrawls meant nothing to her. They were vaguely reminiscent of Alzhedo in their physical beauty, but that's where the similarity ended. From the corner of her eye, she saw that as Steorf pointed out the name of Teshyll to her on one document, all the other pages shimmered. The writings came alive like slender worms and repositioned themselves on the vellum. Every page except the one Steorf held in his hand was a mystery again.

How are we going to defeat him? Tazi wondered morosely.

"Teshyll was a city that provided a centralized farmer's market eight thousand years back when the Teshyll Fields were rich and fertile," Fannah told them. "Calim also kept his harem there in a palace that was one of the greatest examples of gravity-defying architecture ever seen."

Tazi smiled at her friend's keen hearing. Fannah had looked deeply absorbed in preparing a plate of succulent fruit for them all, yet she had been listening closely to their exchange.

"Is there anything left of this city?" Steorf asked and took a bite of a slice of fruit.

"No, there isn't," she informed him. "All that remains of the buildings are a few cornerstones."

Even though she was thirsty, it was hard for Tazi to eat much. She noticed Steorf had the same problem. The overwhelming heat was like a heavy blanket, and putting food in her stomach was the last thing Tazi wanted, but she knew it was necessary for all of them to maintain as much strength as was possible. She forced herself to eat and reminded her friends to do the same.

"Let's close our eyes for an hour or so and pack up," Tazi told them.

Fannah curled up and went to sleep almost immediately. Tazi realized that while she and Steorf might have been sore, the trek was a thousand times more arduous for their blind friend. While Tazi marveled at her mental calmness, she knew that Fannah's body didn't posses the same stamina.

She watched Fannah's deep breathing for a while and lay back with her arms behind her head. She could see golden lizards no bigger than her hand dart between the cracks in the rocks. The lizards were the only wildlife they'd seen since entering the desert. Not even birds, it appeared, ventured into the Calim.

We should count ourselves fortunate, Tazi rationalized to herself, that those lizards are the only creatures we've come across.

She tried to close her eyes, and though she was tired her mind refused to stop turning. A crinkling to her left caught her attention. When she opened her eyes and rolled onto her left side she saw that Steorf was back studying the parchments.

"I thought we were all going to rest," she whispered, not wanting to disturb Fannah.

She looked over her shoulder and saw that Fannah's even breathing hadn't changed.

"I can't," Steorf answered without looking at her. "There's still so much we need to learn from these pages."

Tazi scooted closer to him and touched his hand.

"We do need the information, I won't argue that, but we also need to get as much rest as possible."

Steorf gazed up at Tazi, then at Fannah, and finally at their meager supplies.

"I don't think rest is going to turn the tide for us," he said quietly.

His words struck deep into Tazi. She had been thinking almost the same since they'd left Calimport. The fact that she had failed to purify herself hounded her ruthlessly, but she couldn't let the others see her worries. Fannah's life depended on her, and she wouldn't let Steorf fall victim to that despair either.

"We've come this far," she told him with false confidence. "We've survived every pitfall that has come our way. If Ciredor wasn't frightened of us, I don't think he would've run here. I believe he would have stayed behind in Calimport to kill us. That's worth something."

"I wish that were true," he told her kindly. "I'm afraid he went into the desert because this is where he needs to be to complete his gift to Shar. His time is running out to finish this so he had to come out here. I'd love to believe he was frightened of us, Tazi, but I know he's not."

Everything he said made complete sense to her, but Tazi refused to accept it. To do so would be to accept defeat.

"He should be," she said seriously. "He should be very frightened.

"What else have you figured out?" She added to focus them both on something they could do.

Steorf replied with a faint smile, "I *am* getting closer to the exact distance that the minarets are from Calimport, but I don't quite have it yet. Every time I put these papers down, they're all rewritten the next time I look at them."

His voice was heavy with barely concealed frustration.

"I've been wondering something," Tazi said. "Why do you think Ciredor even wrote this down if it holds so many clues?"

"I've been wondering that myself. We've probably been less than accurate thinking of him as a mage. I think he must be a nightcloak of Shar's, one of her elite priests.

"As far as I know," Steorf went on, "they aren't supposed to take on any special tasks without orders. Ciredor might have been reporting to someone else, and this was the way he did it.

"Or," he added thoughtfully, "he might be operating on his own, and this collection is his written record for others to find after he presents his gift to Shar."

"Something to leave behind for others to find," Tazi whispered, her mind only beginning to guess at the ramifications of what Ciredor might be attempting.

"That may be why he told the followers of Ibrandul that it was a book from their god," Steorf agreed slowly. "He wanted a dedicated group to protect it for . . . afterward."

They were both silent for a time. Eventually, Steorf turned to Tazi. "There is something I would like you to know," he said.

The tone in his voice made Tazi nervous for some unexplained reason. She drew shapes on their ground-cloth with her finger but didn't look at him.

"What is it?" she asked.

"I don't know how this is going to end for us," he started.

Tazi looked at him and placed her fingertips over his chapped lips.

"Don't," she implored.

He gently took her hand away from his mouth and squeezed it briefly.

"I have to," he told her. "Neither of us can say what will happen. I just want to make sure that you understand something, and there might not be another chance to tell you."

"Make sure this is something you're going to be able to live down," she told him lightly. "You know I will forever remind you of it when we get back."

"*If* we get back," Steorf corrected her gravely, "I don't want you to ever forget it."

"All right," Tazi answered, no longer flippant.

"I know how much it hurt you when Ciredor told you that I was on Thamalon Uskevren's payroll."

He watched as Tazi dropped her head. He reached over and cupped her chin in his hand and tilted it up to face him.

"It was true that your father paid me for many years to watch over you as best I could. What you don't know is that I've been watching you far longer than that. I've been watching you since we were children."

"What?"

"Ever since you saved that baby from the midden and Durlan rewarded you with your ring, I've followed you. The mage, Durlan, was one of my instructors back then, and he shared your exploits with me," Steorf explained. "Needless to say, the story made an impression, and I decided one day to see more of you."

Tazi was surprised, and she had thought she was beyond such things.

"My mother, just like your parents, is very conscious of social allegiances. As the premier mage of Selgaunt, she has to be. My childhood was rather secluded," he said, and Tazi detected a note of sadness in his voice. It was an aspect of his younger years she had never known before. "I think I stole out at nights for the same reason as you: freedom. Freedom from duties and obligations and watchful eyes.

"As my prowess and skills progressed, your father approached my mother, Elaine. He was hoping to strike a bargain with her. He felt that my abilities were advanced enough that I might be a guard of sorts for you. He reasoned that since we were of a similar age, I could become acquainted with you and you wouldn't suspect me of anything other than another admirer," he finished.

"Why didn't you just come out and tell me the truth?" Tazi said, torn between anger and an emotion she refused to name.

"First," Steorf replied, "your father rightly suspected that you would resist any offers of protection."

When Tazi remained silent, Steorf said, "Tell me honestly that if you thought I was a bodyguard you wouldn't have escaped from me—and had a bloody good time doing it—the first chance you got."

Tazi lowered her gaze and stifled a giggle, not wanting to wake Fannah.

"I would've done a good job of it, too," she answered when she lifted her head.

"You would've tried," he told her with some of his old cockiness. "But the issue was moot, because my mother refused the whole arrangement. She felt someone would eventually find out about it, and she didn't want to have too close an alliance with any one member of the Old Chauncel.

"That should have been the end of it, but I caught wind of the bargain and approached your father discreetly to accept his offer. He said he was impressed with my ability to 'see past my mother's robes,' but I secretly suspected he was just pleased to get his way. Little did he realize it was me who was getting my way.

"That was how I managed to live the life I wanted for over seven years. You didn't know of the bargain I struck with your father, and my mother never discovered my secret outings. I don't think she would've understood. Elaine so wants me to be the next premier mage of Selgaunt. Our forays just don't fit into that plan."

"But you do have the talent for the job," Tazi told him.

"I know I do. I just don't know if I want it," he answered. "I want the choice to be mine, not something that is simply foisted onto my shoulders. I want the freedom to choose. You, more than anyone else, know the value of choice."

Tazi nodded.

"With you," Steorf went on, "I was free somehow. I recognized that kindred spirit in you. There were many times I wanted to tell you about the deal with your father, but I was afraid of your anger. I hoped you'd never find out. Keeping that secret from you made us both vulnerable to Ciredor. I won't let that happen again. Not any longer."

"I wish you would've told me from the beginning. I'd like to think I would've appreciated the joke on my father," Tazi replied, though she was not entirely convinced by Steorf's confession.

"You don't know that you would've. I didn't want to risk that after I had become so close to you," Steorf said.

"No, I don't know for sure what I would've done," she agreed. "We'll never know nor will we ever get these last two years back that we lost. Now we can only go forward."

"I hope so."

"I think we should start to pack up," Tazi told him.

She wanted to get moving, but she also wanted to have some time to herself, even if it was in the saddle, to mull over Steorf's revelations. She wanted and needed to believe him, but the wound ran deep, like a fault line in the bedrock of their friendship.

Tazi woke Fannah, who was on her feet straight away. It took only a short time to break down their impromptu camp and pack everything onto their mounts. Tazi inspected them briefly and hoped they had had enough rest.

Don't fail us, she thought as she stroked the side of her mount. I can't imagine doing this on foot.

Steorf got them on course, and the three of them traveled for several hours almost in single file. While it made sense to stay as quiet as possible to conserve strength, Tazi knew that Steorf was leaving her to think over what he had told her. She wanted to believe in him again, like she used to.

But how do I go back to the way things were when the trust has been so damaged? she asked herself.

She remembered the answer she had given Steorf: We go forward.

"Steorf . . ." she said, breaking the silence and spurring her mount ahead.

She was unable to finish her sentence. Fannah let out a short gasp as her mount stumbled and fell to the ground. Tazi and Steorf dismounted swiftly and went over to Fannah and her horse.

"Are you all right?" Tazi asked Fannah as she helped the blind woman to her feet.

"Yes," she replied, somewhat shaken. "I seem to be in one piece. What's the matter with my horse? Did it turn a leg in a sinkhole?"

Steorf knelt by the quietly whimpering beast. It had snapped a foreleg in its fall, but there was nothing around to explain why it should have tumbled.

"Should I try to repair the damage?" he asked Tazi.

Her heart went out to the suffering stallion but she knew they had to conserve every bit of their resources and that included Steorf's strength. She shook her head sadly and knelt by the beast.

She drew her small, razor sharp dagger and said, "I'm sorry."

She stroked its neck as she prepared to cut his throat, and the horse jerked as her hand neared its jaw. Puzzled, Tazi lay down her dagger and gently opened its mouth.

"Ugh," she gasped.

It was lined with swollen, black leeches. She expertly slit the animal's neck to end its suffering, realizing there was nothing more to be done for the creature. Its blood pooled black in the sand around Tazi's knees. She rose to her feet.

"We need to check the other two," she told Fannah and Steorf.

Sure enough, both of the other horses' mouths also contained the bloodsuckers, but to a lesser degree. She and Steorf pried the parasites from the animals' mouths. As they were almost totally engorged with blood, the leeches came out easily. They squirmed, bloated, on the hot sand. Tazi stomped on them callously and tried to keep her stomach from turning at the moist sounds they made under her boots.

"How did the horses get infested?" Fannah asked after Tazi and Steorf were done with the vermin.

"My fault," Tazi said, shaking her head once. "I shouldn't have let the mounts drink from that marshy water at our last stop. It looked clear enough, and I only wanted to conserve our water for as long as possible.

"Your mount," she told Fannah, "must have been so weakened by blood loss that it stumbled and snapped a leg."

She went over to Fannah's horse and began to move the supplies over to Steorf's mount.

As she struggled angrily with one of the straps on the packs, she told Steorf over her shoulder, "I'll have Fannah ride behind me, and you can carry the other provisions. Hopefully, that won't put too much strain on the horses."

Steorf helped her with the gear and said, "You couldn't have known. None of us did."

"But I've *got* to know," she snapped. "I can't afford to make any more mistakes out here."

"We won't," he promised her.

Tazi turned away and walked over to where Fannah was waiting for her, looking extremely vulnerable with the massive Calim Desert around her.

"I just can't fail," she muttered.

CHAPTER 13

DESERT LIFE

"How is your mount holding up?" Steorf asked Tazi, breaking the hot silence.

"He's all right," she replied.

She was certain her horse was as exhausted as they were but they had no choice other than to continue forward and drive the animals on with them. The loss of the third horse was wearing the other two animals down very quickly.

The salt flats had given way to rolling sand dunes as far as Tazi could see, and their progress had slowed considerably. Traction was much more difficult and the two horses were overburdened, which didn't make it an easier. Tazi recognized that she was becoming inured by the constant sameness of the desert and was mentally wearing down.

"Blue and gold everywhere," she whispered.

"What was that?" Fannah asked and leaned closer in the saddle to Tazi.

"I'm sorry," she apologized. "I didn't realize that I had spoken aloud."

"It's fine," Fannah told her through chapped lips. "What is it?"

"Everywhere I look, it's always the same thing: empty blue sky over unchanging golden-white ground."

"There is something to be said for constancy," Fannah quipped, but the joke sounded weak to Tazi.

"I could use some change," she said quietly.

The three trudged along. Tazi knew they were getting weaker the farther into the desert they went. Tazi refused to allow Steorf to expend any sorcerous strength on anything other than decoding Ciredor's book. Water was now rationed between them and the mounts since they no longer trusted any of the sporadic water holes they came across to slake their horses' thirst. They had no way of knowing if the sources were infested by leeches or some other waterborne parasite.

One of the insidious facts about desert travel was that they were all losing moisture through perspiration but the desert wind wicked it away almost immediately. They had no way of accurately gauging how dehydrated they were becoming. Imperceptibly, the wind picked up and shifted.

"Calim's Breath," Fannah said.

"What?" Steorf asked.

"Whenever the wind changes direction out here they say it is the djinn, Calim, making his presence known," she explained.

"I hope he's trying to bring us some good news," Steorf commented.

"Look to the east," Tazi told him excitedly.

"What is it?" Fannah asked.

"I see what can only be a pool of water, not too far away," she anxiously described to Fannah.

"I don't think that can be possible," Fannah replied doubtfully.

"I think Tazi's right," Steorf agreed. "It must be a natural pool. I can't detect anything magical about it."

"The only pool of water of any noteworthy size that exists out here is what's known as the 'Walking Oasis.' It's a traveling pool of water and shady trees that appears in a different section of the Calim every year in the spring. By this time of the season, it would be mostly gone, its trees withered and brown."

"But you don't know for certain," Tazi argued. "I think it's worth investigating."

"I do as well," Steorf said. "We could use some more water, as could the horses."

"It isn't far," she said over her shoulder to Fannah. "We'll ride over to it and check it out, and if I'm wrong we won't have lost too much time."

However, no matter how long Tazi and her friends tried to reach the shimmering blue, they never got any closer to the pool. Finally, Tazi had to admit her mistake.

"We might as well stop," she told Steorf, rubbing the sweat from her eyes. "That has to be some kind of illusion created by the heat. We would have been there by now if it was real."

Tazi hunched up her shoulders, fully expecting Fannah to tell her she should have trusted her friend's knowledge of the desert. Once again, Fannah surprised her.

"It was worth the effort," she told Tazi.

"But I was wrong," she admitted.

"When you try for the right reasons, there is no wrong."

Before Tazi could reply to that, both hers and Steorf's mounts suddenly reared up. Tazi struggled to keep her seat, as did Steorf, but Fannah was caught unaware. She tumbled backward and landed hard on the sand.

As soon as Tazi got her horse under control, she dismounted and went to Fannah.

"Are you all right?" she asked her blind friend.

"As you can see," Fannah rose and swatted the dust from her robes, "I wasn't lying when I told you it had been some time since I had been on a horse."

Tazi smiled in spite of everything.

"How can you stay so cheerful?" she marveled.

"Why should I be anything else? At this moment, I am together with my friends," Fannah stated simply.

Steorf walked over with both horses' reins in hand.

"I don't know what's got into these beasts," he said, the strain he was feeling apparent in his voice.

"I don't know, either, but I'm going to take it as a sign that maybe we should walk a little," Tazi decided. "They could use the break of not carrying us for a while, and we can stretch our legs at the same time."

Tazi and Fannah flanked their mount, and Steorf brought up the rear. When Tazi looked back to ask him a question, she could see he was deep in thought. She decided not to interrupt him, as she was certain that he was mentally reviewing Ciredor's writings and mulling over the words he had managed to translate.

He's determined, she thought.

Tazi faced forward and found it hard to see that they were making any kind of progress with no landmarks to provide a frame of reference.

"The way the wind blows and shifts the sands, those dunes look like they're walking," she remarked to Fannah.

"What wind?" Fannah asked gravely.

Tazi realized that there was no wind around them, and she couldn't hear any sound nearby, either. The air was still, but the sands continued to alter their direction.

"I don't understa—" she began then the dunes erupted around them.

The horses reared and whinnied in fear, wrenching themselves free from the grip of their masters. Tazi grabbed Fannah's arm and hung on to her. She could see that Steorf was also turning about wildly. Everything began to slide into the sand.

"It's like water," Tazi screamed to Steorf. "We're sinking at every turn."

"Don't struggle," Fannah told her. "It only makes it worse."

Tazi was close to panicking. She had sunk into the sand almost to her shins, but she realized that she was wrong. The ground wasn't like water. Instead of a constant sinking, the sands shifted and she would found herself immobilized completely as though it had solidified. Then the sands shifted again in opposing directions, and she could feel her feet pulled away from each other.

The horses were screaming, and Tazi turned in time to see that her mount had sunk into the sand so deeply that only its head was still visible. The stallion's eyes rolled madly in its head when suddenly it fell silent.

Horrified, Tazi could only watch as a fount of blood spewed out of its mouth, staining the sands black. As its head was pulled under the dune, one of its forelegs popped up a few feet's distance away, like a log tossed about on the open seas.

"The dune ripped him apart," she yelled to Steorf, who had also been mesmerized by the animal's demise. "These things are alive somehow!"

Her screams snapped him from his stupor, and he somehow managed to wade his way over to Tazi and Fannah.

"We've got to get off these things," he shouted to her. He pointed about thirty feet to the north and said, "It turns back into salt flats over there. I think we might be safe if we can reach it."

"How can we do that?" Tazi asked.

"Don't fight the sands," Fannah told them. "It's in the timing. You've got to move between the shifts."

Steorf's mount gave a plaintive shriek, and Tazi turned to see it thrashing about in the dune. It dawned on her that Ciredor's writings were still in the sack strapped to the surviving horse. They couldn't afford to lose the only potential weapon they had against the necromancer.

Rolling about as though in an earthquake, Tazi literally placed Fannah in Steorf's hands.

"Get her out of here," she said.

"What?" Steorf screamed with an uncomprehending look on his face.

Tazi didn't waste any time in explanation. Judging by the animal's plaintive gurgle, Steorf's horse didn't have much time. She trusted Steorf to get Fannah to the relative safety of the flats. Trying Fannah's suggested technique, Tazi slipped between the shifting grains and reached the horse just in time to see it sink.

"No," she cried in frustration and madly searched with her hands, trying to locate the sack.

She lowered herself deeper into the sand but kept her chin above the surface. Swinging her arms back and forth, she thought one of her fingers hooked onto the sack, but it pulled just out of her reach. She had no choice. Tazi took a deep breath and dived into the dune.

She kept her eyes and mouth squeezed shut, but she could feel the sand fill her nostrils and her ears. She tried hard not to think about that and kept reaching forward with her hands, diving deeper into the dune. She didn't even contemplate what would happen if she didn't find it—her left hand slapped the leather strap of the sack, and she closed her fingers around it.

All that was left was for her to figure out how to get out.

She turned around as best she could, but realized she was only guessing at which way was up. Her lungs were burning, and the weight of the shifting sand was crushing her. Like a swimmer, Tazi tried to kick her legs and stroke her arms in large, sweeping motions but she had no way of knowing if she was even making progress. Instead of panicking, as the horses did, she tried not to resist the dune, but flow with it. She wanted badly to take in a breath of air, but she knew that if she tried, her mouth, throat, and lungs would clog instantly with sand.

Without warning, Tazi felt something grip the back of her *aba*. She felt herself pulled forcefully in the opposite direction from which she'd been traveling, and she fought against the pull as best she could, forgetting her strategy of a moment before. Vague images of some monster dwelling in the sand came to mind, but she was too weak to resist, and she felt herself pulled even harder. Tazi gave in.

She no longer felt the abrasive scratch of sand on her face and risked opening an eye. She was partly free of the dune, and she took in a deep breath that ended in a coughing fit.

"What were you thinking?" Steorf shouted at her, maintaining a firm grip on her shredded robe.

Not expecting an answer, he scooped her up and maneuvered them out of the deadly dune onto the salt flats where Fannah was waiting. Tazi took in deep drafts of air, Steorf's traveling sack still clutched in her fingers.

"How did you find me?" Tazi finally asked as she tried to empty her ears of the caked sand.

"Luck," Steorf told her. "I reached in after you disappeared from sight and managed to grab a corner of your robe."

"How did you get out there so quickly?" Tazi demanded.

"I tried to levitate across, but without a constant surface, I couldn't maintain the spell very well," he explained with a touch of bitterness. "But it did enable me to sort of walk to you."

The three of them fell silent as they watched the hypnotic movement of the dune. Sated from the meal of horseflesh and perhaps realizing that was the only meal it was going to eat there, the dune slowly deflated. Eventually, it rippled away from the flats back southward in gentle waves.

Tazi stood up, shrugged off the tattered remains of her robe, and took inventory of what remained. Her head cloth was long gone, and while her small dagger was still stashed safely in her boot, one of her guardblades was missing.

Steorf still had all of his weapons though his outer-wear hung in shreds as well. Fannah was somewhat shaken but uninjured. Moreover, all that was left of their provisions was the sack that Tazi risked her life to retrieve. Ciredor's manuscript was still inside, but that was all. They had not packed anything else in that bag for fear of inadvertently damaging the pages.

"I guess we keep moving," Tazi finally announced.

Steorf gauged their position by the sun, and they simply kept going.

After what felt like an hour, they mutually decided to rest near a small outcropping of stones. Both Tazi and Steorf had burned their faces. Fannah, much darker skinned than her friends, managed to avoid the painful sunburn. However, that did not protect her from the thirst that infected all of them. Not even the setting sun gave them any relief from that.

While Fannah described to Steorf some succulent plants that they might spot along the route, Tazi got up and wandered a little way from their camp. The night brought the double-edged sword of desert life: freezing darkness after a scorching day. She wrapped her arms around herself, hissing at the painful burns along her bare arms.

This is my fault entirely, she thought morosely. Fannah was right. Without having completed that ritual properly, I have doomed this whole mission.

"I think we should gather up what scrub we can find and build a fire soon," Steorf said from behind her.

Tazi turned and came to a decision.

"I can do that alone. What I need for you to do is take Fannah out of here right now."

"What are you talking about?" Steorf asked.

"This isn't working, and we can't afford to gamble with Fannah's life any longer. You were right," she admitted. "We should've stayed in Calimport, translated Ciredor's writings there, and above all else, kept Fannah safe."

"I am safe," Fannah answered, moving to join Tazi and Steorf.

"No, you're not," Tazi argued. "I couldn't have made you more vulnerable than if I dropped you off on Ciredor's doorstep, which is basically what we're doing right now."

"That's right," Steorf growled. "We would've been much safer in a city where we didn't know anybody and had no way of knowing how many of Ciredor's minions were there. Hundreds, thousands, maybe more. That is exactly what Ciredor expected us to do: stay and hide, not root him out."

"Look at us," Tazi implored them through cracked lips. "We're dehydrated, weakened, no food, no water, and we're on foot in the desert."

"We're alive," Fannah pointed out quietly.

"Who knows for how long?" Tazi muttered darkly. "You two need to return to Calimport. Please see the logic in that."

"Tazi, we know where Ciredor is, or nearly so," Steorf told her. "The hard part is almost over."

"I know," Tazi replied, "and that's why you can go back. I will face him alone."

Both Steorf and Fannah flatly refused.

"That is not an option," Fannah told her.

"I think we're alive because we're together," Steorf added.

Tazi turned away from her friends.

"You won't go?" she finally asked. "Then I suppose we might as well collect what we can to get a fire going."

She could see that her friends were relieved that she had changed her mind. Tazi still felt they were making a mistake, but she saw there was no way she was going to convince them otherwise.

While their fire crackled cheerfully, Steorf was once again engrossed in translating Ciredor's text. Fannah had curled up near the warmth of the flames and had fallen asleep. Tazi sat with her knees drawn up against her chest and her arms wrapped around her shins. With the moon only the barest hint of a sliver like a scratch in the inky blackness, the stars were without competition and shone as brilliant points of light in the desert sky.

Tazi thought that they looked like they were close enough to touch, if she would only stretch out her arm. She had never seen a more beautiful night. As she looked from Steorf to Fannah, she couldn't help but think that they would never share another night like this again.

❀ ❀ ❀ ❀ ❀

"Trouble in paradise, little Tazi?" Ciredor asked, his voice dripping with sarcasm.

He gazed into a scrying sphere he had created and held balanced just above his spread fingers. Within the miniature globe, he could see Tazi, Steorf, and Fannah struggle to reach their decision of unity.

"I think you are correct, Thazienne," he said to the globe. "It is time for your numbers to dwindle. Rather than have Steorf escort Fannah out of the desert, I would prefer that you bring her to me. I do not think we need the boy-mage any longer. Who knows what else he might discover within those pages of mine?"

He abruptly turned away from his scrying sphere. No longer suspended by his magic, it tumbled to the ground, disappearing before it could strike the stone floor.

Ciredor stepped out onto the parapet of the minaret

that was his personal temple. He walked to the edge and closed his eyes. With his head tilted back, he breathed in deeply of the warm smell of sand and dust. When he opened his eyes, he had reached a decision.

Ciredor moved past his unfinished business within the tower and started the walk down to the entrance. He reviewed his mental checklist.

"So many things to do," he murmured, "and so little time left to finish them all. Of course, for some people, time has run out all together, so I suppose I shouldn't complain."

Humming an obscene tune he had learned as a child, Ciredor threw open the doors to the Calim and smiled. As far as he was concerned, all was right with the world.

"I'm afraid your sorcerous companion might throw a kink into things, little Tazi," he continued talking as though he could still see her through his sphere. "I cannot allow anything to disrupt my plans now that they have come together so perfectly. You, dear Thazienne, will be easy enough to deal with when the time comes.

"While you have had your moments and given me some problems with your errant ways," he admitted to the wind, "in the end, you are merely a street brawler, albeit one pleasing to the eye. There might be some use I can put you to before I am finally done. . . .

"Now there is something delightful to contemplate," he added to himself.

Ciredor stepped onto the sand and walked a few paces away from the doors to the minaret. He knelt, placed both of his palms flat on the hot sand, and closed his eyes. The necromancer lowered his head until his brow brushed the rough grains of the Calim and appeared to be lost in deep prayer. His lips moved soundlessly, and the slightest sheen of perspiration formed on his forehead. He passed several long minutes like this.

A low rumbling began in the distance and shook the area. Ciredor lifted his head slowly at the onset of the vibrations. The shaking localized at the minaret. Several feet in front of him sand sprayed in all directions, and two purple desert worms erupted from the ground. They were both close to the same size, and Ciredor guessed they were probably litter-mates.

"Very young," he said appraisingly, "judging by your size."

Each one was about eleven feet long and two feet in diameter. A series of spikes, each half a foot long, rimmed their mouths, and with them, they were able to tunnel beneath the desert sands and rip apart their prey. Their tails ended in glistening spikes that Ciredor knew could inject a deadly poison.

He was pleased with their prompt arrival, even if they were not yet a fraction of their species' full size. The two worms reared and writhed in front of him, apparently uncomfortable, roused from the safety of their burrows and exposed as they were. Their eyes were almost non-existent, typical of creatures that were more accustomed to life underground. Soundlessly, they undulated as he marched around them like a drill instructor inspecting his troops.

"You'll do," he finally approved.

Without warning, the worm on the right lunged for Ciredor perhaps out of hunger or anger at the summons to this location against its will. The mage was momentarily startled by the unexpected disobedience, but his lightning reflexes saved him from the boring orifice of the creature he had called. He dodged to the left, and the worm smashed into the sand where the mage had been standing a moment before. Ciredor's smile disappeared, and he watched to see what the worm would do next.

The renegade monster reared back and prepared to lunge again. The second worm continued to writhe in place but did nothing to help or hinder its sibling. It seemed to be waiting for the outcome.

It didn't have to wait long. Ciredor stood his ground and did not flinch as the worm lunged a second time.

Without using any magic at all, Ciredor caught the worm with both of his hands just below the monster's mouth.

"I don't think so," he snarled as he strained to force the spinning row of teeth away from his face, enjoying the physical challenge.

With a burst of strength, Ciredor wrenched the worm away and threw it to the ground. However, the monster had not yet given up.

It reared up again and lunged a last time at Ciredor. The dark mage feinted to the right, and as the worm once again smashed into the sand, Ciredor jumped on the back of it. Like an unbroken stallion, the worm rose up in the air, bucking from side to side, but it could not shake Ciredor from its back. The mage held onto the worm's neck with his left arm and stabbed his right arm directly into the soft head of the desert dweller. With a triumphant snarl, Ciredor yanked out most of the worm's simple brain stem. The creature slumped limply to the sand.

Ciredor climbed off the dead worm, right arm dripping a putrid slime. He regarded his soiled robes with a moue of distaste. With a practiced gesture, he waved his left hand first over his right arm and over every part of his stained silks. After his enspelled pass, the ebony material glistened in the starlight as though freshly spun. Then he turned to the second worm.

The creature had lowered itself to the ground at the death of its sibling. As Ciredor regarded the creature coolly, the worm slithered docilely at his feet, curling around him like some faithful hound. Absently, Ciredor stroked its side, and the worm nearly quivered in pleasure. When the worm had passed around Ciredor's feet a few times, it hesitantly slithered over to its deceased littermate. The creature raised up its head, obviously preparing to devour the dead relative. Nothing went to waste in the Calim.

"That wouldn't be wise," Ciredor warned sweetly, wagging one finger from side to side.

The worm halted in mid lunge and turned to regard the mage. Ciredor moved over to stand beside the young worm and leaned close to its head.

"I don't want anything to spoil your appetite," he informed the creature, like a mother lecturing a naughty child. "I have something else in mind for you to dine on. You can always come back and have this one later. It's not going anywhere."

Ciredor chuckled, pleased with his own joke.

"Here's what I want you to do," the necromancer commanded, his voice dropping to a whisper.

When he had given the worm its instructions, he patted it along its body.

"Off with you now," he ordered.

The worm reared up and dived into the sand, disappearing completely.

"Such a good little pet," Ciredor said to himself.

He paused to cast a cursory glance at the dead desert worm before turning back to enter the minaret.

"You take care of the mage-child," he said to the absent worm, "and Tazi will make sure Fannah arrives here unharmed. I just don't know what I would do without such dependable servants."

Upon entering the absolute darkness of the tower stairway, cooler still than the desert night outside, a certainty settled over Ciredor. He flung the doors shut behind him and leaned his back against them as they latched.

Once again in his sacred temple, he lowered his voice reverently and said, "Everything is proceeding just as it should. From all the signs you've sent me, it is as though you've already accepted me, Shar."

One side of his mouth turned up in a lopsided grin, and he resisted the urge to rub his hands together.

"It's almost time," he whispered and bounded up the stairs two at a step, like an eager bridegroom.

CHAPTER 14

DEATH IN THE DESERT

As a bloated red sun spread its rosy fingers over the sand, Tazi and her friends decided to move on. She reluctantly realized that they wouldn't consider the absolute logic of returning to the relative safety of Calimport without her. There was no point in continuing to argue with them. It wasted the one thing they hadn't run out of yet: time.

"Well," Tazi said as they threw handfuls of sand on their tiny fire, "at least it won't take long to pack up. See? We're done."

"I've always admired your ability to appreciate the lighter side of things," Steorf complimented her sarcastically.

"Do you feel that?" Fannah interrupted them with a worried look on her face.

"What is it?" Tazi asked, immediately on

guard, though she was not aware of anything unusual.

"A rumbling," Fannah explained to them, "not too deep in the ground. It's getting closer. Do you feel it now?"

"I'm not sure—" Steorf started to ask her when their former fire pit exploded.

The force of the blast knocked Tazi and Fannah to the ground in a spray of sand and debris. Steorf barely managed to keep his footing. Rising up like some leviathan from the ocean depths, the purple desert worm reared its head. Its body eclipsed the rising sun like a storm cloud.

"What is that thing?" Tazi shouted.

Both she and Steorf drew their weapons, and Tazi realized that Fannah was unarmed.

She reached into her boot and called out to Fannah, "Right hand, Fannah."

Her friend extended her hand, and Tazi tossed her razor-sharp dagger so that it landed unerringly with its hilt in Fannah's palm. She saw her friend close her fingers around it.

At least she has something, Tazi thought.

The worm swung its head from one side to the other and an odd realization struck Tazi.

It looks like the worm is trying to decide which one of us it wants to strike at first. Why would that matter?

Tazi didn't have any more time to contemplate the worm's intentions before it made them very clear. The creature cocked its head and snapped it forward at Steorf. The young mage nearly failed to dodge the ring of teeth that smashed at his feet in time. None of them expected the worm to continue its descent.

The creature burrowed under the sand, and all three of them looked about wildly, trying to anticipate where it would resurface. The ground shifted in huge waves beneath them, and Steorf lost his footing. As he tumbled, the worm burst out of the sand to his right.

Steorf rolled furiously to the left, and the creature struck the ground where the mage had lain only a moment before. The creature was undaunted by its failure, and Steorf had to continue to roll as the creature shot after him repeatedly, each time missing the sorcerer by a narrower margin.

Steorf was finally able to roll up into a crouching position and slash across the worm's throat. The desert monster squealed, but the injury, a shallow cut, only made it more frenzied.

Tazi dashed over with her guardblade in hand, Fannah trailing just behind. The worm turned, however, and released a stream of sand from its nostrils, blasting the women. Tazi screamed in pain at the stinging spray. She was temporarily blinded by it.

The worm swung back to face Steorf, all else forgotten. As Steorf slashed at the creature again, Fannah came up behind the slithering beast. Tazi's body had shielded her from the brunt of the sandblast the worm had released, so she was uninjured. The blind woman struck the beast multiple times along its body, with little effect, though it oozed purple at every wound.

As Tazi knelt and wiped away the sand from her bleeding eyes, she was certain her vision was still affected for she saw the worm do a curious thing. It wheeled about on Fannah and moved to strike. Neither Tazi nor Steorf was close enough to stop it. However, Tazi could have sworn that the creature paused when it saw the source of the annoying pinpricks in its side almost as though it somehow recognized Fannah. Rather than strike the nearly defenseless woman with its sharp jaws, the worm shifted its position slightly and batted Fannah away like a horse would use its tail on a fly. Fannah tumbled backward and landed hard on the ground. Tazi could see that she was not seriously injured, however, just had the wind knocked out of her. The worm turned its attention back to Steorf.

The mage had little time to defend himself as he had been more engrossed in Fannah's fate, too. The worm lunged down at him, and he dodged again but was not quick enough this time. The worm's ring of teeth tore away a chunk of Steorf's leather tunic and laid bare a patch of his chest. While he scrambled to regain his footing and draw up his sword, the worm shook its head violently. The section of leather tunic it had torn from Steorf was still stuck to its teeth, and the worm whipped its head from side to side like a dog playing with a rag, trying to rid itself of the annoying cloth.

Tazi used the opportunity to charge at the worm. She struck it in the neck in almost the same spot that Steorf had. She managed to widen its wound, and a burst of purplish pus flowed out.

Tazi instinctively dodged the seepage, and the sand sizzled where the fluids splattered.

"Move!" she yelled at Steorf.

She raised her sword and swung once again at the beast. This time, the creature was prepared for her attack and brought its massive tail around front to parry Tazi's blow with its sharp tail. She tried to strike at it once more, and the creature managed to block her again.

The worm caught her sword by the hilt, narrowly missing her hand with its razor-sharp spike. It flicked her weapon away.

Tazi didn't have time to run. The worm slapped her across the sand with the bulk of its tail. She landed against a small pile of rocks and was momentarily stunned. Once again, though the monster had a clear shot at her, it hesitated.

Steorf and Fannah stood side by side and yelled to distract the worm from Tazi. Obviously they hadn't come to the same conclusions as she had about the worm's intended target.

The creature whipped its head around and dived under the sand again. Steorf and Fannah split up, both running in opposing directions. Tazi watched groggily and suspected that even though the worm had two victims to choose from, it was going to attack Steorf.

He probably makes louder vibrations on the sand than we do since he's bigger, she thought.

The worm burst up in front of Steorf in a spray of sand and grit. It pulled back its head and shot forward, bombarding Steorf with a concentrated blast of sand as it had done to Tazi. Steorf hissed in pain and tried to wipe the sand from his eyes while still brandishing his sword with the other. The more he rubbed, the more he scoured his eyes. This was the distraction the worm was hoping for.

It lunged forward with its mouth of deadly teeth, and Steorf, partially blinded by the sand, only parried its mouth with his weapon. He didn't see the worm's tail poised to strike like some malevolent serpent. Tazi, who had risen to her feet, did see the impending strike.

"Steorf!" she shouted but was too late.

While Steorf had jammed his sword between several of the worm's teeth and used both his hands on the weapon to keep the clicking jaws away from his throat, the worm struck with its tail.

As if it had a life of its own, the creature's tail slashed across Steorf, and the young man's reflexes were a hair slow. He pulled back his body almost enough to miss the gleaming spike at the base of the worm's tail—but the worm was quicker.

The sharp tail sliced across Steorf's chest where it had only moments before exposed his flesh as though this had been its plan all along. Steorf winced at the deep gash and dropped his arms. Tazi ran as she saw that he was completely vulnerable to the worm's attacks.

Steorf recognized his predicament and started to backstep, but he tripped on his own feet. Tazi thought he was moving like a drunkard and wondered if it was a result of dehydration. It didn't matter, she realized, because he was going to perish in a moment. Her heart started to pound harder at the thought of Steorf's plight, and that gave her the burst of speed she needed. She leaped into the air.

"No!" she screamed in defiance.

Breathing hard, Tazi managed to straddle the monster's neck. The creature tried to rear up and toss her from its body with no success. Tazi wrapped her legs tightly around the worm's body and raised her guardblade, point down, high over her head with both hands. Using what was left of her strength, she drove the sword in with a scream.

The worm let out a high-pitched wail. Tazi winced in pain as she felt her eardrums come close to bursting at the sound, but she didn't release her grip on her sword in the slightest. The dying worm slammed its body to the sands and reared up again in a desperate, last attempt to shake Tazi off of itself.

Tazi gritted her teeth, and when the worm slammed to the ground again, she twisted the blade hard to the right and snapped the worm's brainstem. It sagged to the ground, dead.

Tazi tried to slow her ragged breathing and lowered her head, momentarily exhausted, onto her hands, which still held her sword.

After she was certain the worm was dead, Tazi struggled to pull out her blade. She was shocked how utterly spent she had become as she fought to remove her sword from the dead creature. With a sickening sound, the blade popped free, and Tazi staggered back at its sudden release. She didn't even have the presence of mind to clean her blade before re-sheathing it.

Cale would have my hide for treating a weapon so shoddily, she thought after she realized her mistake. Right now, he can have it.

Tazi stopped her wistful thinking as soon as she saw Steorf. For as long as she had known him, he had never looked vulnerable to her. But as she saw him, leaning against some rocks, Tazi's heart missed a beat.

His head of unruly hair was bowed, and Tazi could see that both he and Fannah dabbed at a wound across his chest. Tazi forgot her weariness and ran to kneel at his side.

On closer inspection, Tazi could see that the slash that ran over Steorf's heart was no ordinary wound. The edges of his torn flesh had puckered, and the cut itself was a strange, purple shade. Very little blood ran down his exposed skin, but a milky white liquid seeped out. Tazi looked up at Steorf to see that his eyes were already regarding her.

"What is it?" she asked, already knowing the answer.

Steorf winced and said, "I think that vermin poisoned me with its tail."

"Well, then," Tazi replied matter-of-factly, "get rid of it."

"That's what I've been attempting to do," he said through gritted teeth.

As Fannah passed over a section of the wound with a torn piece of her robe, Steorf bit back on a scream and dropped his head down. Though sightless, Fannah raised her head and evenly met Tazi's worried stare.

"He has been trying," Fannah told her. "I think he is too weak to expel the poison."

Tazi refused to accept that. She gripped his face in both her hands and looked him hard in the eyes.

"If you were able to save me from the spider's venom," she told him, "then you can do this for yourself."

Steorf nodded briefly. He brushed away Fannah's ministering hands and closed his eyes. He laid both of his hands on the oozing gash, and Tazi watched hopefully as his fingers glowed with a faint white light.

That was all that happened.

With beads of sweat rolling down his face, Steorf let out a defeated sigh, and his hands slipped to the ground.

"No use," he whispered. "I can't get it all out. I just don't know the spell very well."

"I'm sorry," Tazi told him, stood up, and reached to get an arm under his.

"What are you doing?" he demanded with surprise.

"What does it look like? I'm helping you to your feet," she said in a tone that brooked no refusal.

Steorf didn't budge. With a burst of strength, he grabbed Tazi's arm and pulled her crashing back to her knees.

"I am dead weight," he said. "In more ways then one."

"I refuse to accept that," she argued.

"Open your eyes, Tazi," he replied. "I don't know how much farther I can walk, and you and Fannah cannot carry me the rest of the way. I am no longer an asset. You have got to cut your losses."

Tazi stood up and faced north.

How many more miles? she wondered. I have to face him with a blind woman and a dying mage, no water, and only one sword. And all I have to do is keep him from presenting my friend's soul to a goddess as some kind of gift.

She shook her head and almost laughed at the absurdity of the picture she had painted for herself.

Turning, she told Steorf, "You are absolutely right. I have to cut my losses."

He closed his eyes almost gratefully at her pronouncement.

"I knew you'd see the merit of my words," he finally said.

Tazi squatted in front of him and replied, "How can I argue with logic?"

Fannah turned with a worried expression, and Tazi leaned across to pat her on her forearm comfortingly.

"I'm going to need your help, Fannah," she told her blind companion. "Could you take Steorf's sack?"

Fannah didn't say a word, but she did accept the bag that Tazi helped remove from Steorf.

"It's the only choice you have," he told the Calishite.

"Now," Tazi added, "If you grab his right arm, I can get his left and we'll get him to his feet."

"What?" Steorf exclaimed.

"You are absolutely right," she told him gravely. "At this stage, I cannot afford a single liability. And you are hardly that."

"But, Tazi . . ." he implored.

"No," she cut him off. "Don't waste your breath. We will have only one chance to defeat Ciredor. Our strength lies in our unity, and that is how we will face him: together."

Tazi took Steorf's left arm and laid it over her shoulders as Fannah took his right. He shook his head but when the women tried to stand, he struggled to help them. They rose, as one, from the bloody sands.

CHAPTER 15

THE LAST WAY

Steorf had been passing in and out of awareness for the past few hours. He spoke less and less coherently to Tazi and started, instead, to mumble strange words and phrases as she and Fannah had helped him across the wasteland.

"The desert nomads say there are six stages of thirst in the Calim," Fannah said. "First, there is the clamorous stage. I think it is fairly obvious that is what he is entering."

Tazi leaned slightly forward of Steorf's dangling head to look at Fannah.

"I think you're right. What else can we expect?"

"If there was not the worm toxin to consider, the next stages, in order, would be: cotton mouth, swollen tongue, shriveled tongue, blood tears, and finally, living death. I am not sure how the desert worm's sting will change any of it, other than to hasten the steps."

Tazi shook her head and found all she could say was the obvious, "We have to find him some water."

"We all need to find some water, Tazi," Fannah reminded her. "This is our fate as well, given time."

Tazi didn't even want to ponder that. She had already begun to feel the painful beginnings of dehydration herself. Her eyes were slowly pulling back in their sockets, and her nose felt like some small, foreign object hanging from her face. She could feel other subtle, and not so subtle, ways that her body was trying to conserve water as well, but the insidious fact was that to do so, her body was picking and choosing what parts of her were expendable and what parts were not. She was not in control.

Steorf's head rolled back, and that motion snapped Tazi from her dreadful realizations. She could see that his eyes opened slightly. He looked at her and Fannah, and Tazi saw an unreadable expression spread across his face. She started to motion to Fannah to slow her pace even more when Steorf had a small burst of strength and shook himself free of the two women.

"Get away from me!" Steorf shouted at Tazi and Fannah.

He stood swaying in the sand. With one hand he rubbed uselessly at his desiccated eyes. His eyelids had dried, and Tazi had noticed how difficult it had become for him to close them. He had taken on a blank stare because of it. He flailed his other hand out in front of him, desperately trying to ward off his imagined attackers.

"What's wrong?" Tazi asked him.

"It's all right," Fannah tried to soothe him, somewhat more aware of the confused state of mind Steorf was slipping into. "We're here."

Neither of the women's words had their desired effect on the failing mage. He staggered a few steps back from them and started to fumble around with his tattered shirt.

"Where's Tazi?" he demanded of his apparitions. "What have you done with her?"

Before Fannah could stop her, Tazi started to move slowly toward Steorf.

"I'm right here," she tried to convince him.

"Don't," Fannah warned her. "He no longer knows who we are."

Steorf tugged at his ripped shirt, and Tazi was startled to see that he was struggling to remove it. Without thinking, she reached over to him and tried to stop his jittery fingers. The moment she touched his hot, dry skin, Steorf swung a fist in her direction. The only reason it didn't connect was because Steorf was so disorientated that his aim was off. Tazi herself was too stunned to move out of his way.

Steorf staggered a bit more from the momentum of his badly executed punch but recovered enough to yell, "Where is she?"

"He needs to be stopped before he hurts himself," Fannah exclaimed, closing in on him from one side as Tazi finally made a move from the other.

Or hurts one of us unintentionally with either his fists or his magic, she thought.

Steorf was clawing at his sword's scabbard. She sprang at him, all the while trying to be careful of his open wound. Tazi hit him in the shoulders with her outstretched hands, and as they both tumbled to the ground, she tucked herself up to somersault away from him. As soon as her feet hit the ground, Tazi scrambled around and slipped her right arm around his throat. Kneeling behind his prostrate form, she grabbed her left shoulder with her right hand and secured him in a head-lock. She slipped her left forearm between her chest and the back of his head and applied increasing pressure until he became still, her chokehold the gentlest way she knew how to take him out.

"I'm sorry," she whispered as she relaxed her hold on him, certain he was unconscious.

She even allowed herself a moment to pass her hand through his hair. The strawlike quality it had taken on was simply one more reminder of their predicament.

"Are you all right?" Fannah asked her.

"Yes," Tazi choked out, "but we can't go on any farther like this."

"Then this is where we'll rest," Fannah replied and kneeled down.

As Fannah began to scrape away a large layer of sand from in front of her, Tazi asked, "What are you doing?"

"I'm removing the top cover of sand, which is the hottest. A few inches down," she explained to Tazi, "the sand will be significantly cooler."

Tazi fell to her knees as well and helped clear away the hot sands. When they had cleared a furrow large enough to hold Steorf, both she and Fannah dragged his inert body over and laid him in it. Tazi felt as though they were lowering him into a grave and tried desperately to keep that image from creeping back into her thoughts.

Tazi could only watch uselessly as Steorf suffered in mute torment. He came around shortly after being placed in the cooling pit, but he shook uncontrollably, caught in the grip of fever chills. When he faced Tazi, however, there was recognition in his eyes.

"What happened?" he asked weakly.

"You got a little confused," Tazi explained gently.

"And?" he prompted her.

Tazi wasn't sure what offered the most temporary relief: that he had regained consciousness at all or that he actually appeared to understand the conversation they were having.

"I think this was your way of getting even with me for years of tricks," she admitted. "You took a swing at me."

"Are you all right?" he asked, his own eyes filling with concern.

She leaned closer to him and whispered, "Not even

on your best day could you ever hope to touch me."

Steorf tried to smile but instead stifled a cry of pain. Though he tried to maintain a brave front, Tazi knew with an absolute certainty that he was dying. Her faint smile died on her chapped lips. She and Fannah busied themselves and tried to make him as comfortable as possible. Fannah removed her outer robe and pillowed it under his head.

"There is not much more we can do for him," Fannah whispered to Tazi.

She looked more closely at him and saw that his wound continued to slowly seep. The discharge was a mixture of the worm's milky venom and a trace of his own blood. What filled Tazi's heart with dread were the red lines of infection that had spidered out from the original injury. Tazi knew that their inexorable march to his heart was what spelled Steorf's doom.

"I will not accept this," Tazi said. She was filled with the absolute need to move. "There has to be something we can do."

"I do not know of anything within the Calim that could cure him," Fannah replied.

She rubbed her forehead, tired.

"Think!" Tazi ordered the Calishite angrily. "There has got to be something here. Anything!"

"There maybe something that might at least alleviate his suffering somewhat," Fannah recalled eventually.

"What is it?" Tazi asked, ready to grasp at any straw offered.

"Before the worm attacked us," Fannah explained, "I had been telling Steorf about a plant that we might come across, and I had wanted him to watch for it. It is called the Calim cactus."

"What's so special about it?"

"The plant is rather unassuming; growing no more than three to four inches tall, and it provides very little nutrition. But it has an extensive root system that runs several feet across just under the sand."

Fannah described the thing deliberately, accurately drawing a mental picture for Tazi with her words.

"How can this help us?" Tazi asked, a seed of hope growing inside her as she committed the description to memory.

"What the plant does to trap moisture is raise its roots above the sands and absorb what water there is before pulling them back underground."

"So the roots are full of water," Tazi deduced, growing excited.

"If we can find some that have buried roots," Fannah cautioned her. "Only those will have liquid in them."

"I will find them," Tazi swore. "I want you to stay with Steorf in case he needs something."

"I don't know what I can do for him," Fannah said, slightly flustered.

"You can be with him," Tazi explained. "Let him know he's not alone."

Fannah nodded and moved back over to Steorf's side. She gathered up one of his hands in hers and squeezed it tight. Tazi wasn't sure what he was aware of at this point. She emptied the sack containing Ciredor's writings and left them in Fannah's keeping.

"I'll need something to put the roots in," she told Fannah confidently.

She stroked Steorf's forehead, shocked by the heat that radiated from him.

"I'll be back as quick as I can," she promised her two friends.

"We will be waiting," Fannah answered.

Tazi turned and marched off to the west. The sun had reached its apex, and Tazi could feel her arms burn under its glare. With only her leather vest and pants, her arms were near to blistering. She occasionally wiped at her eyes, which had become bitterly painful. As she became more and more dehydrated, she could literally feel her eyes pull back in their sockets. Tazi realized that her orbs were mostly comprised of water and she was losing that at an alarming rate, so her body stole from itself. There was nothing to be done about it other than finding the Calim cactus.

Part of her rational mind was convinced that they were going to fail. There was no other logical outcome. But deeper down, in her soul, she hadn't quit, and that was the force that drove her on. It was as though the desert had burned away everything excessive that she carried and left her only her core intact, like a worn stone. The mild winds had smoothed and shaped her and left her determined.

"That's why Fannah knew I needed to pass through the ritual successfully," she said aloud. "Out here, we are nothing but our true selves, whatever they may be."

A little farther to the west, Tazi saw what she thought was some scrub and rocks.

"Please," she whispered in a voice rapidly becoming hoarse, "let that be real. No more illusions."

As she trudged closer, the scrub did not fade from view or remain in the distance. Tazi realized she was actually gaining on it. Heartened, she picked up speed, and soon enough she was in the middle of a small area of brush. Though it was mostly insignificant piles of rocks and quick-moving lizards, there was a little plant life.

Everything she saw was dead. Tazi slumped down on the ground and dropped her head in defeat. She wanted to scream but didn't possess the energy.

Shaking her head, she whispered, "I don't even have enough water for tears. In the end, I'm not even allowed that."

She debated going farther but knew she had reached her limit if she was going to return to her friends.

"If I'm going to die," she finally said, "there's no finer company to be in."

She started to rise wearily to her feet when some movement to her right caught her eye. Several speckled lizards darted in and out of a cluster of stones. Almost as though mocking her, one sat on a small boulder and defiantly licked at the moisture on its own eyeball. Tazi toyed with the idea of trying to catch some of them, but tossed the thought aside.

"Even if I could snare you little demons," she muttered, "all of you put together wouldn't make a meal worth the effort."

Something about their numbers puzzled her, though. Nowhere else in this little haven had she seen any wildlife.

"Just what makes that pile of rocks so special," she wondered aloud, "that you all have to hide there?"

She moved over to investigate, and the moment her shadow passed over the lizards they scattered in every direction on their spindly legs. She didn't bother worrying about whether they might be poisonous or not, if any still remained. She simply thrust her hands into the clutch of stones and started moving them around.

There, nestled in the protective shelter of the gravel, was a small clump of what could only be Calim cacti.

"Thank you," she murmured to no one in particular.

More precious than gold, the group of plants meant possible salvation. Tazi was overjoyed to discover that there was more than one and all of them had submerged roots. She carefully brushed away some of the sand and began to pluck the cacti. They had sharp thorns that tore at her cracked hands but Tazi hardly felt the pain as she pulled out the only desert treasure worth harvesting.

True to Fannah's description, the tiny plants had tremendously long roots and Tazi could feel that they were heavy with moisture. She used her sword to hack the roots free from the thorny part of the plants. Tazi then tossed the cactus tops aside and hoped that they might form new root systems.

"Something for the next lost soul," she explained to a lone lizard before it skittered away.

When her sack was full of the priceless fauna, she stood up and started to turn around. One last cactus caught her attention, and she nearly dismissed it as the plant's roots were fully exposed. From what Fannah had explained, that meant the plant was seeking water and of no use to Tazi—but a strange thought came to her mind.

"It's worth a try," she said as she carefully removed the whole plant.

She carried this one away from the bag crammed with the engorged roots and started the trek back to her friends. She debated about trying one of the roots on the march back, and though her logical mind argued that it made sense since she had expended so much energy to find them, she found she couldn't do it knowing that Fannah and Steorf still suffered without water.

"We'll all have some soon enough," she promised to the little voice of reason that nagged her.

Whether it was because she had simply not accurately kept track of time or her excitement had quickened her pace, Tazi made it back to her friends in short order. Even from a brief distance, one look at Fannah's face spoke volumes to Tazi. There wasn't much time left for Steorf. She rushed to their side.

"Fannah," her voice cracked, "I found them."

"Thank Sharess," Fannah offered in prayer. "I knew she would show you the way."

Tazi found herself tempted to make a joke about Sharess and speckled lizards, but she didn't. She realized that she wasn't sure if someone had led her to the plants or not, so instead of insulting any benevolent forces, Tazi dropped her sack in front of Fannah and laid the intact plant beside Steorf.

"What's the best way to get the water from them?" she asked.

Fannah took a chunk of one of the roots and scored it with Tazi's dagger. It started to bleed water.

"Hold this with both hands," she instructed Tazi, "and suck on it. When you can't get any more liquid out of it, chew up the pulp and extract the last bit of water that way."

Tazi took the first piece that Fannah had cut and held it to Steorf's lips. His face was flushed, and Tazi was alarmed to see that he had stopped perspiring altogether. For a heartbeat, he didn't respond to the liquid Tazi could see rolling into his mouth and she feared the worst.

She leaned close to his ear and implored, "Please take it, Steorf. I won't go on without you."

She held her breath.

Slowly, Tazi could see Steorf's eyes flicker and his tongue gingerly dab at his moistened lips and the strange object he found near his mouth. His eyes opened slightly, and Tazi knew he recognized her. She hadn't lost him.

"Don't talk," she whispered. "Just keep sucking on this. I'll explain it all later."

She placed his hands onto the plant.

"Take this," Fannah told her gently and handed her a section of the root. While Tazi sucked out the life-saving liquid, Fannah asked, "Did you bring any of the little cacti as well?"

"I thought about it," Tazi said between slurps, "but, in the end, I left the tops where I found them. I hoped that they might form new roots and continue to grow. That way, they might be there for someone else one day."

Her idea sounded ridiculous when spoken aloud.

I should have taken them for what little food they would have provided, she berated herself.

Fannah, however, nodded.

"A wise offering back to the desert," she complimented her bewildered friend. "You know more about life than you give yourself credit for."

"I did bring one plant back intact," Tazi said quietly, "because I have an idea. You said the cactus uses its roots to suck in moisture, right?"

Fannah agreed and Tazi could see the same idea now dawn on her friend.

"I found one that was thirsty," Tazi continued, "and I'm

sure it's even thirstier now. Maybe the sun has gotten to me, but I'd like to try something."

Tazi knew Fannah had grasped her train of thought. She turned to face Steorf.

"I have an idea that I want to try out," she explained to him.

He nodded at her with glazed eyes, not really comprehending what she was saying but simply trusting her.

Tazi reached for the cactus and gripped the base of the plant with one hand and held one of its longest roots, nearly three feet in length, against the wound on Steorf's chest. Almost immediately, Tazi could see the milky discharge disappear into the moisture-starved plant. Several minutes passed, and Tazi watched as the root started to swell where it touched Steorf. That swelling slowly grew and progressed up the length of the root, but when the swelling reached the base of the plant, the thorny cactus started to sag. Tazi pulled the dying plant away from Steorf.

She knew that the plant wouldn't be able to draw out all of the poison, but judging from the new width of the root, it had removed a significant portion. Between that and the water, Steorf started to lose the vacant glaze in his eyes. Tazi squeezed his hand and gave him a new section of root.

When all the cacti were gone, Steorf was much more alert. However, though he was somewhat recovered, he was by no means cured of the worm toxin, and Tazi knew it.

"When this is all over," she told him, "I'll get you to a proper healer."

" 'When this is over . . .' " he repeated, marveling at her choice of words.

"Yes," Tazi answered him, "when this is all finished."

"If you are feeling a little stronger," Fannah interrupted, "perhaps you can finish these."

She held out Ciredor's parchments, and Steorf accepted the sheaf of papers. Both Tazi and Fannah helped him to a sitting position. He looked at his two friends, obviously worried.

"I'm not sure I can do this," he finally admitted.

"Yes, you can," Tazi encouraged him. "You were almost finished before you were injured. You can do this now."

Tazi could see how worried he looked. She suspected that since his physical strength had failed him, he was frightened that his sorcerous abilities would, too.

"Fannah needs your help." She lowered her voice so only he would hear her. "I can't translate these papers, and we need to find Ciredor."

"You're right," he said finally. "Give me a moment."

He handed the parchments back to Tazi. She gripped the papers and watched Steorf expectantly.

Steorf closed his eyes and concentrated. For a brief time, Tazi thought he was going to fall short again, but his hands started to glow with a white intensity he had failed to reach on his first attempt after the worm was vanquished. Tazi found she was holding her breath and was wrinkling the parchments in her fists.

"Please . . ." she whispered.

Steorf broke into a sweat, and Tazi recognized what a conundrum he was in. Exhausted from the poison, he was straining what meager reserves he had left to heal himself. Tazi shook her head with the realization that they were using themselves up, one by one.

Slowly, his hands turned brown, and Tazi realized he had nowhere to expel the toxin. She dropped the book and grabbed his hands. Tazi could feel some numbness at the point of contact and even saw her skin discolor, but before any more venom drained away, Steorf opened his eyes and realized what was happening. He yanked his hands free.

"What were you thinking?" he demanded of Tazi, but she smiled when she saw his color was somewhat improved.

"What I have to do," she answered. "Just like you, I'm doing what I have to for us.

"I'll be fine," she assured him as she handed him back Ciredor's writings.

Steorf gave her an unreadable look and started to sift through the dark works. Tazi could see that his eyes were clearer and he was no longer confused. Both she and Fannah kneeled beside him in the sand, their presence the only support they could offer him. Rather than feeling that same lingering frustration, Tazi thought she could actually sense Steorf drawing on their quiet strength.

After some minutes, Steorf said, "Either I'm still out of my head, or this bit here is starting to make sense."

"What does it say?" Fannah asked.

"Most of this is really a treatise to his goddess. In fact, he goes on at some length about her and her virtues."

"Shar is a goddess of darkness, though," Tazi said.

"That is partially correct," Fannah replied. "Darkness is her element, but she rules over hidden pains and buried jealousies."

"Why would anyone follow her?" Tazi asked.

"Who can say what drives the soul or why anyone would do anything?" Fannah cryptically answered. "But I do know that she can bring relief and soothe deep pains."

"She takes away pain?" Steorf asked curiously.

"No," Fannah corrected him, "that's not quite accurate. It is more like she dulls the pain, and her followers simply live with it as a way of life. Sort of a perverse acceptance, really. She hates light and hope, I think, most of all."

"Perhaps it is my pain that has helped me to finally understand Ciredor's writings better," Steorf murmured. "It has brought me closer to him."

"How do you know so much about her?" Tazi wondered.

"Remember," Fannah explained, "Sharess was once under her influence before she broke free. Our church was careful to school us in Shar's ways so that we can always recognize the dark one and never fall victim to her touch again."

Tazi nodded at that.

"Perhaps that's what makes you so special to Ciredor," she considered. "You are the ultimate representation of something Shar lost. A gift of loss to the very goddess of loss herself. I hate to admit it, but in his own perverse way he has probably found the only gift of value anyone could offer her."

Fannah remained silent, and Steorf gave Tazi a cold look. She felt suddenly guilty. She had gotten caught up in Ciredor's thinking. It was the first time Tazi had spoken so objectively of Fannah's worth, as though she had forgotten what was at stake for her Calishite friend. The moment stretched out awkwardly, and Steorf buried his attention back in the writings.

"There's more," he announced triumphantly. "He goes on about Shar for a stretch,"—he pointed to the marks on the vellum he had read—"and here is where he mentions discovering the perfect location for his heart. This has to be about the minarets."

"What does it say?" Tazi asked, eager to have broken the strained silence.

When she glanced at Fannah, Tazi could see her friend had never taken offence. You truly do see the person behind the words, she thought.

Steorf squinted at the text and wiped at his forehead, distracted. Tazi scrutinized him and realized he was still far from well.

"He says that the towers are perfect jewels within the desert and goes on about the views that he has. It seems he sees Spinning Keeps and rubble and somehow this is all so romantic to him."

"What was that last part?" Fannah asked, instantly alert.

"It said something about a Spinning Keep," Tazi told her.

" 'And from the west I can almost see the Spinning Keep of Siri'wadjen, and from the east I can still imagine the former grandeur of Teshyll though it is all rubble now,' " Steorf recited.

"I know where he is," Fannah said. "It makes perfect sense."

"Where?" Tazi asked.

"Ciredor has claimed the minarets in the very heart of both the Teshyll Wastes and the Calim itself, not all that far from where we are," she told them.

"Then this is it," Tazi pronounced. "Now to decide the best way to proceed."

She pondered the question, considering both Steorf and Fannah.

"I have a suggestion," Fannah offered.

"Please," Tazi urged.

"The only path that makes any sense now is to take the Trade Way. It is mostly intact from here, and that will help us immensely."

"And announce ourselves to Ciredor," Steorf added.

Before Fannah could say anything more, Tazi told him, "I think he has always known where we were. When that worm attacked us, I was struck by the feeling that time and time again it turned to you."

She fixed Steorf with a hard look.

"What do you mean?" he asked.

"The creature had more than one opportunity to kill Fannah or me, but it didn't. There wasn't a single time that thing used lethal force against us, but the same cannot be said for you.

"Ciredor sent that thing," she concluded. "Obviously, he views you as the greatest threat, perhaps because of your sorcery."

Steorf lowered his eyes.

"Yes," he said sarcastically, "my all-powerful abilities."

"Maybe there's something in this,—"she held up some of the parchments—"that he didn't want us to find out. We'll never know for certain, but I do know he wanted you eliminated. If he didn't have our exact location, he knew enough. He wanted me to bring Fannah to him," she said, disgusted. "He couldn't even be bothered to take her himself."

"So?" Steorf asked.

"So," Tazi replied with a steely resolve, "nothing has changed. Like I said before, let's bring this to him, and let's end it once and for all."

"The Trade Way?" Steorf asked.

"Fannah?"

The blind woman turned her head from Tazi to Steorf and included them both in her white stare.

"I think it is best. As I told you, the stones were constructed with powerful magic imbued in them. The desert worms cannot penetrate them, in case Ciredor tries to send any others. I think that the walking dunes would have the same difficulty as the worms.

"Of course," she added, "it leads directly to the minarets we seek . . ."

"And Ciredor," Steorf finished.

"Then that's the way," Tazi said. "We will strike at the heart."

She rose to her feet, as did Fannah.

The women reached, in unison, for Steorf. He tried to swat their hands away.

"If you're getting cranky," Tazi teased, "then you must be feeling a little better.

"Save your strength," she said seriously, disregarding his efforts to stand unaided.

She got him to his feet and pulled his left arm over her shoulder.

"Please," she asked him, as much with her soft, green eyes than with her voice.

"I never seem to be able to say no to you," he said, and for the first time in the history of their relationship, Steorf actually smiled at her.

"Which way?" Tazi turned to Fannah, all businesslike again.

"I am a little disorientated," the blind woman admitted. "Which way is the sun setting?"

Tazi and Steorf turned to find the burning orb and were suddenly very aware of a growing gloom.

Finally, Tazi said, "I believe it is toward your left."

"What's wrong?" Fannah asked but then answered her own question. "It has cooled off, but it's too soon. We're not at sunset yet."

Tazi scanned the horizon where the sun should have been and saw only a ghost of an outline. The star was obscured by a swirling haze, ever darkening. In the distance, Tazi heard a faint howl.

"There's something to the west," she announced.

Fannah stood perfectly still, with her head to the side, like a bird listening for a predator.

"Sandstorm," she whispered. "Tazi,"—she turned toward her friend—"we have got to hurry now. Time is almost up. We should be able to reach Ciredor's minarets before the storm falls on us."

Without any further preamble, Fannah took Tazi's arm and started to pull her two companions toward the west.

As she had told them, the Trade Way was not far.

The three came across what must have been a magnificent road at one point in its history. It was wide enough to accommodate three fully packed carts. Time and the desert, however, had taken its toll. Huge chunks of the pavement were broken, and sharp pieces stabbed up from the ground. A few sinkholes had erupted, and the threesome had to carefully maneuver their way around the gaping pits of sand and rubble. Not far from where they stood, though, Tazi and Steorf could see the twin minarets.

"This path is huge," Steorf marveled.

Tazi noticed he was trying not to place all his weight on her, but she tugged slightly on his arm.

"It's all right," she told him.

He looked at her, and in the fading light she could see that his gray eyes were clouded with pain and there were deep smudges under them.

"You need your strength, too," he reminded her. To Fannah, he remarked, "It looks like you could ride six abreast on this road."

"During the Way's halcyon days, I understand it was a marvelous route."

To their left, Tazi and Steorf could see that the swirling sands were getting closer and closer. What surprised Tazi was the amount of sound the storm generated even at a distance. For the most part, the desert had been a deadly, but silent enemy.

Not any longer, Tazi thought.

"The storm is nearly upon us," Fannah remarked, her sharp ears missing nothing.

"We've got to get to the towers," Steorf said, "as quickly as we can."

Tazi watched how rapidly the darkness grew.

"We've run out of time," she declared, and the maelstrom engulfed them.

CHAPTER 16

THE MINARETS

"Where are you?" Tazi screamed.

She, Steorf, and Fannah were on the Trade Way for only a short time when the sandstorm from the west reached them. At first Tazi thought it wasn't too bad. The sun hadn't set yet, and with the three of them side by side, Tazi didn't understand Fannah's extreme concern. It was not comfortable, by any stretch of the imagination, but it wasn't that bad, and the towers weren't that far away.

We can do this, she thought.

"I think we'll be all right," she told Fannah, raising her voice over the wind.

Fannah shook her head in disagreement.

"This is just the edge of the storm," she said. "It's only going to get worse."

As they moved forward slowly, following the

track of the Trade Way, the wind picked up as Fannah had warned, and Tazi started to revise her opinion. She and Steorf had to squint to keep the scathing grains out of their eyes. Tazi was certain she was losing layers of skin to the blasts of sand that only got stronger. The three had no choice but to hang onto each other, and at one point a wild gust tore Steorf's sack off his shoulders and tossed it behind them.

Tazi turned to follow its tumbling course, one hand shielding her eyes.

"I'll get it," she yelled to Steorf.

Part of her still hoped the writings contained some clue of how to destroy Ciredor, and she didn't want to lose their last weapon against him.

"Forget it," Steorf replied.

Fannah simply shouted, "No!"

Nevertheless, Tazi broke from their grip and trotted after the sack, which turned end over end just out of her reach.

The wind pushed Tazi to the left, as though a giant hand shoved her, and she had to compensate for that as she ran. The sack, however, blew farther away. Eventually, as the sun started toward the horizon, Tazi lost sight of it. She slowed down and realized that Ciredor's writings were lost to the desert storm.

And so was she.

Tazi turned around and could only see growing darkness.

She shouted for her friends, but the wind had reached such a frenzied pitch, Tazi couldn't even hear her own voice. She cupped her hands around her mouth and tried again, but there was only the scream of the storm. She stood and swayed as the winds buffeted her body.

Curling her hands around her eyes, she desperately searched for any sign of Steorf and Fannah, but she saw nothing but ever-changing patterns of sand. It was dizzying. There was no end to the desert, no sky, and no ground below. There were only howls. She felt as though she was back within the gate. Her heart was pounding, and Tazi could taste her fear.

That won't do me any good, she told herself sternly. Fannah and Steorf need me.

Without budging an inch, Tazi tried hard to calm herself.

I'm sure I didn't go that far, and as soon as I gave up on the sack I turned sharply around. If I'm right, she reasoned, then I need only to keep walking in a straight line and I'll get back to Fannah and Steorf.

But if I'm wrong, she thought, I'll walk off into the storm.

With that in mind, Tazi started the tricky march back.

The wind continued to push her from side to side, so she tried walking as best she could heel to toe to keep a straight course. She dropped to her knees once and tried to see if she could still feel the paved Way, but the wind and the sand made it impossible for her to tell. She gave up on that and went back to her original plan.

Time lost all meaning to her, and Tazi knew she was close to panicking. It had taken her too long on the way back and she was certain she should have found her friends by now.

She stopped and tried to scan the distance. Having very nearly given in to despair, she thought she heard something just above the whine of the wind.

"Steorf!" she screamed back and listened.

The faint sound grew a little louder, and she cried out, "Keep calling!"

Tazi was certain it was her friends. She lowered her head against the gusts that buffeted her and walked like someone drunk, with great, staggering strides. She looked ahead, and two shadowy shapes remained constant while everything around them was chaos. Tazi marched harder and nearly collapsed into her friends' waiting arms. The three clung to each other for a moment.

"What were you thinking?" Steorf finally shouted into her face.

"Ciredor's book," she started to explain. "I had to try to retrieve it."

"Let the winds have it," he told her. "We could have lost you."

"Not a chance!" she shouted back, a crooked grin fixed on her face.

"We can't let go of each other," Fannah cried. "Not even for a second or all will be lost."

"How are we going to find the towers now?" Steorf asked.

Tazi was momentarily worried as well. She realized they were traveling blind in the storm—and there was her answer.

"Fannah, you're going to have to lead us the rest of the way," she cried.

In the near darkness of sunset, Tazi wasn't sure but thought Fannah nodded to her.

"Hold on," she told Steorf and Tazi.

The three leaned into the wind and lumbered forward. Tazi kept a tight grip on Steorf and Fannah. To her, the disorientation only grew worse the darker it got. There was no frame of reference anywhere, and Tazi turned over all responsibility to Fannah, hoping that her blind friend's sense of touch and hearing, much sharper than either hers or Steorf's would guide them through. Lost in a situation where she was simply passing through time, odd thoughts fluttered through Tazi's mind. Strangely enough, she couldn't seem to get a fable out of her mind.

When she was very young, her father had once told her a story of children lost in the woods. As a grown woman, Tazi could see the story for what it was—a cautionary tale meant to scare her into sensibility—but when she first heard the account, Tazi had wept uncontrollably, leaving her father very flustered with a teary three year old.

As Tazi recalled, her mother had been the only one who could console her by telling her that a guardian spirit looked out for all lost children. In the midst of the storm, Tazi smiled as she followed her spirit to safety.

"Can you see anything?" Steorf yelled to her, jarring her from her reverie.

"Nothing yet," Tazi called back to him. "But if anyone is going to be able to find this, it's Fannah."

"I hope so," he called out and clutched tighter to her arm.

Undaunted by the raging storm, Tazi watched how Fannah never hesitated in their course. She wanted to ask her just how she was guiding them but decided the fewer distractions Fannah had, the better off they'd all be.

The swirling grains and incessant howling were almost nauseating to Tazi. She tried closing her eyes, but it only made matters worse.

Maybe she can feel the pavement under her sandals, Tazi guessed, or maybe she's marching in the original direction we started in, since this tempest can't disorient her in the same way it does us.

Her curiosity got the better of her, and she tried to get Fannah's attention.

"Fannah," she called, and bumped into Steorf.

The mage had stopped walking.

"What happened?" she asked him.

"Look there," he replied, pointing ahead.

Barely discernable in the twilight was a large shape looming in the growing darkness.

"The east minaret," Fannah announced.

Tazi swallowed hard.

"You did it," she called to Fannah.

The three marched side by side up to the entrance. So close to the edifice, Tazi was able to make out some details, despite her reduced vision. The tower was about forty feet tall, as Fannah had said. Tazi reached out and brushed her hand against the surface, feeling stone and brick.

"I think we can let go of each other as long as we're touching the building," she told Steorf and Fannah. "But no one step away alone, understand? We need to find the entrance."

She laid both her hands on the wall and leaned her head against it, desperately needing the feeling of stability the minaret offered to stop her churning stomach.

When she felt better, Tazi joined Steorf and Fannah as they each slid around the building, feeling for a door.

Fannah called out, "It's over here!"

Steorf and Tazi felt their way over to her.

"We're lucky," Fannah shouted. "The doors aren't buried too deeply."

The three fell to their knees and used their hands and arms to rake away what little sand had piled up around the doors. When it was mostly cleared, Tazi tried to pull the doors open, but they refused to budge.

"I think they're locked," she called to her friends.

The wind was picking up in intensity.

Here's a test worthy of a lockpick, she thought, in the dark, in a storm, with that monster on the loose.

Before she could pull out the tools she had stashed inside her vest, Steorf asked, "Are you sure they're locked?"

"In this storm," Tazi admitted, "I'm not sure of a damn thing."

"Let me try something," he yelled.

Tazi placed her hand on his arm.

"Are you sure?" she asked but didn't hear his response.

When Steorf placed his hands on the latches, there was a flash of green so bright it pierced the gloom like a beacon. Steorf was knocked off of his feet as the doors swung open. Tazi knelt down to help him get up.

"Are you all right?" she shouted into his face.

She could see that Steorf was groggy.

"Fannah," she called to her other friend, "grab his arm."

They half dragged Steorf through the doors. Tazi lowered him to the ground, and both she and Fannah fought to close the tower doors, now flapping in the storm. They managed to pull them shut, and the scream of the storm was halved in intensity.

"Dark," Tazi shouted and realized how unnecessarily loud she was.

She checked on Steorf.

"You opened them," she told the dazed mage. "I don't think I would've been able to."

"Ciredor's wards . . ." he whispered, tired from his efforts.

"You and Fannah stay here. I'll go to the top," she told him.

He grabbed her hand and said, "I don't think he's here. I think he simply didn't need anything in this tower, or didn't want anything disturbed. But be careful anyway."

"You know me," she warned him with a wink.

"There should be a brazier at the top," Fannah reminded her. "The stories say that if we get both the minarets' braziers lit, the two towers will be protected from the elements."

"And maybe if Ciredor isn't here," Tazi mused, "we can use that shield to keep him out and destroy his gift. If he can't cast his spell on this special night in this special location, maybe everything will be ruined. Stay here."

Tazi got up and looked around for a torch in the dark, dusty tower. She spotted one along one of the walls and pried it loose. While she felt inside her vest for her chunk of flint, Steorf pointed a finger at the torch and it burst into flames. She graced him with a quick smile, transferred the torch to her left hand, and drew out her sword with her right.

The tower wasn't very wide, and she found the stairs soon enough, passing by a row of very old armaments. She debated about rummaging through the swords and pikes that were lined up against the wall but decided to stay with her blade. After years of training, it was like an extension of her arm.

She started up the steps.

Tazi walked along the outer edge of the stairs out of habit. That was the section of planking Cale had taught her years ago that always had the least chance of creaking, though it would take sharp ears to hear anything with the storm raging outside. The steps were divided in sections of ten, turning at right angles. In the center was an opening that ran the whole height of the tower. If she leaned to the side, Tazi could look up and down the length of the stairway. One wrong step could bring someone crashing down very quickly.

" 'My life is like a broken stair, winding round a ruined tower, and leading nowhere,' " she whispered—a phrase from an old taproom love song she had heard once.

She stopped at the first level and peered at the floor. There was nothing other than a series of bunks that lined the walls. Tazi reasoned that at least one garrison must have been housed there long before.

Between them and the spheres of protection, Tazi noted, travelers would have had it easy.

I wonder what happened to cause this to fall apart? she asked herself.

She made herself a mental note to ask Fannah about it all when they got back to Calimport.

There's that certainty again, she caught herself thinking. Do I really believe we're going to make it, or is it simply because I cannot conceive of death?

The third level was devoid of anything, and Tazi cautiously approached the fourth level. She was careful but had had a sneaking suspicion the whole march up that she wouldn't find anything.

If Ciredor had gone to the trouble of barring the entrance, she thought, he was probably not inside, like Steorf suspected.

She didn't smell his foul presence.

When she entered the rooftop parapet, she could see the sandstorm swirl around the tower, but the sound was still somewhat muted where she stood. Tazi caught a glint of her torch reflected back at her. She moved over to what looked like an open arch and stabbed at the empty space with her sword. The tip of her blade clinked against something, and she guessed that at least part of the parapet was glassed in. Set in the center of the room was a brass brazier resting on a stone base.

Tazi moved over to the brazier and held her torch above it. She studied the roof that was balanced on the deceptively slender arches. Set in a circle at the point of the roof, Tazi could see several blue crystals wink in the firelight. She sheathed her guardblade.

Tazi set the torch into the brazier, and within a minute, a small flame burned where no fire had been in thousands of years.

Tazi watched, awestruck, as the heat of the flames warmed the crystals and they came to life. The sapphire gems shone brilliantly, and outside Tazi could see the sand take on an azure color as light radiated from the minaret. The swirling seemed to diminish slightly, and the howls died down.

"Fannah was right," she said to herself.

Tazi rushed down the stairs and nearly turned an ankle on a loose step in her haste. She caught herself and kept going, cursing herself for not taking the torch with her. At the bottom of the stairs Fannah and Steorf were waiting for her. Steorf was unsteady on his feet, and she could see he held up his hand to illuminate the room.

"It worked," she told them. "Just like you said it would, Fannah."

"So all the stones were there," Fannah remarked.

"Yes," Tazi answered, "they were all mounted in the ceiling. Why?"

"I have heard stories of raiders who stole some of the gems along the Trade Way and sold them for huge fortunes in Memnon and Calimport. The gems, as I understand it, can only be found in the Omlarandin Mountains of

Tethyr," she explained. "So they are basically irreplaceable, and if even one is missing it will not work."

"They're all there. Now let's light the other and see if we can lock Ciredor out," Tazi told them, buoyed by her success in the tower.

Tazi opened the doors to the east minaret, prepared to be blasted by the harsh winds, but the stones were working their magic. It was noticeably calmer, though the sand still swirled and stung their eyes. The west minaret was in view, a sharp outline against the setting sun, and the three didn't need to form a human chain to cross the Trade Way.

As soon as they reached the west tower, Steorf raised his hands to remove the wards. Tazi saw him lower them slowly, and she wondered if he was feeling weaker again, having expended too much of his sorcerous abilities.

"What is it?" she asked.

He turned to her and said ominously, "There aren't any wards on this entrance."

Tazi drew her sword and stepped inside, followed closely by Steorf and Fannah.

They shut the doors behind them, and Tazi said quietly, "I have a feeling we shouldn't get our hopes too high. I don't think this is going to be as easy as it looks."

Steorf turned sharply at Tazi's statement and grew thoughtful.

"What is it?" Tazi asked him.

"I think 'hope,' " he said, "just might be Ciredor's downfall."

Tazi nodded but was only partially paying attention, completely on guard.

"We might have beaten him here," she told her friends. "Stay down here and guard the entrance."

"What?" Steorf whispered harshly. "I'm coming with you."

"No," Tazi stopped him. "If he's not here, I need you guarding the entrance to stop him. If he is here—" she paused—"a few stairs won't slow you down."

Secretly, she knew he was mostly spent, and a part of her was afraid he would only slow her down when she faced Ciredor.

Steorf reluctantly agreed. He pulled a torch down and started to hand it to her but Tazi refused.

"I think it's better if I don't make myself too much of a target. Better to be in darkness," she whispered. "I've got my flint and a bit of tinder in my vest."

She patted the pocket to verify its contents.

"Luck to you," Fannah bid her.

"See you soon," she told them.

Tazi made her way carefully over to the stairs. Out of some childish superstition, she didn't glance back at her friends as she climbed the tower steps.

While the first two floors were nearly identical to the east minaret, Tazi noticed some differences farther up. By the faint light that came from the small lookout windows cut into the stones, Tazi could see some strange markings on the wall. Closer inspection under the weak, blue glow revealed writings very similar to the spidery scrawls that had covered Ciredor's scrolls. Spaced between some of the blocks of writing were nooks that housed obscene statues. Tazi had to gasp as she recognized one carved figure from the tallhouse Ciredor had rented in Selgaunt.

"Pig," she whispered and was startled to hear the quiver in her own voice.

She tightened her grip on her blade and continued up.

She entered the darkened parapet. Though the outside continued to glow faintly, the room was still very shadowy. Tazi held her breath and strained her eyes in the gloom, trying to discover why it was so dark. As best she could tell, Tazi thought that this lookout tower's glass walls were lined with something.

Perhaps Ciredor wanted to shut out the light, she thought. I'll worry about it later.

Tazi realized that she had very little time. The sun had finally disappeared, and she knew Fannah's life was in mortal jeopardy. She moved over to the center of the room and was relieved to see that the brazier was intact.

But that relief faded when she craned her head back to study the roof. The pale light from outside refracted through the crystals, and Tazi could see a hole of light. That meant one crystal was missing. Her heart sank.

"Dark and empty," she hissed. "Not when we're this close!"

Remembering what Fannah had told her about thieves and the rarity of the crystals, Tazi momentarily feared the worst. She stood still, feeling her heart pounding.

"No," she finally said aloud.

She dropped to her knees and began to feel around on the floor.

If nothing else, she admitted to herself, Ciredor is thorough. Either all the gems would be here or none would.

Her first pass revealed nothing but pebbles. Then the thought occurred to her that he might have removed one as he left, sort of like taking a key so the towers couldn't be locked behind him.

She refused to accept that idea, hating herself for even thinking it, and made a second pass on the floor. After a moment, her fingers brushed something hard and cold. She grabbed at the object and felt its many, smooth facets.

"Got you," she whispered.

Tazi stood up and climbed onto the stone support for the brazier. Stretching her full length, she was just barely able to wedge the gem into the empty spot. She jumped down and felt a pain resonate in her joints. Her body was once again telling her it needed water.

"Soon," she whispered. "We're almost done."

Tazi pulled out the sack that contained her flint and a tiny pile of tinder. She made a small mound in the center of the brazier and searched the floor for a bit of stone. When she found a suitable chunk, she held the rock over the pile of tinder and struck her flint against it. It took a few tries, but Tazi got the spark she needed. She blew gently on the combustible fluff, and a small flame erupted. It was enough to heat the brazier, which in turn heated the stones in the ceiling.

But instead of illuminating the room in a blue glow, the stones lit everything with an amethyst hue.

The winds fell completely silent outside, and Tazi was startled by the absence of sound. It was absolutely still. However, what was more startling was what the purple glow revealed about the room she was in. Though the stones hadn't heated to their full intensity yet, the light was sufficient for Tazi to make out what had blocked the glass of the lookout tower. Encircling the entire room were mummified bodies. Tazi was transfixed by the macabre tableau.

The tiny flame warmed the crystals even more, and Tazi could see that it was the crystal that she had replaced that was the source of the purple hue. Unlike the Tethyr crystals that had been set in the tower by artisans of the Shoon Imperium, the one Tazi had fixed in the ceiling was an unholy, amethyst gemstone. The gem flickered to full strength from the heat of the brass brazier and stronger beams of light shot out of it. Each beam struck one of the mummified bodies and illuminated their faces.

Despite her repulsion, Tazi walked around the tower room and studied the dead. She had no way of knowing how long the bodies had been there, since each was dried but perfectly preserved. There were all manner of creatures hanging from the glass. Some she knew. Others were a mystery as to what manner of creature they had been in life. The flutter of one's robe caught her attention, and Tazi could see silver circles glinting on the deep purple cloak. She thought of lizard scales and realized she knew who it was before she saw his face.

"The Mysterious Lurker," she whispered. "This is your reward for trusting Ciredor."

Tazi fell silent when she saw the mummy to her right.

She reached out a shaking hand to the face that even in death she would always recognize: Ebeian Hart.

"How did he do this?" she asked and was once again denied the release of tears by her dry body. "And why?"

She cocked her head to one side and hugged herself, now unable to touch the elf who had meant so much to her. She didn't notice the soft steps behind her.

"What a lovely surprise to find you here," the silky voice whispered, "though it really isn't a surprise at all."

Tazi's blood froze and she turned slowly around with her weapon held high, her sunken eyes open wide.

Standing by the stairwell, Ciredor was a study in black. He folded his arms across his chest and looked affectionately at Tazi.

"My dear Thazienne," he told her easily, "welcome home."

CHAPTER 17

ENCOUNTERS

The silence outside was deafening. The sun had finally set and the new, dark moon had risen in the night sky.

Tazi backed up slightly at the sound of Ciredor's voice. She kept her sword high, but couldn't wipe the stunned look off her face. Ciredor's smile widened.

"Dear Thazienne," he drawled, "you haven't forgotten me, have you?"

Tazi swallowed hard and felt her gorge rise in her throat. Standing before her was the man who had haunted her dreams ever since her last encounter with him. His voice was thick and sweet, and she felt herself reeling. The moment had been inevitable, and still it was nearly impossible to take.

"Ah," he said, "I can see I still mean something

to you after all these years. How wonderful."

He moved over to the brazier and inspected Tazi's handiwork. He crinkled his brow slightly and grabbed the poker that was resting nearby.

The moment he wrapped his hand around it, Tazi raised her sword even more and held it with both hands, but Ciredor paid her no mind and simply used the tool to shift the coals about. The increased air circulation caused the flames to shoot up and the amethyst glowed even brighter under Ciredor's loving ministrations.

"That's better," he said, and Tazi realized he was talking to himself.

It was as though she was no longer in the room with him. She backed up even more and felt a sick thud as she knew she had pushed up against one of the mummies.

Ciredor leaned jauntily on the poker, as though the metal rod was a walking stick, and said, "Nowhere left to go, little girl. And why should you want to? All of my work, and you played no small role in it, is about to come to fruition. You wouldn't want to miss it. Behold."

He waved his left hand like a mummer taking a bow.

Tazi looked around the room frantically and finally understood why Ciredor had left the mummies like guardians around the soul gem. With its light bathing them from one side, their positions against the glass exposed the other side of their bodies to the rays of the new moon. Together, the lights had a monstrous effect on them.

Tazi could only watch, horrified, as each mummy began to stir. She felt withered hands slide up her shoulders and whirled to see Ebeian's empty sockets staring down at her. She stifled a scream.

"Well," Ciredor commented, "I'll leave you two alone. I can tell there's a lot you'd like to say to each other. And I still have much to do before the night is over."

Tazi watched as the tall mage looked up at the ceiling. He flicked a finger at the amethyst gem, and it tumbled loose from its slot. Freed, it plummeted toward the flames. Ciredor never removed his eyes from Tazi as he shot his hand into the fire and caught his precious artifact. The poker fell with a resounding, metal clang on the stone floor.

Ciredor inspected the stone and rubbed it against his tunic like someone about to bite into an apple. He smiled deeply.

"Off to collect my prize," he told Tazi as he turned to go.

"But don't worry," he called over his shoulder, "I'll be back to collect you later. If there's anything left, that is."

He disappeared down the stairs.

Tazi saw that the mummies grew more active after the stone's rays no longer bathed their bodies. She briefly wondered if they were angered that it was gone or if the rock's mystical properties kept them at bay. She guessed the former because she was fairly certain Ciredor's gem was the receptacle for their stolen souls. She didn't have time for further contemplation as one of the mummies' snarls snapped her back to the here and now.

She could see by the firelight that they were all staring at her, perhaps blaming her for the absence of the stone. The circle of mummies started to tighten around her. Tazi turned in a circle herself, ready to strike though she knew she was hopelessly outnumbered.

A shout from the doorway drew some of the undead's attention away from Tazi. She looked over as well to see Steorf and Fannah standing in the doorway to the lookout chamber.

"What is this?" Steorf shouted as several of the mummies had broken away from the circle and started their odd shuffling over to the newcomers.

Tazi could see that Steorf had his sword drawn and Fannah still had the dagger Tazi had given her during the worm attack.

"He's here!" Tazi shouted.

She slashed across the arm of the nearest mummy. The partially severed limb dangled from the creature by a dried piece of tendon. That did nothing, however, to stop its inexorable march forward. Tazi backed up and bumped into the brazier. The mummy that was pursuing her flinched a little at the sight of the flames.

"Of course," Tazi realized, "you're afraid of fire."

She knelt down, and with her free hand she felt around for the poker Ciredor had dropped. When she found it, she stood and placed the metal into the fire.

She shouted to Steorf, "Have you got a torch?"

Steorf saw one mounted to the entrance of the chamber and wrenched it from the wall. He tossed the old wood toward Tazi, and she caught it with her left hand. Still brandishing her sword with her right, she shoved the wood into the red-hot brazier, and it burst into flames. She waved the fire at the mummified remains of the Mysterious Lurker, and he threw his rotted hands in front of his face. She used the opportunity to slip past the lurching horror and gain her friends' side.

"I've got to stop him," a breathless Tazi said to her companions.

A moan made all three of them turn, and they saw that the mummies had grouped up and were shuffling toward the doorway.

"Go!" Steorf shouted. "We'll guard your back."

Tazi was torn for a moment, turning from the darkened stairs to the room of rotted corpses and back again. It was Fannah who broke the spell.

"You have to stop him," she told Tazi. "No one else can."

Tazi looked at her blind friend and squeezed her arm gratefully.

"I'll be back," she told Fannah, handed her the torch, and disappeared after Ciredor.

The guardians growled at Tazi's departure. Steorf cast a quick glance at Fannah and saw that the Calishite gripped her dagger fiercely and held the torch high.

"Are you ready?" he asked the blind woman.

"Yes," she answered immediately.

As one, they entered the room, and the mummies moved toward the intruders with a slow certainty. Steorf beheaded the first one that approached him with one stroke but could feel how exhausted he was after the single effort. The worm poison had taken a heavy toll on him, and he knew he lacked the strength for even the simplest of spells. Fannah stayed close to his side. He wasn't sure if she was clinging to him for protection or to offer it. He realized, however, that it didn't matter.

Fannah waved the torch at the face of a mummified troll that had slithered up beside her. The creature screamed in pain and backed away, batting at the places where the flames had singed its leathery skin. While it was distracted, Fannah flicked her dagger across its throat. Nothing poured forth, as the troll was long since a desiccated husk, but the cut was deep enough to cause its head to sag back.

The weight of its skull and gravity finished the job for Fannah. The troll's head snapped off and tumbled to the ground. Its body stumbled about, directionless.

Steorf smiled at Fannah's handiwork but had his hands full soon enough. Two more creatures shambled over. While a hulking human waved a sword blindly at Steorf, a female half-elf jumped on his back with a shrill scream. She wrapped her arms around his throat and her slender, rotted legs around Steorf's waist. While he slashed at the air between himself and the human, the half-elf clawed at his eyes and bit his ear.

The mummy with the sword made blind slashes at Steorf, which he parried easily. The half-elf was another matter. Steorf had to continue to thrash his head from side to side to avoid her raking fingers. He could feel warm blood trickle down the side of his neck where the female had bitten through his earlobe, and he was momentarily surprised that he had enough fluid in his body left to bleed.

"Enough!" he shouted.

Fannah turned at the sound of his voice. When he saw her, an idea came to him. Steorf began to swing harder with his weapon and forced the human mummy backward.

Thrust after thrust, the creature lost more ground until it tripped on the stone support for the brass brazier and dropped its weapon. The creature stumbled back and fell into the flames. It writhed from side to side and managed to jump up as fast as its hulking body allowed. It made one staggering step before the flames ran up the length of its body. The mummy tumbled to the ground and rolled once before burning completely. An acrid smoke filled the chamber.

Steorf had no time to admire his handiwork. The half-elf managed to get her claws into his chest wound and tear it further. Steorf bellowed in rage and slammed his back, with the half-elf still on him, into the metal doorframe of the chamber.

There was a sickening crack, and when he moved forward the half-elf released her grip and slumped bonelessly to the floor. She toppled forward and Steorf could see that her back had split open. To his horror, she still made a swipe at his boot with one hand.

In absolute repulsion, he brought his heel down on her hand and reduced it to powder.

"You won't be clawing anyone with that," he spat, moving away from the shuddering mummy.

Fannah was cornered by three undead, and she swung her torch in a protective arc in front of her. Steorf saw her predicament and moved to help her. He raised his broadsword with two hands and swung across the mummies like a thresher would a field of wheat, his rage sparking his last reserves of strength. Each mummy was cleanly sliced through the midsection, and they toppled over like a child's set of blocks. Steorf looked at Fannah and saw that she was relieved to hear the mummies' crash, but there wasn't a hint of fear on her face. He grabbed her wrist and pulled her free of the torsos that still tried to clutch at her feet.

"We're almost done," he told her, and she smiled.

"I knew we'd make it," she replied.

"How?" he asked her.

"Because this is part of what I saw within the gate," she answered simply.

Before Steorf could reply, he saw another mummy come up behind Fannah with a raised weapon.

"Duck!" he shouted to the Calishite and roughly shoved her aside.

He parried the monster's blow and brought his knee up into the creature's groin. The force of the blow doubled the mummy up, and Steorf smashed the hilt of his broadsword into the thing's skull. The mummy's head exploded in a puff of dust and rot.

"Behind you," Fannah warned him. "I hear something."

He turned in time to see the Mysterious Lurker staggering toward him with his hands extended.

Steorf was becoming tired, and his reflexes were too slow. Before he could bring up his sword, the old priest wrapped his large hands around Steorf's throat. He dropped his sword and tried to claw the Lurker's fingers away, but to no avail. The Lurker's grip was like steel, and Steorf started to hear his own blood pound in his ears, and small patches of black danced in the corners of his vision.

The undead Lurker's eyeless face remained emotionless as he swung Steorf around by his throat and bent the young mage backward toward the brazier as though he wanted revenge for his burned comrades-in-rags.

Tazi carefully started down the stairs, not knowing where the necromancer might be in the darkness. He must have hidden himself somewhere, she reasoned, since Steorf and Fannah hadn't seen him along the stairs. She slid with her back against the stone wall, smearing Ciredor's graffiti with her leathers. After she had gone down a few steps, she paused and listened. She thought she heard a whisper.

At the third level, Tazi stopped her descent and cautiously peered around a corner. She was certain she'd heard was a low, melodic whisper and that it came from that floor. She gripped her sword with both hands and walked sideways, using the walls as shields whenever she could.

Unlike the east tower, this floor was not empty. She could see that Ciredor had transformed this level into a den of luxury, not unlike how he had kept his secret rooms in Selgaunt. There was a decadence to his selections.

As Tazi turned a corner, she could feel velvet drapes on the walls. He had lined the entire room with the sumptuous fabric and blotted out all the exterior light. Furs were thrown haphazardly on the floor, and she secretly thanked him for his opulent taste. Everything was so well padded, there was no way he could hear her approach.

Nestled in the center of a pile of large pillows, Ciredor was sitting with his legs crossed, but Tazi could see that his heels rested on top of the opposite thighs. She had seen Cale assume the pose once when she had caught him deep in his meditations. She realized that Ciredor, who had his back to her, was not actually sitting on the pillows but floated a few feet above them. She thought she caught a glimpse of the purple gem twinkling just in front of him.

He's mesmerized by the thing, she thought. He doesn't even hear me coming.

Tazi padded closer, holding her breath. She moved her blade back and prepared to slice his head off.

"But I *do* hear your heart beating," he spoke aloud and rotated around to face her.

A flash of green burst from his finger, and Tazi was knocked across the room to slam against the wall. She crumpled in a heap, and Ciredor unfolded his legs and stood to his full height.

"I always hear your heart, sweet Thazienne."

He moved over to her, the gem winking in the candle-light behind him.

Steorf was nearly unconscious as the Lurker began to lower his head toward the flames. The first strands of his blond hair touched the fire and the smell of his own burning body snapped Steorf back to awareness. He tried chopping his hands down on the Lurker, but the mummy was unfazed by the blows. Steorf couldn't think of anything else to try and vaguely wondered what had happened to Fannah. He dropped his arms behind his head to strike the Lurker one more time when one of his fingertips brushed a rod of some kind.

Nearly unconscious, Steorf wrapped his fingers around the object and realized it was the poker Tazi had left in the brazier. With his last remaining strength, Steorf brought the red-hot poker up over his head and stabbed the Lurker through one of his eye-less sockets. The metal sizzled as it slid easily through the desiccated flesh of the one-time priest of Ibrandul. The Lurker flailed his arms about and tried to draw the burning rod from his head.

Steorf withdrew the poker, and as the Lurker raised his arms in one last attempt to kill him, the young mage snarled, "This is for Asraf!"

He stabbed the priest through the heart.

"Revenge does taste sweet after all," Steorf whispered.

The mummified Lurker fell to the floor and squirmed like a bug impaled on a study board. He tried to pull the poker out but the hot metal ignited his purple robes.

The Lurker fell still as the flames consumed him.

Steorf leaned against the stone support and tried to catch his breath. He surveyed the room full of corpses and rotted bones. The fetid smoke stung his eyes, but no tears came.

He rubbed a hand against his bleeding chest and whispered, "Is this what you want for me, Mother? A life filled with death all in the name of justice?"

There was no one left to answer him, and he suddenly realized Fannah was missing.

Steorf looked around the room, but she was not amongst the fallen, either—then he saw that she was outside on the parapet, with the last remaining mummy.

"Hold on!" he cried as he searched for the passageway outside.

When Steorf made his way out, he saw that Fannah had her dagger drawn but she was standing calmly. The mummy had also stopped and Steorf thought it looked as if they were regarding each other in the torchlight.

As he got closer, Steorf let out a startled gasp. The last mummy was his old adversary for Tazi's affection: the elf, Ebeian.

"It's him, isn't it?" Fannah asked.

"Yes," Steorf whispered. "Somehow Ciredor collected his body and reunited it."

The eyeless elf stood and turned from Fannah to Steorf. Even though his dried, leathery face wore no expression, Steorf couldn't help but feel the elf was beseeching him somehow, asking for something.

Steorf ran his tongue over his cracked lower lip and finally said, "Maybe I can save him. Maybe there's some way to reunite his soul with his body."

He wracked his brains for a spell that might accomplish it.

"Ciredor would know," he realized.

Fannah stopped him with one word. "No," she said.

At the sound of her denial, the mummified elf lunged for Fannah. She dropped both the dagger and the torch and accepted what was to come.

Steorf screamed at her to move as he sprang at the elf. The young mage's massive size compared to Ebeian's lifeless shell was enough to bowl the mummy over the railing of the parapet. Steorf leaned over the wall with one hand extended, as though to catch his friend, and he watched as the elf fluttered like a dead leaf to the sands below. He hit the ground with a hollow thud, and Steorf could see by the blue light of the sphere that Ebeian had crumbled to dust.

"No," he whispered, and hunched over his shoulders.

Fannah came up behind him and placed both her hands on his back. He turned at her touch and caught her slim hands in his. When he spoke, his voice was choked with emotion.

"Why didn't you let me save him?"

She freed one hand and stroked his cheek.

"Don't you see?" she told him gently. "You did free him."

"There is no one to save you now, little Tazi," Ciredor told her sweetly.

Tazi blinked hard. The blow she had taken left her dazed. Ciredor squatted beside her, grabbed her hair in his hand, and yanked her head up to stare into her sunken, green eyes. She could feel her terror rising, and once again felt like the battered woman in his cellar two years ago.

"I did so prefer you with the longer locks," he said. "You are fortunate and don't even recognize it. Women with black hair are favored by Shar. They wear their hair long and free to honor her. You should do the same and count yourself lucky."

He released his grip on her and she slumped down.

"Never mind," he told her, turning away. "I'll take care of the details later. You'll be a good girl and just lie there, won't you? I really can't afford for you to disturb my plans this late into the evening."

He turned back to stare at her crumpled form.

"And you're the one who's going to stop me? Did you

really think my goddess would allow someone like you to ruin my plans?" he asked, and kicked her in the side.

Tazi curled up protectively and clutched her ribcage. Ciredor laughed and walked back to his stone.

Through a haze of pain, Tazi could see Ciredor reach out a trembling hand and stroke the jewel.

"It's almost time, and with every sign you send me, beloved Shar, I know that you shine your dark favor on me. I know it," he finished fiercely, then started his low chanting again.

Unknowingly, Ciredor had helped Tazi. When he first flung her into the wall, she had been fighting to stay conscious. With the injury to her side, that was no longer a problem. As best she could guess, Ciredor had broken at least one rib, and every breath was like a knife twist in her side. However, that the pain gave her something to focus on.

Coughing up blood, Tazi placed her hands flat on the ground and pushed herself upright. The room swayed, but she forced herself to focus on Ciredor.

As she struggled to her feet, she heard him whisper, "The time is at hand. . . ."

He clutched the stone to his chest and marched past Tazi. Without so much as a backward glance he started to climb slowly up the stairs.

Tazi seized her fallen sword and staggered after him on shaky legs. She found Ciredor on the stairs and charged up behind him. With a scream of rage, she tried desperately to slash at his back, her pain making her foolish and reckless. Ciredor ducked and whirled to face her. With the glowing gem clasped to his heart, he back-handed her with his right hand.

Tazi's blade flew out of her hand and knocked one of Ciredor's small statues from its niche. She lost her footing and tumbled over the stairwell, hanging over the thirty-foot drop by one hand. Ciredor hummed the rest of the way up the stairs.

Tazi watched the statue fall, as though in slow

motion, and smash to pieces on the main floor. The sense of déjà vu was overwhelming; suddenly she was dangling between the rooftops of Selgaunt, watching her crystal prize smash to bits in the driving rain.

The prize I lost, she thought sadly.

She felt her fingers slip as Ciredor's voice drifted down.

"Where are you, my darling Fannah?"

Tazi's head fell back, and she screamed in rage and defiance.

"I will not let you kill her," she spat.

Somewhere deep within her she found the strength to swing her leg up and hook onto the railing. She dragged herself up onto her stomach, and the pain of her broken rib flashed through her like a white heat. Panting on the landing, her knees bloody and her hands raw, Tazi had another recollection.

This time she was back in the cellar in Selgaunt, battered by Ciredor and in pain from her ring of protection as she foiled his attack. What she felt at that moment was the absolute determination and courage to defeat him. She felt it then and reclaimed that feeling now, the one memory she couldn't own during her ritual with Fannah. She rose to her feet and ran up the stairs screaming the mage's name.

Tazi burst into the lookout chamber in time to see Ciredor toss his beloved jewel into the flames. It hung there, suspended, and pulsed like a beating heart. The room was awash in a purple light. Fannah and Steorf rushed in from the parapet, too late to stop the dark necromancer. Ciredor stood, transfixed, in the glow of the gem, and finished his heinous chant. When he was done, there was an electric charge in the air. Everyone was riveted.

The pulsing grew, and a single black tendril squirmed from the gem. It was absolute in its blackness, but purple scintillated along the edges. It writhed toward Fannah. Tazi watched as the distance closed between her and the fell manifestation. Fannah looked at Tazi with her ice-white eyes and grabbed the black strand.

The tendril pulled her soul into the gem, and Fannah's body collapsed backward.

Tazi screamed in pain. Steorf was a picture of unbridled rage as the poison in his system burned away the last veneer of rationality. He ran to Fannah's side, and with one look Tazi knew she had lost her Calishite friend.

While Steorf howled in anger, Tazi screamed, "No more! The death has to stop here!"

She turned to face Ciredor.

The dark mage was a sight to behold. Bathed in the amethyst glow, his face was almost beatific. Tazi could see that he was caught up in a rapture of desire and hope. The word resounded in her mind over and over.

He hopes, he hopes, he *hopes* . . .

"Now you'll come for me," Ciredor whispered. "You've taken my last gift, my crown, and now you'll take me.

"It is no less than I deserve," he finished, lost to his own desires. "I am ready to serve you, my queen."

Something snapped within Tazi. Even as Steorf struggled to get to his feet, his fury making him blind to everything else, Tazi moved into action. Before either man knew what she was planning, Tazi shoved the enthralled necromancer toward his precious rock.

"I'm certain Shar will take you with open arms!" Tazi shouted. "After all, you carry with you the only gift she could ever refuse: your bright and shining *hope*."

The necromancer stumbled toward the gem but twisted to face Tazi just before touching the flames. Dozens of inky tendrils shot out of the stone. Each one latched onto Ciredor like a leech, claiming a different part of his body, and whatever he was about to say to her was lost.

One by one the tendrils started to pull back into the gem with a piece of the necromancer's flesh in its grasp. His screams were deafening. Blood poured out of every orifice, and Ciredor fell to his knees, weeping bloody tears. As the sated tendrils melted into the gem, new ones snaked out to demand another piece of the fallen mage. Before his consciousness faded away, Ciredor locked eyes with Tazi, and she was certain that the last thing to flicker within his black orbs was fear.

When there was no more of the mage left to feast on, and the last of his blood was lapped up, the tendrils retreated into the stone—but that was not the end of it.

Tazi was certain she could see one purple eye regard her from within the soul gem. She stood her ground, and two new onyx strands slipped from the stone. She could see one move to Steorf and the other came for her, but unlike what they did to Fannah and Ciredor, these strands of black were gentle and hesitant. Tazi flinched as the one moved to her forehead, but its touch was light and almost caressing. She could vaguely see that the other tendril approached Steorf in the same fashion then she saw no more.

She was engulfed in utter darkness. Everything about her was cold, her skin no longer ached with its horrible burns, and she no longer noticed the stab in her ribs. Though she seemed to be alone, Tazi could sense a fell awareness in the dark with her. Then she felt rather than heard a manifestation of the goddess Shar.

I have many things to offer you, Thazienne Uskevren. I would have given them to the necromancer but he proved wanting.

Why do you offer them to me? Tazi asked the presence.

Because you know me so well. With you, it is an instinctual understanding. And who better than one from the house of Uskevren to offer my gifts to?

What do you mean? Tazi questioned.

I feel the anger burning within you, a darkness to rival even the fallen mage, Ciredor. All I ask is that you give in to your feelings. Let me soothe and nourish your hurts and pains. They are such a part of you and have taught you so very much.

Tazi knew the presence was right. In the last few years, her pains had grown, and there was an ache in her heart that never left. But she recognized them as parts, not the whole, of herself. Just as the anger burned in her, there were other lights as well. Pain was necessary but not something to simply accept.

I thank you, but I have to refuse, she told the entity.

Tazi could feel the darkness recede but there was a parting thought.

Very well, Thazienne Uskevren, I go for now. But there will come a day when my touch will not seem so cold. There will come a day when you will welcome my embrace.

Tazi found herself back in the lookout chamber.

The tendril pulled back into the stone. The purple eye was no longer visible.

She turned and saw that Steorf was still caught in the embrace of the other onyx strand. His face was twisted in torment, and Tazi could only imagine what he was suffering to refuse Shar's gifts.

Finally, the tentacle released its hold on him as well and slithered back into the soul gem. With a final, amethyst pulse, the stone shattered into a thousand pieces. Tazi shielded her eyes from the flying shards.

When she opened them again, she saw that the glow faded both inside and outside the tower, leaving her and Steorf alone in the gathering darkness.

EPILOGUE

Tazi walked carefully over to Steorf and hugged him fiercely. It took a moment for him to respond, but when he did, he was just as emotional.

"Easy," she finally told him and freed herself from his embrace. "I think I might have a broken rib or two."

She turned from him, though she didn't let go of his hand. The sandstorm had passed at some point during the battle and starlight now flooded the chamber. Its pure, white light glinted off the shattered remnants of the soul gem, and illuminated the remains of the mummies.

The torn and desiccated bodies had been mended by the destruction of the gem. No longer were their corpses dried and withered. Each of Ciredor's victims' bodies had been restored to what they had looked like in life. Each face bore a peaceful countenance that had formerly been denied to them.

Tazi brought the back of her hand up to her mouth and was finally granted the release she needed. Tears streamed down her face.

"It's over," she choked out.

Steorf took hold of her other hand and moved so that she faced him.

"I've never seen you cry," he told her in a hushed tone. He caught one of her tears gently on his fingertip.

"So much is lost," she whispered.

"Fannah . . ." she started to say, then she squeezed her eyes shut.

She held on to Steorf for a few moments. When she broke from his embrace a second time, she moved to face the chamber of the dead.

"Let me give you a moment alone," he told her. "Then we should probably start our journey back to Calimport, and eventually, Selgaunt."

Tazi nodded to him and he stepped out onto the parapet. Tazi looked carefully near the brazier, but Fannah's body was no longer there.

One of the pieces of the soul gem, no larger than her thumbnail and shaped like a tear, caught Tazi's attention. She picked up the splinter and moved out onto the parapet to join Steorf.

He was gazing at the night sky, and Tazi was struck by how straight he stood, his back no longer bowed in pain. She reached out her hand and touched his face. It was cool under her fingers, no trace of a fever left.

"You're all right," she noted in wonder.

"Must be a parting gift from Shar," he answered vaguely. "Do you want to bury Fannah?" Tazi was certain he was simply trying to change the subject.

She decided to dwell on that later and dismissed the thought for another day.

"She's not there," Tazi informed him, not sure of the meaning behind her friend's disappearance.

"What?" Steorf asked, clearly surprised. "What do you think it means?"

Tazi leaned against the railing with her elbows and twirled the fragment of the jewel in her hands.

"Perhaps it means only that the world is still full of mystery," she answered.

"And hope?" Steorf asked slowly.

"And hope," she replied.

Tazi let her gaze drift off at the miles of ever-changing yet ever constant desert, lit only by the stars. Even though she couldn't see it, Tazi knew that beyond Calimport lay Sembia, and home.

An Excerpt From

Windwalker

**The long-awaited third book in
Elaine Cunningham's
Starlight & Shadows Trilogy**

Coming in Hardcover, April 2003

In many a Waterdeep tavern, ballads are sung of an
ancient city doomed by the evil of its inhabitants.
According to the tale, the city was swallowed by rock and
sea, and the gods raised a vast headstone to mark its
grave.

Most of the revelers who join in drunken refrain have
no idea they're drinking in the shadow of this "headstone,"
which is in fact Mount Waterdeep. Few realize that the
city of Skullport lies directly beneath them and that it is
far from dead. Fewer still hear the subtle messages in the
ever-changing ballads—messages carried from the hidden
city to those whose ears are tuned to dark secrets and
lawless opportunity.

These listeners know that many an adventurer's tale starts in Skullport, and there many will end, unknown and unsung. Skullport rewards the victor but swallows the less fortunate. Its streets and shanties sprawl untidily through a series of enormous stone caverns, and surrounding networks of tunnels delve throughout the northlands and under the sea itself.

In a time not long past, in a remote corner of one of these warrens, a dark figure floated along the ceiling of a narrow stone passage. His innate drow magic kept him aloft, well above the magical wards and alarms that would betray his approach. He pulled himself from one jagged handhold to the next, moving carefully toward the moment that had filled his dreams since the day he'd first met Liriel Baenre.

Gorlist, the warrior son of the wizard Nisstyre and second-in-command of the mercenary band Dragon's Hoard, struggled to tune out the alluring clash of weapons echoing through nearby stone corridors as drow fought drow. The enemy whose death he desired above all others would not be among the sword-wielding priestesses of Eilistraee.

A warning heat began to kindle in the drow's left cheek. He slapped a hand over the dragon-shaped tattoo emblazoned there with magical ink—a talisman that warned of nearby dragons and named with faint, colored light the creature's kind and nature. No telltale glow spilled through his fingers. There was a dragon ahead, but it was a deep dragon, a creature of darkness.

The drow scowled. Of course that would be Pharx, for what deep dragon would allow an interloper so close to its lair? Pharx was a powerful ally; any battle the dragon joined would be short and decisive. Victory was important, of course, but Gorlist had his own vengeance to consider.

With an impatient flick of his ebony fingers, Gorlist dispelled the levitation magic holding him aloft. He swooped toward the tunnel floor like a descending raven and hit the stone floor at a run. The time for secrecy and stealth was past.

Gorlist raced toward his father's hidden sanctum, leaving in his wake blinding explosions of magical lights and alarms that keened like vengeful banshees. The wall ahead shifted, and a ten-foot, two-headed ettin broke away from the stone. The monster rose up before him, blocking the passage with its menacing bulk and a spiked club. Gorlist ran through the utterly convincing illusion as easily as a pixie might flit through a rainbow.

The tunnel traced a curve then ended abruptly in solid stone. Gorlist sped around the tight turn and hurled himself at the wall, leaping high into the air and snapping both feet out in a powerful double kick. The "stone" gave way, and he crashed through the hidden door.

Wood shattered, and spellbooks tumbled to the floor as the concealing bookshelf gave way. Gorlist rolled quickly and came up in a crouch, a long dagger in each hand. With a swift, practiced glance he took in the small battlefield.

His father's chamber was empty.

It was also a disaster. Cracks slithered up the stone walls. Artwork hung askew or lay broken on the mosaic floor, which had buckled and heaved until it was little more than a pile of rubble. Part of the ceiling had given way, and chunks of it lay in heaps against one wall. Dust still rose from the recent stonefall, and water released from some tiny, hidden stream overhead dripped steadily onto the rubble.

Gorlist nodded, understanding what had happened. As he'd anticipated, Liriel Baenre had come to reclaim the magical artifact Nisstyre had taken from her. The wizard had responded with a tiny, conjured quake—a canny move on Nisstyre's part. There were few things the people of the Underdark feared more than a stonefall tremor. It had sent the troublesome wench scurrying out into the open—and to a place that offered Nisstyre every possible advantage.

Bloodlust sang in the warrior's veins as he picked his way through the ruined chamber and sprinted down a tunnel leading to the hoard room cavern. Pharx would be there, ready to protect his treasure. Surely this was the battlefield Nisstyre would choose.

Gorlist was nearly there when a shriek of terrible anguish seared through the air. Without slowing his pace, he seized the flying folds of his cape and drew the magical garment around him in a shield of invisibility.

He burst onto a walkway encircling the vast cavern, squinting into the bright torchlight—or so it seemed to his sensitive drow eyes—that filled the hoard room with flickering shadows. Pharx's lair was dominated by an enormous heap of gold and gems. The hoard glittered in the light of several smoking torches thrust into wall brackets. The object of Gorlist's deepest hatred climbed this pile, moving with a dancer's grace over the shifting treasure.

Liriel no longer looked the part of a pampered Menzoberranyr noble. The erstwhile drow princess was clad in simple black leathers, and the sword on her hip was undistinguished by artistry or magic. Her elaborate braids had been loosed, and thick wavy hair tumbled down her back like a wild, whitewater stream. Gorlist could not see her face, but it was emblazoned in his mind: the patrician tilt of her small, stubborn chin, the catlike amber hue of her scornful gaze. For a moment Gorlist could see nothing but Liriel, and his thoughts held only hatred.

Then his sharp eyes caught an anomaly: a smooth wash of gold amid the jumbled treasure. Beneath the acrid dragon musk lay the stench of burned flesh—a not uncommon scent in a dragon's lair, but under the circumstances, ominous. Shock and fury clenched at Gorlist's throat as he caught sight of the dying drow embedded up to his chest in cooling, molten gold.

There was no mistaking Nisstyre, despite the ravages of a heat so furious it could melt coin as if it were butter.

A large, glowing ruby was embedded in the seared forehead, and its magical light dimmed with the swift ebbing of the wizard's life-force.

Liriel plucked the gem from Nisstyre's forehead and gazed into it like a seer contemplating a scrying stone—which, in fact, the ruby truly was. She greeted the unseen watcher with a smile such as a queen might give a vanquished rival or a hunting cat would use to taunt its prey.

"You lose," she said.

Crimson light flared as if in sudden temper, and abruptly died. Liriel tossed the lifeless stone aside and half-ran, half-slid down the pile toward the dragon-shaped shadow edging into view against the far wall.

So do you, Gorlist silently retorted, pushing aside his disappointment that the female's much-deserved death would not come at his hands.

The dragon staggered into the cavern, and Gorlist's lips shaped a silent, blasphemous curse. It was not Pharx after all, but a smaller, stranger creature: a two-headed purple female. Obviously the dragon had seen battle, and her presence indicated that she had prevailed over Pharx—but not without a price. From his position, Gorlist could see the deep acid burns scoring the female's back.

But Liriel could not see the wounds, and she greeted the dragon with a fierce smile. They exchanged a few words that Gorlist could not hear. The dragon seemed about to say more, but its left head finally succumbed to injury. Enormous reptilian eyes rolled up, and the head flopped forward, limp and lifeless.

For a moment the right head regarded the demise of its counterpart.

"I was afraid of that," the half-dragon said clearly, then the second head crashed face-first into Pharx's treasure.

Liriel threw herself to her knees and gathered the dragon's left head in her arms.

"Damn it, Zip," she said in tones ringing with grief and loss.

The right head stirred, lifted, and said, "A word of advice: Don't trust that human of yours. An utter fool! He offered to follow me into Pharx's lair and help in battle if needed. In return, he asked only that I kill him if he raised a sword against any of Qilué's drow. Best deal I was ever offered."

The dragon turned aside, and her fading eyes held a conspiratorial gleam.

"You're on your own now."

Gorlist followed the direction of the dragon's gaze, and his crimson eyes narrowed. A young human male strode swiftly toward Liriel, his black sword naked in his hand and his concern-filled gaze fixed upon the mourning drow.

"He lives," Gorlist muttered flatly, disgusted at himself and Nisstyre for allowing the human's survival.

When last they'd seen the man, he had been sprawled beside a dying campfire, pale and silent. The drow mercenaries had seen only what Liriel had wanted them to see: the distraction offered by her unclad body and the lie of her pet human's "death." The truth had hidden behind the dark elves' fascination with the deadly game—known among drow as the "Spider's Kiss" in honor of the female spider who mated and killed—that Liriel had tacitly invited them to contemplate. Gorlist granted the quick-thinking female and her devious little ploy a moment's grudging admiration.

But all Liriel's cunning seemed to have vanished with the dragon's death. She cradled the enormous purple head in her lap, rocking it tenderly, all but oblivious to the crescendo of approaching battle.

The drow warrior sneered. So there it was: the princess's weakness. If the loss of a dragon could so distract her, imagine her state when her human friend lay dead at her feet!

Anticipation sped Gorlist's steps as he unsheathed

his sword and crept, silent and invisible, toward the unwitting pair.

Liriel gently put aside the dragon and rose. She jolted back as she found herself nearly face-to-face with her human companion. Her astonishment turned to rage, lightning quick, and in full drow fury she hurled herself at the man, pushing him toward one of the exit tunnels.

"Get out of here!" she screamed. "Stupid, stubborn . . . human!"

But the young man easily removed himself from Liriel's grasp and turned toward the main tunnel. The clamor of swords announced that battle was almost upon them.

"It is too late," he said in bleak tones.

As he spoke, magical energy crackled in a nimbus around him—an aura faintly visible to the magic-sensitive eyes of the watching drow warrior. Before Gorlist could blink, the human began to take on height and power.

The drow caught his breath. Once before he had seen this rather common-looking young man transform into a mighty berserker warrior. He remembered little of the battle that had followed, for the memory had been seared away by the healing potions that had brought him back from defeat and near death.

No fighter, neither human nor elf—or even drow— had ever before bested Gorlist with a sword. For a moment he burned to erase this insult in open combat.

Liriel brandished a familiar gold amulet—the Wind-walker, the artifact that Nisstyre had considered so important. She snatched a battered flask from the human's belt, pulled the cork free with her teeth, and tipped the flask slowly over the golden trinket.

Shock froze Gorlist in mid-step. Nisstyre had coveted the Windwalker for its ability to hold strange and powerful magic. With the help of this treasure, Liriel had brought her undiminished drow powers to the surface, something few drow had been able to accomplish. Yet she was willing to throw away her dark elven spells, so that the magical fires of the human's kindling berserker rage would not consume him.

It was unbelievable, unconscionable! What drow would willingly surrender such an advantage?

For a moment Gorlist was truly torn. He yearned to reveal himself, to defeat the human, to savor the pain the man's death would inflict upon Liriel.

The human began to sing in a deep bass voice. Gorlist could not understand the words, but he sensed the power of ritual behind the song.

Any delay would put his main prize at risk. Better to dispatch the male quickly and savor the second, more important kill. Still shrouded with invisibility, Gorlist darted forward, his sword high.

The human's transformation ended with a surge of magical growth, one so sudden and powerful that it sent him stumbling forward. The stroke that should have cleaved his skull dealt only a glancing blow. Gorlist noted the swift flow of blood and knew that, unchecked, it would suffice.

The ritual song stopped abruptly, but the man's fall was slow, astonished, like the death of a lightning-struck tree. Liriel caught him in her arms, staggering under his weight. With difficulty she eased him to the ground. A small cry escaped her when she noted the white flash of bone gleaming through the garish cut.

Gorlist flipped back his cape, revealing himself and his bloodied sword.

"Your turn," he said with deep satisfaction.

Liriel froze. The eyes she lifted to him were utterly flat and cold, as full of icy hatred as only a drow's could be. In them was no grief, no loss, no pain. For a moment Gorlist knew disappointment.

"Hand to hand," she snarled.

He nodded, unable to contain his smirk of delight. Obviously the princess was not as unaffected as she pretended to be. If her heart had been untouched and her head clear, she would have never agreed to face a superior fighter with nothing more to aid her than steel and sinew.

The stupid female closed the Windwalker, locking away whatever magical advantage she might have taken. She rose and pulled a long dagger from her belt.

They crossed blades. The strength of Liriel's first blow surprised Gorlist—and unleashed a wellspring of fury.

He slashed and pounded at her, raining potential death blows in rapid, ringing succession. Gone was his yearning for a slow death, a lingering vengeance.

But the princess had learned something of the warrior's art since their last meeting. She was as fast as he and skilled enough to turn aside each killing stroke, but her strength was no match for his. Gorlist drove her steadily, inexorably, toward the cavern wall. He would pin her to it, quite literally, and leave her there to rot.

Through the haze of his battle-lust, Gorlist noted the tall, preternaturally beautiful drow running lightly along the far edge of the cavern. Qilué of Eilistraee had arrived, and fast behind her came a band of armed priestesses! His victory must come quickly or not at all.

But the newcomers paid little heed to the furious duel. Lofting a silvery chorus of singing swords, they rushed to meet the mercenaries that yet another band of females herded into the open cavern.

Liriel had also noted her allies' arrival. She made a quick, impulsive rush toward them, in her relief forgetting the uneven floor. She tripped over a jeweled cup, stumbled to one knee. Gorlist lunged, his sword diving for her heart.

But Liriel was faster still. She rose swiftly into the air, and the warrior, deprived of his target, found himself momentarily off-balance. Before he could adjust, she spun like a dervish and lashed out with one booted foot.

To his astonishment, Gorlist felt himself falling. The floor of the hoard room seemed to drop away, throwing him into a maelstrom of faint, whirling lights and magical winds.

Before his heart could pick up the beat stolen by shock and rage, he was flung out into cold, dark water. He fought off the urge to take a startled breath and swam doggedly for the surface.

It was all too clear what had happened. Eilistraee's priestesses had killed some of his fellow mercenaries and stolen the medallions that granted magical transport to the tunnels surrounding the hidden stronghold. Judging from the number of females in the hoard room, Gorlist had lost at least thirty fighters. Most of them had been aboard ship and ready to set sail. Worse yet, Liriel knew of this plan and knew just where to find the hidden magical gate. Her "retreat" from his assault had been calculated, every step and stumble of it! The knowledge of this pained Gorlist nearly as much as the burning of his air-starved lungs.

Gorlist burst free of the water and dragged in several long, ragged gulps of air. He dashed the back of one hand across his eyes, then squinted toward the bright light of battle.

The situation was grim. A small crowd of drow children—valuable slaves bound for a dark elven city far to the south—huddled together on the dock. Their wary, watchful red eyes reflected the light of the burning slave ship.

Gorlist's second ship was still intact, but that was the best he could say for it. His minotaur boatswain slumped over the rail, its broad, brown-furred back bristling with arrows. The crow's nest flamed like a candle. The drow archer stationed there had tried to leap free and had become entangled in the rat lines. His garish crimson leathers identified him as Ubergrail, the best archer in the Dragon's Hoard. He hung there, slain by his own crimson arrows—Qilué was known for her disturbing sense of justice—and looking like a bright insect caught in Lolth's web. Other, nameless dark shapes bobbed in the water around Gorlist, giving silent testament to his band's defeat.

But a few males still stood and fought. Heartened, Gorlist swam steadily for the ship. He pulled himself up one of the lines leading to the rail, one that would place him nearest the fighting.

When he neared the top, he summoned a burst of levitation magic to speed his way. He shot up over the rail. Dispelling the magic, he dropped to the deck in a crouch, close to a comrade's side.

As he rose, the "comrade" whirled toward him. A black fist flashed toward Gorlist's face and connected with a force that snapped his head to one side. He instinctively moved with the blow, using the momentum. Drawing his sword as he turned, he blinked away the stars that danced mockingly before his eyes.

When his vision cleared, he beheld his opponent—a tall, silver-haired drow male who crouched in guard position, waiting for Gorlist to gather himself for battle. The stranger's foolish chivalry and silvery hair proclaimed him a follower of the hated goddess Eilistraee.

Gorlist's lip curled in a sneer, and he made a contemptuous beckoning gesture with one hand.

The silver-haired drow lifted his sword in challenge, shouting, "For the Dark Maiden and our lady Qilué!"

The mercenary fisted his beckoning hand and twisted it palm down, releasing a dart hidden in his forearm sheath. Immediately his opponent shifted his sword to deflect the projectile. It exploded on impact, sending a slick of viscous black liquid skimming over the blade.

In less than a heartbeat, the metal of sword and hilt melted and flowed into a steaming, lethal puddle—too quickly for the drow defender to understand his doom, or to toss aside his blade. Flesh and bone dissolved along with the molten steel, and the drow stumbled back, staring in disbelief at the ragged shards of bone protruding from his wrist. His back hit the aft mast hard, and he started to slide down it.

Immediately Gorlist lunged forward and thrust his sword between two ribs—not deep enough to kill, but enough to hold the wounded drow upright. His victim didn't seem to notice this new injury.

"Look at me," Gorlist demanded softly.

Stunned eyes flashed to his face.

"Isn't it enough that we must answer to the females of Menzoberranzan and their accursed Lolth? What male would cast off this yoke, only to worship Eilistraee?"

"Tzirik," the drow said in a rapidly fading voice. "I am Tzirik, redeemed by Eilistraee, beloved of Qilué."

These words filled Gorlist with fierce joy. He slammed his sword forward, felt it bite into the wooden mast behind the traitorous male, then wrenched it free.

"That was a rhetorical question," he told the dying drow, "but thank you for sharing."

"You! Drider dung!" shouted someone behind him, delivering the insult in strangely accented Drowic.

Gorlist's moment of dark pleasure shattered. He spun to face the speaker, who strode toward him, a sword gripped in her left hand. The warrior was furious, female, and—as if those things were not trouble enough—*fairy*.

Gorlist might have notions foreign to most of his Underdark kin, but he shared in full measure their hatred of surface elves. This particular fairy elf was tall, with moon-white skin and sleek ebony hair – a bizarre reversal of drow beauty. A streak of silver hair, the mark of Eilistraee, hung in a disheveled braid over one mail-covered shoulder.

Gorlist ran a few steps toward the female. He stopped suddenly, letting her close the distance between them, then delivered a high feinting jab. She ducked and answered with a lunging attack, a quick move that sent her silvery braid swinging forward. Gorlist parried the darting sword with a rising circular sweep of his blade, catching her weapon and moving it out wide. Reaching under the enjoined swords, he seized the fairy elf's braid, determined to rip it from her scalp.

A dagger appeared in the elf's right hand. Up it flashed, severing a few inches of braided hair. The lock in Gorlist's hand flared with sudden light then flowed into a new and deadly shape. Suddenly he was holding a small viper. Its tongue flashed like miniature lightning as it tasted the drow's scent, and its head reared back for the strike.

Gorlist hurled the tiny monster to the deck. It landed with a splat, breaking apart into a hundred tiny silver balls. These rolled together and reshaped into a tiny dragon. The diminutive monster hissed and leaped into flight, hurtling straight for the tattoo burning silver-bright on Gorlist's face.

The drow refused to be drawn by either distraction. He kept his sword in guard position, swatting the little dragon aside with his free hand. The thing let out an indignant soprano squawk and flapped out of reach.

Gorlist and the elf exchanged a few blows, taking each other's measure, testing defenses. The female was tall—nearly a head taller than he, with a reach that exceeded his. Worse, she seemed to understand the ever-shifting patterns of drow swordplay. She met each attack with a casual, almost contemptuous ease. For several moments they moved together in perfect coordination, like light and shadow. All the while the silvery dragon circled them like a seabird following a fish-laden ship.

Suddenly the dragon faded into mist, which expanded into a bright, hazy cloud. This settled down over the embattled pair—a deliberate and mocking reversal of the globe of darkness that drow often employed in battle. The last thing Gorlist saw with any clarity was the smirk on the fairy elf's face.

He squinted into the too-bright mist. The elf's outline was still visible, and her sword reflected the defused light as it swooped toward his hamstring. Gorlist leaped high above the blade, throwing himself into a spin to gain distance from the second, third, and fourth attack that any drow would surely have planned and ready.

This impulse saved him: a second, unseen weapon scraped along his leather jerkin, and the stroke that would have disemboweled him merely drew a stinging line across his backside.

Gorlist landed and lunged in one quick, fluid movement, but his sword plunged through shadow without substance—the elf was gone, leaving an illusion behind. He overextended, but instead of adjusting his footing, he threw himself several steps forward in hope of outpacing the bright globe. His abysmal luck held. The Lolth-spawned light clung to him.

A dark form appeared in his path, and Gorlist pulled up short, nearly toe-to-toe with one of his own mercenaries. Instantly they fell apart, snapping into guard position with mirror-image precision. The mercenary's eyes widened with horror as he realized he faced his commander. He lowered his weapon and immediately dropped to one knee, baring his neck as a sign of submission.

Gorlist also turned away. Holding his sword with both hands, he whirled back, putting all his strength into the blow. The blade hewed through flesh and bone, and the mercenary's head tumbled across the deck. Before the body could fall, Gorlist snatched the medallion from the severed neck.

"Surrender accepted," he muttered as he draped the medallion around his own neck.

He bolted for the side of the ship and vaulted over the rail. The fairy's globe followed him all the way to the water. He dropped into the wonderful darkness and was instantly swept into the magical passage.

Gorlist emerged in a familiar stone tunnel and immediately kicked into a run. The ships were lost, but perhaps the mercenaries he'd left behind were faring better.

He ran through several passages before he heard the song: a jubilant paean to Eilistraee voiced by Qilué's priestesses.

Fury surged through him, speeding his steps into a headlong sprint. But even as he ran, Gorlist acknowledged the truth:

The Dragon's Hoard band was defeated. He was alone, without resources or allies. Everything Nisstyre had built over years of effort was gone.

Or nearly everything.

Gorlist veered off into a side passage, one that led to his own private stash. It would provide a new start. One way or another, Liriel Baenre would die. He would leave no means untested, scorn no alliance—no alliance, no matter how deadly or distasteful.

Gorlist knew what he must do. As soon as he could, he would return to the hoard chamber. He would find Nisstyre's ruby, and he would seek out someone who hated Liriel nearly as much as he did.

R.A. Salvatore's
War of the Spider Queen

New York Times best-selling author R.A.
Salvatore, creator of the legendary dark elf
Drizzt Do'Urden, lends his creative genius to
a new FORGOTTEN REALMS® series that delves
deep into the mythic Underdark and even
deeper into the black hearts of the drow.

DISSOLUTION
Book I
Richard Lee Byers sets the stage as the delicate power structure
of Menzoberranzan tilts and threatens to smash apart. When
drow faces drow, only the strongest and most evil can survive.

INSURRECTION
Book II
Thomas M. Reid turns up the heat on the drow civil war and
sends the Underdark reeling into chaos. When a god goes silent,
what could possibly set things right?
December 2002

Return of the Archwizards

When ancient wizards of extraordinary power return
from centuries of exile in the Plane of Shadow, they
bring with them an even more powerful enemy and
a war that could destroy the world.

REALMS OF SHADOW

An Anthology

Twelve all new stories spanning thousands of years brings the
war against the phaerimm and the dark designs of Shade to life.
Featuring stories by R.A. Salvatore, Troy Denning,
Ed Greenwood, and Elaine Cunningham!

THE SORCERER

Return of the Archwizards, Book 3
By Troy Denning

Tilverton is no more. Phaerimm surround Evereska. The High
Ice is melting. Floods sweep through Anauroch. Elminster is
still nowhere to be found. The greatest heroes of Faerûn are
held at bay, and a flying city has taken up permanent residence
in a world on the brink of destruction.

November 2002

Don't miss the beginning of Troy Denning's exciting
Return to the Archwizards series! Now available:

The Summoning • Book 1
The Siege • Book 2

Shandril's Saga

*Ed Greenwood's legendary tales of Shandril
of Highmoon are brought together in this trilogy
that features an all-new finale!*

SPELLFIRE
Book I

"Director's cut" version in an all-new trade paperback edition!

The secret of Spellfire has fallen into the hands of Shandril of
Highmoon. Now the forces of the evil Zhentarim are after her.

CROWN OF FIRE
Book II

All-new trade paperback edition!

Shandril and Narm are on the run from the Zhentarim. As
they make their way toward Waterdeep, aided by a motley
band of fighters and mages, the danger grows.

New!
HAND OF FIRE
Book III

*Ed Greenwood's latest novel brings
Shandril's Saga to its thrilling conclusion!*

The forces of the Zhentarim and the terrifying Cult of
the Dragon converge on Shandril, but there may be a worse
fate in store for her.

FORGOTTEN REALMS®

Travel with Drizzt Do'Urden behind enemy lines in the first book of an all-new R.A. Salvatore series

THE HUNTER'S BLADES TRILOGY

Book I: *The Thousand Orcs*

The *New York Times* best-selling author of *Sea of Swords* returns with an exciting new trilogy that pits the dark elf Drizzt against his most dangerous enemy. And this time he stands alone.

October 2002

The *New York Times* bestseller
now available in paperback!

SEA OF SWORDS

Paths of Darkness series

For the first time since *The Silent Blade,* Wulfgar and Drizzt cross paths again, both bent on recovering the hammer that's been stolen away on a pirate ship that sails the Sea of Swords.